Belinda Alexandra's bestselling historical fiction has been published around the world, including in the United States, Spain, France, Germany, the United Kingdom, Turkey, Hungary and Poland. She is the daughter of a Russian mother and an Australian father and has been fascinated by world culture and travel since her youth.

She lives in Sydney with her three black cats and a garden full of interesting wildlife. Her hobbies include flamenco dancing, piano and foreign languages. A lover of all creatures, Belinda volunteers with several animal charities.

www.belinda-alexandra.com

belinda_alexandra_author
BelindaAlexandraAuthor
hellobelindaalexandra

Also by Belinda Alexandra

INTERNATIONAL BESTSELLING AUTHOR

BELINDA ALEXANDRA

THE
MASTERPIECE

HarperCollinsPublishers

HarperCollins_Publishers_
Australia • Brazil • Canada • France • Germany • Holland • India
Italy • Japan • Mexico • New Zealand • Poland • Spain • Sweden
Switzerland • United Kingdom • United States of America

HarperCollins acknowledges the Traditional Custodians
of the lands upon which we live and work, and pays respect
to Elders past and present.

First published on Gadigal Country in Australia in 2024
by HarperCollins_Publishers_ Australia Pty Limited
ABN 36 009 913 517
harpercollins.com.au

A catalogue record for this book is available from the National Library of Australia

ISBN 978 1 4607 6305 6 (paperback)
ISBN 978 1 4607 1562 8 (ebook)
ISBN 978 1 4607 3897 9 (audiobook)

Cover design by Michelle Zaiter, HarperCollins Design Studio
Cover images: Woman © Mark Owen / Trevillion Images; all other images by
istockphoto.com
Author photograph by Elizabeth Allnutt
Typeset in Bembo Std by Kirby Jones
Printed and bound in Australia by McPherson's Printing Group

For Lilli

PROLOGUE

EVE

Nice, June 1946

I arrived at the Villa des Cygnes at what they call on the Côte d'Azur the 'Magical Hour'. That time of the evening when the sun sinks over the Baie des Anges, the sky turns pink and gold, and the sea darkens to a deep shade of purple. From the height of Mont Boron, I could take in the sweeping expanse of the Mediterranean, the picturesque harbour and terracotta rooftops of Nice. But one doesn't stop to admire the view when one's father's life is at stake.

What I did notice as my fingers gripped the locked iron gates to the garden was the dilapidated condition of what must have once been a grand house: a Neo-Pompeian style summer residence. The pink stucco was crumbling in places, and the Rococo balustrading that surrounded the rooftop terrace looked as if it might disintegrate and come crashing to the ground at any minute. My gaze travelled to the statues of Greek gods and goddesses that stood on either side of the overgrown path. Under the circumstances, their blank stares were unnerving, as was the Medusa mascaron situated above the villa's entrance door. My heart beat fast against my rib cage

1

and my hand trembled as I pressed the buzzer near the gate. No sound emitted from it and I wondered if it could only be heard inside the house.

I looked desperately around for any sign of life. I had no evidence, only a hunch, that Kristina Belova might have returned to the villa. But what would I do if she wasn't here? My mind flashed to my father held in a lice-infested cell in Fresnes prison, chains around his wrists and ankles. When there was no response to my second press of the buzzer, I stepped back and considered how I might hoist myself over the gates. Before I had to think too much further, the front door opened and the stooped figure of a man appeared. His black butler's uniform hung off his skeletal frame and his face was so pale it was almost ghoulish in the fading daylight. I shivered slightly when he shuffled down the path towards me. But as soon as he drew close, I could see that he was no apparition, he was simply ancient. At least ninety years of age.

'Can I help you, mademoiselle?' he asked, in the breathless voice of a man of failing health.

'I am Eve Archer. I'm here to see Madame Bergeret,' I said, using Kristina Belova's married name.

The butler looked taken aback. 'Has she invited you?'

'I sent a telegram and didn't receive a reply. I've come all the way from Paris.'

He touched his breast pocket, but then seemed to think better of it. 'Madame Bergeret doesn't wish to see anybody.'

The way his gaze shifted, I sensed that what he said was only a half-truth. I thought of the painting that had turned up at the Hôtel Drouot auction. Kristina was working again, and someone had put her artwork on the market. So why would she not wish to see anyone? I was prepared to talk to her through a crack in the door if she preferred. But talk to her I must.

'Please, I must see her. It's about Serge Lavertu. He's in grave danger.'

My father's name seemed to startle the butler like an electric shock. 'Serge Lavertu? He's alive?'

Something wasn't right. Did this man not read the newspapers? If he had, he would have known my father was indeed alive, but not for much longer if the Ministry of Justice had its way. It was either going to be the guillotine for a double murder or the firing squad for a war crime. Unless I could persuade Kristina Belova to come to Paris to testify on his behalf, my father was doomed.

'Yes, he is alive,' I said. 'Please, I need to speak to Madame Bergeret tonight.'

The butler's gaze travelled to my small suitcase. It would have been more prudent for me to have found a hotel in town and come to the villa in the morning, but my panic had made me act in haste. After another pause, he reached for the key in his pocket and opened the gate.

'I am Lorenzo Amato,' he said, with the pride of an Italian manservant who takes his role seriously. 'Follow exactly in my footsteps. The garden is booby-trapped.'

Then, to illustrate his point he indicated a large pile of rubble that once might have been an outbuilding. 'The Germans took over the villa in 1943 and left it mined when they retreated,' he explained. 'After the liberation, a looter decided to use the toilet in the guest quarters. He pulled the chain and "boom!" – the building collapsed on him.'

I flinched. The newspapers were full of descriptions of hapless people who had set off undetected mines simply by turning on a light switch or straightening a painting.

'And the house? Is the house clear?'

We reached the front door and Lorenzo opened it, ushering me into the entrance hall. 'It was cleared by the British. They think they got everything … well, except the cellar. But nobody goes down there anymore.'

A fluttering sound made me look upwards through the middle of a grand spiral staircase. Straight above us was a hole that tore right through the ceiling and roof. Black specks that I recognised as bats circled overhead. The rest of the hall looked as rundown as the exterior of the house with a broken chandelier and peeling paint.

Lorenzo put my suitcase down and indicated for me to sit on a sofa carved with so many laurels, medallions and rosettes, it could have come straight from the Tsar's winter palace, although the ivory silk upholstery had seen better days before it had been attacked by moths.

'Now we wait,' he said, turning on a floor lamp and sitting down next to me.

He drummed his fingers on his lap and looked about him as if we were two people on a bench expecting a bus.

I anticipated some explanation for his odd behaviour, but when none was forthcoming the tension grew too great for me. 'What are we waiting for?' I asked.

He pointed to the second floor. 'When the light fades completely, Madame Bergeret will stop painting. She will take some tea while I prepare supper. I have the samovar boiling now.'

While it wasn't unusual for an artist to be disciplined about her work, something about the degree of orderliness felt odd. It was beginning to dawn on me that Kristina, as well as Lorenzo, might not have much contact with the outside world. Perhaps it explained why she hadn't come running to my father's aid herself.

Lorenzo must have noticed the look of consternation on my face. 'It is not Madame Bergeret's natural temperament to be so particular about time,' he explained. 'She was always the loveliest and most accommodating of people. Keeping strict time is her way of coping. The war has affected us all.'

I shifted in my seat. It was true that Kristina had suffered tragedies of her own. 'Yes, indeed,' I said.

My sympathy seemed to make Lorenzo warm to me a little more. 'I have served the Belov family for nearly sixty years,' he said. 'I was first hired by Madame Bergeret's grandfather. I've known her since she was a baby. Now I am all she has left.' He sighed. 'And I am such an old man.'

The remaining daylight suddenly dimmed as if someone had switched off a light. The tinkle of a little bell sounded from upstairs.

'Excuse me,' said Lorenzo, rising. 'Please wait for me here.'

He disappeared into another room for a few minutes, returning with a tray and some tea things and an oil lantern.

'This way, Mademoiselle Archer,' he said, leading the way up the stairs slowly. Despite his unsteady gait he did not grab the balustrade but carried the tray with as straight a posture as he could muster and with a sense of dignity that was striking. I got the impression that he lived for this moment each day.

On the upper floor was a large room lit by a row of sconces down one side. From the frescoes on the ceiling and the French doors that opened onto a balcony, it might once have been a ballroom. Propped up on the floor, tables and chairs, were dozens of paintings of all sizes, colours and configurations. They sat among piles of books, newspapers, and an array of objects including a carousel horse and a broken violin. I wasn't sure if it was my imagination, but I thought I caught sight of a tiny caramel rabbit hopping from behind one painting to another. The clutter seemed at odds with Kristina Belova's organised schedule.

Lorenzo put the tray down on a side table. Thinking that we were alone in the studio, and that Kristina must be coming to join us from somewhere else in the house, I stepped closer to study a portrait of a man with black hair brushed away from his handsome face. He seemed familiar to me, and then I remembered I'd seen him in another portrait in my father's art gallery. He was Max, Serge's business partner and Kristina's husband.

A sudden tingle ran down my spine, alerting me to the fact that we weren't alone in the room after all. Lorenzo cleared his throat. I turned, and for the first time noticed the tall woman with her back to us. She was cleaning paintbrushes in a bowl of water. Her platinum-blonde hair hung down her back in a loose plait. All of a sudden, she turned and looked over her shoulder. Had she felt my stare at her back? Her gaze settled on me, and my breath caught in my throat.

'Madame Bergeret,' said Lorenzo, 'may I present to you Mademoiselle Archer.'

I was struck instantly by Kristina's large blue eyes, the sparkling type that looked as if they had pieces of the stars in them. She was even more beautiful than she appeared in her self-portraits. Maturity had given her face character, and the lines around her eyes and mouth accentuated her sculpted features. For someone who had been in a death camp, she looked remarkably healthy. It was both a surprise and a relief.

Despite my best intentions of approaching the pressing subject with care, I gushed, 'I have heard so much about you, Madame Bergeret. I've come because Serge Lavertu urgently needs your help.'

I did not refer to Serge as my father — that was a secret I didn't share with anybody. Even Serge himself did not know it.

Kristina studied me intently. 'Yes?'

A queer feeling clenched my stomach. 'Serge Lavertu,' I repeated. 'Your art dealer. Your friend.'

She glanced uncertainly at Lorenzo.

'Serge Lavertu,' he said slowly, announcing every syllable carefully. 'He is alive. It is wonderful news!'

Kristina seemed to be on the verge of smiling but then her face twitched. For one dark moment I thought that some deception might be taking place. Perhaps she did not want to be associated with an art dealer who had allegedly sold a French national treasure to Hitler. But then I noticed the look of genuine struggle in her eyes.

I turned to Lorenzo. With an awful, tragic fatalism, the old man shook his head.

I looked back to Kristina whose eyes glistened with tears. 'I'm sorry, Mademoiselle Archer. You see ... I don't quite remember Serge Lavertu.'

She bowed her head by way of apology and then I saw it. The missing patch of hair above her ear and the jagged scar that ran across her exposed skin. Kristina had incurred some sort of head injury.

I felt the blood draining from my face as the terrible truth dawned on me. The only chance I had to save my father had gone terribly wrong. How much can one's circumstances change in a mere thirty days? Only a month ago my life had felt wonderful. After years of struggle, I had been on the pathway to success. How smug I had felt on the morning of Lucile's birthday party. How excited I'd been about the day ahead. If I had only known what trouble had been heading my way, I might not have got out of bed at all.

PART I

CHAPTER ONE

EVE

Paris, May 1946

Odette bustled into the room, parting the curtains with a forceful 'swoosh'. I was bathed in morning sunshine and given a view of the Eiffel Tower at the same time.

'Are you awake, Mademoiselle Archer?' she asked, peering into my face. 'Shall I bring your coffee and newspaper now?'

I blinked slowly until my eyes adjusted to the light. 'Yes, thank you, Odette.'

We regarded each other for a moment as if we were creatures from two different planets. We were both twenty-one years of age. Both reasonably attractive, but not exceptionally beautiful. Our complexions were lit by that certain glow of youthful health that, with some help from cosmetics and smart clothes, could put us on the right side of charming. But our similarities ended there. While Odette was content to be a humble maid, I had enough ambition to fill every room in the Hotel Ritz.

'How is Madame Damour this morning?' I asked. 'Violet or red?'

Odette laughed as she went to the armoire and took out a gold satin dressing-gown for me. 'I would say she is at green today – quite happy and content.'

'Good,' I said, slipping out of bed so Odette could help me into the gown. 'That's the best state of mind to be in when it's your birthday.'

'Let's hope it lasts,' said Odette, heading towards the door. 'I'll bring you the newspaper now.'

I sat down at the dressing table and brushed out my hair. There was so much to do for Lucile's fiftieth birthday party that evening, but I allowed myself the luxury of a moment of feeling pleased with myself. It was just over a year since I had come to Paris, and six months since I had started working for Lucile. I had utterly transformed her life and elevated my own in the process. I now wore clothes from the top couturiers in Paris and slept on linen that smelled of violets. It was a long journey from where I had started.

My gaze drifted to the top drawer of the dresser where the letter was stored, the letter my mother had written the year before the war began.

You made me happier than anyone else could have …

When the policeman had handed me the note written on a flimsy slip of pale blue paper, I'd thought at first that my mother had penned those words to me. For a moment her abandonment of me was almost forgiven. Until I realised that the letter was directed to a man she had known in Paris – an art dealer named Serge Lavertu. She wrote longingly and lovingly of old times with him. The only part of the letter that referred to me was a postscript at the bottom, which seemed to be an instruction that I go to him for help.

Eve is a bright young girl who has a lot of you in her. Please help her make her way in the world.

It apparently hadn't occurred to my mother – who to be fair wasn't in a good state of mind when she wrote the letter – that her daughter had no means of getting to Paris. Then with the war and the German occupation, it was impossible to enter France anyway. When I finally did arrive, Serge was in no position to help me and so, once again, I was left to fend for myself.

'Here you are,' said Odette, returning with a cup of coffee and the newspaper. 'Shall I put them by the window as usual?'

'Yes, please.'

She placed the items down and then gave me a curtsy before leaving.

I wonder if she would still be so deferential if she knew the truth, I mused, taking my place at the window where I liked to admire the Eiffel Tower for a few minutes every morning. We all have our gods, and that wrought-iron lattice tower that had risen from nothing to become the icon of a city was mine.

Lucile liked to tell people that I was the daughter of a beloved friend who she had taken under her wing. The story was that I was born in the picturesque Hunter Valley in Australia, the offspring of landed gentry. She would further embellish the tale by adding that my fluent French and poise were the result of attending an exclusive boarding school in Sydney. It couldn't have been further from the truth, but when one woman pays another to be her companion, details are bound to be exaggerated. I hadn't been born on a vineyard, let alone to landed gentry. I'd grown up in a mouldy terrace house in Sydney's inner city, squashed between the crumbling Italianate office of a funeral director and a general goods store. But my mother was French, and even though we had lived in cockroach-infested squalor and our rent was always overdue, she insisted on holding her head high, impeccable in her threadbare clothes.

I sipped my coffee, picked up my pen and studied the newspaper, looking for appropriate articles to highlight. It was the second spring after the war had come to an end. Signs of life were beginning to sprout like the shoots of tulips pushing through the soil after a long, hard winter. The headlines reflected that optimism and restoration of order: the 'French Empire' was now to be called the 'French Union', and those accused of collaboration during the war would now be tried with proper legal processes instead of being summarily shot at dawn. Even the Galeries Lafayette was selling underwear stamped 'Renaissance Française'. Granted the products were in short supply and had all the utilitarian charm of Soviet-issue clothing, but still, these were signs of better times ahead.

A breeze drifted in through the window and frolicked over my skin. I found my mind turning to my mother again. She was the one who had taught me to ignore the reality around me and to set my sights on better things. So I had studied assiduously all those elements that made for a good and elegant life. First it was the magazines that Mrs Kent, the grocer's wife, gave to me after she'd finished with them. I examined the clothes, hairstyles and recipes as if my future depended on them. After I left school I worked in a haberdashery shop, where I learned to distinguish mother-of-pearl from Trochus-shell buttons, and Guipure lace from Chantilly. Later I found a position in the prestigious millinery department of Mark Foy's. For the entire years of the war, I trained myself to recognise the customers who had style and those who didn't. Oh, how I loved those well-dressed, pleasure-seeking Sydney elites! Money was of no consequence to them. They had so much of it, they had to hire other people to keep track of it. They were marvellous. Their demands were high and they knew what suited them.

I finished my coffee, put aside the newspaper and opened the armoire. Today I would wear a striped silk dress with a harem-style skirt. I ran my hand over the soft, smooth texture of the material. Balenciaga had designed it. The man had done quite well for himself despite the war. I held the dress against myself and admired my reflection in the mirror. I wasn't rich, but nobody could tell that unless they looked at my bank account. I'd learned to walk, talk and even think like a fashionable socialite. So much so that when I arrived in France I was surprised to find that not everyone in the city possessed an innate sense of style – that French *je ne sais quoi* as they call it. Due to my excellent references, I found a job as a junior draper with the fêted decorator Monsieur Rémy Lavigne. But when his clients all started to request the services of 'la femme Australienne', he became threatened, and was probably relieved when Lucile came along and made me a better offer.

★

Lucile was already seated for breakfast in the dining room when I entered. I was pleased to see how smart she looked with her soft boyish haircut, the one that she had initially resisted because *everyone* was still wearing victory rolls. The striped dress I had chosen for her gave structure to her otherwise scrawny figure.

'Good morning,' I said brightly, kissing her on both cheeks and handing her a copy of *Le Figaro* marked with asterisks on the articles I wanted her to read.

'Oh Eve,' Lucile said, glancing at the newspaper and pulling a face that did not flatter her hawkish features. 'Not more politics.'

'*Ma chérie,*' I said, 'political discussions are the lifeblood of France these days. They dominate every cocktail party and formal dinner, even with ladies present. You must learn to discuss the events of the day with facility and brilliance. It's not enough to be simply decorative anymore. A woman must be well informed.' I nodded towards her outfit. 'You look lovely by the way. Not a day over thirty.'

Lucile blushed with delight. I felt both affection and frustration towards her. I was at a loss to explain how a woman able to afford the best of everything, and having more leisure time on her hands than the rest of the household combined, seemed to have managed to have raised being a wallflower to an artform. She was neither very young nor very old. Not particularly tall but not short either. Not dark nor fair. There was absolutely nothing about Lucile that stood out. Without my help, if you blinked, you wouldn't notice her at all. She had already bored two wealthy husbands to their deaths and was unlikely to find a third. Left to her own devices, she would have sat in her apartment and faded away like her absurd button collection. However, it wasn't my role to criticise her lack of *savoir faire* but to encourage her development of it.

'Happy birthday!' I said, passing her my gift: a box containing a bottle of Schiaparelli's perfume 'Shocking', wrapped with a bright pink bow.

'Oh, you shouldn't have, Eve,' she said, taking the perfume from the box and spraying a puff in the air. 'I didn't expect anything.'

I really shouldn't have, I thought, as notes of rose, narcissus and honey floated through the air. The perfume had cost me almost my entire allowance for the month (Lucile and I never mentioned the word 'wages'), but after watching the cream of French society give each other rationed goods like cigarettes and canned peas for the past year, I thought it was time to splash out.

16

I had just picked up my baguette to butter it when Odette bustled into the room.

'Madame Damour! Mademoiselle Archer! Look what's arrived!' she said, holding up a copy of *Elle* magazine opened to the page with a photograph of Lucile standing in the foyer of the apartment. I went to Lucile's side so I could read the article over her shoulder.

'What a triumph!' I said, my eye travelling over the photographs of rooms with white wainscotting, whisper-soft pastels for the upholstery and delicate but well-crafted furniture.

Lucile turned the page and I gave a muffled cry of delight. There was a photograph of me standing with my arms folded and looking most pleased with myself.

Mademoiselle Eve Archer is the genius behind the apartment's transformation, the caption read.

'How lovely,' I said, downplaying my moment of fame, while secretly thrilled at the acknowledgement.

When the Germans invaded Paris in 1940, Lucile had fled to her country house in Chantilly where she had lived out the war in relative tranquillity by turning herself into a recluse. Meanwhile, her city apartment was sequestered by the German army. At first the officers had behaved as gallant, respectable Aryans, but as soon as they realised they were losing the war, they turned into brutes and barbarians. Lucile returned after the liberation to find her apartment ransacked and vandalised. She immediately called for Monsieur Lavigne, for whom I was working at the time, to repair the damage. At first I didn't understand why he sent me to assist such a wealthy customer rather than going himself. While I stood in the middle of Lucile's drawing room and surveyed the broken porcelain that littered the floors, the slashed upholstery and the holes in the walls where light fittings had been ripped out, she had stood beside me, weeping into her handkerchief.

'Perhaps you could show me around, Madame Damour?' I suggested. 'So I can report back to Monsieur Lavigne.'

'Yes, of course,' she sniffed, indicating for me to follow her down a corridor. But her self-control didn't last long. In a moment she was in tears again. 'I've heard reports that the *Boche* swung from the chandeliers while their scarlet women paraded around in my ... *delicates!*'

I tried my best to put that image out of my mind.

When we came to the door of the main bedroom, Lucile was hesitant. As soon as I entered it, I understood why. Apart from the shredded carpets and upturned bed, someone had written obscenities on the walls in what I guessed was excrement, but that I assured Lucile was most likely brown paint.

We next turned our attention to the library, which – apart from the defaced portraits of Lucile's late husbands – had been left mainly intact. It seemed even drunk debauched German officers appreciated the value of books. Lucile took out a photograph album full of pictures of herself and her second husband at home, so I could get an idea of what the apartment looked like before the maelstrom.

'I'd like it returned to its original glory,' she said, her eyes brimming with tears. 'Do you think it's possible? Do you think you could find all these fabrics again?'

I examined the photographs and swallowed hard to disguise my reaction. The apartment had been the most papered, panelled, tapestried and tasselled interior I had ever seen. There was not a square inch of breathing space anywhere. No logical line for the eye to follow, no pause to take in any particular object. As if the frilly curtains weren't hideous enough, every lampshade was beaded *and* fringed, and every piece of fabric was patterned. The unmatched cabinets and dark Turkish rug added to the gloomy, funerary effect. I understood instantly why Monsieur Lavigne had sent me rather than come himself. Lucile had terrible taste — expensive, but terrible taste. His sensitive palate would not have been able to bear it.

I looked around the room once more then gently squeezed Lucile's arm. 'Rather than seeing what has happened here as a tragedy,' I said, 'let's see it as an opportunity.'

'An opportunity?' Lucile asked, looking confused.

'Yes,' I said. 'To let the modern in.'

★

'It was a good idea of yours to send Madame Damour to the beautician today,' said Odette, helping me arrange the furniture in the drawing room for the party.

It was easy to do because one of my rules in redecorating the apartment had been that there wasn't to be any chair, sofa or side table that couldn't be lifted by two women. That ensured that all the furniture added to the elegant, airy atmosphere I had strived to attain.

'Let's plump these cushions, shall we?' I suggested.

While I didn't encourage too much intimacy between myself and the servants, and my loyalty always had to be with Lucile, I couldn't help but agree that things worked more smoothly when she was out of the way. Since my employment I had come to realise that the slightest amount of pressure could turn her from a placid woman into a tyrant. Which made the task she'd hired me for — to turn her into one of Paris's most stylish hostesses — all the more challenging. A good hostess was something like a circus ringmaster, able to showcase her various guests while keeping a smile on her face even if the big top should collapse, a lion escape or a financial backer skip town.

While Odette dusted, I took a moment to admire the pièce de résistance of the apartment: a rare and valuable pastel painting by Degas that Serge had found for us. The painting had been discovered after the artist's death. It was of a ballet dancer standing in the wings waiting for her moment of glory.

My mother had taught me the ballet steps she had learned as a young girl. We had no money for lessons, but I dutifully followed her strict instructions and developed a posture so regal that it earned the ire of the other children at school. *Look at her! All haughty and high and mighty! She thinks she's better than us, even though her mother is a filthy drunk who forgets to feed her so she has to hang around the rubbish bins looking for scraps to eat.*

'Better than them? Of course you are better than them,' my mother told me when I went crying to her. 'They are nothing but the low-born descendants of convicts. But you, my dear, are French.'

The taunts of those children meant I grew up not trusting people. My sense of style developed into an armour I held up against the world.

I adored my mother, but I was frightened of her too. It was true that she was fond of the bottle, and the alcoholic haze in which she existed meant she often made promises and broke them in the same sentence. She wounded my heart so many times that it now sat like a rock in my chest. It only opened when I saw something beautiful. Luxury was the crack that let in the light.

'Why do we keep this thing?' asked Odette, polishing the one piece that remained from the previous version of the apartment: a Baroque mirror studded with five bullet holes, each surrounded by a circular web of shatter marks, giving the impression that five spiders had taken up residence on the glass.

'Because it's a conversation piece,' I said, coming to stand next to her. 'It tells a story. Everyone in Paris is talking about how they passed the war. Some were part of the Resistance. Others were sent to concentration camps. This mirror tells Lucile's story.'

Odette looked at me blankly, so I gave her a more straightforward reason. 'Keeping evidence that the apartment was destroyed by the Germans supports the fact that Lucile wasn't a collaborator.'

'Oh,' said Odette, the wisdom of my decision slowly dawning on her.

She moved on to dust the piano while I stared at myself in the war-scarred mirror. I thought about the German who had fired his gun at the glass. Why had he shot at his own reflection? What inner demons had been haunting *him*?

★

I walked in the direction of the Place Vendôme to pick up a necklace that Lucile would be wearing that evening. The spring sunshine was glorious and the vibrant pink geraniums spilling out of window boxes lent colour to the beige buildings. But in the shadows, the air still carried a grave-like chill. I passed a woman with her hair twisted into an elegant chignon. The way she carried herself with an erect posture and walked one foot perfectly in front of the other was pure Parisian chic. But the damask tablecloth draped over her shoulders in place of a shawl wasn't. Although such incongruousness was a common sight even in the seventh arrondissement, it never failed to astonish me. A freezing cold winter exacerbated by shortages in fuel for heating and textiles had sent people throwing decorum to the wind. They had gone about wrapped in anything that would keep them warm, including curtains, bed quilts and tablecloths, and now that the weather was warmer they seemed unable to shake the habit. Only the stupendously rich could afford new clothes, and the number of women in suits with padded shoulders, straight skirts and feathers in their hats made it seem as if the clock had stopped in 1939.

In the Jardin des Tuileries, there were so many women pushing prams or playing with infants on picnic blankets spread out on the lawn that it gave the impression the city was being overtaken by tiny squirming human beings with pudgy faces. I'd read in *Toujours Magazine* that 'baby shows' were now more popular than dog or cat shows had ever been. On the other side of the park, a crowd had gathered around a *fromagerie* and were peering in the window. The wistful expressions on their faces got the better of my curiosity. I walked towards them and looked over a man's shoulder to see what had taken everybody's attention. At first I thought I was hallucinating, for there behind the glass was a selection of cheeses such as I had not seen anywhere but the black market since my arrival in Paris. Camembert, Roquefort, Crottin ... all artistically arranged from mild to strong.

'It's incredible!' exclaimed one man, practically salivating.

The others nodded in agreement. While bread, butter and vegetables had been slowly reappearing in stores, the memories of near starvation were deeply etched on the onlookers' faces. The patisserie next door wasn't quite so lucky. The cakes in its window were all still made of cardboard with little handwritten cards in front of each that read 'Model only'. The only real pastries they had on offer were some dry-looking croissants and tarts. As I walked on, it was clear that the Paris I had come to was not the city my mother had described to me, back when she'd run away to live the bohemian life in Montparnasse.

'Tell me the story again,' I would beg her when I was a young girl. 'Tell me about my father.'

I would sit enthralled as she described Paris in the twenties, about her bad-tempered concierge who wore a monocle and smoked a pipe, the artists' ball where she went in a leopard costume and got into an argument with a woman dressed as a panther. I imagined the glamour of the cafés where she conversed with artists. Then she would tell me about my father, Serge Lavertu. 'He was so elegant, so chivalrous, a truly unique human being. You couldn't help but adore him.' Not only did her stories magically make the stained walls of our draughty house disappear, but they kept her away from the bottle.

'Tell me another story. Tell me another ...'

I wanted her to keep talking forever. When my mother was sober, she was an angel. But when she was drunk, she was a devil. I knew the drink would eventually kill her, but at least the stories bought us time.

★

The neoclassical buildings of the Place Vendôme appeared before me. If ever there was an area of Paris that demonstrated that France's postwar economy was bankrupt, it was here. The prestigious square's haute couture milliners and dressmakers were kept afloat by American dollars. It was no longer European royalty sniffing the expensive bottles of Fleur de Rocaille and L'Heure Bleue at the Institut de Beauté, but 'Joan from Atlanta' and 'Barbara from Sacramento' who found the devaluation of the franc had worked in their favour and they could afford French luxury now.

The concierge at Mauboussin gave a courteous bow when he opened the door for me. I drew in a breath. The lights rained down on the displays of sparkling jewellery. Such colours! Such forms! Mauboussin's ability to create new shapes and combinations of stones was unending. My eyes drifted from the glass case housing the 24-carat emerald Napoleon had given Joséphine – on show but not for sale – to the spectacle of gold and ruby bracelets designed by the master, René Sim Lacaze.

The store represented the best of the decorative arts at which the French still excelled. It was not a place you came to find quaint clusters of diamonds and pretty arrangements. You had to love colour – emeralds, rubies and sapphires set against black onyx or brilliant platinum.

Sylvette, the store's most stylish *midinette*, smiled when she saw me approaching her counter. Even in her black uniform she managed to stand out, with her beauty spot at the corner of her mouth and her naturally rosy pout. The only artifice she wore, and to great effect, was a turquoise and platinum clip in her blonde hair.

'*Bonjour*, Eve,' she said, taking out a purple velvet presentation box from the drawer under the counter and opening it for me.

'Oh!' I said, feasting my eyes on the dazzling white gold choker. It was everything I had imagined it to be when I ordered it. Each of its waved links – fifty in all to signify each year of Lucile's life so far – was decorated with a cabochon-cut pink tourmaline and a pearl joined together by rows of sapphires and brilliant cut diamonds. My instinct told me that it would be necklaces that would take over from bracelets as star pieces in the next year, and that's why Lucile's new choker had to be especially exquisite. She had to lead the way in something.

'What will Madame Damour be wearing this evening?' asked Sylvette.

'A black silk-faille off-the-shoulder evening dress.'

Sylvette nodded her approval. 'The perfect choice.' She reached under the glass counter and produced a rose gold ring set with Burmese rubies, aquamarines and diamonds.

'Try it on,' she urged me.

I slipped on the ring and the two of us gazed at it like two clucky grandmothers doting over a newborn baby.

'It's a pity you and I, so appreciative of beautiful things, can't afford them,' Sylvette lamented. 'Not unless we find a rich man.'

I flinched. I had unpleasant memories of a rich man. His name was Anthony and he had spotted me working at Mark Foy's. But our love affair didn't end well.

There now, don't look so sad. You knew it couldn't last, Eve. I must marry someone who my family knows. Someone who moves in the same circles … Here is a ticket for Paris. No, I insist you take it. You always said you wanted to go there … Together? Oh no, that is impossible. One day you'll meet a man who will sweep you off your feet and you'll forget all about me. You'll see …

Abandoned by my mother. Abandoned by my lover. If there was one thing I'd learned about life it was that the only person I could rely on was myself.

I reluctantly slipped the ring off my finger and handed it back to Sylvette. 'One day I hope to be very rich,' I told Sylvette, 'and have an apartment full of beautiful things. But it won't be because of a man. It will be due to my own efforts.'

'We can only dream,' she replied, putting the ring back under the counter and closing the presentation box. 'Shall I have the necklace sent around?'

'Yes, please do,' I told her. 'I have other errands to do and the last thing I need is to be robbed.'

★

After I saw the florist about the arrangements for the evening, I made my way to Saint-Germain-des-Prés. The rickety medieval houses, narrow winding streets and profusion of dusty second-hand bookstores had little in common with the grander arrondissements of Paris. I had no real business there that morning; it was simply one of the places in Paris where I felt close to my mother. But like the rest of the city, Saint-Germain-des-Prés was changing. It was American students who spilled out of the cafés now, wearing berets and discussing existentialism and the poetry of André Breton. The French students wore swing skirts and motorcycle jackets and listened to the Glenn Miller Orchestra on their radios. The Americans wanted to be French, and the French wanted to be American. Together, the sheer number of students in the quarter had brought about a kind of revolution. A bill making prostitution illegal had just been passed. The government needed all that brothel accommodation to house the influx of students.

I stopped in front of an antiques store with a chalkware bust of a beautiful woman in its window. The eyes of the sculpture looked alive and gave the appearance of being trained on some distant horizon. It made me think of my mother.

When she was sober, my mother would teach me how to dine like a lady and dance the tango. Her beauty and charm made it easy for her to win jobs as an inhouse model or a sales assistant in the fancier sections of the department stores. At those times, there might be a new dress for me or a pretty doll in a box. Then, just as I was fooling myself that this time her abstinence was permanent, I'd return home from school to find something burning on the stove and my mother passed out on the couch. Captain Sutherland from the Salvation Army would come over and pray for my mother, who would contritely pour the remaining alcohol down the sink. But the cycle would always begin again.

I looked over my shoulder at the art gallery wedged between a book binder and a café. The larger paintings hung from the floor to the high ceiling while smaller ones were propped on a long browsing shelf that ran down the centre of the room. Serge was there at his desk, bent over his account books with his wire glasses perched on the end of his nose. The diffused light from the glass ceiling gave him an angelic glow.

The first time I had come to see Serge I'd fully intended to give him the letter my mother had written to him and reveal that I was his daughter. But then I discovered his circumstances had greatly changed during the war. He'd lost his prestigious gallery on Rue la Boétie due to the Nazi Aryanisation laws during the occupation and he had filed a lawsuit to get it back. For now, he was living in the humble shop where he and his business partner, Max Bergeret, had started out their career selling art supplies. Max had disappeared during the war and his wife, the artist Kristina Belova, had been sent to a concentration camp. Serge had not been able to find out what happened to them. The most valuable paintings in his inventory had been looted during the war and he was barely making enough money to support himself. I couldn't bring myself to add to his burdens by informing him of my mother's death and thrusting a daughter on him whom he knew nothing about.

But then something unexpected happened. My keenness to learn about everything cultured led me to ask Serge about art and my interest sparked something in him. Before I knew it, he was inviting me on weekly visits to the Louvre, explaining which paintings had been hidden from the Nazis during the war, and the importance of colour, line, form and texture. He showed me that the *Mona Lisa* was not meant to be viewed straight on, but just left of centre — *the subject's eyes are the focal point of the painting and from this angle we connect with her* — and that the young male nude painted by Jean-Hippolyte Flandrin was so moving because the reason for his heartbreak was unknown: *Is he shipwrecked? Is he a shepherd who has lost his flock? Or a young man who has lost his beloved?*

There wasn't any underlying flirtation in Serge's attentiveness, which would have been horribly awkward. His interest was altruistic and genuine, and I soon sensed that he was very different from other men. He was calm, steady and, most of all, *consistent*. He turned up to meet me when he said he would, and when he promised to find a unique and beautiful painting for Lucile's apartment, he searched diligently until he discovered the Degas. The more I began to treasure my time with him, the more paralysed I felt about revealing my secret. What if I told him I was his daughter and his attitude towards me changed? What if he abandoned me as the others had? After all, there was some reason that my parents had not been together. My mother had alluded to it in her letter:

I understand the reasons you couldn't love me the way I loved you, and I forgive you for them …

Now I felt the only way I could be accepted by him was to become worthy enough of him and to make myself someone of note in Paris.

★

Serge looked up from his books when I pushed open the heavy wrought-iron and glass door to his gallery. His face instantly brightened.

'Ah, Eve,' he said, laying down his pencil and taking off his glasses. 'The sight of you lifts my spirits! How is Madame Damour enjoying her new painting?'

'I'm not sure she quite notices it, to be frank,' I told him. 'But her guests surely will tonight. And I stop to admire it every time I pass it. The dancer seems poised, ready for her life to begin. Yet I can almost feel her heart hammering in her chest.'

Serge smiled. 'The appreciation of art is a lifelong education. Don't give up on Madame Damour developing a keener eye just yet.'

My gaze travelled over the walls of Serge's gallery. Apart from a few impressionist landscapes, his stock was almost entirely modern paintings, including some emerging American artists. My eye settled on the portrait of a handsome man with kind eyes.

'It's Max,' said Serge. 'A portrait painted by his wife soon after they met. The Artistic Recovery Commission returned it two days ago. It was found in a salt mine in Altaussee.'

I understood the mental torture Serge was enduring of not knowing what had happened to Max. But I also knew that death of any kind left questions that could never be answered. *What were the person's last thoughts? Did they suffer?* My mind flashed back to that day at the hospital when the mortician had pulled back the green sheet. Despite having jumped from the Harbour Bridge, my mother had not broken one bone in her body. Her golden hair lay around her grey face like a mermaid's. She looked like she was only asleep, and I half-expected her to open her eyes and talk to me. But of course, she didn't. Once they are gone, there is only a deafening final silence.

'Ah, look at me,' said Serge. 'You have come to visit and already I have made you sad. Come upstairs. I'll show you something else I have discovered.'

I followed Serge up the stairs to the apartment. He'd never taken me there before and my nerves tingled with anticipation. The fact that my mother had once been a visitor to those private quarters meant they held a particular fascination for me.

Serge waved me inside. My eyes took in the bronze chandelier in the hall and the stained-glass window of the room beyond as I followed behind him. *My mother saw all of this*, I told myself. There was an intoxicating smell of old books, beeswax and sandalwood in the air. I looked down at the worn parquet floor, imagining my feet stepping in the same places as hers.

'Well, tell me what you think of this?' asked Serge, indicating a painting leaning on an easel. 'It was returned to me by an old client of mine who swears he bought it unwittingly from another dealer with no idea of its provenance.'

I moved closer to the painting of a beautiful young woman with blonde hair sitting in front of a dressing table and brushing her hair. There was something intriguing about her bright blue eyes. The brushwork was vigorous and dazzling. The painting had an immediate effect on me, both alluring and hypnotic. It showed not only technical mastery but a high degree of creative imagination.

My eyes dropped to the signature: *Kristina Belova*.

'It's a self-portrait,' said Serge. 'She was only eighteen when she painted it.'

If that was how Kristina Belova had painted at the start of her career, I could only imagine what she would have achieved if the war had never happened. She was beautiful, no doubt, but it was a sense of inner elegance that made the painting exceptional.

'It's stunning!' I said. 'Truly! I must convince Madame Damour of the value of it to add to her collection.'

Serge looked at me. 'You have good taste, Eve, but this one is not for sale. The portraits are all I have left of them. I intend to hang Max and Kristina together in this room. They can be inseparable as they were in life.'

I was ashamed of my insensitivity. 'Of course,' I said. 'I'm sure that's what they would have wanted. You never told me exactly what happened to Kristina.'

Serge indicated for me to take a seat while he went to the little kitchen in the corner of the room and put a kettle on the gas stove. 'It seems Kristina survived the concentration camp and was sent to a hospital in Switzerland afterwards. After that there is no trace of her,' he said. 'Some people in the art world conjecture that she killed herself after what happened to her daughters.'

Serge had tried to sound factual, but I noted the crack in his voice. He hadn't mentioned Max and Kristina's children before. Still, having already been less than tactful only a moment ago, I held my curiosity at bay and didn't press him for more details. I turned back to the painting, once again struck by its beauty and sense of movement. War destroyed everything that was good.

The kettle whistled and Serge cleared away ink bottles, writing paper and books from the side table before taking the kettle off the flame. He returned with a pot of steaming rosemary tisane. Its woody scent perfumed the air.

'Tell me more about Kristina's art,' I said, accepting the cup he offered me.

'She was a Russian but worked in France,' Serge said, blowing into his cup. 'She managed to combine French modern influences with the Slavic love of brilliant colours. Her talent was never widely appreciated as much as it should have been, but her art was sought-after by discerning collectors – those who recognised genius when they saw it.'

'Yet another artist ahead of her time?'

'No artist is ahead of their time, Eve. They are all perfect for the era in which they are painting. It's the viewing public that must catch up in their ideas.'

'That's an interesting theory,' I said.

Serge sat back in his chair and glanced about the room forlornly. 'I had a dream the other night that I received a letter from Kristina. She wrote that she and Max were alive and well. They had decided to live on an island in the Pacific where the people were kind to each other and nature, and didn't perform horrific acts out of greed.'

'That sounds like a beautiful place. Perhaps Kristina *is* alive somewhere, nursing her broken heart. People are still showing up even now. Only recently, I read in the paper about an American GI being found in a jungle in Borneo. He had no idea that the war was over.'

A door at the other end of the room was slightly ajar. As I spoke, I caught a glimpse of a mahogany bed and an oriental screen. The last time my mother had seen Serge was in 1923, just before she left for the other side of the world, trailing after a no-good actor who promised her everything and gave her nothing. I thought of the letter she left before she took her own life.

'Serge,' I said, leaning forward and hearing my own heartbeat thump in my ears, 'why did you never marry? Did you not want children yourself?'

His brow furrowed as he considered my question. 'Some people are not made for family life and I'm afraid I'm one of them. No, Eve, I have never wanted children.' Then as if to make light of the subject, he added, 'Anyway, can you imagine children in a gallery? All those grubby finger marks on the artworks? Precious sculptures smashed to smithereens?'

I smiled too, despite the wave of pain that surged through me. If Serge had not wanted the joy of young children with all their carefree laughter and playfulness, what on earth would he want with an adult one? I might not damage his artwork, but I came with more complex problems.

Peering over the rim of his teacup, Serge studied me. 'When the light falls on you a certain way, you remind me of someone,' he said. 'But among the ghosts of the past, I can't think who that might be. And yet it is there in the tilt of your head and the way your mouth quivers the second before you smile.'

I turned to the faded gilded mirror above the mantelpiece. Black spots were dotted around the edges where the silver had worn away. The reflection of Serge and me together fitted perfectly within the frame, like a family portrait. Both of us sitting there, meticulously elegant with our cups poised in our fingertips. The perfect picture of a father and daughter.

CHAPTER TWO

KRISTINA

Nice, June 1946

Kristina stood by the air vent, listening to the muffled voices of Lorenzo and the young woman, Eve Archer. Their words were indistinct, and she only caught snippets of their conversation, but it was obvious that Lorenzo was explaining her condition to their visitor. Kristina wished he'd given her enough time to talk to Eve herself before he'd whisked her away. But her dear butler was like that – protective and adamant that she shouldn't be 'disturbed'. All she had been able to ascertain was that a Serge Lavertu – a man she knew to be a friend of her beloved husband – was in trouble and needed her help. But Eve might have been able to tell her things – factual gaps in her life that Lorenzo either didn't know or was hiding. She trusted that Lorenzo had her best interests at heart, but it was difficult for her to rely on the recollections of a nonagenarian who couldn't remember where he'd put the bread most days. She knew her name: Kristina Bergeret, née Belova. Her age: forty-one. Her occupation: artist. Beyond those facts, the rest of her life felt uncertain. As fleeting as the sinking sun disappearing into the sea.

The villa for one. She knew her grandfather had built it and when her parents were alive it was splendid: the paintings, the tapestries, and the glass cabinets filled with Limoges porcelain. Before the Russian Revolution, it was an escape from the bitter winters of Saint Petersburg. Afterwards, it was a place of refuge out of the reach of the murderous Bolsheviks. Gazing out of the tall windows at the sweeping view, in the room where she stood now, were once princes and princesses, dukes and duchesses, counts and countesses, all assembled for one of her mother's famous five-o-clocks. Kristina smiled as she recalled her mother. Always so beautifully dressed and mannered. Always so punctual. Yet married to her father who was perpetually late. In Kristina's mind's eye she saw him out in the garden with his trim beard and gentle eyes, tending to his roses with the devotion of a monk at his prayers. *Is that the time, my dove? Already?* This house had been a happy place – the light, the colour, the freedom. It had once been pure joy to be alive.

Kristina walked out onto the balcony where the balmy breeze caressed her skin. She considered that it was probably a mercy her parents didn't live to see the Germans strip the place of its beauty and leave every room and glass case empty. There were some who believed it a mercy – as her physician Docteur Gabriel did – that Kristina couldn't remember it either.

While she recalled her childhood and her youth vividly, her memory stopped at a very specific time in 1923. After that it was all vague and blurry. Occasionally a face or a brief memory would appear out of the mist, but it always retreated as quickly as it had come.

'To have lost so many years of your memory prior to the war is highly unusual,' Docteur Gabriel had said. 'It leads me to believe that your trouble is the result of that injury to your head, and that those memories may never come back. At least you have your art, and you are painting again.'

Yes, thought Kristina, *I have my art. But I want to remember. What my mind has done in making me forget is cruel, not kind. The past is a mirror we look into to make sense of who we are today.*

She stepped back inside and breathed a sharp intake of air. A sweet gentleness pressed against her heart and she sensed it must be Nadia and Ginette, her daughters, whom Lorenzo had told her about. She strained to imagine their faces clearly, but her head started to ache. In frustration, she pressed her fist against her forehead. The Germans took so much more than artworks and heirlooms. The familiar sense of fear and dread welled up inside her and she tried to utter words she couldn't speak.

Her attention turned to the portrait she had painted of Max. Handsome, warm-hearted Max. Uniquely charming, nothing could banish his gaiety or embitter him. The moment they met she knew something miraculous was happening, something intoxicating and enchanting. Her memories might have stopped in 1923, but those that she still had were beautiful ones to keep.

CHAPTER THREE

KRISTINA

Paris, June 1923

In the drawing rooms of the more conservative arrondissements of Paris, many said the artists of Montparnasse were a rather louche lot who wasted their time mingling in cafés and participating in drunken debaucheries and illicit love affairs. While there was some truth in the *joie de vivre* of the quarter, it was untrue that they were all lazy or not serious about their work. Picasso painted through the night to take advantage of the stillness and silence, and woe to anybody who dared disturb him after he'd gone to bed in the morning. Derain and Braque worked out their creative frustrations by boxing, while Marie Laurencin absorbed the genius around her with utter dedication, determined to become a master herself. Even Kristina Belova, a humble art student, could be found working in the lecture room of the Académie de la Grande Chaumière long after everybody else had gone home.

She locked eyes with her reflection in the mirror perched on her desk, while at the same time trying to keep the right amount of tilt to her head. She wasn't admiring her beauty, nor scrutinising her face for flaws as another young woman might do. She was attempting to capture herself in oil paint and was finding the task much harder than she had anticipated. She wasn't sure if she wanted to idealise herself or capture the truth. If the former, then she should depict a smart modern woman who sensed she was on the brink of something grand. If the latter, then her portrait should be of an intelligent, well-educated eighteen-year-old frustrated by her limitations.

She put her brush down with a sigh and placed her hands over her eyes. She knew she must stop squinting. It only happened when she was painting, and her eyes were the feature on which most people commented. 'Blue like a mountain lake,' her father said. 'Blue like a mysterious Siamese cat,' was her mother's description. A lock of her blonde hair slipped over her forehead. She'd discovered there was more green in blonde hair than yellow, and that it picked up the colours of nearby objects. She stared at the top of her head. The fine hairs that framed her face would have to be painted delicately.

She returned to her palette and worked on in silent contemplation. She had been taught to paint by a series of Russian tutors, and her subjects until five years ago had been summer dachas and ballet classes in the style of Élisabeth Louise Vigée Le Brun. A distinctly modern self-portrait was not something she would have dared attempt. The Russia that she knew was steeped in folklore and ruled by superstition. Her nanny employed all manner of rituals and customs to ward off evil. If she had ever discovered Kristina staring into a mirror for too long she would have been horrified. Reflective surfaces were magical and not to be taken lightly. They were used for scrying. They were portals to another world.

A door suddenly slammed. There was no breeze coming from the window or else Kristina wouldn't have had sweat dripping down her back. She went to the door and looked up and down the hall. There was not a soul to be seen. *It is the ghost of Modigliani*, she told herself, as it was rumoured that he still wandered the building and the whole of Montparnasse, his loud laughter following him as he vanished around a corner or up a flight of stairs. Kristina wouldn't mind meeting his restless spirit, although it was said that in real life, for an Italian at least, he was quite unsociable.

She returned to her desk and picked up her brush. She dreamed of being a great artist but did not want to live and die tragically as Modigliani had – a mind and body destroyed by absinthe and hashish; a trail of broken hearts left in his wake including the suicide of his pregnant mistress. Apart from her desire to paint, what Kristina desired for the rest of her life was quite ordinary. She wanted to have someone to love and who loved her. She wanted to be happy.

'Kristina.'

She looked up to see her friend Sonia standing in the doorway. The arched eyebrows she had taken to pencilling on every morning accentuated her angular face and made her look dramatic. She was wearing a tubular dress that hung straight from her shoulders to below her knees. It was one of her own creations and suited her svelte figure and short brown hair. She'd made a similar dress for Kristina in sapphire blue, only of a looser fit, because nothing was going to flatten Kristina's curves no matter what fashion dictated.

Kristina glanced at the clock on the wall. It was almost six o'clock.

'I lost track of time,' she said, packing away her materials. She quickly washed her brushes and hands, and then fixed the pins in her hair.

'You ought to cut it,' said Sonia.

'Not after your mother nearly killed you for chopping off yours. She'd send me straight back to Nice.'

Sonia's mother, Madame Vertinskaya, was the only reason Kristina's parents had allowed her to study art in Paris. Sonia wanted to become an interior designer, but her family had not fared well after the Russian Revolution and did not have the means for her to live in Paris. Kristina's father offered to pay for an apartment for the three women if Madame Vertinskaya would act as a guardian for his daughter.

'Hardly, my mother thinks the world of you,' said Sonia, parading around with her head held high as Madame Vertinskaya was wont to do. '"Why don't you try to be more cheerful, like Kristina. Why do you look so dour all the time?"'

Sonia's imitation of her mother made Kristina smile. Madame Vertinskaya was a good woman of integrity, but she was also rather conventional.

'What do you answer when your mother says things like that?' Kristina asked.

'I tell her it's not fashionable to be cheerful and that it's much better to have an air of disdain about you.'

Kristina pursed her lips to stifle a laugh and followed her friend out the door.

Outside, the heat was even more oppressive. It bounced off the pavement and hit them in the face like a bomb blast. It was hot in Nice but at least the town had the sea breeze in the evenings.

The women passed a street vendor whose horse was wearing a straw hat with holes cut out for its ears. 'Look, fresh strawberries,' Kristina said, pointing to the vendor's cart.

'I haven't eaten all day,' said Sonia, wincing and rubbing her stomach.

'You worked through lunchtime again?'

'No, I want to fit into the silk evening dress I'm making.'

'Why don't you make the dress to your size?' Kristina asked. 'After all, wasn't comfort the point of women liberating themselves from corsets?'

Sonia sent her a withering glance, but Kristina was spared one of her acid remarks because she was one of the few people Sonia genuinely liked.

'Come, I'll buy us some,' Kristina said, opening her purse and handing the money to the vendor. 'It's not good to drink on an empty stomach.'

The strawberries were juicy and full of summer sweetness. They finished them off before they reached the corner of the street. They were about to cross over to the Café de la Rotonde when a voice called out to Kristina. It was Peggy Truesdale, an American student from her drawing class. Peggy caught up to them, her plump face moist and red beneath her sailor's cap.

'I'm meeting friends at Le Dôme,' she said. 'Are you going there too?'

Café du Dôme was directly across the street from La Rotonde and drew a crowd of American college students in white pants and blazers and their flouncily dressed girlfriends. Kristina wouldn't have minded because Peggy was fun. She played the ukulele and took lessons in Grecian dancing. But Paris's most serious artists – or at least the artists Kristina most hoped to emulate – favoured La Rotonde.

'No, we are headed to La Rotonde,' said Sonia, answering for Kristina. Her tone had a degree of hostility that would put anybody off.

Peggy, who was as warm and friendly as a ray of sunshine, looked taken aback. Kristina was about to introduce the women to each other when she realised there was no point. Sonia could be abrasive, disagreeable, and a bully when the urge took her.

When she cut someone it was because she'd made up her mind to not like them and there was no use trying to persuade her otherwise.

'We are meeting friends there tonight,' Kristina said to Peggy, feeling embarrassed by Sonia's deplorable attitude. 'But I hope you have a nice time and I look forward to seeing you in class tomorrow.'

Peggy nodded and headed across the road to a group of smiling young people who waved first to her and then to Kristina and Sonia.

'More money than sense,' muttered Sonia. 'Why would a woman with such a round face even think of wearing a sailor's cap. It made her face as big as the moon.'

'I think she's pretty.'

'Pretty is not chic. There is a difference. That girl has loads of money and still manages to look like she stepped straight out of a cornfield.'

Kristina sighed and let the matter go. Her father often said that to be happy, one had to always be searching for what was good in people. It was no surprise then that Sonia was one of the unhappiest people Kristina knew. She had never got over her family's loss of wealth and status and Kristina knew half of what she said was out of bitterness.

They reached the doors of La Rotonde and straightened their dresses and readjusted their cloche hats to appealing tilts before going inside. They were immediately hit by the overpowering smell of garlic and tobacco. Despite it still being early, the café was already full and the animated patrons sitting around the marble-topped tables were noisy. Kristina felt the men's eyes turn towards them. Two fashionably dressed women − one very tall and blonde, and the other dark and petite − always made an impression.

The head waiter, Pierre, managed to cut through the din. 'Ah, you are here, beautiful ladies! Straight upstairs. And if any of those rascals give you trouble, let me know and I will kick them in the pants!'

La Rotonde had just been extended and instead of gathering in the back room, the artists now met in the upstairs dining room which became a cabaret and dance floor after nine. Kristina and Sonia knew that Pierre had sent them there because he thought they were decorative, not because he respected them as an upcoming artist and an interior designer. 'Ladies', as a general rule, did not patronise La Rotonde. The women who went there were either artists' models or actresses and opera singers not yet established in their careers. But Kristina understood that a female artist must expend an inordinate amount of energy to gain even a fraction of the recognition of a male one. By not participating in the discussions taking place in cafés like La Rotonde, the other women in her classes were missing out on making the connections that would help them get exhibited or introduced to important art dealers. She looked forward to the day when she would show Pierre one of her more accomplished paintings and see the surprise on his face.

The accents echoing around the room made it sound like Kristina and Sonia had just stepped into the League of Nations: French of course, but also Russian, American, Japanese and German. There was none of the French xenophobia that one might find in upper-class drawing rooms.

Kristina scanned the room and immediately felt like an imposter. At a table in the far corner, Pablo Picasso and Man Ray were deep in conversation. At the table next to them were Tsuguharu Foujita and Francis Picabia. Jean Porel, a portrait artist and a regular at the café, was sitting with two other young men Kristina knew as Louis and Hector. They were looking at a sketchpad and squabbling over some point of difference. Jean saw them and waved them over.

'We need you ladies to settle an argument,' he said, pulling out chairs for them and inviting them to sit down.

Hector, who had a twirled moustache he took great pride in, waved to the waiter to bring Kristina and Sonia drinks. Kristina ordered eau-de-vie while Sonia ordered a Turkish coffee with vodka.

'What were you arguing about?' Sonia asked.

'What we always argue about,' replied Louis, his eyes magnified behind his thick glasses. 'Who is the better artist and who is the better lover.'

'Women are the best judges of lovers,' said Sonia, 'so it's stupid for you to argue that point among yourselves. I want to know how you judge the best artist.'

'Much the same way we judge lovers.' Jean laughed. 'A perceptive eye and a steady hand.' He held up the sketchpad where someone had drawn a portrait of Jean.

'That's very good,' Kristina remarked.

'It's mine,' said Louis with pride.

Hector shook his head. 'The challenge was to draw a portrait of Jean without once lifting the pencil. So far none of us have succeeded in doing it.'

'Let Kristina have a try,' said Sonia.

The men looked at each other and laughed good-naturedly. The waiter brought the drinks and placed them before the women.

'I'm serious,' said Sonia. 'Let Kristina try.'

'All right,' agreed Jean, pushing the sketchpad towards Kristina and lifting his chin. 'See if you can capture my beauty.'

Drawing a detailed image in a single line was something Kristina's father had urged her to do since she was a child. But it had always been a game and never a competition. She took a sip of her fiery drink to steady her nerves and focused on her goal like a golfer about to take a shot. The table fell silent as her pencil touched the paper. The trick, she had learned, was to work rapidly so that self-doubt didn't get the better of her, but not to hurry so much that she might miss an important line and bring the whole process undone. Looking from Jean to the pad, her hand seemed to move as if it had a life of its own.

She finished in under two minutes and held up an authentic rendering of Jean's angular face with shading that reflected the fading summer light in the room. He took the sketchpad from her and stared at it in awe.

'I would not have believed it if I hadn't seen you do that with my own eyes,' Jean said.

'You are indeed an artist,' agreed Hector. 'We must show Max.'

He stood up and yelled across the room to a party of well-dressed men and women. 'Max! Max!'

At first Kristina thought he was addressing the dandyish-looking man at the head of the table. But it was the man who'd had his back to them who turned around.

When he realised he was being called, he stood up, cutting a striking figure in a white linen suit and with the sort of stiff brush-like hair, cut short, that stood up on its own and that Kristina found marvellous to paint. His facial features were fine with a sloped nose that flared slightly at the nostrils. Kristina thought he would make a wonderful subject for a portrait. She judged every new person she met that way.

'Who is he?' Sonia asked.

'Max Bergeret,' Hector whispered. 'An art dealer.'

Sonia turned to Kristina, who shrugged. The art community in Paris was small and if you hadn't actually met a member of it, you at least knew of them. But she had never heard of this Max Bergeret.

'Max,' said Jean, 'may I introduce you to Mademoiselle Kristina Belova.' He held out the sketch to show him. 'Look what she did. In less than two minutes and without lifting her pencil.'

Max studied the sketch and raised his eyebrows, impressed. 'I see a dedicated yet confident hand, Mademoiselle Belova,' he said in a warm voice that brimmed with good manners. 'It takes many hours of dedicated practice to develop such a skill.'

'Sit down,' Jean invited him.

While Jean grabbed an extra chair, Max introduced himself to Sonia, and then when everybody was settled again, he fixed his sparkling grey eyes on Kristina. 'So where are you studying in Paris?'

'The Académie de la Grande Chaumière.'

'A fine school. How are you finding it?'

Kristina barely heard herself answer that she was enjoying learning about colour theory and developing her drawing skills. She was experiencing the same sort of light-headedness she felt whenever she was suddenly inspired by an idea – a rush of adrenaline that kept her up all night to finish a painting.

'She has only been in Paris two months,' said Sonia, 'and she has already completed twenty fine paintings, gouaches and drawings. There is hardly any room left in the bedroom we share.'

Max looked from Sonia to Kristina and smiled. 'Is that so? Are you so prolific?' He edged his chair closer to hers with an expression of genuine interest on his face. 'Then I wonder if you would permit me to view them?'

Kristina's fear that she was an imposter vanished. She was a serious artist and the fact that an art dealer in Paris was already interested in her work was proof of that.

'Of course,' she said, looking in her purse for a pen and piece of paper so she could write down the address of the apartment. 'But I will have to ask Madame Vertinskaya first for permission to have a visitor.'

'Is Madame Vertinskaya your concierge?' Max asked.

Kristina shook her head. 'No, she is Sonia's mother. We live with her.'

Max's cheeks pinked slightly. Kristina assumed he was used to more independent women and was surprised she lived with an older guardian.

'Of course, I would not wish to intrude,' he said.

'Oh, you wouldn't be intruding at all,' Sonia was quick to respond. 'But my mother has old-world manners. Apart from her Sunday "at homes", she accepts guests only by invitation.'

'Your mother sounds delightful,' Max said. 'I find old-world manners charming.' He took the paper from Kristina with the address on it. 'I will write to her and ask when it is convenient to call on you to see your artwork,' he told her.

Kristina was relieved that he was so accommodating but worried that he might be going out of his way. She was about to suggest that perhaps she should take the best examples of her work to his gallery and, if he liked them, he could then pay them a visit to see the rest. But at that moment, a loud burst of laughter came from the table where Max had been sitting. They both turned towards the commotion. An exotic-looking woman with red hair beckoned to him.

'I best get back to my friends,' he said, standing.

His face – so open a moment ago – was suddenly hard to read. He was watching Kristina closely as if expecting her to say something, but she didn't know what. She felt grateful enough that he had interrupted his meal to look at her sketch. Yet, even after he returned to his table, she felt his attention still on her. It took all her willpower not to turn and look at him.

When eight o'clock came around, Sonia nudged her. 'We'd better be going, otherwise my mother won't let us hear the end of it.'

Madame Vertinskaya allowed them to stay out until eight o'clock, believing that they were both studying with fellow classmates. And in a way, they were. But if she knew Kristina and Sonia were hanging around La Rotonde, they'd probably never be let out of the apartment again.

'You leave us like two Cinderellas,' said Jean, his voice slurred from the effects of one too many drinks.

Outside on the street, Sonia pinched Kristina's arm. 'You have to push yourself more, Kristina. It isn't enough to paint beautifully, you need to know how to sell your work. You should have told Max Bergeret about the praise you've been getting at art school and the prizes you've won.'

Kristina knew Sonia was right. To be a successful artist involved much more than knowing about the mixing and handling of paints or the ordering of a composition. One had to know how to negotiate. Something she wasn't very good at.

'Anyway, we shall see what he thinks of your paintings,' Sonia continued. 'And if he doesn't exhibit your work, then he is a fool, and we will find a better dealer for you.'

Kristina linked her arm with Sonia's. Her friend could be a devil sometimes, but if she liked you, she would be your greatest champion. 'Thank you,' Kristina said.

'Don't thank me,' Sonia said with a wry smile. 'You don't understand my motives. I only want more space on my side of the bedroom.'

They were both quiet the rest of the way home, letting the possibility of success linger in their minds. As they passed

Notre Dame, the streetlights twinkled prettily to life. It was a sight Kristina had witnessed many times before, but that day it was as if she was seeing it all for the first time.

★

Russians do not entertain by halves. On the afternoon Madame Vertinskaya had arranged to show Kristina's paintings to Max Bergeret, she and her maid, Faina, travelled back and forth from the kitchen to the dining room with plates of lemon and spice cakes, raspberry tarts, black bread and caviar, along with candied violets and pots of sour cream, strawberry jam and honey.

'He's French,' said Sonia, watching the preparations from the doorway. 'For him, afternoon tea is a fruit tart and cheese.'

'It's lovely for you to go to all this effort, Madame Vertinskaya,' Kristina said more gently, 'but he may not stay that long. He is a busy man, I imagine.'

Madame Vertinskaya frowned. 'Nobody who comes to our home will ever be able to say that they left it hungry.'

'That's for certain,' said Sonia.

There was a knock at the door and Faina went to answer it while the other three women straightened their hair and clothes. Kristina heard Max's voice as Faina ushered him inside. When she led him into the room where the feast had been laid, he stopped short in surprise. He was carrying a bouquet of lilies and a box of chocolates, which, after Kristina introduced him to Sonia's mother, he handed to the older lady. 'Thank you for welcoming me into your home, Madame Vertinskaya.'

She smiled broadly. 'First, we eat, and then you look at Kristina's paintings. Pleasure before business, as they say.'

Max's eyes opened wide as if he was perplexed and Kristina wondered if it was because Madame Vertinskaya had mixed up the saying. It was supposed to be 'business *before* pleasure'. She noticed he was younger than he appeared at La Rotonde – perhaps in his mid to late twenties. He dutifully took the seat Madame Vertinskaya offered him as the guest of honour, while the rest of them sat down. It occurred to Kristina that he must feel outnumbered, and perhaps this was not the right way to go about getting a dealer interested in her work. But as the meal progressed and Madame Vertinskaya piled more food onto his plate and topped up his wineglass, he seemed to relax. He listened with sincere interest to her stories of life in Russia before the revolution. She had not told anyone those stories in a while, and it reminded Kristina how hard things were for the people of her parents' generation who felt they no longer had a country. It was easier for Sonia and her to adapt and consider France their home.

After the meal was finished and Faina had cleared the table, Madame Vertinskaya sent everyone to the parlour where Kristina and Sonia had put the best of the paintings, pastels and drawings on display. Now that her mother had done the job of softening up Max with food and wine, Sonia took over the role of saleswoman, edging Max towards a portrait Kristina had painted of her own mother from her last visit back to Nice, which Sonia was adamant was her best work. In it, Kristina's mother was fashionably dressed for the opera in a red silk evening dress and black gloves. Her face was composed but there was a glint of rapture in her eyes, as if she was already listening to the opening act of *La Traviata*.

Max moved closer to study the portrait, his expression betraying nothing of his thoughts. Then he turned his attention to Kristina's other works, looking at each one for a long time. He turned to her, and something in his face made her think he was on the verge of apologising. Her stomach sank. Perhaps he didn't think her work was good enough, and she very much wanted him to approve of her paintings.

'Your work is exceptional,' he said finally. 'You capture inner worlds – and not just that of your subject, but I suspect, your own as well.'

His praise made Kristina feel as if she had been lifted off the ground. Her parents were always so effusive in their praise of her work that it seemed in their eyes she was the greatest artist since Da Vinci. Her teachers liked her work too, but focused mainly on the technical application of paints and the use of brushes to achieve effects. To receive approval from someone who could determine her future as an artist was more than flattering, it was vital.

'Thank you,' she said.

But Sonia had less restraint. 'Her work is worthy of an exhibition, don't you think, Monsieur Bergeret?'

His eyebrows shot up as if Sonia had startled him. Kristina was about to protest that an entire exhibition of her work was premature. The most she was hoping for was that Max would take one or two pictures to sell in his gallery.

But before she had a chance to correct Sonia, Max answered, 'Indeed, Mademoiselle Belova's work is fresh and bold. It's worthy of an exhibition which Bergeret and Lavertu would be happy to undertake.' He turned to Kristina. 'If a commission of fifty per cent is agreeable to you, I can send a removalist van on Friday to pick up the works.'

A commission of fifty per cent or higher was common among the best dealers, so Kristina was about to agree when Sonia put her hand on her arm.

'And the costs of the framing and the catalogue?' she asked.

He gave her a respectful nod. 'Our firm will cover those.'

Max took out a docket book from his pocket and wrote down the number of works he would be collecting. Sonia winked at Kristina, who had to concede that she was right about being assertive.

Madame Vertinskaya signalled to Faina who entered with a tray of vodka glasses.

'Let us drink to the success of Kristina and to the good health and happiness of all of us,' she said.

★

After the removalist collected Kristina's artworks, she waited a further fortnight for word from Max. She was sure he would let her know once her paintings were framed and ready to be exhibited. She arrived eagerly at La Rotonde each evening hoping to see him, but he never appeared. Jean, Louis and Hector had all gone south for the summer so she couldn't ask them if they'd seen him. She considered asking the other artists, but a niggling doubt stopped her. She didn't want to make a fool of herself in front of them, especially after Peggy expressed surprise that Max would have taken all of Kristina's work.

'You must owe him a lot of money!' she said. 'Unknown artists usually pay for their exhibition spaces. It's unheard of for art dealers to offer an unproven artist a solo show.'

Kristina's mind travelled back to the night she had met Max. Jean had not actually introduced him as an art dealer – it was Louis who had, and he was prone to exaggeration. She spoke to the head waiter, Pierre, and asked if he knew anything about Max Bergeret.

'Ah, yes, that good-looking young man. I see him occasionally, but I don't know what he does.'

When there was still no word from Max the following day, Kristina walked to Rue la Boétie – the elegant narrow street that was often referred to as the 'Florence of Paris' because it was where the best private art galleries were located. In the windows she spotted works by Renoir and Cézanne, Matisse and Picasso, Utrillo and Derain. She read the names of the galleries in the gold lettering above their doors: Rosenberg, Bignou, Hessel and Wildenstein. But after reaching the end of the street without finding Bergeret & Lavertu, it occurred to her that Max's partnership might be a subagency of one of the larger galleries. She turned back and walked into a gallery with one of Monet's water lily paintings on an easel near the door. An elegant woman in a black suit and smelling of champagne and Chanel No 5 approached her. 'It's beautiful, isn't it? It's poetry in a painting.'

'It is exceptional,' Kristina agreed. 'But I'm looking for an art dealer named Max Bergeret. I don't know which gallery he works for.'

The woman blinked and then shook her head. 'I do not know of this Monsieur Bergeret. Wait a moment, I'll ask my husband.'

An elderly man appeared from the back room, his hair heavy with pomade and his pin-striped suit sharply cut.

'Ah, you are mistaken, mademoiselle,' he said. 'Bergeret and Lavertu are not art dealers. They have an art-supply store.'

'An art-supply store?'

The man took an address book from a drawer under the counter and thumbed through it. 'Here you are,' he said, taking a piece of paper and writing down the address. 'You'll find them in Saint-Germain-des-Prés, not far from the École des Beaux-Arts.'

Kristina stared at the piece of paper. Saint-Germain-des-Prés was a working-class suburb on the Left Bank. Kristina knew it well because of Les Deux Magots, a café popular with artists and writers. It was an area of shabby streets, rag and bone vendors and the briny smell of fish shops. The sense of triumph she had been feeling since Max's visit collapsed into dread, and she swallowed down a sickening feeling that she had been swindled.

★

Kristina found Bergeret & Lavertu wedged between a bookbinder and a café. In its windows were canvases and stretchers. The walls of the shop were lined with glass cabinets like those found in pharmacies, containing dozens of jars of paint pigments. She exhaled a breath and entered, nearly toppling over a stand of paintbrushes in her fury.

A young man of perhaps sixteen was sorting pastels at the counter. He looked up when she entered but before he could greet her, Kristina noticed the doorway to a back room and through it spotted the portrait of her mother. She rushed into the room expecting the worst, but was surprised to see her works had been suitably framed and arranged in such a way that the eye travelled easily. One of her larger paintings of the Seine had been placed in a grouping of six of her smaller works of the bridges of Paris, as if they were in dialogue with each other. If they had been in a proper gallery, she would have been impressed with the good taste and care with which they had been displayed. But from the bars on the window and the pipes that ran up and down the corners of the walls, there was no denying they were hanging in the back room of a shop.

'May I help you, mademoiselle?' the shop assistant asked, coming up behind her.

54

'These are my artworks!' she said, sounding as bewildered as she felt.

The assistant's eyebrows shot up. 'They are? You are Mademoiselle Belova?' He wiped his hands on his apron, flustered, and then shook her hand. 'Your sense of colour is exquisite! But my goodness, what an argument you caused. I thought the world was coming to an end!'

'An argument?'

The assistant smiled wistfully and with a gesture of his hand, indicated for her to follow him up a flight of stairs. Kristina was too confused to protest. She entered an apartment on the second floor that was empty of furniture. On the walls someone had drawn in chalk a dining table, a floor lamp and a sofa. Above these were the words *reconnaissance de dette*, which was the French equivalent of I.O.U.

She turned to the clerk and shook her head, not understanding what any of this had to do with her paintings.

'Monsieur Bergeret pawned Monsieur Lavertu's favourite items of furniture in order to buy quality frames for your paintings,' the clerk said. He pointed to a corner where an armchair and desk had been drawn on the wall. 'Even his rosewood desk and his favourite armchair. Monsieur Lavertu is very particular about his things, and he was livid. That is, until he saw your paintings. Then he almost wept.'

'He almost wept?'

'From the beauty of the paintings, Mademoiselle Belova. He was overjoyed that he finally had a real artist to represent.'

The clerk's description of Monsieur Lavertu's reaction to her work nearly softened her resolve, but then she reminded herself of the seriousness of the situation. 'Messieurs Bergeret and Lavertu are not art dealers,' she said. 'This is an art-supply shop.'

The clerk frowned as if personally wounded by her dismissal of his employers. 'They have a good eye for art. They have taken paintings in lieu of payment in the past, and always managed to sell those works at a good price.'

Kristina wondered if perhaps all might not be lost. If Max had sold paintings in the past, perhaps he was not a complete amateur. 'Where does he sell them?'

'Here … or at the markets.'

'The markets!' she groaned.

This was truly a disaster. Her career seemed to be over before it had even begun.

There was a noise behind them, and Kristina turned to see Max coming into the room carrying a box on his shoulder.

'Mademoiselle Belova!' he cried when he saw her. He put down the box and reached out his hand. 'What a delightful surprise. One of the paintings doesn't have your signature on it. If you could sign it now, I'll be able to sell it.'

'You won't be selling anything,' she said. 'I thought you were an art dealer. A *professional* art dealer. I went looking for you on Rue la Boétie.'

'Ah yes,' he said, his face reddening.

'You deceived me.'

He touched the back of his head and rolled backwards and forwards on his feet. 'Not intentionally. I didn't realise you thought I was an art dealer until I arrived at your apartment.'

'Then why did you come to see my paintings?'

'Because I like art — and I thought you were very pretty,' he said contritely. 'When I realised you thought I was there to possibly represent your art, I didn't know what to do. Taking the whole collection and selling the works at good prices seemed the only honourable way to handle the situation.'

If it wasn't her future as an artist at stake, Kristina might have found the absurdity of the situation amusing.

'You can't sell my artwork from the back room of your shop!' she said.

'Why not?' he protested. 'All the great artists started selling their works in cafés and at the markets. Picasso used to do sketches in exchange for his supper. You are in good hands with my partner, Serge Lavertu. He is in London at the moment looking for opportunities to sell art there.'

The bell on the shop door rang downstairs and the clerk – who had been watching the exchange between Kristina and Max with some curiosity – reluctantly excused himself to attend to the customer.

The sincerity in Max's face took the edge off Kristina's annoyance. 'I'll have to meet Monsieur Lavertu first before I consent to dealing with either of you,' she told him.

'Certainly,' he agreed. 'But I think you will be impressed by him. He has a sense for good art like nobody else I know.' His eyes met hers and he said earnestly, 'I feel we have got off on the wrong foot. Is there any way I can make this up to you?'

Kristina studied his handsome face. His defined jaw. That marvellous shock of hair. She had a sense she was being drawn into something, seduced by that velvet gaze of his. But his eyes were also full of laughter – and goodness. This was not a man who meant her harm.

'You can,' she said.

A look of relief spread across his face. 'I can? How?'

She cocked her head. 'I need a model. You can pose for me. And you can call me Kristina.'

★

An artist must study things carefully to paint them, and they visualise the world differently. While others see objects and people, they see collections of lines, shadows, shapes and contours. In that regard, one might say they see the world as it really exists. Clouds are not white but blue, yellow and green. Skin is not only pink but also burnt sienna and ultramarine blue.

'Turn your face slowly towards me,' Kristina told Max. 'Now don't smile with your mouth, only your eyes.'

It was their first session together and Kristina was making sketches in preparation for painting Max's portrait. They had commandeered the back room of his shop among her other paintings where they would not be disturbed. Sitting still did not come naturally to Max. Nor did silence.

'A true artist uses only a few brushstrokes to evoke, not only a scene, but a feeling. That is the skill you have,' he said.

Kristina didn't answer. Not because she didn't agree, but because she was too busy capturing the shape of his nose and studying the curve of his cheek. His magnetic eyes locked with hers. Strangers look at each other for a split second before averting their gaze, friends maybe linger a moment or two longer, but an artist and her model must get comfortable with staring at each other for extended periods of time. As her pencil scratched across the paper, she thought that drawing someone was possibly the best way to get to know them, and the more she drew Max, the more she began to fall in love with him.

He shifted slightly and she noticed the beads of sweat on his forehead. Even in the back room the air was hot. It intensified the earthy smell of the oil paints and crayons drifting in from the shop. A pearl of sweat traced down her spine as softly as a fingertip.

'You can open the top button of your shirt if it is more comfortable,' she told him.

Max reached up and undid the button, tugging it away from his neck with an air of relief. Then he ventured a step further and undid the buttons of his sleeves and rolled them back to his elbows, leaning forward as he did. The sight of his strong arms and the position of his torso moved something inside of Kristina. His laughing eyes grew intense and his jaw stiffened. He was a different man from the dapper Max he had been only a few seconds before. Kristina saw in the way his muscles twitched and the blood rose to the surface of his skin that he was a man of passion.

'Hold that position,' she said.

For the next hour, as the temperature rose still further, Kristina and Max continued to study each other. When she thought she had captured as much as she could for one sitting, Kristina put her pencil down.

'I'd like to block out the portrait tomorrow afternoon,' she said. 'Once I've begun something I don't like to stop until I see where it is going.'

Max sent her a beguiling smile. 'I am exactly the same,' he told her. 'Let's go to dinner.'

★

The heat was milder under the chestnut trees in the courtyard of La Closerie des Lilas. The café was busy but quieter and prettier than La Rotonde or Le Dôme, and was therefore favoured by writers, poets and lovers. Golden light spilled through the leaves over Max's head and shoulders, and Kristina listened with fascination as he described his childhood growing up in a village in the Fontainebleau district. She knew of it only from the Neoclassical paintings of Jean-Baptiste-Camille Corot and was captivated as he described adventures in verdant forests of magnificent oak trees with his large entourage of siblings – four girls and three boys.

'Your description reminds me of my childhood at my family's dacha in Finland,' she told him. 'My summers were spent running barefoot through the grass and jumping into rivers with a dozen cousins.'

The waiter brought their potato quenelles, smelling richly of olive oil, rosemary and oregano. A pair of diners sitting next to them caught Max's attention. One was moustached and square-faced and sitting back in his chair, laughing good-naturedly, while the other, fair and fine-boned, leaned forward, imploring him about something. Both had American accents.

'What do you think they are discussing?' Max whispered to Kristina.

She took a sip of wine before answering. 'The fair-haired one is asking the other to read his manuscript. He is convinced he has written the great American novel and wants the other one to introduce him to his publisher.'

'Ah, you can read feelings so well?' replied Max.

'I can speak English.'

Max laughed. 'Really? Ah, then you must help me improve mine,' he told her. 'Once I gain a reputation in Paris as an art dealer, I'm going to travel to America.'

'America? Why?'

'To sell your art, of course. I have already taken a great painter under my wing, and I must make sure she is a success.'

'I haven't committed myself to you,' Kristina said. 'I might get a better offer elsewhere.'

'You might,' he conceded. 'But I assure you that you couldn't have more passionate champions than Serge and me.'

Kristina already knew that she and Max were meant for each other. They may have spent only a few hours together in an overheated studio, but in that time she had got to know Max better than most people do after years together.

'Well then, I shall put my trust in you,' she said. 'If only because you remind me of my father.'

He raised his eyebrows. 'I hope in good ways?'

Kristina nodded. 'I can see that, like him, you are someone who is quick to laugh and slow to anger. I like that. He would thoroughly approve of you trying your hand in America. He has always taught me that it's important to yield to new experiences, and to be ready to set out for adventure. I think that's why he has borne the loss of our life in Russia so well.'

Max watched her for a moment, and then reached across the table and put his hand on hers. It was far from any touch Kristina had known, and it made her feel quite unlike herself. Max stood up and she did too, without quite knowing why. Then, as if driven by some unseen force, they leaned forward and kissed each other tenderly on the lips. For a moment, they seemed to be floating on air, their bodies moving together, upwards and onwards as if their joy could defy gravity. They were sealing a pact. There would be no other dealers. No other lovers. It would only be Kristina and Max for eternity.

CHAPTER FOUR

EVE

Paris, May 1946

When I returned to the house after visiting Serge, the smell of real tobacco and the sound of a man's smooth baritone voice coming from the parlour told me that Lucile's nephew, Georges, was paying a visit.

'Ah, there you are, Eve,' he said, rising from his chair when I entered. 'I was just telling Odette here that we would have to send a search party to find you somewhere in Galeries Lafayette.'

From the enthralled look on the maid's face, it was clear they'd been discussing more exciting topics than my whereabouts. I guessed Georges had been entertaining her with stories from the war years he'd spent working in Buenos Aires – that city of sleek cars, bright lights and sultry women. Georges was nothing like his timid aunt. If suaveness and sophistication could be bottled into a fragrance it would be named 'Georges No 5'. His twinkling steel-blue eyes and upper-class French accent, blended with the inflections of an English education and the romance of South America, made women swoon. If I hadn't already been burned by another wealthy man as charming as he, I might have succumbed myself.

'Thank you, Odette,' I said, pulling off my gloves and holding them out for her to take.

At first she appeared not to hear me. Then when she realised I was addressing her, she gave me an embarrassed smirk, took the gloves and hurried away.

'I'm afraid your aunt is at the beauty parlour today,' I told Georges. 'She won't be back before five.'

Georges stood up. He was tall for a Frenchman and towered over me. 'It's you I came to see, Eve. I felt I ought to forewarn you that your intimate dinner of ten is now going to be twelve.'

It was nearly four o'clock. It was impolite for Georges to be thrusting new guests on me. Despite his reputation as a lady's man, he was a lawyer and quite serious about his cases, I had been told. He was cluey enough to know that planning for an elegant dinner party took precision and last-minute invitations were a great inconvenience. But refusing him was next to impossible because his voice was like a narcotic. I would have gladly listened to him reading out the Métro schedule.

'Some friends of yours?' I asked.

'Goodness no! I would never be so inconsiderate to you, or risk sending my aunt into a flap with even a glimmer of spontaneity. These are self-invited guests. And rather unpleasant ones, I'm afraid.'

I didn't like the ominous tone in his voice. 'Who are they?' I asked, indicating for him to sit down.

'The dreadful Marthe de Villiers and her husband, Cyrille. Hasn't my aunt ever mentioned them to you?'

I took the armchair opposite him. I could count Lucile's social circle on my fingers and toes, and I had never heard of Marthe and Cyrille de Villiers. 'No, she hasn't.'

'Marthe's father is one of the richest men in France,' Georges explained with a hint of distaste twisting his lips. 'But he was wise enough to see war coming and moved his investments and family to Switzerland. Marthe and Cyrille have been in Lucerne for the past seven years. Now they are back, and ready to wreak havoc on Paris. Before the war, Marthe's mother was one of the most popular socialites in Paris. She died last year, and Marthe's determined to step into her shoes as Paris's most revered hostess. She saw the article in *Elle* and I am sure she wants to investigate what you have done with Lucile's apartment.'

I was all for a bit of healthy rivalry to perk up one's game. But as it didn't take much to upset Lucile's applecart, a woman like Marthe having the gall to invite herself without speaking to Lucile or myself directly was like a slap in the face before a duel. To be a successful hostess in Paris, I had observed, a woman had to have one of three advantages – she was likeable, she was feared, or she was of great importance. In Marthe's case it seemed I could safely discount the first.

'Why do you describe Madame de Villiers as "dreadful"?' I asked.

'Why?' he exclaimed. 'Because she blighted poor Aunt Lucile's life. Their fathers were business associates, which meant that as young women they were often thrust together at social occasions. Marthe was a bully, and what little confidence Aunt Lucile had was quelched by her antics. She seemed to forever place Aunt Lucile in situations that made her look dumpy and grumpy. Once at the opera, Aunt Lucile was wearing the most exquisite blue silk dress and cloak. All eyes turned to look at her. But Marthe deliberately tripped her, sending her sprawling in a most undignified manner down a flight of stairs. She played innocent, of course, and pretended to be deeply concerned that Aunt Lucile had hurt herself.'

'What an atrocious woman!' I cried.

'Unquestionably,' agreed Georges.

My mind quickly dissected the situation. So, Lucile had been bullied? That would certainly explain her timidity. Some considered childhood bullying a rite of passage, but I knew the damage it could do. When I was at school, those children whose parents couldn't afford to give them lunch were issued special tokens to purchase food from the canteen. Nobody at my school was rich, but as one of the few token-holders, I stood out as the poorest of all. Sometimes the hunger was easier to bear than the humiliation and the teasing. Even though I now had an armoire full of couture dresses and a gold watch to wear, I still felt like the lonely poor girl on the inside.

'I'll tell Marthe de Villiers that she is not welcome here,' I said. 'She's obviously someone who picks on easy targets and I won't put up with dirty tricks. Lucile deserves to have a lovely birthday party.'

Georges regarded me with renewed appreciation. 'You genuinely care about my aunt, don't you?'

I felt the colour rise to my cheeks. Of course, Georges must have known that I wasn't some rich girl from the landed gentry of Australia. He managed Lucile's finances. He would have figured out I was a paid companion but was gentlemanly enough to have never said a word. He certainly never spoke to me as if he saw me as a servant.

'Well, yes,' I replied. 'She's been generous to me. I know she can be a bit of a fuddy-duddy sometimes but now you've given me a possible reason for it, I feel even more protective of her.'

'She was terribly lonely before you came along, even when she was married,' said Georges. Then a smile came to his face, and he leaned forward. 'I have a better idea. If you snub Marthe it will only make her more determined to defeat you, and you must remember she has much more social influence than Aunt Lucile.

You might find my aunt is suddenly uninvited to important social events after you've worked so hard to get her name on those lists. I say let Marthe come here and *you* take her on. As they say, "Hold your friends close, and your enemies closer".'

'Me? But I'm a nobody in Paris. I don't have a franc to my name, and I guess you know it.'

Georges shrugged. 'So what? What you have, Eve, is worth so much more than money.'

My curiosity was piqued. 'And what's that?'

He steepled his fingers and smiled. 'You, Eve, have an ability to influence people. You know what their secret desires are and how to fulfil them. Who would have known that dear Aunt Lucile harboured a longing to be a socialite? Until you came along, she shunned social engagements and could barely get the courage to speak up to her own servants. You've given her confidence, and she has blossomed.'

'But not blossomed enough to challenge Marthe herself?' I asked.

'I'm afraid not.'

Odette knocked and entered the room, carrying the presentation box holding Lucile's necklace from Mauboussin. 'This just arrived for Madame Damour,' she said.

I took the box from her and opened it to show Georges.

'That really is splendid,' he said, nodding his approval. 'You have excellent taste, Eve. The sight of it will have Marthe de Villiers breathing fire.'

He stood up and asked Odette to bring him his hat. 'I must get going now. I have a client to see before dinner tonight.'

I walked him to the front door. 'Before you leave, Georges, I have a legal question I want to ask you on behalf of … *a friend.*'

His face, smiling a moment ago, turned serious. 'Am I correct in assuming that you mean a friend of the male persuasion?'

He appeared so put out by the idea that it almost seemed as if he was jealous. But the idea was ridiculous. A man who could have any woman he wanted would not be worried about who I might be seeing. 'No, nothing like that,' I said. 'An older man and a mentor.'

Georges sighed and took his hat from Odette. 'Ask your question, Eve, but with the full understanding of the ridiculousness of my profession.'

'This friend of mine was a successful art dealer before the war … a Jewish art dealer. His gallery was requisitioned by the Germans and sold to a French art dealer who doesn't want to give it back, not unless my friend pays an exorbitant amount of money. The case seems to be taking a long time to get to court. Is there any way to speed up the proceedings?'

Georges rubbed his chin. 'The French government has put in place restitution laws, but the process is time-consuming, difficult and, I'm afraid to say, sometimes futile. What is your friend's name?'

'Serge Lavertu.'

'Ah yes,' Georges said. 'I know of him. Well, I can certainly see what I can do.'

'Thank you.'

He grimaced. 'Don't thank me, Eve. It bores me to be thanked. Human beings are fundamentally selfish and rarely do things entirely out of pure intentions.' His eyes rested on my face for a moment. 'As it turns out, I have a favour to ask of you.'

'Really? What could it be?'

'I must attend the Anglo-French Legal Conference dinner in July. I'm normally quite happy to go to those tedious functions by myself. But it seems the wives' committee this year is being quite insistent that every single man must come accompanied. As I can't think of any woman who wouldn't mistake the invitation as some sort of sentimental gesture, I'd appreciate it if you would do me the honour.'

'A sentimental gesture?' I replied with mock horror. 'Could there be anything ghastlier?'

'Exactly!' Georges grinned.

'Well, of course I'll go with you. It will be my pleasure.'

He studied me. 'It will get them all talking, I suppose. You won't mind that?'

'I don't care,' I said, as Odette opened the door for him and he stepped out into the hallway. 'It doesn't matter what people say, as long as it isn't true.'

He gave me a slight bow before turning to leave. 'Once again, Eve, you've shown yourself to be the most astute woman in Paris.'

I laughed and waved as he strode down the corridor. Then suddenly remembering the point of his visit had been to warn me about Marthe de Villiers, I called after him, 'You didn't say anything about Monsieur de Villiers. What should I expect of him?'

Georges turned back to me. 'He is a nothing. About as appealing as a typhoid-carrier.'

I grimaced and Georges mirrored the expression back to me. 'Yes, he has exactly the same effect on me,' he said. 'The man sets my teeth on edge. Well, goodbye, Eve. I am looking forward to this evening.'

★

Soon after Georges left, the flowers arrived and I turned my attention to studying the arrangements from every angle. I moved an occasional table to position it directly under the

Degas painting in the drawing room and placed a vase of lilies on it – the kind of flowers that might be thrown to a dancer after a splendid performance.

I looked around the room with an air of satisfaction. The clusters of roses, tulips and hellebores were tasteful and intimate. The candles were a decadent touch – they were rationed and expensive, but they were also practical. The electricity supply in Paris was erratic and I was worried it might suddenly shut off in the middle of dinner. Then I went to my room to dress for the evening. As I combed my hair at the dressing table, I remembered my visit to Serge's gallery and that he'd said I reminded him of someone. I had assumed it was my mother, although our features couldn't have been more different. But now I believed it was himself. I stared at the mirror at my pale, translucent skin with the pinches of colour in both cheeks, my chocolate-brown hair and green eyes, and thought that if he hadn't been my father, and we were the same age, Serge and I could have been twins. Yet, he couldn't see the resemblance.

For the first seven years of my life, I had thought my father was an out-of-work and out-of-luck actor named Efron Archer. He didn't live with my mother and me, but turned up at random intervals, drunk and berating my mother for 'ruining his life'. Even at my young age, I sensed that Efron was the cause of his own demise. What my mother felt for him, I could never detect. It was only after he died of cirrhosis of the liver that she told me that my natural father was Serge Lavertu. My eyes travelled to the dresser drawer again, and against my better judgement, I took out the letter she'd left and reread it:

Dearest Serge,
I know it will be a shock to receive this letter after so many years. But I'm descending into a darkness that I fear I will not

come out of again. Not this time. I am a cat who has used up her nine lives.

But I cannot depart this world without telling you that you made me happier than anyone else ever could. What joy we had together in our younger years in Paris and Nice. But the darkness grips me more urgently now and I have no strength left to fight it. So, I must tell you two things. Firstly, I understand the reasons you couldn't love me the way I loved you, and I forgive you for them.

The second thing is we made a daughter together. I named her 'Eve' after the last painting I posed for. I did not tell you about her before because I didn't want to make you feel responsible. But now some aspects about myself have come into sharp relief, and I wonder if in doing so, I deprived you of something essential to your own being.

I must go now. If anyone could have saved me, it would have been you. But alas this beast is too strong for a mere mortal like me.

With all my heart,

Madeleine.

PS. I will ask Eve to go to you with this letter. Eve is a bright young girl who has a lot of you in her. Please help her find her way in the world.

I was at work at the haberdashery when my mother took her life. We had received a bolt of pearl-pink crepe de Chine that day, and as my mother was writing her final letter to Serge, I was imagining myself wrapped in glorious Vionnet-style gowns. In the weeks leading up to her suicide, she had been in constant states of rage and bitterness and I had taken to staying out late with friends after work to avoid her. I often wondered if my rejection was the final straw that led to her fatal decision.

I closed my eyes to fight back the tears. I did not want to make my face puffy and red for the party.

'Mademoiselle Archer,' came Odette's voice at the door. 'Are you ready for me to do your hair now?'

I pressed the heels of my palms hard against my eyes and composed myself. 'Yes, Odette,' I said. 'You may come in.'

★

I waited until Lucile was dressed and ready to receive her guests before I broke the news that her old nemesis was coming to dinner.

'Marthe!' she said, her voice as high as a soprano's. 'Marthe de Villiers! She's coming here? Tonight?'

The beautician had done a wonderful job with Lucile, shaping her eyebrows and creating a pretty bow shape to her lips. Now she had a crimson flush from her throat to her forehead and was starting to look hot and shiny. It was clear she was still intimidated by Marthe.

'Now, remember what I told you,' I said, thrusting a glass of champagne into her hand. 'Never let anyone get the better of you.'

Lucile glanced at her reflection in the bullet-scarred mirror in the drawing room. 'The better of me?' she repeated, before taking an undignified gulp of champagne.

I was worried she was about to fall apart on me. It was like being a captain who finds their major hiding under a camp bed moments before an important battle.

A knock at the apartment door made Lucile jump out of her skin. I had to practically drag her to the foyer, but thankfully it was a smiling Georges who met us when Odette opened the door. He looked even more debonair than usual in his black evening suit. With him were Alice Dabescat and her husband Olivier, and their adult son, Ronan.

Georges sidled up to me. 'I thought I might come a bit early for moral support.'

'Thank you,' I whispered back.

'Well, isn't this all delightful!' said Alice, looking around at the flowers and the dozens of flickering candles. 'And don't you look wonderful!' she told Lucile, looking her up and down with admiration. 'And so do you, Eve,' she added. 'But then you always do.'

I was wearing a silver and white lamé evening dress draped around the neckline. Alice was frowzily dressed in a shapeless taffeta gown, but what she lacked in fashion finesse she made up for in personality. Her liveliness and quick wit could perk up any party, and unlike most society people in Paris, she didn't have a mean bone in her body.

Olivier, a serious man with a long upper lip and grave face, launched into the headline news of the day. 'The Russians have been secretly taking over Paris. They are buying the best buildings and homes in the finest arrondissements. Proletarians, indeed! Their officers are better dressed than the French in gold braid, and I've seen them at the Club Scheherazade, spending as freely as the Imperial family ever did.'

Lucile glanced at me, and I gave her a nod of encouragement. I'd told her to never speak about politics emotionally, but with an open and astute mind, sticking to the facts and always offering a fair solution to the problem.

'The Soviet Union doesn't allow French government officials outside their embassies without strict permits. We must insist on reciprocal rights for all,' she pronounced with eloquence.

Georges looked in my direction and lifted his eyebrows.

'Won't you please come this way,' Lucile said, guiding the guests towards the drawing room.

The Dabescats followed her, Alice oohing and aahing at the apartment's new décor. Georges stayed behind with me.

'Now tell me more about the guest of honour this evening,' he said. 'I've been hearing excited whispers in every home I've visited this week. People have been guessing, but nobody really knows.'

'Her name is Fanny Toussaint,' I told him. 'She is not yet famous but soon will be. In the past year she won the Prix Premiere at the Paris Conservatoire, and also came first in discus and shot-put at the European Championships in Oslo.'

'A concert pianist and an athlete? A highly unusual combination,' remarked Georges.

'I'm pleased you agree,' I said. 'It's one thing to have someone celebrated at your table, but an even bigger thrill to have someone who is on their way to being famous. For Lucile to be able to claim some part of Fanny's trajectory of success will give her kudos. If you are in agreement, I'd like Lucile to pay Fanny's tuition. The girl works at her music and sports with utter devotion. I promise you there will be a payoff in the future.'

Georges nodded. 'How could anyone refuse such an intriguing proposition? Just as I'm sure I've learned everything about you, Eve, you surprise me yet again. Is there nothing you don't think of? If you should ever tire of working for my aunt, I should very much like to have you on my legal team.'

Another knock at the door heralded the arrival of Fanny and her mother. I was pleased to see that the young woman's squared-jawed face and broad shoulders were softened by the Cartier earrings I'd sent her.

'Ah, Fanny,' said Lucile, reappearing in the foyer. 'How wonderful to see you, dear. Come, I have some people I want you to meet.'

I was glad that Lucile had relaxed into her role as hostess, but it was a misstep to not have acknowledged Fanny's mother. The woman looked about awkwardly at the Qing-dynasty vases like a tourist seeing the Arc de Triomphe for the first time. She was clearly uncomfortable in the surroundings.

Georges flew into action. '*Bonsoir*, Madame Toussaint,' he said gallantly. 'I am Madame Damour's nephew, Georges Camadeau. Allow me to accompany you to the drawing room.' He offered his arm, and the mesmerised Madame Toussaint took it. 'Now do tell me,' Georges continued as they moved away, 'where does your daughter get her talent in shot-put from?'

Jeanne and Henri Perret arrived soon after. They were an attractive couple in their late forties and too rich for their own good. They had a tendency to monologue endlessly on topics that were of no interest to anybody but themselves: their personal sleep schedules; their obsession with deep-sea fishing; where their children were going skiing for the winter season. Lucile had implored me to invite them as she'd known them for years, but if she wanted to be a successful socialite, I was going to have to wean her away from them. At one exclusive luncheon, the hostess confided in me that it was an unspoken rule among the top hostesses to never sit bores next to interesting people. 'They kill the mood. But if one sits bores together at the same end of the table, they seem to enliven each other with their monotonous conversations.' After that, I noticed that Lucile was nearly always placed with the Perrets and other social bores and that had to stop.

I followed the Perrets into the drawing room, leaving Odette and another maid, Marie, to wait for Marthe and her husband. It was rude enough that they had invited themselves and at such short notice, but to be over half an hour late was unforgivable. I could never be sure how long the electricity supply would last and if they didn't come soon, we'd all be eating a cold dinner.

'Tell us something about your life in Australia, Eve,' Olivier said to me, once we were all gathered with a glass of Veuve Clicquot in our hands.

I did not enjoy telling lies, but I launched into my well-rehearsed life story about growing up on a vineyard in the Hunter Valley and the pretty homestead that had survived bushfires, hailstorms and floods.

'And the wine?' asked Ronan. 'What kind of wine did the vineyard produce?'

'Fine semillon wines,' I answered on cue. 'Zesty and crisp with complex flavours.'

'But they have dangerous snakes in Australia, don't they?' asked Jeanne with a shudder.

I never quite understood how a people who had lost over half a million of their fellow citizens in the war could be so afraid of God's own creatures, who were generally shy and avoided human contact. But for the sake of the dog and pony show, I was about to launch into my well-worn tale about waking up one morning with a snake next to me on the pillow when Odette ushered a couple into the room. I hadn't heard them arrive.

'Monsieur and Madame de Villiers,' Odette announced.

Marthe de Villiers was the same age as Lucile, and handsome with a long neck decorated with a white gold necklace and diamond pendant. Her gleaming silver hair was set off by a sparkling sapphire tiara. But there was something wrong about her dress, the skirt of which consisted of yards of pleated cream silk. It was more a ballgown than an evening dress. And the tiara especially troubled me. Why would you crown yourself to attend another woman's birthday party?

Showing more bravery than either Georges or I had credited her with, Lucile immediately stood and greeted the couple. 'You look marvellous, Marthe,' she said. 'The Swiss air has done you wonders.'

Although there was the tiniest crack in her voice, it was such a gracious and disarming approach that I was proud of her.

'I couldn't have done it better myself,' Georges whispered in my ear.

'And you, Lucile,' replied Marthe, squinting at her, 'look enchanting.'

I saw a glimpse of relief in Lucile's eyes that perhaps the hatchet had been buried and she no longer had to fear Marthe. After all, they were both now mature women with life experience. But the moment was cut short when Marthe added, 'Black is no longer for widows, I see. I've noticed all the *young* girls donning it.'

Marthe's backhanded compliment was followed by a horsey laugh that pinched every nerve in my body. Lucile looked crestfallen. She opened and shut her mouth, like a goldfish swimming aimlessly around a bowl.

Cyrille stared forlornly at his jacket and tails. He was shorter than Marthe and as colourless as Georges had described, with grey-blond hair and such unremarkable facial features it would be impossible to give detectives an accurate description of him should he go missing. 'I'm sorry we are overdressed. Marthe insisted it was a white-tie occasion,' he said.

Marthe touched her tiara and looked around the gathering. 'Oh, black tie is positively quaint. We aren't the last to arrive, are we? There are more people coming? It is your birthday, after all.'

Having paralysed Lucile with her venom, Marthe then set her gaze on Alice. 'Oh, hello, dear. You look rather swish in that gown. I believe that shade is called "shrimp-orange". I remember how popular it was before the war.'

It should have been my cue to leap into defensive action but I found myself glued to the spot, gaping in horror at what Marthe was doing. It was such an obvious approach for a bully that we could have been children in a schoolyard and not adults in a drawing room. I wanted to ask her to leave, but I remembered Georges's warning. I glanced at him for inspiration, but he seemed equally engrossed by the exchange.

'If only Aunt Lucile was astute enough to make witty comebacks this could be a thrilling bout,' he said out of the corner of his mouth. 'At Madame Florence Gould's soirées, the biting repartee between the social divas is the main attraction.'

Marthe turned her sights to young Fanny, and I froze. The girl was my trump card. She was going to play Ravel's 'Scarbo' after dinner, a piece that required great virtuosity and was rarely played at recitals because of its notorious difficulty. I anticipated every salon in Paris would try to snatch her once they heard about it, but Fanny would remain loyal to Lucile if she was paying her tuition. I couldn't let Marthe spoil my plan by scaring Fanny off.

'What should I do?' I asked Georges.

'It's time to get into the match, Eve,' he said.

Without further thought, I blocked Marthe from reaching Fanny like a fencer lunging for an attack. '*Bonsoir*, Madame de Villiers,' I said. 'I'm Eve Archer. I'm so sorry that you misunderstood the dress code. If you feel at all uncomfortable, Lucile will happily lend you one of her gowns. She has a lovely one designed by Christian Dior. Do you know him? He used to design for Lucien Lelong but now he is stepping out on his own.'

Out of the corner of my eye I spotted Georges giving me a silent clap. But my counter-parry seemed to have little effect on Marthe. She waved me away as if I were no more than a bothersome mosquito. 'Oh yes, the little Miss Nobody from Australia.'

I was temporarily stunned by her audacity. Despite all the diamonds in her tiara, the woman was as rude as a fishwife. Then Olivier, apparently oblivious to the dark side of society hostess rivalry, inadvertently came to my defence. 'Mademoiselle Archer's photograph is in *Elle* this month. Everybody will try to snatch her away from Lucile to redecorate their homes. Lucile had better be careful.'

Georges signalled for Marie to bring Marthe a glass of champagne while the rest of the room fell into a tense silence as they awaited her reply.

'All this white and glass, and the chrome finishes?' she replied, looking around and wrinkling her nose. 'It's a fad, nothing more.'

I countered with a running attack inspired by what Serge had told me that afternoon. 'The décor *is* modern. It always takes time for the *general public* to catch up with new ideas.'

Marthe's mouth quivered, and I half-expected her to lash at me with her tongue. But at that moment, the butler I'd hired for the evening rang a bell to invite us to the table. Marthe and I were forced to disengage. She was not a subtle enemy; she was a wrecking ball. I was glad I'd had the foresight to have placed her next to Georges at the table. His unruffled charm would be a good distraction for her and give me time to regroup. I would keep my eye on her husband, Cyrille, and use my own charm

78

to glean information about Marthe from him that might be useful. When facing a formidable opponent, one must be quick to discern their Achilles heel.

'You're my dinner partner tonight, Monsieur de Villiers,' I told the odd little man, linking my arm with his. 'Shall we go to the table?'

His eyebrows rose in surprise and delight. 'It would be my honour, Mademoiselle Archer.' Then leaning in close to me, he whispered, 'You were very brave to have taken on my wife. She's not a woman for the faint-hearted.'

I found the remark coming from Marthe's husband funny. Against my better judgement, I chuckled, which seemed to delight Cyrille even more.

*

Berthe the cook had outdone herself. Lucile might not be the most exciting hostess in Paris, but no one could criticise the food served at her table. The consommé was so clear you could see the gold rosette on the bottom of the soup bowl. The marrow on toast with a sprinkle of salt was all panache without being showy. It was quite a feat considering flour and bread were now rationed again. When the plates of tournedos with sauce béarnaise were laid out on the table, someone nudged my foot with their own. At first I thought it was Georges trying to get my attention, but he was engrossed in conversation with Fanny. Whoever it was nudged my foot again. I studied the faces of the others, but nobody gave the slightest indication it was them. Most likely the culprit was long-limbed Olivier stretching his legs and not realising he was kicking me. It wouldn't do to look under the table, so I tucked my feet under my chair.

Marthe sat back and patted her lips with her serviette. 'Paris has changed so much,' she said. 'I am scandalised by the prices in the shops. The lack of food is a disgrace.'

It was Lucile's role to introduce the topics of conversation and allow each guest the opportunity to express their opinion, but Marthe had taken it upon herself. I glanced in Lucile's direction and nodded, encouraging her to take back control of the evening. She went to open her mouth but Olivier, without meaning to, spoke over the top of her so that her words were drowned out.

'What can we do?' he replied with a shrug. 'The fishermen have discovered that they can make more money selling the fuel the government has allotted to them than to go out to sea and catch fish.'

Lucile cleared her throat, ready to try again, but this time Jeanne spoke. 'Do you know what happened the other day while I was waiting for my daughter outside the Ritz? I threw my cigarette butt away and it was swooped on by a well-dressed gentleman.'

'There's a market for cigarette butts,' said Henri. 'This is what we have come to, I'm afraid.'

It was as if Lucile had become invisible at her own birthday party. Georges stepped in and attempted to turn the focus back to his aunt. 'Come now, here we are in this splendid apartment, celebrating Aunt Lucile's birthday and eating a fine meal. Why should we talk about rationing again?'

'You are correct, Georges,' agreed Alice. 'I lost a good ten pounds during the occupation.'

'I did too,' said Jeanne. 'I had to walk everywhere.'

It was a good try on Georges's part, but it seemed the ball simply kept rolling further and further from Lucile. Apart from Marthe and Cyrille, who brought with them ill intent, the others at the table were people Lucile counted as allies. How would she ever survive in the vipers' nest that was *Tout-Paris*?

Cyrille leaned into me. 'My wife wouldn't have been able to stand the occupation. She hates walking. She has to be driven everywhere. Sometimes I think she doesn't have legs.'

'Indeed,' I said, but my attention was on Madame Toussaint. Her brassiere strap was slipping down her arm. I tried to catch Odette's attention so she could discreetly slip it back into place for her, but she was too busy clearing the used dishes from the table.

'I heard there was a shortage of women's underwear during the war in France,' Cyrille said. 'It was almost impossible for a woman to get a brassiere.'

I assumed he had noticed Madame Toussaint's predicament and felt some need to focus on it.

'Yes,' I agreed. 'They are a rather intricate form of apparel with nearly twenty different parts. I suppose those parts were needed to make bombs of some sort,' I added, trying to use humour to distract his attention.

He gave an insipid laugh and took a sip of his wine. There was something off about him, a bit creepy. Like one of those society men you read about in the papers, the ones who have been murdering virgins for years and storing their bodies in their wine cellars. I regretted engaging with him on the topic of women's underwear and tried to turn the conversation to Marthe's shortcomings.

'So, your wife doesn't like to walk about the world's most romantic city,' I said. 'Is there anything else about the city she finds disagreeable?'

But before he could answer, Fanny piped up, rather loudly for a dinner party.

'It's outrageous that mothers can't buy enough milk for their babies,' she said. 'It should be a crime to use milk in any kind of cooking. It should all go to the babies.'

While it was admirable that she cared so much about her fellow citizens, introducing a topic in such an emotional way was not acceptable at a formal dinner party. We weren't in a Left Bank café where passionate debates were settled by punch-ups and knife fights. I'd have to speak to her about her etiquette. I glanced at Lucile. It was her opportunity to continue Fanny's topic but to soften the tone in which it was discussed. But to my horror she remained mute in her chair, looking for all the world like a deflated balloon. It gave Marthe the opportunity to fan the flames.

'The black market is France's disgrace,' she said, eyeing the rich food in front of us. 'Those with money to buy it do not have the right to make their fellow citizens go hungry.' She turned to Lucile. 'But I'm sure none of tonight's dinner was bought on the black market?'

'No, of course not,' replied Lucile passively.

Sometimes I thought Lucile was one of those people who went through life in a bubble, oblivious to the workings of the real world. If Berthe and I hadn't traded on the black market for the ingredients for the dinner, we'd have been having Oxo and hot water. As for Marthe being so high and mighty, very likely the reason her cook didn't have to buy on the black market was that the family owned farmland, an advantage Lucile didn't have.

'Not all the black-marketers are criminals,' said Georges. 'Most of them are ordinary people with families to feed too.'

'I suppose you've used that defence in the courtroom, Georges,' Marthe replied. 'That's a lie people tell themselves to ease their guilty consciences. And you know it.'

If Lucile didn't step in and defuse the brewing argument, the night was going to be a disaster. Then I remembered what Cyrille had told me about Marthe hating to walk and came upon an idea.

'You are quite right, Madame de Villiers, to remind us all that we must not live selfishly,' I said. 'Why don't we all pledge not to go anywhere by car for the next month and to donate the gasoline to the hospital for their ambulances instead. Who is with me?'

The idea brought amused chatter to the conversation. Lucile looked slightly alarmed but raised her glass.

'It's a splendid idea,' said Alice. 'It will alleviate my guilt over the sumptuous camembert I bought today.'

'Well, I don't mind a month of walking for a good cause,' said Olivier.

I looked in Marthe's direction. She would be damned by her own words if she refused. She lifted her glass and squinted at me.

Touché! I thought.

★

After dinner, Fanny played masterfully for us as I knew she would. Ravel's 'Scarbo' wasn't the usual lyrical, after-dinner music that tended to make guests drift off into their own worlds. The movement was dark and foreboding. Its jagged, violent dissonance had us all on the edge of our seats. Frenetic and relentless, I knew the contrast of Fanny's girlish innocence and the psychotic intensity of the piece would astound everyone.

'Bravo! Bravo!' both Alice and Olivier cried as they rose to their feet when Fanny finished. They were both music aficionados, and I counted on them spreading the word about

83

Lucile's 'discovery' of Fanny. The other guests also clapped enthusiastically except, unsurprisingly, for Marthe, who frowned, puzzled at how Lucile had managed to discover such a unique talent.

'You know that piece was born of a competition, don't you?' asked Georges, sidling up to me afterwards as the guests broke off into little groups for conversation.

'Yes, Ravel deliberately set out to write something that could break a virtuoso. He wanted the movement to be even more difficult than the almost unplayable "Islamey" by Balakirev.'

Georges lit himself a cigar. 'Ravel was a show-off though. At least Balakirev was sincerely trying to convey the grandiose beauty of the Caucasus Mountains and the unique folk music of the region. Ravel was simply trying to outdo him.'

'Show-off or not,' I replied, 'everyone knows Ravel's piece. He had the last word.'

'As have you, my dear,' he said, nodding in the direction of Marthe. 'She appears to have quite a case of indigestion after that performance.'

I laughed and looked around the room to see what Lucile was up to, but found myself accidentally locking eyes with Cyrille. He lifted his glass of Cognac to me, and I had no other option but to lift mine back to him.

'Typhoid-carrier indeed,' I whispered to Georges. 'Anyway, I suppose I'd better help Lucile mingle. The music was a triumph. This is her chance to make up for lost ground.'

Ronan and Henri were standing in front of the Degas painting. It was exactly the opportunity I was looking for. I indicated for Lucile to join me as I approached the men.

'What do you think of it?' I asked them. 'Isn't it beautiful?'

'It is quite splendid,' agreed Ronan. 'I didn't know you collected moderns, Madame Damour.'

'She's just started,' I said. 'With the help of a wonderful art dealer named Serge Lavertu. I can put you in contact with him if you like.'

'That Jew?' came Marthe's voice from across the room. 'The one that deals out of Saint-Germain-des-Prés? Oh Lucile, you could do so much better.'

Her words made me flinch. I couldn't bear to hear her disparage Serge that way.

'The painting brims with life and movement. It was bought straight from Degas's studio. Serge Lavertu is a dealer who is adored by both artists and collectors,' I told her.

With great show, Marthe came and put her face close to the painting. 'I can't believe you bought a painting from that poky gallery on Rue Seine near that café where all the students meet. Next time you are thinking of acquiring a painting, Lucile, you must allow me to introduce you to my nephew, Martin La Farge. He has a simply beautiful gallery at number twenty-one Rue la Boétie.'

My face froze. That had been Serge's gallery before the war. It was Marthe's nephew who was refusing to give his property back.

CHAPTER FIVE

KRISTINA

Nice, June 1946

The lights in some of the rooms in the villa were still working, and Kristina listened as Lorenzo showed Eve to one of the guest rooms on the third floor. She was glad he had done so. It would have been rude to have sent the young woman away late in the evening when she would have had no hope of finding accommodation in town, but it also meant Kristina would have a chance to speak with her the following day. She picked up her pet rabbit, Flora, and turned to her own bed in the corner of the ballroom that now served as her studio. It was a four-poster with leaf finials and the linens were pink toile de Jouy. It made her feel like Sleeping Beauty when she climbed into it – the princess cursed to sleep for a hundred years until awakened by the kiss of a handsome prince. The villa was too high above the bay for her to hear the waves, but she liked to imagine that she could. There were no curtains in the room, and Kristina could see the moon through the tall French windows. Its luminescent brightness gave her some peace. The ocean and the moon had been formed billions of years ago and could not be erased. Those elements existed before humankind, and they would remain long after the last person disappeared from the earth.

She turned off the bedside lamp and settled into the pillows. Memories floated towards her but as she was about to grasp them, they floated away again. That first kiss with Max was where her memory stopped. It was like a line, a precipice, a border. But there was one other memory that sat right on the edge of the abyss. Max was laughing, telling a joke, and Kristina sensed a glimmer of a figure next to him. Tall and with an air of distinction. A tenderness rose within her, but it was fleeting and gone. She knew it was Serge Lavertu but she could not recall his face.

She looked to the stars. When she was a child, her father had told her that what she was seeing in the night sky was not the actual stars, but the light those stars had emitted decades earlier and that had taken years to reach Earth. 'Whenever you are looking at starlight, you are looking at the past.'

What has been can never not have been, Kristina thought. Surely everything that had happened to her still existed somewhere besides her damaged brain? The same way that Nice would still exist even if she caught a train and went to Paris.

Yes, the past still existed somewhere, even if she couldn't remember it. That was a hope to hold on to.

CHAPTER SIX

KRISTINA

Paris, July 1923

'Well, that's done,' Kristina said, signing off on her portrait of Max. 'Come and have a look and tell me what you think.'

He stood and shrugged the stiffness from his shoulders before coming around to her side of the easel. His eyes looked over the painting with wonder and she was rather proud of it herself. She had spent the last two sittings making small changes, and then rethinking and redoing them. Now she felt she had captured not only his image but his essence in the beautiful tonal colours. The expression on his face in the portrait was forthright but friendly; he was masculine but illuminated by a soft glow.

'It's superb,' he said. 'But you know that whatever an artist paints is also a self-portrait. I see you in the painting as well as myself.'

Kristina liked that idea, and signed it at the top in addition to the bottom so there could never be any doubt who had created the painting.

Max circled his arms around her and kissed her neck. Her blood heated and her body felt as if it was a jar full of butterflies.

But their ardour was brought to a sudden stop by the sentimental strains of a violin being played upstairs. Kristina recognised the piece. It was Elgar's 'Salut d'Amour' – Love's Greeting.

'Serge is back,' Max said. 'He came in late last night and must have woken up now. Let's go see him.'

He took Kristina's hand and they hurried upstairs. The door to the apartment was open and there was a man wearing a silk dressing-gown and cravat playing the violin. Kristina felt a surge of curious excitement. He wasn't classically handsome, like Max, but he was elegant, with smooth porcelain skin and shapely hands with long tapered fingers. His eyes were closed, and he had a sweet smile on his lips as if he were dreaming of his beloved.

'Serge!' said Max. 'Welcome back!'

Serge opened his eyes and grinned broadly when he saw Max. He put down his violin and the two men embraced like long-lost brothers. They had none of the air of men who saw each other as a threat and held themselves at arm's length. The smiles they sent each other spoke of a history of challenges and triumphs, youthful pranks and shared confidences. For a moment Kristina was left on the outside, playing the part of an interloper. She felt both touched and vexed until the men broke away from each other and turned to her.

'And you must be Mademoiselle Belova?' said Serge, taking both of her hands.

'Kristina, please,' she said. 'I have heard so much about you that I feel I know you already.'

His bottle-green eyes moved over her face. They were beautiful and she was captivated by them. But it was his expression, so honest and refined, that most endeared him to her.

'Call me Serge,' he said. 'I feel the same way about you.'

'I knew you two would get along,' said Max, grabbing Serge by the shoulder. 'Kristina finished her portrait of me just this moment. Come see it.'

As the trio trundled down the stairs again into the back room, Kristina was hit by a sudden wave of insecurity. Max liking the portrait was one thing – he was in love with her. But Serge would be more impartial. Max had been firm that out of the pair, Serge was the more discerning critic. It was suddenly important to Kristina that Serge approve of her work.

'I'd like your straightforward opinion,' she said, as she turned the easel towards him. 'I don't want you to flatter my vanity or spare my feelings. I need to know what I do well and what I must improve on.'

But her fears dissipated when Serge's eyes lit up at the sight of the painting. 'Oh my,' he said, 'you've done what I most admire in a portrait. You cropped it closely to keep it intimate and you haven't settled Max into one mood but suggested several different possibilities. That is exactly what separates a portrait from a mere painting of a person. It's the quality that will bring viewers back to look at the work many times.'

Max stood beside him. 'She is quite a discovery, isn't she? Look at the energy of expression, the clear but subtle sensuality, and the observant eye.'

Their combined praise made Kristina feel that she was entering a new epoch in her life, moving from a starry-eyed student to a serious artist.

'But we can never sell this portrait, Kristina,' said Serge suddenly, his tone serious.

Her heart sunk to her feet. What fault had he found?

But when he turned to her his eyes were crinkled in a good-natured smile. 'You've captured Max completely. The painting is more Max than even Max is. How could you or I ever part with it?'

★

A few days later, having been given the permanent use of the back room at Bergeret & Lavertu as a studio, Kristina was on her way there when, for reasons she couldn't explain except that she was in love and therefore prone to spontaneity, she took a different route from her usual one and found herself in the middle of a flower market. The air was a summery mix of sweet lavender and peonies. She was weaving her way through the vendors and the cheerful faces of sunflowers and the showy heads of dahlias, when she spotted Serge standing in front of a stall. He was waiting for the seller to wrap a spray of carnations and veronicas.

'Hello,' she said, stepping up beside him.

'*Bonjour*, Kristina. How lovely you look today!'

There was a smile in his voice as well as on his face. To have elicited so warm a greeting filled her with pleasure.

Serge turned back to the flower-seller and indicated a bunch of flamingo-pink roses. After the vendor had wrapped them, Serge handed the bouquet to Kristina. 'Something to match your prettiness,' he said.

Kristina accepted the flowers graciously but could feel the heat of a blush rise from her neck and travel upwards over her face. Even though she knew that in France pink roses symbolised nothing more than sweetness and femininity, to Russians, they alluded to a blossoming romance.

'Besides me, who are you buying flowers for?' she asked him, doing her best to regain her equilibrium as they fell in step and headed in the direction of the shop together.

91

'Myself,' he said, 'for my desk. They will soften the fact that I will be spending the day with my nose in accounts books and other administrative tasks.'

Kristina thought well of men who appreciated flowers because her beloved father was one of them. Her mother always said that a man who cared for a garden would nurture his family, and a husband who appreciated nature's beauty would equally love his wife in all her seasons.

They came upon the vegetable-sellers whose carts were almost as colourful as the floral displays. The red tomatoes, green beans and yellow corn were like bright blobs of paint on an artist's palette.

'Max doesn't help you with the dreary tasks?' she asked Serge.

He resisted a grin, and she guessed the answer to her own question. Out of the two of them, it was Max who was the charmer and showman. In Serge she detected a quieter spirit with a strong sense of aesthetics. She didn't believe for a minute that he would prefer to be dealing with accounts and figures rather than beautiful artwork, but perhaps he did it out of a loyalty to his partnership with Max.

'You two remind me of my parents,' she told him as they made their way further into the market. 'My mother is the practical one, my father the dreamer. It was thanks to my mother that we weren't left destitute after the revolution.'

Serge looked at her with interest, so she elaborated.

'My father was a member of the Duma and tried to persuade the Tsar to form a constitutional monarchy and modernise Russia. But my mother saw the Tsar's days were numbered, and gradually moved small amounts of valuables out of the country. My family lost their lands and houses in Russia, but we now live a comfortable existence here in France thanks to her prudence.'

'You are lucky, Kristina,' he said, with a satisfied tone that hinted that he was flattered by the comparison. 'Everywhere in Paris you can find a former duke working as a chauffeur or a kitchen hand. Once I even caught a taxi driven by a former princess.'

'Princess Sophia Dolgorukova,' said Kristina. 'I know her. She is a very resourceful woman. In Russia she was not only an accomplished pilot and racing-car driver, but she was a well-respected doctor. Unfortunately, her qualifications are not recognised here.'

They had been so engaged in conversation, that neither of the pair realised that they had moved to the far side of the market where second-hand goods were sold. Dingy worn-out shoes, blackened kitchenware and faded top hats were laid out on rugs.

'Paris is gaiety and poverty side by side,' Kristina said. 'In Russia it's famine and splendour.'

Serge's gaze lingered on her face. 'I hope you are happy in France. You must miss your country?'

'The country I miss no longer exists. It's my cousins who couldn't get out in time that I mourn the most. I miss having a big family.'

Serge looked thoughtful, as if her words had caused him to recall memories of his own. The slight downcast glance of his eyes made her think those must be unhappy recollections, and she didn't want to be the cause of his sadness when they seemed to be getting along so well.

'I'm lucky in many ways,' she said, injecting cheerfulness into her voice. 'If we had remained in Russia, I would have never met Max — or you. Studying in Paris to be an artist would have been out of the question. I'd have been married off to some dreary duke or count instead of being able to choose someone for myself.'

'Have you chosen Max?' he asked her. 'What will your parents say about that?'

Kristina and Max had discussed getting married, but if Max hadn't indicated their plans yet to his best friend then it wasn't her place to do so. But if she were to have answered him, she would have told him that she was sure that her parents would approve of Max. Apart from the fact Kristina believed that he was impossible to resist, her father was a romantic who had married for love rather than fortune. And, as for her mother, she would see it was better for Kristina to marry a Frenchman determined to make a name for himself, than an impoverished Russian aristocrat who could only live in the past.

Looking for a way to change the direction of the conversation, she turned towards a bric-à-brac stall selling a bizarre arrangement of odds and ends: wheelbarrows, dressmakers' mannequins and broken costume jewellery laid out in wooden trays. She shivered. The sight reminded her of all the Russians who'd fled to France and had been forced to sell everything they owned at cheap prices to the second-hand dealers just to survive. Many of them had been people she had grown up with, including the Vertinsky family. If Sonia's uncle and Kristina's parents hadn't stepped in to help, Sonia and her mother would have been left destitute.

'Oh dear, look at that,' said Kristina, pointing to a poorly executed sketch of Sacré-Coeur.

Serge smiled wistfully. 'I've found some treasures in these places,' he said, casting his eye over a stack of old paintings. 'Max and I once discovered two African statues that some students had stolen from the Louvre and sold cheaply to pay their rent. We returned them of course, but I never overlook the humble market. You never know if you might find a Renoir or a Rembrandt someone has exchanged for a cooking pot simply because they didn't realise the painting's true worth.'

Before he could say more, there was a commotion and then a scream. It sounded like the cry of a human baby. They both turned to see a black and white rabbit running between people's feet and a woman chasing after it, brandishing a broom and a knife. The rabbit ran straight up to Kristina. She saw the terror in its eyes, and without a thought scooped it up and tucked it against her chest.

'You caught it,' the woman said, reaching out her arms. 'Thank you.'

Kristina's eye travelled from the broom to the knife. She'd seen how the French killed rabbits, pinning them down on their backs with a broom and slitting their throats. The rabbit's heart beat like thunder against her own. She froze, unable to make herself hand it over, knowing what its fate would be.

'I didn't know rabbits could scream,' she said, turning to Serge. 'What a terrible sound.'

'Well, yes they do,' the woman said, stepping closer to her. 'Right before you kill them.'

Kristina moved back behind the protection of Serge.

'Give it to me,' the woman said. 'I've got a customer who's paid good money for it.'

People stopped to look at them, sensing a scene was about to unfold. By rights the rabbit belonged to the woman, and she could call the police if Kristina refused to give it back. Serge looked at her quizzically, and then reached into his pocket and took out his wallet. He pressed several crisp notes into the woman's bloodstained hand. 'Why don't you buy your customer a pie from that baker over there and a good bottle of wine?' he suggested. 'Compliments of a stranger.'

The woman's eyes grew big when she saw the sum of money Serge offered her. She closed her fingers around the notes. 'You're crazy, the both of you,' she said, before walking off.

The onlookers tittered and jeered. 'Did you see how much he paid for that rabbit?' one man exclaimed, sounding scandalised. 'That could feed my family for a week!'

Kristina had the sense that the crowd around them was swelling.

'We'd better get this rabbit away from here,' said Serge, placing his hand on her shoulder and guiding her through the bystanders. 'They die of shock easily. Especially the males.'

'Are you talking about rabbits or the French?' she whispered.

*

'That was the most expensive rabbit I have ever bought, Kristina,' Serge said when they reached the shop and he opened the door to the apartment upstairs. He took out a straw basket from a cupboard and lined it with a blanket. Kristina passed the rabbit to him, and he gently nudged it under the blanket. 'What do you intend to do with it? I gather you're not planning to cook it yourself?'

'I don't know,' she told him. 'I just couldn't let that woman kill it. The poor thing came to me for help.'

'Russians don't eat rabbit?'

'Not usually,' she said.

'I've heard that your countrymen are superstitious about forest animals.'

'Russians are superstitious about everything,' she replied, watching him with interest as he went to the kitchenette, found a carrot in a box of assorted vegetables and began slicing it into pieces. 'But in truth, my family doesn't eat any type of animal.

My father was a good friend of Count Leo Tolstoy and shared a lot of his views, including humans not having the right to take the lives of animals.'

'Ah Tolstoy,' said Serge. 'A great writer and a great man. Did you meet him?'

'Several times. But I was far too young to appreciate his greatness. I was more taken by his long beard and the fact that an aristocrat preferred to wear peasant clothing.'

The rabbit poked its head from under the blanket and looked around, its tiny nose twitching. Serge returned and began feeding it a slice of carrot at a time.

'What are you going to call your new friend?' he asked, stroking the rabbit's head. It was friendly and not afraid of him.

'I should call him "Leo",' she said, 'in honour of Tolstoy.'

Serge nodded his agreement. 'With such an auspicious name, you should also paint his portrait.'

The idea made Kristina laugh. 'I should paint yours,' she said, 'with Leo.'

'You mean like Leonardo da Vinci's *Lady with an Ermine*?' he asked, a grin tickling his lips.

'Exactly, only yours will be titled *Frenchman with a Rabbit*. Portrait painting is the best way to get to know someone. And as you and I are both fond of Max, we should get to know each other and be friends.'

She leaned back and surveyed the room. Max had managed to sell three of her paintings and some by other artists, so Serge's furniture had been restored from the pawn shop.

'I've told you about my family,' she said, turning back to Serge. 'Now tell me about yours. You grew up in Fontainebleau too?'

'Yes, you are quite right,' he said, his voice turning flat. He scrutinised her for a moment and then said, 'I imagine your parents love you very dearly, Kristina.'

'Well, yes,' she said, surprised at the way he deflected her question. 'How did you come to that conclusion?'

Serge leaned his chin on his fist. 'You have the comfortable manner of a well-loved daughter. One who is curious and unafraid of the world.'

'And you?' she asked. 'I hope you were loved too?'

His brow furrowed. 'I understand that I was a much longed-for child who came into my parents' lives too late,' he said. 'Unfortunately, they both passed away from tuberculosis when I was six years old, so I barely knew them. After that, I was passed from relative to relative, none of them really wanting to take responsibility for a frightened and lonely child. Finally, a great aunt who lived in Barbizon took me in. You probably know of the town? It was a favourite place for the impressionist painters to work.'

'Yes, Max told me all about it,' Kristina said. 'You sometimes played with Claude Monet's grandchildren.'

'*Max* played with them. I was mostly kept indoors.'

Serge seemed disinclined to continue. Understanding that she was encroaching on a memory that was painful, Kristina stopped her questioning there. She could ask Serge more about his childhood when she knew him better.

The rabbit, having finished the last carrot slice, climbed out of the basket, jumped into Serge's arms and promptly fell asleep.

'It's certainly very trusting,' Kristina said, 'considering what that woman intended to do to it.'

'It's young,' said Serge, stroking the rabbit's head. 'It doesn't yet know that human beings are treacherous.'

'Not all are so cruel,' Kristina said. 'I can't imagine that *you* could be treacherous. Not a man who appreciates fine art, likes flowers and is kind to animals. Could you?'

Serge fell quiet as if he was searching every corner of his conscience so that he could give Kristina the most honest answer possible. 'No, I can't be treacherous,' he said, after a while. Then turning the question over in his mind once more, added a caveat. 'Unless I was defending something – or someone – I dearly loved. I might commit murder under those circumstances.'

Kristina liked his answer. 'I think when it comes to protecting someone we love, we are all capable of that.'

★

The following evening, Sonia was busy finishing a design for her first client, so Kristina went to La Rotonde to meet Max on her own. No sooner had she stepped in the door than Pierre stopped her and pointed up the stairs. 'You can't go up there today. The cubists are fighting.'

Above the sound of the piano accordion came shouts of aggression. A loud crash gave her the impression a table had been overturned.

'If they don't settle it soon,' said Pierre, 'I'll call the police. It won't be the first time, but it will be the last.'

The cubists were like their paintings: stocky, thick-necked and strong. But Kristina knew that despite the show of violence, they would be shaking hands and singing songs of camaraderie again before the night was out.

'I'll wait here until the mood passes,' she told Pierre, sitting down at a table where she could keep her eye on the door for Max.

'I'll bring a drink,' he replied. 'Compliments of La Rotonde.'

Kristina had no sooner removed her gloves when the sound of a woman singing rose above the din. It wasn't nasal or husky, like the usual street singers who performed at the café. The mezzo-soprano voice had a pleasant timbre, and a tremolo placed on certain notes made it rich and romantic.

A trained singer? Kristina turned around and craned her neck to see over the heads of the patrons. On the other side of the room was a golden-haired woman wearing a slinky dress that showed off her bony shoulders. She was no more than four foot eight but graceful with a long neck and a ballerina's poise. She was singing a song, the words of which Kristina had never heard before: *One evening, if I should die please don't cry, just go on pretending you loved me …*

It was nostalgic and haunting, and the singer closed her eyes as if nobody and nothing else existed in her universe. When she finished, there was loud applause. With a mischievous smile, the singer moved among the patrons, holding out a cloche hat lined with magenta silk, to collect coins for her performance. As she drew closer, Kristina deduced from the cut of her dress and the way the fabric shimmered in the dim light, it was most certainly a Chanel design. What was such a luxuriously dressed woman doing collecting coins for singing at La Rotonde?

'Mademoiselle!' she called out to the singer and held up two notes.

The performer smiled and veered towards Kristina as if drawn by a magnet. Now she was closer, Kristina could see that she must be about her age. Her square face was perfectly symmetrical – a rare quality Kristina had discovered from having painted so many portraits. Kristina herself was always complimented on her beauty, but the intense study of her own face had revealed that one of her eyes was a touch rounder than the other, and her chin curved ever so slightly to the left. The young woman before her was as perfect as a doll.

'You sing magnificently,' Kristina said as the singer took the notes and slid onto the stool next to her.

'Thank you,' she replied in an upper-class Parisian accent. 'I've seen you before. You're with the artists, aren't you?'

Kristina wondered how she could have missed the extraordinary young woman while she had noticed her.

'I *am* an artist,' Kristina said.

The singer's eyes opened wide. 'Really? What's your name?'

'Kristina Belova.'

The young woman held out her hand. 'I'm Madeleine.'

'Madeleine ...?'

'*Just* Madeleine,' she replied firmly. Then, perhaps afraid she had sounded too harsh, she gave Kristina an explanation. 'I have a new life now. No ties to a past or a family. Those things don't matter to me ... *anymore*.'

She crossed her legs and Kristina noticed that Madeleine's embroidered shoes had jewelled heels but holes in the toes. The sight of the tattered footwear made her want to cry. She was filled with two strong desires at once – to paint this unique creature, and to help her.

*

It was Kristina's habit to start work early, especially when painting a portrait. She felt a sort of agitation when she was about to paint someone – as opposed to a scene or a still life – as if her soul was about to join with that of her subject in a kind of alchemy. It was especially so with Madeleine, who Kristina sensed was hiding deeper, darker layers underneath the effervesce of her surface.

On the day that she and Madeleine had agreed to make a start on a portrait of the young singer, Kristina arrived at

Bergeret & Lavertu as the sales clerk, Noël, was lifting the shutters at the front of the shop.

'*Bonjour*, Mademoiselle Belova,' he said.

Max and Serge were visiting collectors that day, and Kristina knew that the shop would be quiet until later in the afternoon, so she took advantage of the silence to think out her approach to Madeleine's portrait. She only worked on a white canvas when she had a clear vision of what she wanted to achieve, finding that having a wash of colour already on the canvas helped not only with tonal values, but gave a sense of depth to a subject. Artists often painted over old canvases to save money, but in the case of her approach to painting Madeleine, the idea of a picture underneath a picture suggested a mystery that would be perfect for the subject. She selected a canvas that she had covered in a light red wash several weeks earlier. It would be the perfect foundation for Madeleine's bold spirit. She set up her easel and crayons, then she glanced at her watch. Madeleine was already half an hour late. Although Kristina didn't expect someone who made their living at night to be up at the crack of dawn, when an hour passed by and there was still no sign of Madeleine, she began to worry that the young woman had changed her mind and would not come at all. Then, just as she considered giving up and going to a life-drawing class at the academy, there was a cheerful cry of '*Bonjour!*'

She looked up to see Madeleine bustling in the door, bringing with her the sweet smell of freshly baked pastry. She thrust out a paper bag to Kristina.

'The *only* place to get *pain au chocolat* is on Rue Montorgueil. I spent all the money I earned last night on these, but I thought we should only have the best.'

Madeleine opened the tapestry bag she had strung over her shoulder and produced a bottle of fine champagne and two glasses. She popped the cork with a bright laugh and poured a glass for herself and Kristina before proposing a toast.

'To an exciting adventure,' she said, her eyes twinkling.

Living with Madame Vertinskaya, Kristina still ate hearty Russian breakfasts of buckwheat porridge and cottage cheese pancakes served with fruit and a dollop of sour cream. And tea – always steaming hot tea served from the samovar. She had not acquired the French custom of sweet pastries and coffee, let alone drinking anything alcoholic so early in the day. But Madeleine was in high spirits and Kristina had no intention of dampening them. She took a sip of the bubbly champagne and glanced at the red-painted canvas, congratulating herself on having chosen exactly the right base colour.

'Sit for a while,' she said to Madeleine, offering her a chair. 'You don't have to pose or be still. I'm going to look at you and make some sketches and play with some ideas. And while I do, I want you to tell me about yourself.'

'Well, where shall I start?' asked Madeleine, taking another sip of her champagne before she launched into amusing stories about her bad-tempered landlady who wore a monocle and smoked a pipe, and the artists' ball where she went dressed as a leopard and got into an argument with a woman dressed as a panther. As Kristina's charcoal scratched against the surface of the canvas, she paused every so often to take in another aspect of her subject. It was clear that Madeleine was comfortable telling stories about everyone else while avoiding the topic of herself. Kristina wanted to capture that contradiction: Madeleine's bright smile and her animated gestures and yet that flash of fear in her eyes. Kristina decided that she would not paint Madeleine looking directly out of the frame as she had with Max but have her gaze slightly to the right. Max was an open book, but Madeleine was a puzzle to be solved. Like her, Kristina had come from a privileged background, but that world had been a safe place for her to cultivate her mind and expand her view of life. The way Madeleine's eyes darted around the room when she spoke suggested her experience had been quite different. Kristina had the impression she was not only a runaway, but that she was being pursued.

★

By the time Kristina finished her preliminary sketches, it was one o'clock in the afternoon and the heat in the back room was stifling – it was pointless to continue. A little woozy from the champagne, she stood up.

'I think that's enough for the day,' she said to Madeleine. 'Let me buy you lunch.'

Max and Serge would have gone directly to La Rotonde after seeing their clients. They hadn't met Madeleine yet, and Kristina was curious to see what they would make of her.

'Do you mind if we go through the cemetery on our way?' she asked Madeleine as they set out. 'The linden and ash trees are so beautiful at this time of year. I want to sketch their dappled light on the graves for a study I have to do for my class.'

'If we must,' answered Madeleine. 'I haven't been to a cemetery since my grandmother died.'

At last a snippet of information about Madeleine's family. Kristina sensed the memory was as fragile as a butterfly so she did not grab for more and hoped it would come to her of its own accord. But it fluttered away, and Madeleine said nothing further.

When they reached the cemetery, Kristina sat down on the edge of a grave and pulled out her sketchpad.

Madeleine looked about uncomfortably. 'My grandmother used to say that the dead still talk to us, and because she was deaf, she used to ask me to sit by my grandfather's grave and write down for her what he was saying. Do you think it's true? Do you think all the dead in this graveyard are talking to us?'

Kristina shaded her eyes with her hand and looked up through the sparkling light at Madeleine. Her mood was melancholic, poles apart from the exuberant spirits she had displayed when she had been posing. It was like the song she had sung at La Rotonde: a tumble from high to low notes in one bar.

'If they talk to us,' Kristina said, repeating something her mother had told her, 'it's because they want to guide us. It wouldn't be anything to be afraid of.'

Madeleine's face softened as if Kristina's words had soothed something that had been bothering her. 'My grandmother was the only person who ever loved me. She's buried in the family vault at Père Lachaise. But I never go there.'

'Well, perhaps you should some time,' Kristina offered gently.

Madeleine's eyes filled with tears. 'I hate to think of her dead. What is the purpose of life if it ends so dreadfully, with disease and decay?' Then looking at Kristina with a desperate earnestness, she asked, 'If I die, will you come and listen to me?'

It was a strange thing to say. *Why is she so fixated on death?* Kristina wondered.

'I should certainly hope that you would sing to me,' she said, trying to infuse some levity into the conversation. Then standing up, she grasped Madeleine's hand. 'The purpose of life is to be brilliant while it lasts. No one lives forever. But I don't think it's something you and I need to ponder on too much today. Come on, let's have lunch.'

But Madeleine didn't move. Instead, she looked directly at Kristina as the light came back to her face. It was as if she was the sun and had only been temporarily covered by a cloud.

'You are very kind,' she said, smiling through her tears. 'If I should die before you, Kristina, I'm going to become an angel and watch over you.'

★

Once they arrived at La Rotonde, Madeleine was back in her element. Every man in the café turned to look at her and it seemed the world gravitated around her. Max and Serge were on the terrace. Max smiled boyishly as he held out chairs for them while Serge seemed lost for words, as if struck dumb by Madeleine's beauty.

'Madeleine is my new model,' Kristina told them. 'She sings magnificently and poses with the discipline of a ballerina.'

The waiter brought them a basket of bread and a bottle of wine. Madeleine tore off the tiniest portion of the bread and chewed it carefully while Serge poured everyone a glass.

'So you sing?' he asked Madeleine, recovering his composure. 'What style?'

Madeleine burst into an operatic aria that had everyone in the café look in their direction again.

'Truly?' asked Serge. His face beamed as if he was being drawn into a magical circle from which there was no escape.

Madeleine giggled. 'I trained for the opera, but I am a *chanteuse réaliste*,' she said. 'I write songs about the sorrows and joys of life.'

'You *write* your own songs?' Serge asked.

'Yes, the music and the lyrics.'

'We must see you perform,' said Max.

'I'm singing at Le Coucou tonight. You are welcome to come,' Madeleine said, her gaze drifting from Max and Kristina

106

and settling on Serge, who looked back at her as if he had discovered a rare and unusual painting.

'What made you switch styles from opera to cabaret?' he asked.

Madeleine took a sip of her wine before answering. 'I wanted to go to the conservatorium and sing opera on the stage, but my family wouldn't hear of it. So I ran away and, you know, a girl's got to make a living.'

Kristina listened with fascination as Madeleine told Serge that her family had been so adamant that she should not make a spectacle of herself by performing on stage, that they had sent her away to a convent in the Loire Valley, but she had escaped and come back to Paris.

Within a few minutes, Serge had elicited more information from Madeleine than Kristina had managed to squeeze out of her all morning. But that was Serge, she thought. He had a kind of grace that drew people to him.

'If you need more modelling jobs,' offered Max, 'I would be happy to introduce you to some artists.'

'Don't steal her from me so quickly,' said Kristina with a laugh. 'I'm desperate for good models. They'd rather pose for men. They don't believe I will make them famous.'

Max put his hand on Kristina's back. 'Now, I have some good news for you. Serge sold your *Girls at the Piano* to the American collector, James Terry. He is taking back one of your still lifes to show an art dealer in Los Angeles. While France might be conservative, the Americans are more open-minded so you might find success there.'

'You're art dealers?' asked Madeleine with a bright smile. 'Kristina didn't say anything about that. She only said that you were both exceedingly handsome men. And she was right!'

Max laughed but Serge's face blushed as red as the wine. Kristina was sure of her relationship with Max and didn't mind Madeleine's flirtatiousness. But to her surprise she felt slightly put out that Serge seemed so taken with her new friend.

'Well, Kristina is so beautiful herself,' said Max, squeezing her hand, 'it's hard to believe she is a living, breathing person. The first time I met her, I was sure I was looking at Botticelli's *Venus* come to life. I am the luckiest man alive.'

'I'd say Kristina is also lucky to have a man who looks at her the way you do,' replied Madeleine. 'Let's toast to that!'

The four raised their glasses and the conversation turned to the Americans who were populating the Left Bank, driving up the rents yet buying paintings by the truckload.

'They say the American collector, Gertrude Stein, is always on the lookout for a new artist to discover and that the walls of her apartment are filled with works by Cézanne, Bonnard and Matisse,' said Serge.

'The Americans have such wonderful salons,' agreed Madeleine. 'Such panache! Such flair! I've been to one where the guests sat in hassocks instead of chairs and we ate with our fingers.'

As the conversation continued, it occurred to Kristina that they made a pleasant and spirited foursome.

'I have an idea,' she said, taking Max's arm and looking at Serge and Madeleine. 'Max and I are planning to spend the rest of summer at my parents' villa in Nice. It would be wonderful if you two would join us. We'd have so much fun together and I could continue to paint Madeleine.'

Madeleine's smile broadened so wide that for the first time Kristina realised she had a gap between her upper front teeth. It was a trait the French found so charming that they referred to it as *les dents du bonheur*: lucky teeth. And it did seem to Kristina to enhance Madeleine's beauty rather than detract from it. But while she was beguiled, a look passed between Max and Serge.

'I wouldn't want to impose,' Serge said, a note of hesitancy in his voice.

'You wouldn't be,' Kristina insisted.

He nodded uncertainly at Max. 'Perhaps you intended to have Kristina all to yourself. You don't need us in the way.'

'Of course, it's all right,' said Max, topping up the wineglasses. 'What a splendid way for you and Kristina to get to know each other better and Madeleine is more than a welcome addition.'

Madeleine elbowed Kristina in the ribs and whispered, 'I hope you aren't trying to matchmake me with Serge. I don't deserve a man like that. He's too good.'

Kristina turned to her, sure she must be joking. But when she looked into Madeleine's eyes, she saw in the depth of them a lost soul and that she had meant every word. Despite her abundance of beauty, charm and talent, Madeleine truly thought Serge was too good for her.

CHAPTER SEVEN

EVE

Paris, May 1946

The dining room was bright with sunshine when I entered it the following morning. The table was polished and laid for breakfast. The air was still and no one's reflection but mine shone in the Venetian mirror above the sideboard. There was not a clue to suggest that only a few hours before, the room had been filled with guests. It was as if they had all been otherworldly beings who had crossed a threshold of some magical place and now they had vanished. Not even an essence of them remained. I thought life was something like that. One day we would all be gone for good, and we should enjoy the party while we could.

'You are looking very thoughtful this morning, Eve,' said Lucile, coming in and sitting down at the table. 'You would think after all the food we ate yesterday I wouldn't want breakfast this morning, but I'm famished.'

She looked radiant and not at all tired. When she sat down and examined the newspaper I had laid next to her setting, she did so with an air of confidence. The sight of her happiness instantly lifted my mood. Despite all Marthe's attempts to derail the evening, the party had gone off remarkably well, and Lucile appeared to have turned a corner in a view of herself. I felt her victory as if it had been my own.

'You were superb last night,' I told her, sitting down opposite while Odette brought in the breakfast. 'And wasn't Fanny Toussaint wonderful? I imagine that Olivier and Alice will be spreading the word about her today.'

'The necklace was a success,' Lucile said, 'but what about the black dress? Marthe said—'

'Marthe was green with envy,' I assured her. 'Don't worry about anything Marthe said. She was simply trying to spoil your triumph.'

Lucile took a slow sip of her coffee. 'So you think she was jealous?'

I had never seen such a devilish glint in her eye. I didn't think she had it in her. But when one's life has been blighted by a bully, why shouldn't one feel pleasure when the tables were at last turned?

'I told you that all your hard work with the apartment and your style would pay off one day,' I said. 'Soon *you* will be the most admired hostess in all of Paris. But most importantly, I hope you will be the happiest.'

Lucile beamed at me. 'You did it all. I don't know what I would do without you, Eve.' She reached across the table for my hand. But then a thin line etched itself between her brows. 'But what about the Degas? Perhaps it didn't have quite the effect we'd hoped it would?'

It was the first time Lucile had expressed any true doubt in my judgement. She might have been reluctant to cut her hair or get rid of her heavy furniture, but in the end she had always conceded to me. But this questioning was something different. I thought of how Marthe had been adamant in her dismissal of the painting. No doubt she was the one who had planted the seed.

At first I had an impulse to doubt myself too. Marthe was born to the high life while I was the one who had studied it. The first time Anthony had played a recording of the opera *Samson and Delilah*, I felt things I hadn't been able to put into words. After that, I listened to every opera record I could. I longed for a world of beauty and sophistication. But perhaps my attempts at elegance and taste would always have something false about them, like a glass bead trying to pass as a pearl? But then I straightened myself. When it came to art, I had confidence that I'd had the best teacher possible in Serge.

'I believe we're in safe hands with Monsieur Lavertu,' I said firmly. 'If anyone understands the French restitution laws, he does. The art market after the war is fraught with risk. The provenance for all of Monsieur Lavertu's inventory is impeccable. No other gallery owner in Paris can offer us that. They were all conveniently negligent with their record-keeping during the war, but provenance can still be proved by people – *Jewish* people – who had their paintings stolen. If we buy a painting from another dealer, there might be a chance that you will have to give it back to whoever the painting was looted from, or sell it back at a deflated price.'

'I see,' said Lucile. But not with as much conviction as I would have liked.

★

The rest of the morning was spent in preparing Lucile for the luncheon she was going to at the home of Simone Cabasset, a socialite of middling importance in Paris. She looked fetching in the polka-dot pencil dress I had selected for her, but I had to stop her several times from straightening her fashionably asymmetrical hat. I wasn't worried that I wasn't accompanying her. I had yet to establish myself as someone worth inviting and it would be good practice for Lucile. If she made some dreadful faux pas, the consequences would not be as disastrous as they would be if she was going to the home of a star hostess.

There was a knock at the front door and Odette answered it. The next minute, a string of florist delivery boys brought in bouquets of roses. Odette, Marie and I scrambled to find vases for them all, placing them on tables and shelves in the drawing room and Lucile's bedroom. When we were finished, there were so many flowers that the apartment had taken on the atmosphere of Empress Joséphine's rose garden.

'Who sent these?' I asked one of the delivery boys before he headed out the door. 'Is there a card or note?'

The boy shook his head. 'The sender did not give a name, mademoiselle. He only said that we should deliver the best roses in Paris.'

Georges was my first suspect. Perhaps he wanted to bolster his aunt for her birthday. But his charm was subtle. He was more likely to send one bouquet of very fine and exotic flowers rather than fill a room with roses. The gesture was wildly extravagant and much more something a lover would do than a nephew. It wasn't easy to find roses in Paris because the lack of food had seen many flower gardens converted to vegetable farms. It certainly would not have been any of Lucile's tight-fisted siblings, the ones who neglected her shamelessly and never invited her anywhere. For one uncomfortable moment, I thought it might be Marthe, trying to unsettle Lucile in some way. But then I decided against it. These were long-stemmed red roses. The very best kind. They made the room smell like an orchard of peaches and lemons. I was sure even Marthe wouldn't spend so much money on a practical joke. No, the flowers were from a man on a mission.

I turned to Lucile and clapped my hands. 'You have an admirer!'

Colour flooded her face. 'I can't believe it!' she said, reaching for one of the bouquets and gingerly touching the flowers as if to check they were real. 'Who do you think it is?'

I shook my head, completely confounded. It wouldn't have been any of the men from the previous evening. Besides Georges, Ronan was the only single man there, and he wasn't interested in women. 'The sender has remained anonymous. I'm sure he'd only do that if he was confident that you would guess his identity.'

'But I have no idea who it could be,' said Lucile.

'Truly?'

'I tell you everything, Eve. You know exactly where I have been and who I have seen.'

Her words assured me of her faith in me again. 'Whoever he is, he is very rich and very determined.'

'What should I do?' she asked, her eyes bright with excitement.

I had to admit to myself that being showered with thousands of francs worth of flowers was outside my experience. In my mind, it was the kind of thing that only happened in the pictures. I thought back to the wealthy female customers I had served when I worked in the department store. What would they have done in such a circumstance?

'There is nothing to do,' I said, aware that time was flying by and that Lucile would need to be leaving for her engagement. 'We must wait to hear more from this mysterious admirer.'

I fixed her hat one more time and led her towards the door.

'I can't wait to tell the others about the roses,' she said. 'I haven't … well, I haven't had an admirer for a long time.'

The wrinkles on her brow had softened and her eyes sparkled. The years seemed to have dropped off her. *What a bit of romantic attention does for a woman!* I thought.

★

After Lucile left, I sat at the bureau and organised her correspondence. Odette came into the room and handed me an envelope addressed to Lucile. The paper was of the finest linen and it smelled of jasmine.

'It came by special delivery,' she said.

'Thank you, Odette.'

But she seemed hesitant to leave.

'Is there something I can help you with?' I asked.

She beamed. 'I just want to say, Mademoiselle Archer, it's wonderful what you've done with Madame Damour. I've worked for her for five years now and I've never seen her so happy or look so lovely. Her mood today is definitely bright pink. She looked like she is in love.'

It was probably the most gratifying compliment I had been given and I could see from Odette's face that it was heartfelt. Although every instruction I had ever read on running a household counselled against getting too close to 'the staff', I picked a rose from one of the bouquets and gave it to her. 'Why don't you put that in a vase in your room for you and Marie to enjoy.'

'Really?' asked Odette, gazing at the rose.

'You have my permission.'

After she left the room, I turned my attention to the envelope she had given me. I gasped with astonishment when

I saw the cream card and elegant calligraphy. My eyes raced over the words. It was an invitation for Lucile to attend the Fouquets' ball. The event was one of the most important ones of the year. Lucile had been snubbed when the invitations had gone out the previous month. Now there was a personally written note from Madame Fouquet herself, apologising for the 'oversight'.

'Oh!' I said, rising from my seat when I read that Lucile had also been invited to the private dinner before the official events of the evening. The pre-ball dinner would only be attended by the most important people in Paris. Lucile had a secret admirer *and* an invitation to the most prestigious ball of the year! My fears about Marthe undermining me vanished. Then, just when I thought things couldn't get any better, I found a second invitation behind the first. The sight of my name caused my heart to miss a beat. I paced the room barely able to breathe from the excitement. Lucile's star was rising faster than I'd expected and I was following in her path. We would both need wonderful dresses for the occasion ... Balenciaga should make them. But there wasn't much time. I looked through my address book for the number of his atelier and when the receptionist heard that the dresses were for the Fouquets' ball, she made an appointment for the next day. I put down the receiver and stared at it. What I had dreamed of was coming true. I thought of what Olivier had said about other society women wanting me to decorate their homes. Of course I would always be kind and loyal to Lucile, grateful for the opportunities she had given me, but the way she was ascending in society she wouldn't need me much longer anyway. I sat back and closed my eyes so I could savour the sense of triumph. Lucile and I had both been tortured by bullies – *but look at us now*, I thought.

The telephone rang and I jumped. Without waiting for Odette to take it, I picked up the receiver. 'The Damour residence, good morning.'

'Eve?'

It was Serge. There was background noise and he sounded agitated. I began to panic. We always corresponded by letter. He never called me.

'Is everything all right?' I asked.

'I'm at the Hôtel Drouot,' he said, naming the famous Paris auction house. 'A painting came up for sale and I bought it.'

I thought of my conversation with Lucile earlier that morning. I hoped it was something spectacular. Something no other dealer in Paris would be able to obtain.

'It's by Kristina Belova,' he said, sounding on the verge of tears. 'It was painted only a few months ago. It means that—'

'She is alive!'

'Yes!'

I'd been cynical when I had thought people never came back from the dead. Kristina Belova proved an exception to the rule. I was beginning to sense that the whole day was blessed by the sublime and everyone's wishes were coming true.

'I would love to see it. Can I come by today?' I asked.

'I'm still at the auction. I'm just about to go back inside. Perhaps Thursday?'

'Thursday then,' I said, distracted by Odette coming into the room and handing me a velvet presentation box with the Mauboussin logo on it.

'Shall we say about three o'clock?' asked Serge.

'Perfect, I'll see you then,' I said, before ringing off.

I lifted the lid off the presentation box and saw inside an exquisite amethyst and rose diamond bangle.

Mon Dieu! I thought, lifting it out and admiring the way it sparkled.

I wondered who might have sent Lucile such an exceptional gift. Tucked into the silk of the box was a note. I hesitated. Perhaps the gift was from Lucile's secret admirer. If it was an intimate note, then I should not be looking at it. But Lucile was so sensitive and easily shaken that perhaps I should, so I could advise her on the best response? I wavered before giving in to my second impulse and opening the note. But when I stared at the first line, I saw the bracelet wasn't a gift for Lucile. It was for me.

Dearest Mademoiselle Archer,

I hope the roses have brought you as much joy as you have given me. You have completely cast me under your spell. Today I find myself thinking over the events of last night so much that I can concentrate on little else. The touch of your hand on my arm, your secret smile that was meant only for me. I have ordered all the servants to leave me alone so that I may pursue my daydreams of you undisturbed.

Tonight, my sweet, tonight. I have booked a private dining room at the Ritz where we can continue the beautiful dream we have started. There is so much more I want to give you than this humble token of my deep admiration. Please meet me there at eight o'clock.

Yours fondly …

A sharp bolt ran up my spine when I read the signature at the bottom.

Cyrille de Villiers

★

118

That evening when I sat down with Lucile for dinner, I had no appetite and had to force myself to eat. It was eight o'clock and I did my best not to imagine Cyrille de Villiers and his pouty lips waiting for me at the Ritz. The image was so sickening, I felt bile shoot up my throat, and had to cover my mouth with my hand.

'Are you all right?' asked Lucile, looking up from her plate. 'What's wrong?'

'Something caught in my throat,' I said.

'Oh,' she said, not really concerned about me but rather eager to talk about her luncheon. 'The ladies were very excited about the roses. We all took guesses at who my admirer might be.'

I thought it very unlikely any of them would have imagined that insipid Cyrille de Villiers was behind the gesture. This was truly a disaster in the making. Each of those ladies would tell at least five of their friends, who would in turn tell another five of theirs, and soon the gossip would compound at the same rate that rabbits breed. Every salon and drawing room in Haute-Paris would be discussing who had sent Lucile the roses.

'Blanche d'Alcy thinks it is Gaston Modot. Mona Faber is sure it is Louis Le Bargy,' Lucile continued.

Both men were rich and rather dashing widowers. While it was charming that the ladies now had high expectations for Lucile, they could not have been further from the mark.

The telephone rang and Lucile and I both jumped with surprise.

'It's rather late, isn't it?' she asked.

We never received telephone calls in the evening. Even when Lucile's brother-in-law had become gravely ill, nobody had thought to call Lucile. Only Georges came the following morning to inform her that his father had died. I knew there was only one person it could be. My stomach felt as though it was full of frantic birds wanting to escape.

Marie appeared in the dining room.

'Who is it?' Lucile asked.

Marie shook her head. 'There was someone on the line, but they said nothing then hung up.'

The telephone rang again.

'Perhaps I should answer it?' I suggested, rising from my chair.

Neither Lucile nor Marie protested, and I went out into the hall and picked up the receiver.

'Hello, who is calling please?'

There was a pause before Cyrille's voice came on the line. 'Mademoiselle Archer? You couldn't get away?' His voice was tight, like a string on a violin that had been tuned too high.

I hung up immediately, cringing. Just hearing his voice made me feel as if the man had drooled over me. I left the telephone off the hook and returned to the dining room.

'Who was it?' Lucile asked.

'There must be something wrong with the connection. There wasn't anybody there.'

Marie cleared the plates. Lucile watched her impatiently and after she left, leaned towards me, her pupils large with excitement.

'It's him! It must be! My admirer.'

I shook my head to discourage the idea.

The telephone rang again. Marie must have seen it off the hook and replaced it.

'I'll answer it,' said Lucile, getting up. 'He's hoping I'll do that. That's why he's ringing so many times.'

She ran out into the hall before I could stop her. Even if it *had* been an admirer for Lucile, I was sure that such a display of eagerness wasn't the right response. We weren't girls in a boarding school.

'You'll do nothing of the sort,' I said, chasing after her and grabbing her arm.

She raised her eyebrows at me.

'If it is him then it is most ungentlemanly of him to call you at this hour. You can't show any interest in a man like that. You must scorn him.'

Lucile searched my face as if she couldn't believe what I was saying. 'Why?'

'Because it's not respectful. The flowers are all very nice, but a man can't buy Lucile Damour with flowers.'

For one moment in my imagination, Cyrille de Villiers vanished and in his place stood a true admirer. Perhaps Gaston Modot or Louis Le Bargy. What would I have said to Lucile then?

'Men do not value women who come at a low price,' I continued. 'Of course, no one expects you to play coquettish games, but you shouldn't appear desperate either.'

Lucile's chin trembled. 'It's easy for you to say, Eve. You are young. There will be many men for you. But when you get to my age you can't be choosy. And I'm so … lonely.'

Her statement plucked at my heart strings. But she was wrong to think that young women were never lonely.

'On the contrary, you can afford to be choosier!' I told her.

I turned her to face the mirror that hung in the hall. It didn't have bullet holes in it; it was a grand Louis XV mirror with a gilt frame carved with scrolling foliage. 'Look at how you have transformed. Look at how beautiful you are,' I told her. 'Your spirit must now match your looks. Lucile Damour will not be at any man's beck and call simply because he sent her flowers.'

Lucile's shoulders relaxed and I could feel the tension in her dissipate. 'Yes, Blanche d'Alcy didn't get married until she was fifty-six and I have already had two husbands. "A woman is like wine, she gets better – and wiser – with the years," Blanche always says.' She looked at the telephone, then after a second's pause, turned in the direction of her room. 'Thank you, Eve. Well, I think I'll go to bed early tonight.'

I watched her go, feeling utter repulsion for Cyrille de Villiers. He had sent all those flowers and the bracelet without a second's thought about the consequences for Lucile or me. Lucile had gone to the luncheon and told everyone about her admirer, which now made the whole situation ten times worse. I would have liked to have confided in her about Cyrille's unwanted attention, but now that was impossible. It would break her heart and the embarrassment might make her turn on me.

*

Cyrille de Villiers turned out to be a man who was not easily put off. Although I had returned the bracelet to Mauboussin first thing the following morning, I received a note from him asking me to meet him in the Jardin des Tuileries, at the tenth bench on the Grande Allée. He didn't even have the sense to choose somewhere discreet.

With no one to rely on but myself, I knew I would have to confront him to put an end to his pursuit. He was placing me in jeopardy not only with Lucile's feelings, but the wrath of Marthe should she ever find out. When I returned the bracelet, I asked Sylvette whether I should approach Marthe about her husband's behaviour. Her words were not only firm but ominous: 'Don't ever involve the wife,' she said. 'She will always blame you for leading her husband astray, no matter how many times he may have done this before. And worse for you, to save face, Marthe de Villiers will set to work convincing everyone else of your guilt too. She could destroy everything you've worked so hard for.'

The Jardin des Tuileries was beautiful with the sun-dappled pathways and flowerbeds full of sweet-smelling jonquils. But I barely noticed as I hurried along. Despite my efforts to calm myself, I kept seeing Marthe behind every tree or in the face of every woman strolling around the pond.

Finally, I spotted Cyrille sitting on a bench with his hat in his hands. His hair was pomaded into ridiculous curls and he was wearing a red rose in his buttonhole.

He jumped to his feet when he saw me. 'Mademoiselle Archer, you came! Shall we have a stroll and then lunch? Perhaps at Le Taillevent? The restaurant is new and will take my reservation at a moment's notice.'

The man felt like a rash crawling over my skin. He truly had no idea when to stop. I shook my head. 'I can only stay five minutes. Please let me make this brief—'

'You sent back my gift,' he said, smiling lopsidedly. 'I understand. *Women prefer to play a little hard to get.*'

The last part was said in garbled English which did nothing to heighten his attractiveness. *Women prefer men who don't make their skin crawl*, I thought. But I took a breath and forced myself to be tactful. 'I think there has been a misunderstanding—'

'I find myself reliving every moment of the other night,' he continued, as if I hadn't spoken. 'I can still smell your perfume. The wonderful way you brushed against me when we said "goodnight".'

What was it about some men — especially the repugnant ones — that made them feel so entitled to a young woman's regard? I was quite certain I had not 'brushed' against him.

I realised that this was not a man in his right mind and had to make my rebuttal firmly, or things would only get worse. I had to force myself to look directly into his eager eyes, although I would have far preferred to set my attention anywhere else.

'Monsieur de Villiers! I want to be very clear. You have misinterpreted my actions. I had no intentions towards you other than the courtesy I would have shown to any guest. So please stop this useless pursuit of me. I'm sure you will come to your senses, and you have my word that I will not mention this lapse in your judgement to anyone.'

I gave him a minute to let my clear communication of disinterest set in, but to my dismay – and fury – he only smiled like an imbecile.

'Perhaps a little holiday,' he said, reaching his spiderly hand towards me. 'Perhaps a trip to Normandy. Just the two of us.'

It had been a mistake to meet him and try to make him see reason. I felt like a gazelle who had spotted a lion on the horizon. I was seized by a sudden urge to run. For there would be no point for a gazelle to try to reason with its predator. I turned and started to walk quickly away.

'We can go by train,' Cyrille said, trotting after me. 'Or by car. With my private driver if you wish to be … *discreet.*'

I began to walk faster but Cyrille kept up with me. Finally, I was out of breath and had to stop.

'I've made my feelings very clear, Monsieur de Villiers. I find you continuing to pursue me this way most *ungentlemanly.*'

He giggled stupidly. 'Darling, after all the glances we exchanged the other night, after all I have imagined for our future, I know I am not mistaken about your true feelings.'

Despite my intentions of calm – and the precarious position this stupid man was putting me in – his last statement hit a nerve.

'I am very sure of my own feelings, Monsieur de Villiers.'

I turned and walked away again, but he sped up in pursuit of me. I turned down a path and crashed straight into a huddle of women. They scattered in all directions, clucking and screeching like farmyard chickens.

'Oh, I'm so sorry,' I said.

'Eve?'

I turned around to see Blanche d'Alcy, Lucile's friend, among them. Then I recognised Mona Faber too. The entire group were all dressed in flounces and feathers like women from the previous decade.

'Where are you off to in such a hurry?' Blanche asked.

My heart was pounding and I had to catch my breath. 'I have to order some new stationery.'

'Isn't it wonderful news about Lucile?' said Mona. 'An admirer! She's very excited.'

I felt dizzy. The discombobulation caused by my situation was something akin to being very, very drunk.

'Oh, he's just one of many,' I said.

They gathered around me as if I was the farmer's wife tossing out seed.

'Really?' asked Blanche. 'Do tell us more.'

Before I could make up a story, Mona frowned and pointed at something behind me.

'Isn't that Cyrille de Villiers over there?' she asked.

We all turned to see him peering at us from behind a tree. He tipped his hat and stalked off in the opposite direction.

'He's a funny man, isn't he?' said Blanche. 'Apparently he has quite an eye for the young ladies. I heard there was some trouble in Switzerland. That's why he and Marthe are back here, to make a new start.'

'Trouble?' I asked.

'Yes,' said one of the others, a woman so tiny she could have been mistaken for a child. 'He'd given some jewellery belonging to Marthe to some maid or another. There was a formidable row about it, apparently. I haven't heard the full story, but I believe Marthe had him committed to a mental asylum for treatment.'

I clenched and unclenched my hands. Whatever the 'treatment' was, it clearly hadn't worked.

'What happened to the girl?' I asked.

'She was arrested,' said Mona.

'Arrested!'

'She deserved it, I'm sure,' said the tiny woman. 'We all know that type – ready to take advantage of a situation by leading a sick man astray.'

'I'm very sorry, ladies,' I said, 'but I must hurry with my errands.'

I made it to the edge of the park and clung to a tree. Less than two days ago I'd felt on top of the world. Now I was seized by a fear that things were about to go horribly wrong.

★

For three days, my nerves were on high alert. It was as if everything I touched sparked with static. I jumped every time the concierge came to the door with a package or a letter. But when Cyrille made no further attempt to contact me, I thought that by some miracle he had come to his senses, and it was with a lighter heart that I went to visit Serge to see the new painting.

This time when I entered his gallery, it was not Serge at the front desk but a pleasant-looking woman of about sixty years of age wearing a flecked-wool suit. Her hair was swept into a high smooth bun and she gave off the pleasant scent of rosewater.

Serge had told me about Inès Bonne, his faithful secretary who had kept an inventory of his artworks that were plundered by the Germans during the war. Madame Bonne had hidden the list in a violin and kept it at her mother's place. It was this precious list that Serge was now using to retrieve his treasures.

'*Bonjour*, mademoiselle,' Madame Bonne greeted me when I entered.

'*Bonjour*, madame. I'm Eve Archer.'

She rose from her chair in that elegant way that sophisticated French women have perfected, and that I had learned to imitate.

'Monsieur Lavertu said you would be coming today, Mademoiselle Archer. He has gone out in search of real coffee and said that you should wait for him upstairs. May I show you the way?'

She arched her arm through the air like a ballerina taking a curtsy. I was so in awe of her natural grace that even though I knew the way to Serge's apartment myself, I followed her like one under an enchantment.

'Monsieur Lavertu goes to court in two months' time to try to get his gallery back,' she said as we climbed the stairs, our footsteps clacking in perfect unison. 'It was beautiful before the war, with elegant exhibition rooms and softly filtered light streaming through the windows. He always had a refinement about him, and his knowledge and taste are far superior to any of the other dealers.'

I listened to her with interest and a great deal of pride. *I'm not such an imposter after all*, I thought. *I have good taste in my genes.*

Once we were inside the apartment, Madame Bonne ushered me to the sitting room. By the fireplace was a painting on an easel covered with a red velvet cloth.

'Monsieur Lavertu always shows off his art with éclat,' she said. 'I'm afraid you'll have to wait till he gets back to see the new Kristina Belova painting he acquired. I'm quite sure he spent his very last franc on it.'

I took the seat she offered me and, with a wistful eye, looked around the room trying to see it as my mother had. How many hours had she and Serge sat in conversation in these high-backed chairs and sipped coffee from the same set that Madame Bonne was arranging now on the dining table? But I couldn't be sure of any of it except for the walls and ceiling. Perhaps the chairs and coffee set were replacements for those that had been stolen by the Nazis. I caught sight of a painting behind Madame Bonne that hadn't been there before, but I instantly recognised my mother's face in the model. I stood up and walked towards it.

It was a painting of my mother in a way I could never have imagined her depicted. Her face was lit with both joy and fierce rebellion. She was wearing a suit of armour and wielded a sword. Gigantic angel wings sprouted from her back. She was flying away from two men in the far distance – a young one holding an apple in one hand and a snake in the other; the second man was white-haired and bearded and holding a staff. It was Adam and God. My eye fell to the signature. It had been painted by Kristina Belova. Then I saw the small name plaque at the bottom of the frame, which read: *The Flight of Eve*.

My heart stuck in my throat. This was the painting my mother had told me about. The last one she had ever posed for and after which I had been named.

'It's magnificent, isn't it?' said Madame Bonne, coming up behind me. 'It's just been returned after spending the war with a fascist dealer in Holland.'

'It's beautiful,' I said, barely able to get my words out. 'But weren't Adam and Eve expelled from Paradise because Eve was tempted by the Devil?'

'Not in Kristina Belova's depiction. Eve, fed up with both God and Adam, is leaving to find a better world than the one they have created for her.'

'It's a masterpiece,' I said.

'It certainly deserves to be considered as one,' sighed Madame Bonne. 'Unfortunately, "masterpiece" is a title that seems reserved for works by male painters.'

Footsteps sounded on the stairs and the next minute, Serge burst in the door. 'Ah, Eve, you are here,' he said, handing a small tin to Madame Bonne.

'This painting,' I said. 'It's extraordinary.'

'Yes,' he said, not quite looking at it. 'But I'll talk to you about that painting later. Meanwhile, while Madame Bonne brews the coffee, come and have a look at this extraordinary painting that turned up at the Hôtel Drouot auction.'

My heart pinched a little that he seemed more interested in the new painting by Kristina than he did by the return of the one of my mother. For a fleeting moment, I wondered if it had been Kristina who had come between them. But she had been the wife of Max, and Serge did not seem the type who would cuckold his best friend.

He lifted the red velvet cover from the painting and at once I recognised Kristina by her beautiful eyes and high cheekbones. It was another glorious self-portrait, but the subject was clearly a changed woman. Those eyes that had sparkled in her younger days were flat and tired. She had outlined herself in heavy fluid lines as if to emphasise the weariness of her being. Her expression was stern, and many different colours had been worked into the contours of her face and neck. Yet there was still an air of pride and nobility about her. Her golden hair was neatly pulled back in a chignon. Her blue dress was simple but tailored. It was only the background that gave the painting a sense of effervescence with the vibrant colours in the palette of Matisse. It certainly had the hallmarks of genius, but as Madame Bonne had so sadly pointed out, would probably not be given that status by art critics simply because Kristina was a woman.

'It's wonderful,' I said. 'But somehow, despite the bright colours, sad.'

'Yes,' agreed Serge, his eyes shining. 'Yet she is alive and painting better than ever.'

'Do you know where she is?'

'Not yet, but from the colours in this painting I'm hoping she has returned to her family villa on the Côte d'Azur. I have written to an old friend of mine in Nice to make some inquiries for me.'

'You don't think she'd be pleased to hear from you directly?' I asked.

Serge's cheeks flushed and he shook his head uncertainly. 'I don't know.'

I found his hesitancy odd. From the way he had described Kristina and Max, it seemed they had been the greatest of friends. Had something happened during the war? Something that made him doubt Kristina would have warm feelings for him?

Then, as if to change the topic as quickly as possible, he returned his attention back to the painting of my mother.

'The attention to detail is very typical of Kristina. Although she has paid homage to Charles-Amable Lenoir in style, she has subverted his tendency to paint women as beautiful, delicate and frail. She has made the mythical Eve look capable of commanding an army and achieving victory.'

I peered at the painting, trying to see the world from my mother's perspective as she posed. An artist and their model spend hours together. The two women must have known each other well. The subject had been treated with both admiration and tenderness. It was not a piece of art painted by one female rival of another.

'Who is the model?' I asked. My voice trembled despite my efforts to control my emotions.

'Madeleine.'

I was shocked that he said my mother's name impersonally, as if he had no feelings for her at all.

'Madeleine who?' I asked, although I knew perfectly well. There was some part of me that hoped by seeing me in close proximity to the painting of my mother, he would repeat his sentiment of the other day that I reminded him of someone. *I'm a product of the both of you*, I yearned to tell him.

'No one ever knew,' he said. 'She never used her last name.'

Our eyes met, and a slight frown came across his face as if he was on the verge of making the connection. But then Madame Bonne gave a gentle clearing of her throat to indicate the coffee was ready and Serge immediately turned his mind to other things.

'Oh, that delicious aroma,' he said, rubbing his hands together. 'Let's drink to better things and better days.'

Although I drank real coffee at Lucile's, I could see the pleasure that Serge and Madame Bonne took in sipping a drink that had once been a mainstay of French life but that was still hard to find two years after the occupation. They could have been sharing a bottle of fine Beaujolais from the way they inhaled the coffee before taking a sip, saturating their palates for just a moment, and then exhaling as they swallowed.

I expressed my appreciation of the rich full flavour. But my heart, which had been opened by Kristina's depiction of my mother, had once again retracted in my chest.

CHAPTER EIGHT

KRISTINA

Nice, June 1946

After Lorenzo took away Kristina's breakfast tray, she told him to send up Eve Archer and to bring Flora some parsley from the garden. She must have frightened the poor young woman with how confused she had been at the mention of Serge Lavertu's name. But she did want to help her – and Serge. She knew that he had been Max's best friend but that was it; the memory became unclear after that. But perhaps if Eve gave her more details, she might start to recall things. In fact, she wondered if the appearance of Eve Archer might be exactly what she needed to help her recover her past.

The sound of the buzzer at the front gate rang shrilly. She went to the window that faced the street and peered furtively out to see that the dark-haired woman was back again. Sonia Vertinskaya. She was fashionably dressed in a shantung jacket and pleated skirt. She came at least once a week, but Kristina told Lorenzo to never let her inside the villa, even though the two of them had been good friends when they were young. Sonia's appearances filled her with such a strong sense of foreboding that she felt her life was in danger each time she came.

'Madame Bergeret?'

Kristina turned around to see Eve Archer standing in the doorway holding the bunch of parsley she'd asked for. The poor girl looked like she hadn't slept a wink. She had dark rings under her eyes and was as pale as a ghost.

Kristina took the parsley from her. 'Please, sit down,' she said. 'So, you know I have amnesia?'

Eve nodded.

'I'm hoping we can help each other,' Kristina continued. 'You see, I was thinking this morning that if you tell me what you know, it might help me to start to remember.'

She stopped herself. How desperate must she be to ask a complete stranger to help her piece her life together? But as she looked again at Eve, she realised there was something familiar about the young woman. 'You're Australian, aren't you?' she asked. 'Lorenzo told me. When did you come to France?'

'Just a year ago.'

'Then you and I have never met before?' Kristina sat down. 'But it's the strangest thing, I feel like we already know each other.'

'You and my mother knew each other,' Eve said cautiously. 'Her name was Madeleine and you painted her.'

Kristina thought for a moment that she could hear the beating of wings. She saw the glint of metal flash across her mind. It was like trying to remember a dream – it was there for a second, and then it was gone.

She shook her head. 'I'm sorry. Do you have a photograph?'

Eve reached into her pocket and pulled out a small photograph of a pretty woman with blonde hair and a sad smile. But it still sparked nothing in Kristina's memory.

'You painted her as Eve of the biblical story—'

Before Eve could finish, Flora appeared from behind a painting and scampered up to eat the parsley Kristina was holding.

'My pet rabbit,' she explained, lest Eve thought there were wild rabbits scurrying about the house. 'Lorenzo says I've always liked rabbits. He brought this one to keep me company. Her name is Flora.'

The expression on Eve's face suddenly changed. 'Flora!' she said. 'Why did you give her that name?'

Kristina was startled by Eve's reaction. She tried to recall what prompted her to name the rabbit that. She thought her original idea had been to name her Fleur because the rabbit was fond of eating flowers, but for some reason, Flora had been the name that stuck.

Kristina shook her head. 'I don't know. It seemed to suit her. Why, what's so unusual about the name?'

Eve stood up, her eyes frantic.

'Because that's the title of the painting Serge is accused of selling to Hitler.'

CHAPTER NINE

KRISTINA

Nice, August 1923

'It's Americans you see everywhere, these days,' said Kristina's mother, Yelena, when Kristina and Sonia joined her for breakfast on the terrace of the Villa des Cygnes. The light floaty dress Sonia had made for Yelena made her look like a young woman, even with her grey hair and the lines on her forehead. 'A stroll along the Promenade des Anglais used to be considered sufficient exercise,' she continued. 'The Americans are far too impatient for that. They need to be active – swimming or out on the golf course, no matter the weather. Now every hotel must have a gymnasium.'

'Well, that's good for us, Mama,' Kristina said, trying to steer the conversation away from a topic that might upset Sonia. The reason there were no Russians out strolling on the promenade was because they were too busy working as chauffeurs and governesses. 'I shall be able to sell my paintings to rich Americans and Sonia will be able to decorate their homes.'

Yelena eyed the young women's clothing. 'What are those outfits you two are wearing by the way?'

'Beach pyjamas,' replied Sonia, twirling around in the silk loungewear she had made for herself and Kristina. 'You don't approve?'

'I approve very much,' replied Yelena, taking Leo the rabbit out of his basket and placing him on her lap. 'You look like two Chinese dolls. As long as you stay under your parasols and out of the sun. I don't like this fashion for tanning. The young women who spend all day lying on the sand are going to look like peasants before they are thirty.' She touched her nose to Leo's twitching one. 'Isn't that true, my darling? You are clever and stay inside.'

Kristina and Sonia exchanged a smile. The moment Yelena had laid eyes on Leo it was as if she had found another child. She sewed him little jackets and bowties to wear. He had a pen in the nursery upstairs and Kristina's father had fashioned some runs for him to race around on. At dinner, the rabbit sat on a cushion on the table and ate with the family. Kristina was attached to Leo too but had decided to leave him in Nice with her parents when she returned to Paris. She could not offer him the same sort of attention and lifestyle as he was enjoying in Nice.

Max and Serge arrived wearing white shorts and shirts and holding tennis racquets. They looked like movie stars – or the active Americans Yelena so disapproved of.

'You must have got up early!' Kristina said with a note of surprise. Max had gone to bed the same time she had, but she knew that Serge had stayed up late with Madeleine.

Before she could probe further, her father sauntered in dressed in a white linen suit, his beard and moustache immaculately groomed. He handed Yelena a bunch of freshly cut lilac roses from the garden.

'What type are these?' Yelena asked, sniffing the roses. 'Their perfume is divine! It makes me think of sweet lemonade.'

'Sterling Silver,' he answered. 'They are quite unusual and not at all easy to grow.'

Mikhail was the epitome of a male Russian aristocrat – tall and slender with clear blue eyes and fine features. Kristina had always believed it was impossible for any mortal to match his natural elegance.

'They are the perfect mix of pink and blue,' Yelena said, admiring the colour.

Everybody sat down and Mikhail launched into his favourite topic. 'Like all lilac or lavender roses, they share the same symbolism as the fabled blue rose. Nobody has yet produced a blue rose. It is a quest for the mystical and the seemingly unattainable. Meanwhile, we have these roses to delight and inspire us. They are a symbol of enchantment. Speaking of enchantment, where is pretty Madeleine this morning? Isn't she joining us?'

'Haven't you noticed that "Pretty Madeleine" doesn't eat breakfast and likes to sleep in late?' Sonia asked.

'Because she is used to working late at night,' Kristina said.

She had not counted on Sonia joining them at the villa for August. Madame Vertinskaya had come to Nice to stay with her brother and Kristina had assumed Sonia would stay with him too. Now the pleasant holiday she had envisioned with Max, Serge and Madeleine had turned into a constant jousting match between Sonia and Madeleine. Every time Madeleine opened her mouth, Sonia made some disparaging remark. After dinner the previous evening, she had said to Madeleine in front of everyone, 'Your "little girl lost" act might fool the others, but it doesn't work on me.' To which Madeleine responded, 'Your "poor little victim" act bores the rest of us to tears.'

But Kristina suspected there might be another reason Madeleine was sleeping in that morning apart from habit or a desire to avoid Sonia. And that thought caused her to smile as she sneaked a glance at Serge. On the top floor of the villa was an observatory and, above it, a roof-top terrace. Restless and unable to sleep from the heat the previous night, Kristina had risen from her bed with the intention of viewing the full moon from her father's telescope. She had been upset by the argument between her two friends and gazing at an object so far from Earth seemed like the perfect remedy for her frayed nerves. But as she mounted the stairs, she'd heard the soft strains of music from the terrace. It was 'Casta Diva', the prayer to the goddess of the moon for peace, from the opera *Norma*. Kristina climbed to the terrace to see Serge and Madeleine illuminated by the moonlight. They had their backs to her and didn't hear her approach. Madeleine's singing and Serge's violin-playing were sublime, and Kristina stopped a moment to listen. When they finished the piece, she stepped forward with the intention of joining them. But then Madeleine had laid her head on Serge's shoulder. It was in that moment that Kristina realised they might be very good for each other. Madeleine would draw Serge out of his shell, and Serge would be a steady influence on Madeleine. Kristina went back to bed and slept peacefully.

'Well, we are on holidays,' said Yelena, pouring everyone a cup of tea. 'If Madeleine wants to catch up on sleep, I have no objection to it.'

The tea was Yelena's special blend of cinnamon sticks and cloves with orange peel and dried pineapple. It was sweet and aromatic and made Kristina think of her childhood whenever she drank it.

Yelena noticed Kristina's pleasure. 'Flowers might enchant us but tea is truly magical,' she said. 'It can produce a state of tranquil meditation – or give us courage if we need it.'

They all lapsed into silence for a moment as they savoured the tea.

'I have something amusing for us all to do this afternoon,' said Mikhail. 'Édouard and Beatrice Fould have invited us to their villa to view their art collection.'

The suggestion put Serge into an unprecedented state of euphoria. 'The Foulds!' he exclaimed. 'Their collection is famous all over France!'

'Of course it is,' said Sonia. 'They are wealthy Jews, aren't they?'

'They are members of the Fould banking family,' said Mikhail. 'They are generous benefactors of art to French museums, but are most widely known – and admired – for their establishment of hospitals, schools and low-cost housing for the poor.'

'If we are going to visit the Fould estate then I had better iron my suit,' said Serge, rising from his chair.

Mikhail looked amused at Serge's eagerness to make an impression and waved his hand. 'Don't bother. You will be surprised at how relaxed Édouard and Beatrice are.'

An hour before they were due to leave, Kristina went upstairs to wake Madeleine and see if she would like to join them for the visit to the Fould estate. Knocking softly on the door, she waited for an answer. When none came, she gently pushed the door open to discover that the pretty toile de Jouy guest room allocated to Madeleine now resembled a jumble sale. Clothes were strewn about the room, some inside out and rumpled. Madeleine lay face down on the bed, still dressed in her gown of the previous evening. The air reeked of alcohol and Madeleine's unwashed body odour. Kristina's eyes fell to the empty wine bottles on the floor. She picked one up and realised it was a vintage Château Latour from her father's cellar.

How had Madeleine found it? She was sure Serge had nothing to do with Madeleine's drinking spree. He had looked bright-eyed at breakfast. It was Madeleine. She had come back to her room and got drunk alone.

'Madeleine,' she whispered. 'Are you all right?'

At first there was no response, then gradually Madeleine stirred. She turned her head and set swollen eyes on Kristina. 'They took my baby. They took her away right after she was born.'

'Who?' asked Kristina, crouching down next to the bed.

Madeleine's eyes were glazed over. 'I won't tell you his name because I don't want him to harm you. But he is dangerous.'

Kristina waited for more, but Madeleine lapsed back into sleep again.

'The taxis are here, Kristina!' Max called from downstairs.

Unsure what to do, she felt a shiver of panic race through her. Should she call a doctor? But Madeleine was breathing steadily and calmly. After a moment's thought, Kristina poured a tall glass of water from the jug on the dresser and left it beside Madeleine. She opened the window to let fresh air into the room. Then she collected the bottles and hid them in a cupboard before tidying the clothes as best she could. On her way downstairs, she said to the maid, Suzanne, 'Mademoiselle Madeleine isn't well today. Could you please check on her in an hour?'

She's young and silly, Kristina thought, as she hurried to join the others. *But what was that about a baby?* After a moment's pause, she shook away her worry. *It's nothing*, she told herself. *It was a bad dream. Madeleine will be all right.*

She couldn't bear to think otherwise.

★

The Foulds' white semicircular mansion was perched on a hill overlooking the sea. Its modern design was complemented by an extensive Mediterranean garden, thickly planted with palm and olive trees. The two taxis transporting Kristina and her parents as well as Serge, Max and Sonia travelled down the gravel driveway through an avenue of looming cypress trees. At the front door, Kristina stepped forward to press the gold doorbell. The resulting chimes were so delicately musical, she imagined there must be a dozen servants on the other side tapping spoons against crystal glasses. A butler, far more formal in manner than her family's dear Lorenzo, welcomed them into a sun-drenched foyer.

'Monsieur and Madame Fould are on their way down,' he told them, leading them to a drawing room with a breathtaking panoramic view. The Bergere chairs and marble-topped tables were opulent. Everywhere Kristina looked, there were stunning objets d'art: silver urns, jade figurines and ceramic sculptures. She and Max raised their eyebrows at each other. Despite the magnificence of the surroundings, Kristina, who was sensitive to such things, thought that there was something missing. Not in the décor of the house – it was exquisite – but in the atmosphere. A sense of the absence of something – as if the house were holding its breath and waiting for something to complete it.

A striking middle-aged couple entered the room. Silver-haired Beatrice Fould, wearing a simple coral sundress, was the epitome of understated good taste. Her husband, Édouard, dressed in white trousers, a navy jacket and striped cravat, reached out to clasp Mikhail's hand. His bushy eyebrows, flat nose and long jaw gave him the appearance of a friendly camel. Kristina immediately thought how interesting it would be to sketch him.

'Welcome, Monsieur Belov,' Édouard said, correctly using the Russian masculine form of the family name. 'My wife and I are pleased you have come with your family and friends.'

Mikhail introduced the Foulds to each of the members of the party, before presenting Beatrice with the bouquet of prize cabbage roses he had brought with him.

She accepted the flowers with grace. 'They are exquisite,' she said, admiring the ruffled blooms. 'The flowers in Nice are always beautiful, but these are exceptional.'

Édouard signalled to the butler. 'Let's have some tea here, shall we? We can go into the garden later, when the sun isn't strong enough to cook us like pancakes.'

With much aplomb, the butler set out a tea table with a Sèvres porcelain set trimmed in imperial blue and gold and decorated with sepia paintings of Ancient Egypt.

'It's so unusual,' said Yelena, admiring a teacup bearing an image of the Sphinx.

Beatrice passed her the sugar bowl to examine. 'This design has quite an interesting history,' she said. 'The first set was presented by the Tsar of Russia to Napoleon as a diplomatic gift. The second set was produced as a divorce present from Napoleon to Empress Joséphine, but she thought it was far too severe for her taste and it was returned to the Sèvres factory. It was later offered by Louis XVIII to the Duke of Wellington. It now remains with his successors. This is a copy, of course, but quite a conversation piece.'

'Beatrice is considered one of the foremost experts on porcelain,' said Édouard proudly.

'It's a passion of mine,' she explained with an apologetic shrug. 'I do hope I'm not boring you?'

'Not at all,' Yelena assured her. 'You have before you an audience of appreciators of the fine arts. We love nothing more than to hear about a piece's history.'

'Splendid!' said Édouard. 'That is exactly what I was told about you. I so wish that I had invited you all here when ...'

His gaze travelled to his wife, and he was unable to finish his sentence.

'We don't have many visitors we can show off our art collection to these days,' Beatrice said, giving the impression that the Foulds were the kind of close couple who finished each other's thoughts. 'It was different of course when David was alive. The house was always full of people then. He was so liked by everybody.'

Kristina now understood the sensation of absence she had experienced earlier. She remembered reading that the Foulds had lost their son – and only heir – at the Battle of the Somme.

Kristina's mother reached out and touched Beatrice's arm. 'Such a sacrifice,' she said. 'I lost a dearly loved nephew in that war. It was a terrible waste of bright young lives.'

Beatrice nodded to show she appreciated the sympathy, but she quickly changed the subject. 'Édouard had a wing added to the house for his art collection and he has promised to build a similar one for my porcelain. Let's finish our tea and then we'll take you on a tour.'

As Édouard and Beatrice led their guests through the house, stopping every so often along the way to point out a cloisonné-style vase or jar in a glass display cabinet, Kristina and her companions trotted along with all the excitement of children in an Easter parade. In one room, Beatrice drew everyone's attention to a salmon-coloured vase painted with wisteria and peony blossom designs. Kristina noticed Sonia was staring at a pair of eggshell porcelain lanterns next to it. They were painted in delicate famille verte enamels. At first she thought her friend was admiring them, but when Sonia turned, her face was contorted with bitterness. Kristina had never seen Sonia look quite so dark, but she understood what she was most likely feeling. She remembered visiting Sonia's family's summer villa in Crimea, which was even grander than this house. Back then, Kristina had been in awe of the multitude of servants and the magnificent Afghan carpets that filled the home. Madame Vertinskaya had once talked as passionately about her extensive collection of amber as Beatrice was now speaking about her Syrian glassware. The only difference was that Sonia's family's fortune was gone.

Through a corridor with picture windows that overlooked a Florentine garden, Édouard led the group into a gallery the size of a ballroom. Max and Serge gasped at the Flemish and Dutch masters, Mikhail was drawn by the stately English portraits, while Kristina and Yelena gravitated to the French eighteenth-century works. Sonia stood aloof by one of the windows.

'Look!' cried Kristina with delight. 'François Boucher's painting of Madame de Pompadour.'

It wasn't so much the Rococo painter Kristina admired, but the subject. Not merely the mistress to the French king, Madame de Pompadour had been a patron of the arts and a follower of the Enlightenment. She had been determined to turn Paris into the capital of Europe for taste and culture.

Beatrice came up beside her. 'She was a lover of fine porcelain and championed Sèvres.'

'The painting is wonderful,' said Serge, joining them. 'The volume and the structure of the ruffles of her clothing, the suggestion of artifice in her make-up. It's intimate but doesn't give too much away – as a good mistress of the king wouldn't.'

'For someone so young, you have quite an eye,' Édouard said to Serge. 'And quite a knowledge of ladies. Come here, will you, I want your opinion on these two portraits by Carriera.'

The two men walked around the gallery together, sharing their admiration for the art. Serge's earlier keenness to make an impression had dissipated into easy and intimate conversation.

Kristina thought it looked like the pair had known each other forever.

'Well, Édouard seems to have stolen your friend,' Beatrice said to Max. 'So perhaps you can give me your opinion on the Vermeer he is so fond of. Am I wrong to dislike it?'

Max pointed out some strong points so as not to offend Édouard but also put himself in agreement with Beatrice indirectly. 'Vermeer is not thought of as a painter of beauty, rather he is admired for his subtlety, and nuance of depiction of light. However, while I appreciate his mastery, I am not fond of his work myself. I find it a touch wooden.'

Kristina smiled to herself. Max could charm the birds from the trees.

They spent more than two hours in the gallery and Édouard and Beatrice seemed delighted by their company.

'I'll tell you what,' said Édouard suddenly, 'I have in my collection an extraordinary painting. I'd like you all to see it.'

A flutter of excitement ran through the guests. Kristina had thought the Foulds' artworks so exquisite she couldn't imagine there could be one particular painting that could outshine the entire collection. It was with great curiosity that she followed the Foulds through a series of corridors that seemed to narrow as their journey continued. When they finally came to a set of double doors, Édouard took a key from his pocket and turned the lock. The room was dim until he walked across and pulled aside the heavy drapes, leaving the natural light to filter through sheer white curtains. The walls were lined in red silk damask and devoid of any artwork, except one medium-sized painting at the opposite end of the room. Kristina instantly recognised it as a Renaissance work from the colours and style. She followed as Édouard led them towards it.

As soon as they saw what it was, they let out gasps of surprise and delight. The subject was Flora, the classical goddess of spring and flowers. She was pale and elegant with sloping shoulders and sensuous curves visible beneath her diaphanous gown. A band of flowers sat on her head and she held a cornucopia of roses, from which she was tossing flower stems to the pretty nymphs gathered around. Kristina was struck by the brilliance and the luminosity of the work, as well as the harmony and sense of movement. This wasn't just any Flora. Kristina's eye travelled over the grace of line and took in the detail by which the flowers and other plants had been rendered. This was Sandro Botticelli's Flora, the same one who appeared in his masterpiece *Primavera*.

'Marvellous!' exclaimed Serge, trembling with excitement. 'A Botticelli! I was unaware a companion painting of *Primavera* existed.'

'Yes, most definitely a Botticelli,' said Édouard, 'but one that was lost for centuries. It wasn't painted at the same time as *Primavera*, but later, and on canvas instead of wood, as was *The Birth of Venus*. But it's much smaller than that work – a third of the size.'

Max studied the painting closely. 'There is no Medici family symbolism in it,' he said. 'No crests on the clothing or anywhere else in the painting.'

'Indeed,' agreed Kristina. 'Although the model still seems to be Lorenzo di Pierfrancesco's wife, Semiramide, and she is smiling as she was in *Primavera*.'

'That is interesting,' agreed Édouard. 'But the painting was included in the Medici family's inventory.'

'How did it go missing?' asked Sonia, suddenly interested in the conversation again. 'Was it stolen?'

'Yes, it was stolen,' said Édouard, 'most likely by Botticelli himself.'

'Why would he steal his own painting?' asked Yelena. 'And from the patron who had commissioned it?'

Édouard pointed to a blackened corner of the painting. 'To burn it.'

After suitable expressions of surprise from the others, he turned to Serge. 'You are a competent art historian. You explain why.'

Serge tore his eyes from the painting and spoke as if he was under a spell. 'After the decline of the Medici family's power in Florence, Botticelli came under the influence of a charismatic Dominican friar, Girolamo Savonarola, who encouraged the burning of mirrors, non-religious paintings, dice, playing cards, fancy clothes and luxury items. He preached that anything beautiful was offensive to God. It's believed by many that Botticelli added to the flames those of his paintings that would have been considered "pagan" by the friar. It was to make a break from his hedonistic past and his association with the Medici family. From then on, he would only paint religious subjects.'

'The bonfire of the vanities,' said Mikhail. 'But how did this painting survive?'

Édouard smiled broadly. 'It appears it was plucked from the fire by an ardent admirer of Botticelli's work and hidden away. After its rescuer's death, it was probably sold off or given away by relations who didn't know its worth.'

'But how did you obtain it?' asked Max.

'David found it in a junk shop in Portugal. The vendor had no idea it was a Botticelli. But David knew instantly by the style, attention to detail and the technique of applying the paint in thin, uniform layers using very fine pigments. Botticelli's favoured binding emulsion was *tempera grassa* – egg and oil. But in his final glazings he liked to use natural resins.'

Kristina thought of her conversation with Serge in the flea market in Paris. Perhaps he was right to frequent such places!

'But,' began Serge, pausing as if he was uncertain that what he was about to ask was appropriate, 'your son recovered it some years ago and yet it has not been exhibited. I haven't read of its discovery anywhere.'

Édouard's face clouded. 'The director of the Louvre and a select group of art experts are aware of it. The painting is bequeathed to the museum upon my and Beatrice's death.' Looking at his wife, he added, 'We believe that great art is for all people, not only those who can afford it. But this treasure ...' He sighed and then with a voice trembling with emotion said, 'You should have seen the delight on David's face when he presented it to us. The memory of that expression has comforted me through my darkest nights. No, this painting will remain with us until we are both no more. Then it will take its place at the Louvre where it can be enjoyed by all.'

Beatrice put her hand on his arm and Édouard patted it. In that gesture, it seemed to Kristina they had spoken volumes to each other without uttering a word. They had the best of everything, the utmost luxury that money could buy, but they would give it all up in an instant if it meant they could have their son back.

Mikhail stepped forward and clasped Édouard's hand. 'Then we are honoured that you chose to allow us to view this masterpiece today. It is a memory all of us will treasure and we will not breathe a word of its existence to anyone.'

Kristina knew that her father had spoken from his heart. Her parents' first child was a boy named Pavel who had died at six years of age, two years before she was born. Although she'd never had any lack of love and attention from her parents,

Kristina understood that the hardest part of leaving Russia for them had not been the loss of riches, but the loss of places that held memories of their dear little boy – the rooms in the house in Saint Petersburg he once filled with his childish laughter, the pond where he launched his first miniature sailboat, the swing in the garden where he used to tell his papa to push him higher and higher.

Kristina reached for Max's fingers and squeezed them. There would be tragedies and triumphs in their future too, and she wanted to go through them with him and for them to never be apart. They had talked about getting married after she made her first major sale. But somehow the moving scene she had witnessed between people who knew heartache made her want to become his wife as soon as possible. She would speak to Max that night. He could ask her father's permission and they could be married before they went back to Paris.

Afterwards, as promised, the Foulds gave their visitors a tour of the gardens. But while Beatrice pointed out palm trees from the Canary Islands, South America and Australia, Édouard and Serge lingered towards the back of the group, still engrossed in discussing art.

'So, you prefer modern works?' Kristina overheard Édouard ask Serge. 'David did too. But I never listened to him.'

'It's not that I don't value all great art,' replied Serge. 'It's that I prefer to discover and nurture new talent. *Living talent.*'

'David's words exactly!' said Édouard with a hearty laugh. 'Perhaps you will guide me. Who should I start with?'

'You should start with the artist right here in front of us, Kristina Belova,' Serge said. 'She is as yet unknown, but her art is exquisite. I'm expecting great things for her.'

'Mademoiselle Belova?' replied Édouard. 'Well, I should certainly like to see her work on your recommendation.'

For Édouard Fould to display an interest in Kristina's work was far beyond her expectations and she was grateful that Serge had such faith in her. But it was hard to feel confident about herself after having spent two hours looking at the works of the greatest painters in the world. Could one of her paintings possibly hang in such an esteemed collection as the Foulds'?

Kristina glanced at Sonia. A few weeks earlier, when Kristina had been recounting to her friend all the things that were wrong with one of her paintings, Sonia had slammed down the book she was reading and said, 'Picasso doesn't lack confidence in putting himself forward, and he doesn't have half your talent. Max Ernst considers himself a genius, and maybe he is, but you are a genius too. Why do women have to squeeze their talent into little boxes so as not to make anybody uncomfortable? Or to avoid being accused of thinking too much of themselves? Nobody pays attention to humble painters in the art world, Kristina. You'd better start thinking like the men if you want to amount to anything.'

So when Serge called out for her, she straightened her posture and put on her best smile before turning and walking towards him and Édouard.

'Monsieur Fould would like to commission you to paint a portrait of Madame Fould,' Serge told her. 'I suggested you could start on it as soon as you finish your current portrait of Madeleine.'

Madame Fould stopped her tour and looked from Serge to Kristina. 'You are a painter? I didn't realise. I would certainly be most flattered.'

'Kristina is truthful in her portraits, Madame Fould,' said Serge. 'She aims to catch the authentic essence of someone, so she's not a drawing-room painter. You won't be able to influence her version of your soul as she sees it.'

Beatrice's eyebrows shot up. 'And I am not a drawing-room subject, I assure you, Monsieur Lavertu. I will give Mademoiselle Belova licence to paint me, warts and all. In fact, I shall demand it.'

Kristina marvelled at Serge. He had increased her cachet and stirred Beatrice's excitement at the same time. She would have been so grateful to have received a commission from the Foulds that she would probably have painted Beatrice any way she directed. But Serge had turned the tables and made it seem as if it was Beatrice who was lucky to have Kristina paint her portrait.

Her eyes met Serge's and she held his gaze, marvelling at his business acumen. Pleasure spread across his face before he gave her a conspiratorial wink.

★

The following day, Kristina sat under a parasol sketching the scenes of the beach while Sonia lay exposed next to her, slowly turning the colour of a coffee bean. Kristina's parents were back at the villa. Max was picking up pebbles and throwing them into the sea to the delight of a group of children he had befriended. Serge and Madeleine played in the water. Sometimes joyfully splashing each other, other times swimming gracefully side by side.

'They are like dolphins together,' Kristina said.

Sonia turned over onto her back and Kristina could not resist a jab.

'And you are a little *piroshok* that must be turned over until it is golden and puffed.'

'I am absorbing the warmth before we go back to Paris,' Sonia replied.

Kristina's gaze travelled from Max and the children back to Serge and Madeleine. They were bobbing in the waves together now, talking intimately about something with looks of sympathy on their faces, but they were too far away for her to hear.

'What do you think they are saying to each other?' Kristina asked.

'They are talking about paintings. Whenever I hear them speak, it's always about art.'

'Well, that's good,' Kristina said.

Whenever Serge talked about art to Kristina she felt caught in a beautiful spell. The first night in Nice, he had admired the Jan Van Huysum's still-life paintings of flowers in Mikhail's study. The way he described the sweeping variegated arrangements, it was as if the paintings had come to life. She could feel the velvety blooms and the cool drops of moisture under her fingertips, and hear the minute flutter of the butterflies hovering nearby.

Kristina looked back to Sonia who was now reading *Le Petit Écho de la Mode*, a fashion magazine full of advertisements for anti-wrinkle creams and bust-lifting potions.

'Do you think they are in love?'

Sonia lifted her hand against the glare of the sun and squinted at her. 'Who?'

'Serge and Madeleine.'

'It isn't Madeleine he is always looking at,' she replied curtly. Then after a pause, she added, 'It's *you*, Kristina.'

'Don't be ridiculous. We're good friends, that's all.' Then in a desire to change the topic, Kristina said something she hadn't intended to reveal to Sonia until the deed was done.

'Max is going to ask Papa for my hand in marriage this afternoon,' she said. 'Will you be my bridesmaid?'

'No,' Sonia replied emphatically. 'I don't believe in marriage.'

Kristina cringed. It was as though Sonia had thrown a bucket of cold water over her. She could be her best friend one minute, then say something awful the next.

'Perhaps you should be less … *blunt*,' Kristina told her.

'I always say what I think, you know that.'

'Why don't you believe in marriage?' Kristina asked. 'You've never said so before.'

'It is my observation that marriage does not make a woman happier. The union might appear to start off well, but eventually it drains the life out of her. By the time she realises what has happened, there is no escape.'

'Well,' Kristina said, 'that's not how Max and I will be.'

'No?'

Kristina did not like Sonia's cynicism. In fact, ever since she and Max had become close, Sonia had become even pricklier. Kristina stood and walked in the direction of Max and the laughing children. He looked up and smiled, waving for her to join them.

The expression on his face reassured her. She wanted to marry him as soon as possible.

★

Kristina could not have wished for a more perfect day for her wedding. The sky was clear, and a mild sea breeze softened the heat and gave her full-length veil a fetching lift. When she and Max stepped out of the Town Hall, their friends and family following after them, she had a sense that everything was happening at once. It was a new chapter in her life. She was no longer just an art student, but a wife, a serious artist and perhaps, sometime in the future … a mother. The joy, the excitement and the trepidation made her tremble, but when Max took her hand and squeezed it, her body settled. She had united herself with the love of her life, a man who shared her dreams and her passions. There was nothing to fear as long as she had Max by her side.

Later, over a lunch of mushroom *piroshki*, stuffed cabbage and Niçoise salad on the terrace, Kristina found herself quite relaxed. The wedding party was small. Max's family had not been able to come for the celebration due to his father's poor health, so the afternoon was an intimate affair consisting of Kristina's parents, Serge, Sonia and Madeleine. The two young women had called a truce for the day, and although they studiously avoided each other, there was at least no outward combat.

A prickle of unease returned briefly when Kristina looked at Serge, who, while smiling at a story Madeleine was telling him, seemed lost in deep reflection. As Yelena was occupied with overseeing the wedding feast, Serge had been left in charge of Leo. The rabbit was sitting in his arms placidly and Kristina remembered how on the day they rescued him, she had suggested to Serge that she paint him with the rabbit. But he'd seemed reluctant whenever she brought it up afterwards and the idea had been dropped. Was it because she'd also said that painting their portrait was the best way to get to know someone? As if suddenly aware Kristina was looking at him, Serge turned and his eyes met hers and held them earnestly. There was a question in his gaze that she didn't understand and didn't know how to answer. Then she remembered Sonia's observation that Serge often looked at her. Feeling she might be on dangerous ground, she quickly looked away.

Madeleine suddenly flung her arms open. 'I want to sing for our lovely couple,' she said, '"Plaisir d'amour".'

The gathering encouraged her with applause and Madeleine stood up, swaying slightly on her feet. Although she appeared tipsy from the rosé Mikhail had chosen for the occasion, she wasn't blind drunk. Kristina had not seen a repeat of the lone drinking binge, and that fact had availed her fears for Madeleine's future and convinced her of Serge's positive influence.

Madeleine sang beautifully with perfectly turned trills. But Kristina had never listened to the words of the popular love song closely before and was surprised to find them melancholic, all about how the pleasure of love is brief, while the grief at the loss of it lasts a lifetime.

When Madeleine finished and sat down to the appreciative murmurs of her audience, instead of looking pleased with herself, her eyes clouded in a way that gave Kristina the impression of heartache. She wondered what could be wrong when Madeleine had been in high spirits only a few minutes ago, but before she could think further about it, the wind picked up, sending serviettes and flower arrangements flying.

'Let's move inside,' suggested Yelena. 'I'm about to serve the wedding cake.'

★

That night, lying side by side on the bed in the room that Mikhail had filled with white lilies and Yelena had decorated with fine linen, Kristina and Max finally had a moment to be alone.

'The day went by so quickly,' said Kristina.

Max traced the curve of her cheek with his fingertip. 'The day may not last, but we are married forever,' he said.

'That's true,' she agreed. Then her mind drifted to Serge. 'Do you think Serge enjoyed himself? There were moments when he looked ... so sad.'

Max rolled on his back and folded his hands behind his head. 'I suppose he is sad … a little,' he said. 'We've been together since we were boys. We are as close as brothers, perhaps even closer for I see more of Serge than I do of my own siblings. We came to Paris together.' He flashed her a cheeky grin. 'But we can't do marriage together.'

'Are you really the only family he has?'

Max nodded. 'Serge's aunt hired tutors for him and made sure he received a good education. He was fed and clothed but that was about it. There was no affection. One day I was walking by the river when I saw him on the other side, playing his violin. I knew he was made fun of by the other young people in the village because his family was Jewish, but something about him intrigued me. I asked him to play for me and we became firm friends despite him being a few years older than me. Over the years we have helped each other with our shortfalls – my lack of education, his lack of sociability. I suppose that things must change now makes him sad.'

Kristina was surprised to learn Serge was Jewish. It was the first time Max had mentioned it. Serge never practised any religion or celebrated any Jewish holidays. She had thought he was Catholic like Max. 'I can see that you are very good for each other,' she said. 'I hate to think that I've come between you.'

Max shrugged. 'Things had to change sometime. He told me he's found an apartment not far from the shop.'

Kristina sat up on her elbow. 'But I never expected him to move! The apartment above the shop is his home too. Why doesn't he go on living there as before? It's large enough for us all.'

'And if Serge should find someone?' asked Max, lifting his eyebrow.

Kristina assumed he meant Madeleine and laughed. 'Then we can all live together.'

Max smiled back. 'You sincerely like him, don't you?'

Kristina nodded. She had been an only child – she understood absence. She felt it still. In the past, August meant the Villa des Cygnes was filled with cousins with whom she'd have shared her room. Giggling, snoring, loud and fun cousins. The villa felt so quiet without them.

'You will tell him tomorrow, won't you?' she asked. 'Before we leave. To put his mind at rest.'

Max nodded and reached for the table lamp, switching it off before taking Kristina in his arms. 'Thank you. I will tell him.' He slipped his hand down her hip and her skin tingled at his touch as he lifted her night dress over her head. 'But right now,' he whispered, 'we have something else to occupy our minds.'

Kristina sighed with desire as he pressed himself against her. 'Yes, we do,' she said.

CHAPTER TEN

EVE

Paris, May 1946

After visiting Serge and seeing the new self-portrait by Kristina Belova and the extraordinary painting she had made of my mother, I returned to the apartment. I let myself in and heard the voices of women and at least one man moving between the rooms. Lucile's squeaky soprano tone was immediately recognisable. But a chill rippled up my spine when I realised the *très chic* inflections of the other woman sounded distinctly like Marthe de Villiers. What was she doing here?

The man's voice was unfamiliar. 'Ah, this one is very pretty indeed, Madame Damour, but unfortunately of little value on the market.'

The tone was elegant and even, like a pristine river flowing over rocks and gently smoothing their edges. The kind of voice a skilled seducer uses when he wants a woman to do his bidding.

'Nineteenth-century prints have a warmth about them. I suggest you keep it,' he continued.

The trio came out of the library and into the foyer. Marthe's eyes narrowed at once when she saw me, but the man only turned to me with curiosity. He had the face and proportions of a blond Greek god, slightly aged with a touch of grey around his temples and a fan of wrinkles around his topaz green eyes. His almost supernatural masculine beauty was marred only by his nose being bent slightly sideways. Had the damage been caused by some sporting activity – polo perhaps? Or had he got into a fight? The cultured confidence the stranger exuded didn't give me the impression of a man who was a brawler.

'Eve!' Lucile said, her voice bright with excitement. 'I'm so glad you are here. This is Monsieur La Farge. Marthe brought him today to assess my art.'

Assess the art? A ripple of panic ran through me. No such plan had been discussed with me. Lucile's art was awful. She had dozens of paintings in the academic style, either by minor artists or distant ancestors. Not only were they mediocre, they were so haphazardly assembled that they could not be described as a collection. When I'd completed the redecoration of the apartment, she had wanted me to have them rehung. After much discussion, and my threatening to leave, we had finally compromised on rehanging them in the bedrooms and library. But I thought Lucile and I had settled the matter that Serge Lavertu would be advising her on acquiring new paintings in the future. Now I saw that Marthe's underhanded tactics would require constant vigilance. The hold she had over Lucile had not been broken as I'd hoped after the birthday party.

'*Enchantée*, Mademoiselle Archer,' said Martin, taking my hand and chivalrously kissing it.

I had to struggle to maintain my composure. So, this was Martin La Farge? The man who was causing Serge so much heartache. He was not what I expected. I thought a man who might cheat another man out of his business would have the decency to look like a criminal and not like some sort of Prussian prince.

Marthe cleared her throat. 'When I rang you, Lucile, you told me that Eve was out for the day?'

'Well, I'm here now,' I said.

'I must compliment you on the splendid décor, Mademoiselle Archer,' said Martin. 'The pictures in *Elle* didn't nearly do it justice.'

Marthe snorted. 'It's a little sparse, don't you think?'

Martin diplomatically didn't answer. The décor might be utterly beautiful, but it was Marthe who buttered his bread.

'Monsieur La Farge has invited us to his gallery for a special viewing of some paintings he would like to offer us,' said Lucile. Then looking at me uncertainly, she added, 'They seem frightfully expensive.'

Lucile calling Martin's gallery 'his' sent a shot of anger through me. I pursed my lips and Martin gave me a puzzled look. After all, in his mind, we'd only just met.

'When you pay a high price for the priceless you are getting it cheap,' he said. 'It is the best of the best that will always rise quickly in value.'

'What is the best of the best in your opinion?' I asked him.

He paused for a moment before answering. 'Titian, Velázquez and Rembrandt, of course.'

'The Nazis took those, didn't they?'

'Yes indeed, Mademoiselle Archer. France lost a great deal of its heritage during the occupation. But much of the art is being recovered now and is coming back to us.'

'To its rightful owners, I hope?'

'Yes, wherever possible to its rightful owners,' he said. 'But that's not always possible.'

'Because they're dead?'

Martin considered me for a moment as if I were an intricate bomb he had to defuse. 'Yes unfortunately, because many of them are dead,' he said in a tone of infinite regret.

'Not only "dead",' I said, '*murdered*. Entire generations deliberately and methodically destroyed – all so others could get their hands on their fortunes.'

'Well, thank you for drawing our attention to an unpleasant subject, Eve,' Marthe interrupted tersely. 'Do you have a point?'

Lucile looked bamboozled by the conversation, and I reminded myself that it was more important to get her back on side with me than it was for me to argue with Martin La Farge. I took a more measured approach. 'Madame Damour isn't looking at acquiring art for investment. She's becoming a connoisseur and a collector. A tastemaker. I don't think she wants works that prompt her to wonder how the original owners died. That wouldn't exactly be *pleasant*, would it?'

Marthe gave me one of her withering stares, but Lucile's docile demeanour changed with my fiery words. 'Yes, that's right,' she said. 'I am a shepherdess and not a sheep.'

Coming out of Lucile's mouth, the declaration seemed absurd. Martin's eyebrows twitched but he remained tactful. 'And what is Madame Damour looking to collect?'

Lucile glanced uncertainly at me.

'Modern art,' I said. 'And, from now on, only living artists.'

I hoped that by suggesting an area of art-collecting that involved speculation and no guarantee of profits, he might be put off.

'Ah, I see,' he said, keeping his eyes on my face. 'While it's admirable to want to support new artists, not all of them will be successful. There was a time when Louis Demy, Fabrice Belmondo and even Kristina Belova were considered to be the shining new stars. But who has heard of them now? An experienced dealer must separate the wheat from the chaff, and that's where I can help. It takes a Vollard to discover a Renoir, a Kahnweiler to recognise a Picasso.'

His description of Kristina Belova as a forgotten artist rattled me. I had to admit I had never heard of her before I met Serge, and he spoke about her as if she was the most talented artist of the twentieth century.

Lucile, with a sudden eagerness to be helpful, spoke up. 'Eve acquired a Degas from the art dealer, Serge Lavertu. It's hanging in the drawing room.'

At the mention of Serge's name, everything seemed to fall into place for Martin. He looked me over anew, reassessing just how much sway I held in the household.

'Yes, Serge Lavertu,' he said, with an air of dismissal. 'I should very much like to see the Degas he sold you, *Madame Damour.*'

Like a child leading the way to the tree on Christmas Eve, Lucile eagerly guided Martin to the drawing room. At the same time, someone knocked on the apartment door. For an awful moment I thought it might be Cyrille and rushed to open it before Odette could. To my relief it was Georges.

'Come quickly,' I whispered, bustling him towards the drawing room. 'Martin La Farge is here. Marthe brought him.'

We stepped into the drawing room to see Martin squinting at the Degas from every angle through the lens of a monocle.

'A later work, I see,' he said, rubbing his chin, 'when the artist was losing his eyesight. Not a bad execution by any means, but a touch rough. It's not one of his better paintings.'

He glanced at Lucile. 'If you wanted to start your modern collection with a Degas, Madame Damour, I would have recommended one of his early works, back when he was a master in depicting movement.'

Marthe smiled with the satisfaction of an executioner who has just released the guillotine blade, while Lucile looked grim, like the person who had just lost their head.

I wanted to defend the choice but knew I was no match for Martin's expertise. Then Georges, who seemed to have assessed what game was being played, spoke up.

'How fascinating,' he said, 'to watch a dealer at work. I have always thought it was something akin to Saint Peter standing at the pearly gates of heaven to keep the great unwashed out of the lofty world of art. But now I see it is much like watching a plumber criticising the work of another.'

Martin spun around at the sound of Georges's voice.

'Ah, Monsieur Camadeau,' he said matter-of-factly. 'We have only met once before, so you may not remember me. I am Martin La Farge.'

'I assure you that no reminder is necessary, Monsieur La Farge,' Georges replied. 'I remember the occasion of the inquiry very well.'

'Inquiry?' repeated Lucile.

I had a satisfied feeling that the tables might be turning on Martin and his aunt. Anything that had even the slightest whiff of illegality or scandal about it was extremely off-putting for Lucile.

Martin coolly answered, 'Yes, that ridiculous inquiry. It was long ago now.'

Georges circled the room slowly, the way I imagined he did the courtroom floor before firing a question. 'Dear Aunt Lucile, don't you know Monsieur La Farge was accused of having the heads of one of Degas's dancing girls repainted before he sold it. The buyer wanted "a pretty painting" for his wife who loved the ballet. He insisted on a Degas, but he knew his wife would not appreciate the monkey-like face that the artist had given his dancer. So, Monsieur La Farge had her "improved".'

Martin waved his hand as if the accusation was of no consequence. 'The adjustment was no more than one or two brushstrokes. The practice is not unheard of.'

'And nobody would have been any the wiser if the couple in question hadn't divorced and she'd tried to sell the painting to a collector who called in Serge Lavertu to authenticate it.'

Martin's arrogant smile remained firmly on his face. 'The court didn't find me in the wrong, Monsieur Camadeau. You seem to be leaving out that part. *You* lost the case for the collector. I hope you didn't charge him a fee.'

'What is the point of all this?' asked Marthe, waving her hand impatiently. 'We are talking about *this* Degas in front of us right now, which is clearly second-rate and the reason why Martin should take over buying art for Lucile. Eve doesn't have the competence required and is easily deceived. We're not talking about serviettes and stationery here, we're talking about extremely complex and expensive items.'

'Eve is the sharpest woman in Paris,' said Georges. 'She wouldn't have bought Titian's *Madonna of the Rabbit* without the rabbit.'

'Whatever do you mean, Georges?' Marthe asked.

'Why don't you ask your nephew?'

'Georges,' said Marthe, exasperated, 'you might find your obtrusiveness amusing, but I find it very ill-bred. You haven't even told us why you are here.'

'Do I need a reason to visit my favourite aunt and her lovely charge?' he replied.

Martin took his monocle out, wiped it clean with a monogrammed handkerchief and replaced it in his breast pocket. He then took out a silver case from the inner pocket of his jacket and snapped it open to take out a card.

'It seems I have come at an inopportune time and am interrupting a family gathering,' he said, handing the card to Lucile. 'Perhaps, Madame Damour, you could call my secretary and come and see me at my gallery. I have a selection of *very good* paintings that I believe would be perfect for a connoisseur's collection.'

His actions were measured and calm, but the colour of his face screamed out his indignation. I was on the verge of adding fuel to the fire by correcting him that it was Serge's gallery, but I kept my silence, glad enough that he was leaving.

'I'll come with you,' Marthe said to Martin, frowning first at Georges and then at me.

She was not yet ready to concede defeat. When she passed by, she purposely bumped into me. I understood that everything had shifted now. It was no longer drawing-room parrying between Marthe and me, but open warfare.

With my nemesis and her accomplice gone, I turned to Georges. 'What was that about rabbits?' I asked him.

Georges took a cigarette case from his pocket and proceeded to light one. Then through a screen of smoke, he said, 'Martin La Farge is the sufferer of a rare condition known as leporiphobia.'

'Lepor— what?' asked Lucile, looking disturbed as if whatever Martin suffered from might be contagious.

'Leporiphobia,' repeated Georges. 'He has a fear of rabbits. He's been known to have them painted out of pictures he dreads them so much.'

'But surely not a Titian. Surely not a master?' I exclaimed.

'Perhaps not. Perhaps a fine forgery though.' He turned to Lucile. 'I suggest you avoid dealing with the man, Aunt Lucile. He is most unsavoury.'

I was glad Georges had arrived when he had. If Lucile wouldn't listen to me, perhaps she would listen to him.

Leporiphobia, I thought, mulling it over. It was as if I'd discovered Martin's Achilles heel, although I had no idea how I could use the information. But it did amuse me. One of the richest art dealers in Paris – and the man who was harming Serge – was scared of bunnies.

★

The following morning, feeling that I needed to shore up Lucile's confidence in Serge after Marthe's underhanded tactics, I went to Serge's gallery to discuss with him the next acquisition in Lucile's modern art collection. She was already being talked about because of her discovery of Fanny Toussaint and the article in *Elle*. Unfortunately, she was also being talked about because of the truckload of roses she'd been sent by a secret admirer.

I could have taken the Métro to Saint-Germain-des-Prés, but the weather was so pleasant I decided to walk. The trees were now in full leaf, and in a florist's window were vases of lily-of-the-valley, lush with green foliage and pretty bell-like flowers. It was as if Paris was recovering some of her legendary charm and sending out a message of her return to happiness. Yet not far from Serge's gallery I was overcome by a sense of foreboding. I looked over my shoulder with the distinct feeling that I was being followed. Then, low and behold, an unwelcome voice sounded beside me.

'Mademoiselle Archer.'

I turned to see Cyrille de Villiers by my side. I groaned and continued walking, only at a far less leisurely pace. But he stuck to my side like a determined fly on a humid summer's day.

'You have probably been wondering why you haven't heard from me,' he said.

'I was hoping you had come to your senses and were going to leave me alone,' I replied.

'I have acquired an apartment in Auteuil, not far from the Bois de Boulogne,' he continued with a suggestive smile. 'The architecture is exceptional, and the concierge is *discreet*.'

'How lovely for you. But I have an important errand to run.'

'I thought perhaps you would like to see it. I believe it will be to your taste. The fireplaces are marble and the views are spectacular. I haven't furnished it – that I'll leave to you with an account set up with Madame Allarie's Antique Gallery.'

I stopped in my tracks. 'This is an outrage, Monsieur de Villiers!'

'You would prefer modern furniture, perhaps?'

'No! Your proposal of a –' I could barely bring myself to say the word without wanting to heave '– a … a love nest! Have you lost your mind? How dare you make such an improper suggestion to me!'

We had stopped in front of Les Deux Magots with its green canopy and bistro chairs. A few people sitting at the outdoor tables glanced in our direction, no doubt intrigued at the sight of a middle-aged man and a young woman arguing. Out of the corner of my eye, I saw a well-dressed man put his newspaper down and half-rise from his chair.

'But, darling …' said Cyrille, taking a step towards me.

I recoiled, terrified he was about to kiss me. 'Don't you dare touch me! Go home to your wife!'

Cyrille's doughy features sharpened at the mention of Marthe. 'Never mention her,' he said, baring his teeth. 'Never mention my wife!'

It was like watching a man transform into a werewolf. Cyrille was even more unhinged than I thought. He reached out and grabbed my arm so tightly I thought he would break it.

'Let go,' I said. 'Stop it!'

'Take your hands off her, Uncle Cyrille,' came a stern voice behind me. 'Go home to Aunt Marthe.'

I turned, and with a strange dream-like shock, realised it was Martin La Farge standing next to us. I had not recognised him as the man rising from his table. The day before he had been wearing a three-piece suit, now he was more casually dressed in a tweed waistcoat and cap and looking even more handsome. His command was given so emphatically that Cyrille let go of me and stood on the spot as if he was a chastised boy who'd been caught pulling a girl's plait. Then without any protest, he trudged off.

Martin turned to me and we were both silent for a moment, as if trying to decide who was in the more awkward position. Him, for having such a lecherous uncle, or me for having to be rescued by a man I had humiliated the day before.

It was Martin who spoke first. 'I'm sorry, Mademoiselle Archer, my uncle is not a well man. He has a piece of shrapnel in his brain left over from the Battle of Verdun. It's a tragedy. He was a brilliant man before the war. It's very hard on Aunt Marthe.'

'Ah,' was all I managed to say. It was not an easy moment to feel empathy for your enemy's suffering. It felt unwise to let down your guard and yet lacking in humanity if you didn't.

'I'm sorry to hear that,' I said as graciously as I could.

'You look shaken,' he said, indicating the table where he had been sitting. 'Shall I order you something?'

Although it felt awkward to join him, it would have been worse to decline his offer. His manner was chivalrous, and if he harboured any ill feeling towards me after our encounter the previous day, he wasn't showing it. I took the chair he offered and let him order a coffee and a tartine for me.

'Have you been to Les Deux Magots before?' he asked. 'It's something of an institution in Paris. Before the war it was a gathering place for artists, writers and intellectuals.'

I shook my head. My mother had only ever told me about Café de la Rotonde in Montparnasse and the artists who met there.

'Where do you get your love of art, Mademoiselle Archer?'

Martin watched me carefully with those mesmerising eyes of his and I had to remind myself that this was a man who could not be trusted. I was not about to tell him that Serge Lavertu had taught me everything I knew.

'I have studied art in galleries since I was a child,' I lied. 'I have faith in my own judgement.'

'And you lean on Serge Lavertu as an expert?'

He said it casually without a tone of accusation, but I felt my skin prickle as if I was being goaded into making an unwise move in a chess game.

'Yes, I do.'

The waiter brought our coffee and my tartine with blackberry jam and white cheese. My mind searched for something more I could say. But I was a novice up against a grandmaster.

'I suppose that Monsieur Lavertu told you that we are in dispute with each other over his gallery?'

His tone was full of regret. But all my senses sharpened with the warning that I was about to be told a lie. It's difficult to deceive a woman who was once a neglected child left to provide for herself, one who grew up knowing that nothing was ever given for free. It was better to speak plainly to let him see I knew the lie of the land.

'Yes. He said it was taken by the Nazis and given to you during the war and that you won't give it back,' I told him.

Martin was unruffled by the sharpness of my tone. He took a sip of his coffee, then said, 'There are two sides to every story, Mademoiselle Archer. I bought the gallery legally. I offered to sell it back to Monsieur Lavertu for half the price it is worth. Is that not a reasonable compromise? Should I be out of pocket for something neither of us could control?'

I needed to attack before I was checkmated. 'I would say it depends how much you paid for the gallery when you bought it? Did you pay a reasonable price or was it sold to you at a bargain? And how can you claim to be "out-of-pocket" when you made millions of dollars selling artwork to the Nazis?'

Rather than looking surprised by my move, Martin offered a tempered smile. 'Mademoiselle Archer, I don't wish to belittle you, but you are not French and you were not here during the war. You have no idea what life in Paris was like during the occupation. Yes, I sold art to *German* customers, but that was perfectly legal. If I hadn't traded old masters for modern paintings then thousands of works by Picasso, Chagall, Van Gogh and others would have been destroyed as "degenerate art". Even your revered Degas would have gone up in flames. I went before the tribunal after the war and was proven innocent of any wrongdoing.'

He said he didn't want to belittle me, but it felt like that what he was doing.

'And the owners of the modern art you sold – were they saved too?' I asked.

The waiter passed our table and Martin signalled to him to bring us two more coffees. I couldn't help thinking he was giving himself a moment to consider his reply. Indeed, when he turned back to me he was smiling again, almost laughing.

'It seems that you and I have got off on the wrong foot, Mademoiselle Archer. If you wish to deal with Serge Lavertu, that is entirely your business. But I would be more than happy for you to visit my gallery too. I assure you that my many years of experience in art dealing could prove valuable to you. I know a sophisticated woman when I meet one. You have excellent taste ... but perhaps not the funds to acquire the quality of things that align with it. You see, if you were to encourage Madame Damour – who very clearly relies on your advice – to buy from me, there could be a healthy commission for you, a *very* healthy commission. Five per cent.'

Five per cent! A commission on a 300,000 franc painting would be 'healthy' indeed. But I couldn't justify it. I would be using Lucile when she trusted me, and I would never betray Serge.

Then another, more sinister, idea occurred to me.

'How do you know whether or not I was in France during the occupation?' I asked. 'Have you been investigating me?'

'Investigating you?' replied Martin with a derisive laugh. 'Don't overestimate your importance, Mademoiselle Archer. My aunt told me. It seems she is very interested in you and how you and Madame Damour met, and frankly I don't blame her. She has known Madame Damour since they were children, and she is only doing what any caring friend would do.'

I had a sense of something being pressed on me – subtly, chivalrously, but as sharp as the tip of a knife.

'I have nothing to be ashamed about,' I said. 'I have helped Lucile rise in society. I have been the perfect *companion* to her.'

'Indeed, a drapery *salesgirl* is a perfectly honest position. But a salesgirl who poses as something else is quite another thing. Paris society will not accept that.'

Marthe's research on me was quite extensive, it seemed. I knew that I mustn't falter, that I must call the bluff that was being played.

'I think Coco Chanel would disagree.'

Martin's eyes narrowed. They had gone from haughty to having a distinctly predatory quality. 'Madame Chanel had millions of dollars before anyone in society would let her into their drawing room. Imagine if the Fouquets were to find out that you are not a gentleman's daughter after inviting you in good faith to their intimate pre-ball dinner. That would be a great offence to them. Paris society does not want penniless girls posing as rich ones and trying to lure their sons into marriage.'

The audacity of the man! I would return him the favour. 'You and your aunt can say what you like. Perhaps you won't mind me sharing that Cyrille de Villiers was pursuing me.'

'There are two sides to every story,' Martin replied. 'Someone looking at that little exchange earlier with my uncle *might* see a young woman being harassed by an older man. But then again, they might have seen an ambitious young woman taking advantage of an unwell man for his money, just as she has with Lucile Damour.'

I could feel my colour rise. It was clear what objective Martin La Farge was pursuing. 'There are not two sides to a story in this case,' I said. 'There is one person telling the truth and one person telling a lie.'

'Perhaps then you should consider which one is more likely to be believed.'

He said it with such mildness, it was as if he were a kind uncle giving me advice. And yet, what was intended was not benign at all.

'Are you threatening me, Monsieur La Farge?'

Martin shook his head. 'Threatening you? No! In art dealing you must be precise in your terms. "Impasto" is not the same as "intaglio".' Then leaning across the table, he looked into my eyes and said, 'I'm not threatening you, Mademoiselle Archer. I'm *blackmailing* you.'

CHAPTER ELEVEN

KRISTINA

Paris, October 1923

When Kristina and Max returned from their stay in Barbizon, Serge greeted them with good news.

'I acquired a painting by Georges Braque at auction and sold it to Édouard Fould. Two promising cubists have now signed contracts to be represented by us. We are on our way.'

While Kristina had hoped it would have been one of her paintings that paved the way for the success of Bergeret & Lavertu, she was genuinely happy for Max and Serge. 'Let's go to La Rotonde and share the good news. Who knows? You might steal Picasso away from Vollard!'

Sonia, who had also received a lucrative assignment decorating the Foch Avenue apartment of an American banker, joined them.

'It will be your turn soon, Kristina,' Max whispered to her. 'Your success is just around the corner.'

Kristina tried not to be discouraged despite the lack of sales of her art. She was returning to Nice at the end of October to paint Beatrice Fould. Serge assured her that painting an art collector was a wise move for an emerging artist. 'Think of

Renoir's portrait of Paul Durand-Ruel or Tarbell's of Henry Clay Frick and his daughter.'

'Where is Madeleine?' Kristina asked Serge. 'I wrote to her from Barbizon twice but didn't hear back. I have a wonderful idea for a painting with her as the model. It came to me in a dream.'

Serge froze and stared at his glass at the mention of Madeleine's name. 'I don't know,' he said. 'I haven't seen her.'

His reaction troubled Kristina.

'Do you think Madeleine and Serge had some sort of argument?' she asked Max when Serge's attention was elsewhere. 'They seemed happy together when we left.'

'Perhaps they did,' said Max. 'But they are adults, Kristina. It's up to them to put things right. And while Serge might have been a good influence on Madeleine, I don't think she has brought him any peace of mind.'

'Yes, I suppose you're right,' answered Kristina, feeling foolish that she might have made the mistake a lot of people did when they were in love – expecting everyone else to settle down as happily as she and Max had.

It wasn't until a few days later that Kristina linked Madeleine's absence to the Australian who'd started appearing at La Rotonde a week before they'd all left to go south. Suntanned and muscular, he'd perfected the air of an adventurer, with a lock of hair that permanently flopped over his forehead and a cigarette jammed between his perfect white teeth. He was always surrounded by admirers – men and women – who seemed enthralled with his stories about wrestling crocodiles and his time spent as an overseer on a tobacco plantation in New Guinea.

'*Bonsoir, charmantes demoiselles,*' he'd called out to Kristina and Sonia one night as they passed his table. He spoke such terrible French that Kristina assumed him to be English.

'Who is that?' she asked Sonia.

'Efron Archer,' she replied. 'He's the star of a pirate film they're making at the new studios in Billancourt. He's Tasmanian.'

'Tasmania? Isn't that part of Australia?'

'Not according to him,' Sonia said as they continued up the stairs. 'I don't think he's particularly intelligent, but he is very *photogénique*, don't you agree?'

Kristina hadn't given Efron Archer another thought until she saw him at La Rotonde with his arm around Madeleine. She leaned against him like an adoring puppy and drooled at every word he uttered. Now she understood Serge's discomfort at the mention of Madeleine.

'Hello, Madeleine,' Kristina said. 'I've been sending you letters to come pose for me.'

'Efron got me a part as an extra in his film,' she said, her eyes sparkling. 'I get to walk in front of the camera holding a basket of fruit.'

Her voice was slurred. She was drunk again. But in front of her was an enormous plate of pasta and she'd eaten over half of it. Kristina had never known Madeleine to have such an appetite. She'd put on a bit of weight, which made her look even prettier.

For his part, Efron was all adoration and affection towards Madeleine, stroking her hair and gazing into her eyes.

'Won't you sit down?' he asked, sending Kristina a killer smile. As Sonia had said, he was incredibly handsome. But she couldn't understand why Madeleine would choose him over Serge, who had so much more to offer.

For Madeleine's sake and out of politeness, she accepted Efron's invitation. Seeing he had captured a new audience member, Efron started telling Kristina stories of his outlandish adventures.

'Pearl fishing in New Guinea is what made me a man,' he said, squinting as if reliving a distant memory. 'It's lucrative but demands nerves of steel. You can go through a hundred shells and not find a thing. Then just when you are about to give up, there it is in the hundred and first shell – the elusive pink pearl.'

Efron held his palm up, and against Kristina's better instincts, she stared at it as if that rare commodity might actually appear in it. *He really is a good actor*, she thought.

'But after watching too many brave divers disappear into the deep dark sea and never come up,' Efron continued, 'I gave my fortune to their families and set out on my way to China with no more than two pounds in my pocket.'

From there, Efron's stories grew taller, going from managing the most successful nightclub in Shanghai to being discovered as a professional tennis player, then a champion boxer and a famous trapeze artist with a travelling circus, until one evening, while saving a young woman from a gangster, his wrist was broken. As he spoke he rocked back in his chair, and Kristina was sure that if Max had been with her, he would have kicked it out from under him. Max couldn't stand a boastful man. Likewise, Sonia would have called Efron out on his falsehoods. But as Efron went on, sharing his fanciful stories to Madeleine's rapt attention, Kristina found herself feeling sorry for him. His fingers trembled with a nervous energy as he spoke. She sensed the desperation in his tales. He was nothing more than an overgrown boy who wanted people to like him.

But when he claimed to be a child-survivor of the *Titanic* – 'There was a fearful explosion and then the ship started cracking. I'll never forget the moment when the lights went out ... and then the screams' – even Kristina reached her limit of patience.

'I'm so sorry,' she said rising. 'You'll have to save that one for next time. I promised to meet Sonia for dinner.' She glanced at Madeleine. 'Please do come and see me about posing. I have a wonderful idea and you are the only model I can imagine using for it.'

'Of course I will,' said Madeleine. 'I'll come tomorrow. But not before eleven.'

Kristina left La Rotonde with an uneasy feeling pinching her stomach. If ever two people needed someone to take care of them, it was Madeleine and Efron. Leaving them together felt like leaving two young children to play with matches. If they became enmeshed with each other, she could only see it leading to disaster.

★

'He's not a lout, like everyone thinks.'

It was the first thing Madeleine said to Kristina when she arrived the following afternoon after keeping her waiting for two hours.

'He is an *artiste*. If only people really knew him, they'd understand how wonderful he is.'

Kristina thought Efron was an artist of the braggadocio school. The painting she was planning was epic and she would need Madeleine every day for the next few weeks. She hoped a steady job and time away from alcohol might help wean her off Efron. Her friend was obsessing about a man who could only bring her trouble.

The work Kristina had planned would pay homage to the French realistic painter Charles-Amable Lenoir, who was known for his romantic mythological paintings. In it, Madeleine would pose as Eve – not the humiliated woman of the Bible,

178

the culprit for the fall of humankind, but a defiant one. She would be powerful like a gust of wind, with intensity and determination in her eyes. Eve would be escaping the tyranny of God and Adam of her own accord and setting out on an adventure of independence. She would wield a sword like Joan of Arc and have the wings of an angel.

Perhaps, thought Kristina as Madeleine arranged herself on the podium for the first sketches, *if Madeleine sees herself in this painting the way I see her, it will change her perception of herself.*

Kristina was so focused on this hope that in the weeks that followed, she managed to block out Madeleine's ceaseless chatter about Efron. Until one day, Madeleine said something that prickled Kristina's nerves.

'When Efron puts his arms around me, I feel protected and safe. He is wild and he is strong, *like a man is supposed to be.*'

Kristina looked up. 'I hope that wasn't a dig at Serge,' she said tersely. 'Because he is both strong *and gentle.*'

'Serge! Serge!' Madeleine laughed, her voice brittle. 'Dear Serge. Doesn't he have you fooled, Kristina?'

Kristina felt her blood boil, but she knew if she got angry at Madeleine, her flighty model might run away just when she was at a crucial stage of the work. She didn't need to defend Serge. His character spoke for itself. She suspected Efron was simply doing for Madeleine what he did for the adoring fans of his films – playing the part of the hero without actually being a hero. He was the type of man who was only interested in a woman to massage his inflated ego. When he got bored with that role, he'd move on.

But the next day, when Madeleine arrived and took off her coat, Kristina saw purple welts up and down her arms and was horrified.

'Did Efron do that to you?'

Madeleine averted her eyes. 'No, of course he didn't. Efron would never lay a hand on a woman. I bruised my arms moving furniture around my room.'

Those bruises were not from moving furniture, Kristina was sure of that. She could see the imprint of fingers as if someone had grabbed Madeleine by both arms. But if it really hadn't been Efron, then Madeleine was in trouble of some sort. Did she owe money to a thug? Kristina knew things like that were common in Paris – a criminal would force a female entertainer to pay him 'protection' money when the only person she needed protection from was him.

'Why don't you come and stay with us?' Kristina offered. 'There's a small sitting room we could turn into a bedroom for you. It gets delightful sunshine in the morning.'

Madeleine shook her head. 'After the portrait's done, I'm leaving Paris. In fact, I'm getting away from France for good.'

Kristina was startled by the news. 'What? Where will you go?'

Madeleine rubbed at her hands. 'I can't tell you,' she said. 'It's better you don't know. But I'm going with Efron. He said he's ready for a new adventure.'

Kristina wanted to run into the shop where Max was sorting out stock and ask him to make Madeleine come to her senses. But he had told her not to interfere, and Kristina reminded herself that Efron might not be serious. His 'new adventure' might just be another one of his fantasies.

The sound of Madeleine gagging surprised her. Madeleine's face had turned a sickly shade of green and she reached the sink just in time to throw up into it. At first, Kristina assumed her friend had drunk too much again, but then another idea occurred to her. Madeleine had never had much of an appetite before, but the other night she had tucked into a large plate of pasta. The way she blushed under her scrutiny made Kristina more certain of her suspicion.

'You're pregnant.'

'I'm not feeling well,' Madeleine replied. 'I'd better go home. I'm sorry. I'll come back tomorrow.'

'Madeleine, please let me help you. You can't possibly rely on Efron to be responsible. He can't be a father to your child.'

'He's not the father,' said Madeleine softly.

Kristina frowned. 'He isn't?'

'Efron is all bluff,' she said coyly. 'He doesn't function very well in that department.'

Kristina had heard that alcoholics were not the best lovers. Then the truth dawned on her. 'Serge?' she asked.

Madeleine's face turned dark. 'Do not tell him, Kristina.'

'But—'

'*Do not tell him*, Kristina. If you do, I swear I'll kill myself.'

Kristina recoiled, terrified. Why was Madeleine making such a vicious threat to herself and her unborn child?

Madeleine's eyes filled with tears. She threw her head back and blinked hard. 'My parents didn't send me to a convent like I told you. They sent me to an asylum. They said I was mad, but I'm not mad, Kristina. My father did things to me that no father should do to his child. And when I had the baby, they gave it away. Well, they won't be giving this one away.'

Kristina saw things more clearly now. So this was the real reason Madeleine was running away. 'If you won't let us help you, who will you turn to?'

Madeleine shook her head. 'My brother used to be my defender, but years of beatings from my father have turned him into a monster too. He'd sooner kill me than have his reputation ruined.'

Kristina looked down at Madeleine's arms. 'So he was the one who did that to you?'

Then another idea came to her mind. 'Why don't you go stay with my parents in Nice and have the baby there?'

Madeleine straightened herself and took her coat from the back of the chair. 'I'll think about it, Kristina, thank you. But for now I just want to go home and lie down for a few hours. I'll come back tomorrow. We'll talk about it more then.'

Kristina helped Madeleine get her arms into the sleeves of her coat. *She's too emotionally frail to have a baby*, she thought.

Before she left, Madeleine glanced at the painting, which was almost finished. She smiled. 'It's wonderful, Kristina,' she said. 'It's your best work yet.'

★

After Madeleine left, Kristina paced the studio. She could not settle her feelings of impending disaster. She had promised Madeleine not to tell Serge about the pregnancy, but how could she keep that promise when two lives were at stake?

She went out into the shop but Max was no longer there.

'He said to tell you that he's gone with Monsieur Lavertu to Rouen to see a collector. They will be back later this evening,' Noël told her.

'Why didn't he tell me he was leaving?'

'He thought you were painting and didn't want to disturb you.'

Kristina returned to her studio and began pacing again. She wavered between different courses of action – go to Madeleine now and plead again with her to go to her parents' villa in Nice, or wait for Serge? In the end, she thought it best to wait for Serge.

When he and Max returned, they were both in high spirits. They had their arms around each other and were singing old French drinking songs.

They stopped and smiled when they saw Kristina.

'We sold three of Armand Rouvel's paintings!' Max said, holding out a bouquet of marigolds to her. 'We wanted to celebrate. It's the biggest sale we've ever made. We are practically millionaires.'

'You're drunk,' she said, not to admonish them but to express her dismay. Max was in no fit condition to do anything, and lay down on the sofa and fell promptly asleep, snoring loudly.

Serge looked at Max fondly and then turned to Kristina. 'Not quite millionaires yet. But far richer than we were yesterday. We stopped in Argenteuil to celebrate.' Then noticing her expression, he asked, 'Is everything all right?'

She was relieved to see Serge was not quite as drunk as Max.

'It's Madeleine,' she said. 'Let's sit down. I have something important to tell you.'

She poured out the whole story, assuring Serge that Madeleine was quite certain the baby was his child.

He shook his head in wonder. 'A baby? My child?' He looked around the room for a moment and then returned his attention to Kristina. 'Of course I won't abandon her,' he said. 'Even if Madeleine doesn't want to be with me, I can still be the child's father. Somebody needs to provide for them, and it won't be Efron.'

Kristina's heart lifted but then she thought of the cruel way Madeleine had laughed at Serge. Surely she'd see that whatever had happened between them, Serge was putting her and the child first. She could only hope Madeleine would come to her senses and appreciate Serge for the fine man he was.

'I'll go see her first thing tomorrow morning,' said Serge. 'I believe I know what I can say to her.'

'I'll come with you and wait at the café opposite her apartment,' Kristina told him. 'You can call on me if you need me.'

They covered Max with a blanket and retired to their bedrooms, although Kristina suspected neither of them would sleep. Before they parted on the landing, Serge turned to her.

'You know I would marry Madeleine, if she would agree. I may not be perfect, but I believe I would make a good father.'

'You would make a wonderful father,' Kristina said. 'I have no doubt at all about it.'

Afterwards, as Kristina lay in bed, she thought about Serge's words. There had been a doubt – not in his own constancy, but seemingly in his worthiness to be a father. She thought about what it must have been like for him growing up without parents and only a distant and strict aunt to watch over him. Perhaps he lacked confidence because he'd never learned what being in a real family was like, as she and Max had. She squeezed her eyes shut, praying with all her might that things would turn out well for him, Madeleine and the baby.

★

Madeleine's apartment was on Rue Saint-Vincent. Kristina waited at the café across the road while Serge spoke to the concierge, who didn't look anything like the concierge of Madeleine's stories who had worn a monocle and smoked a pipe. She looked more like somebody's sweet grandmother.

Serge waved Kristina over, his face grave. She knew instantly that something terrible had happened.

'She's gone,' Serge said. 'Madame Seigner says she left with Efron late yesterday afternoon.'

'Yesterday!'

Kristina knew then that pursuit would be useless. They could be anywhere with that sort of lead – about to board a ship at Le Havre, or hiding in Belgium or Switzerland. Her heart sank. Why hadn't she acted sooner? She thought of the painting and how Madeleine had looked at it. Madeleine had known then that she wasn't coming back.

'Why do you think Efron was so keen to run off with her?' she asked Serge. 'Do you think it's because *he* is in some sort of trouble?'

Serge clenched his fists as if trying to control himself. 'Efron lives in a fantasy world. He probably thought running off with Madeleine was nothing more than a pirate adventure. He has no sense of responsibility.'

'But Monsieur Archer gave me a good sum of money for the rent,' Madame Seigner said, as if trying to calm them. 'He seemed like a nice enough man. Better than that other one.'

Kristina frowned. 'What other one?'

'The rich one in his fancy car. I know that type. The sort that look down their nose at you. He was always demanding that he be let up to Madeleine's apartment, but I stood up to him. Then the night before last he caught her coming home. They argued and then he tried to drag her into his car. For such a tiny thing she put up a fierce fight. Monsieur Petit came out of the café and beat him off.'

'What were they were fighting about?' Serge asked.

Madame Seigner shook her head. 'Poor Monsieur Petit is deaf from the war and didn't hear what they were saying. But he said Madeleine looked frightened for her life.'

Kristina now understood. Madeleine had been telling her the truth when she'd said it wasn't Efron who'd caused the bruises. At least there was some comfort in that.

'I think it was her brother,' Kristina said. 'She told me yesterday that he didn't want her in Paris, and that he thought she was ruining the family reputation. I can only imagine what he thought of her taking up with Efron. It would have got into the papers sooner or later.'

'She left with only a suitcase,' Madame Seigner said. 'The rest of her things are in her apartment. She told me I could keep them. Shall I show you?'

Kristina and Serge followed the concierge up the creaking stairs to an apartment with patched furniture draped in expensive shawls and unwashed windows with silk curtains. There was a narrow bed and a lopsided lamp. The bedside table was covered in empty wine bottles. It made Kristina want to cry to think that Madeleine must have sat in this dingy place and drank alone. She felt like a negligent friend for not having tried harder to save her.

She opened the drawer of the bedside table and, under some spools of cotton and lace, found a photograph. It was of an old woman with a kind face and a baby in her arms. Behind them was a grand house with a mansard roof and an equestrian statue of Marcus Aurelius near the door. The woman must have been the grandmother Madeleine had spoken about.

Kristina gave the photograph to Serge. 'Please keep it. I can't bear to look at it.'

'Are you Kristina by any chance?' Madame Seigner suddenly asked.

Kristina turned to her. 'Yes, I am.'

'Madeleine told me if you came to relay a message to you.'

Kristina felt a flutter of hope. Perhaps Madeleine had left a forwarding address after all. 'What was it?'

'She said to tell you that she was sorry.'

The bell rang downstairs and Madame Seigner excused herself to answer it. Kristina saw Serge standing by the window as still as a statue, his face in his hands.

'Serge?'

She placed her hand on his shoulder. It was then Kristina felt him trembling and realised he was weeping. Great racking but silent sobs.

'The child!' he wept. 'The child!'

Kristina thought her heart would break. It would have been terrible for any child to be born into the situation Madeleine was facing, but this was *his* child.

'She might come back,' she whispered to him, 'like a swallow in the spring. And she will bring the child with her.'

But even as she said it, there was a feeling of dread in Kristina's bones. If Madeleine came back, she thought, it would only be in the form of an angel.

CHAPTER TWELVE

EVE

Paris, May 1946

Blackmail is a ghastly business. It leaves you trapped between two worlds – your inglorious past and your now uncertain future. I knew that it was probably better not to give into a blackmailer's demands because if you did, they would always come back for more. But if you didn't, what then? The overhanging threat was so present in my mind that it didn't matter if Lucile and I were dining on roquefort or brie, a soufflé or a quiche, I couldn't taste the difference. My attention to detail narrowed to one single focus – would Martin La Farge carry out his threat to reveal my origins?

So when on the last day of the month a letter arrived from Martin, asking Lucile and me to come view a new American artist by the name of Joan Mitchell that he had set aside 'exclusively' for us, I did what my mother used to do whenever an eviction notice arrived – I hid it in my desk drawer and pretended I'd never seen it.

'What's wrong with you?' Lucile asked while we waited in the luxurious fitting room of Cristóbal Balenciaga on Avenue George V. The place smelled of lilies and our feet sank deep into the plush silver-grey carpet. 'You've been distracted all week.'

I could not afford to make Lucile nervous at this point, not now she had spent a fortune on our gowns for the Fouquets' ball at my insistence. Balenciaga was a temperamental Spaniard and a perfectionist who did not like to be hurried, and yet he'd agreed — at a premium price — to give us what we wanted in time for the ball.

'I'm only thinking how splendid you look,' I told her, 'and how I should organise your first soirée as soon as possible.'

The dress Balenciaga had designed sat perfectly on her frame. He was not simply a designer but a master couturier who understood clever cutting and minimal seaming and darting. The result was a steel-grey dress with an empire line and azalea pink sash that made Lucile look regal. My dress was equally as stunning. Drawing on his Spanish roots, Balenciaga had given me a skirt of glistening white satin veiled in black tulle with a matching ruffled top that was a nod to a flamenco costume. But I felt like I was walking a fine line, and if Martin decided to push me over the precipice, I might never get to wear it.

After the fitting, we went to dine at the Ritz. The atmosphere of the hotel was so bright and breezy it was difficult to imagine that it had been occupied by the Luftwaffe during the war. Indeed, while Hermann Göring might have been in prison at Nuremberg awaiting his sentence for war crimes, the French fashion designers, industrialists and journalists who had collaborated with the Germans were still in attendance, eating caviar and Châteaubriand béarnaise. As we were led to our table we passed a spectacular floral arrangement of orchids, lilies and moonflowers that must have cost a few thousand francs.

As the smartly uniformed waiter took our order for sole poached in white wine and asparagus in Hollandaise sauce, I looked around me and began to calm. People were glancing in our direction and admiring us. From the blush that pinched both her cheeks, it seemed that Lucile had noticed too. She was transformed and she knew it. I hoped her gratitude might cement her attachment to me in the event Martin chose to reveal my identity. With her loyalty, we might weather the storm together and even find it to our advantage.

Then Lucile did something unexpected. She pulled out a small velvet box from her purse and pushed it towards me.

'It's a gift for you. For your birthday,' she said.

'My birthday?' I repeated with surprise and saw that the box was embossed with the gold logo of Fosco jewellers. It *was* my birthday, but I had hardly paid attention to the date. I'd never celebrated it, even as a small child. It hurt too much to have a mother who raised my expectations of cake and other delights, only to disappear into an alcoholic stupor when the time of the proposed celebration arrived.

I opened the box. Inside was a platinum ring set with rose-cut diamonds. It was exactly to my taste and Lucile must have gone to a great deal of effort to choose it.

'It's lovely,' I said, feeling flushed and a little emotional. I hadn't expected such a gesture from Lucile. I put the ring on and showed it to her. She smiled with delight.

'You don't have a family and my own siblings don't care about me,' she said. 'But you and I have each other. You've become very dear to me.'

'Thank you,' I managed to say. 'That was very kind of you, and I feel the same way.'

The gesture seemed to signify a change in the nature of our relationship, and that I meant more to Lucile than a mere paid companion. The sick feeling I had been carrying around vanished. I would tell her about Martin's threat, but I would do it after the Fouquets' ball when she wasn't so nervous. Then together we would decide on a strategy of how to respond to any revelations that Marthe or Martin might divulge.

We stood up to leave and as we walked through the foyer, we passed a man reading *Le Monde*. The front page of the newspaper was dominated by one headline:

Lost Botticelli Masterpiece found: To be returned to France.

It sounded like important news. I would have to ask Serge about it when I next saw him.

★

None of the mansions I had visited as a junior draper – and many of them had been grand – had ever been as palatial as the Fouquets' mansion on Avenue d'Iéna.

Lucile and I strolled down the red carpet with Georges between us. I was almost afraid to look at the magnificent Italian Baroque façade or at the dozen servants waiting for us dressed in fine livery. It was a reception worthy of Emperor Napoleon. The grand hall was hung with art from every era. When we entered, my eye settled on a painting that, from its subject matter of a servant girl wearing a scarf of the most extraordinary ultramarine, I took to be a rare Vermeer. My gaze travelled upwards to a Genoese chandelier large enough for twenty-four lights and heavy with crystal drops. It cast sparkles over the gilded mosaics on the walls.

'It's quite the show, isn't it?' Georges whispered in my ear. 'I've heard that on one of the upper floors there is an indoor swimming pool fashioned in the style of a desert oasis.'

I nodded, wondering if I had been gaping. After being formally welcomed by the Fouquets – he, a distinguished-looking gentleman with a handlebar moustache, and she, a birdlike creature exquisitely dressed in a sequined gown – we were directed up a marble staircase like we were a procession of courtiers from Versailles: the women in tulle dresses and dripping with diamonds; the men in white tie with ribbons and sashes. Indeed, as I looked around me, I recognised the faces of comtes and comtesses I had only ever seen in the society pages.

A thrill of triumph tingled in my veins. Despite all Martin La Farge's hints at my demise, I had not given into him, and here I was, a part of it all.

After an aperitif of Perrier-Jouët champagne, we were led into a dining room with walls of pale turquoise and gold mouldings. An Aubusson rug with an ostrich-feather design covered the floor. Lucile was seated close to Madame Fouquet, and Georges next to a woman with the striking brunette looks of an Italian. I was delegated the least important seat at the long table, but I didn't care. My place setting was as beautiful as anyone else's with sterling-silver flatware and monogrammed plates. Down the length of the table wove pink Juliet roses set on gilded branches. I looked around me, wanting to commit every detail to memory.

The elderly man opposite me leaned across the table. 'Do you know the music for this evening was specially composed by Francis Poulenc?'

I had noticed the strains of a flute and piano sonata. Something graceful but bittersweet.

'Poulenc is one of my favourite composers,' I told him, at the same time imagining how wealthy one would have to be to have a world class composer create music for your party.

The dinner was woodcock accompanied by Romanée-Conti, the most expensive and sought-after wine in the world. I lifted the crystal glass to my lips and savoured my first taste. Flavours of violets and sweet cherries burst on my tongue.

The man across the table must have noticed my pleasure. 'They call it velvet and satin in a glass,' he said.

'That's a perfect description.'

The woman next to him, dressed fantastically in a gold brocade gown with a puff of flaxen hair framing her face, joined our conversation. 'The wine comes from the Côte d'Or where the soil has more limestone and less clay, and the grapes receive the perfect amount of sunshine for ripening. But the vineyard is small and cannot be expanded. And so, only a limited amount of bottles are produced each year.'

'That means most people in the world will die without ever tasting this sublime offering,' the man said.

After the dinner, the sound of the musicians tuning their instruments came from the ballroom, and the ladies, Lucile and myself included, went to Edith Fouquet's boudoir to fix our hair and dresses before heading to the ballroom. I stood still for a moment dazzled by the intricate furniture with mother-of-pearl inlays and the cherub fresco on the ceiling.

'May I help you, mademoiselle?' a maid asked.

It took a moment for me to realise that she was speaking to me and that I was a guest in her eyes, not a servant. I had stepped into a whole new life and I didn't want to go back to my old one.

When we were all ready, we met with the men on the landing and linked arms with those who had been our dinner partners, before heading down the stairs to the ballroom. The other guests were arriving, and a great thrum of voices rose up from the entrance hall. The ballroom was even more beautifully decorated than the dining room, with great pyramids of topiary roses and pots of white gardenias. The scent of the flowers mingled with the odours of fine perfume and expensive cigars.

I saw Marthe arrive with Cyrille and our eyes locked for a moment. She would have heard by now that Lucile and I had been invited to the Fouquets' exclusive dinner while she hadn't. I was sure it infuriated her, but it was too late for her to reveal what she knew about me. To do so now would only cause the Fouquets embarrassment.

The string quartet accompanied the guests who danced waltzes and foxtrots. The beautiful couples glided past me, their feet barely touching the gleaming floor like floating characters in a Chagall painting. An elderly gentleman I recognised as the British ambassador asked me to dance and gallantly steered me around the dance floor. I spotted Lucile waltzing with Basile Fouquet himself! Then I spied Marthe talking with a group of people but constantly glancing at Lucile with undisguised envy.

Well, that look makes up for all the years you taunted her, I thought, with a certain satisfaction.

'May I have this dance, Mademoiselle Archer?' came a familiar voice from behind. I turned around and smiled at Georges.

'You certainly may, Monsieur Camadeau.'

I let Georges steer me around the dance floor in a slow foxtrot.

'How are you enjoying the evening?' he asked.

'I am enjoying it very much. I've never been to such an extravagant ball before.'

'And yet you dance so beautifully. You've taken to Parisian society like a duck to water.'

We performed a pivot and feathered to a less crowded corner of the dance floor where we could hear each other better.

'What is it you truly desire, Eve?' Georges asked. 'A bright young woman like you can't possibly want to stay with Aunt Lucile forever?'

'What do I desire?' I replied, gesturing around me. 'I want to live like this every day. In a beautiful house with beautiful music and beautiful things to look at.' But then remembering what it was like to live in a dingy house with broken furniture, I added, 'But I don't want to be an outsider looking in. I want to belong.'

'Well,' said Georges, as we turned and weaved, 'from the admiring glances of several young men who have been watching you all evening, including the very, very wealthy Hubert Thirard, I would say you'd have a number of volunteers willing to provide that lifestyle for you.'

'You know as well as I do, men like that don't marry young women like me.'

'Like what? Heiresses from some exotic place across the other side of the globe?'

I squeezed his hand a little harder. 'You must know that story isn't true. In fact, I regret letting Lucile convince me to tell it. You see, I don't want to be provided for by a man. I want to succeed on my own terms. I don't think it's shameful at all to work your way up in the world. But now she's made me tell it, I'm in a rather precarious position if that lie ever gets found out.'

'I see,' said Georges, twirling me in another change of direction. 'What if you met a man who didn't give a toss whether you were a descendant of the French Sun King or not, and wanted to support your dreams simply because he liked you and believed in you.'

'Like Madame Chanel's Boy Capel, you mean?'

'Something like that.'

I thought about Georges's idea. Boy Capel had set Chanel up in business but had married someone from his own class. That sounded uncomfortably like my own unequal love affair

195

with Anthony, and I was not going to put myself through that heartache again. I shook my head firmly. Whatever I did, I would do it on my own.

The music changed to a waltz, and a young man requested the next dance with me. Georges graciously took his leave. My new partner introduced himself as Hubert Thirard, and I realised he was the wealthy heir Georges had mentioned. He was attractive and extremely courteous, but his deferential manner made me realise how much I enjoyed bantering with Georges.

After several more dances with gallant young men, I needed to cool down. I noticed two women were going up a staircase to the next floor. I remembered what Georges had said about the indoor swimming pool. I discreetly followed them, but the women disappeared down a corridor and I realised they were most likely house guests of the Fouquets and were going to their rooms. I looked around, hoping no one had seen me. I was about to go back down the stairs, when I noticed a glimmer of light coming through the gap of a door that had been left ajar. I caught a glimpse of luscious silk drapes that invited me to take a closer look. I pushed the door open and discovered a room with a Venetian Rococo desk at the centre. A porcelain lamp sent a soft glow over the blue-green walls, the shade of which made me think of verdigris. The Savonnerie rug was soft under my feet as I approached the desk and cast my eye over the sterling-silver pen and the ivory letter-opener. From the tray of monogrammed writing paper, I imagined it was where Edith Fouquet wrote her correspondence and gave out the orders to the servants for the day.

Laughter spiralled up the staircase from the party downstairs, and I was about to leave when I heard someone come in behind me. I turned to see Marthe standing in the doorway.

'So, you think you have won, do you?' she asked, stepping towards me. 'You think you have transformed Lucile from an ugly duckling into a magnificent swan, and yourself from a shopgirl to a society princess? I assure you, that is not how this world works. Everyone has a place they are born into and "rising in society" is nothing more than a myth.'

Confident in my Balenciaga gown and fortified by fine wines, I stood my ground. 'What you say might have been true before the war, but it's not true anymore. There are too many former collaborators in French society for them to put on such airs now.'

At that moment, the lights went out. I could hear cries and gasps from the ballroom.

'Another blasted blackout,' a man said. 'Get the candles,' a woman's voice called.

To be in complete darkness was unnerving, but it was also a welcome interruption from Marthe and it gave me time to think. I tried to remember exactly where she was standing. If I could pass her and get to the door by the time the lights returned, I could avoid her for the rest of the evening. But then the lights came back on, and I blinked. It was no longer Marthe standing before me but Cyrille.

'Mademoiselle Archer, we are alone at last,' he said under a wheezy breath.

The glow from the lamplight did not flatter him the way it did the room. It made him seem ghoulish. I tried to skirt around him towards the door, but he closed it before I could reach it.

'I would like to go, Monsieur de Villiers,' I said, feigning a composure I did not feel. 'Please stand aside.'

But he remained in the doorway and fixed a look on me that gave me the chills.

'I don't understand what you want. Where did your wife go?' I asked.

Then remembering the effect Marthe's name had on him that last time I'd seen him, I shrunk back a little. But this time he simply smiled.

'She'll be downstairs, I imagine,' he said. 'Doing what she does best. She's given me her blessing, you know. She understands that a man has his desires. In fact, she told me to give you this.'

He fiddled in his pocket before producing the white gold and diamond necklace I'd seen Marthe wearing at Lucile's birthday party. Then noticing the horror that must have shown on my face, he added, 'Don't tell me you don't like it? It's worth a fortune. Here try it on.'

He lurched towards me as the full gravity of the situation bore down on me.

'Now listen,' I said. 'I don't know what game you and your wife are playing but it has gone far enough. There are a lot of people downstairs, and they will hear if I scream.'

As if to mock me, the dance orchestra at that moment switched to a swing band. Nobody was going to hear me over the sound of trumpets and trombones.

I moved towards the door again, but Cyrille placed himself between me and it.

'Why are you in such a hurry? I saw the way you let Georges Camadeau look at you when you danced with him. Georges is a young man who hasn't come into his full inheritance yet. He doesn't have even a pinch of the money I do. Marthe said that's what young girls like you want.' He reached into his pocket, pulled out some notes and tossed them in the air, laughing as he did. 'It's a bargain you see, you get money and I get you.'

'You are out of your mind,' I said, making for the door again. But this time Cyrille grabbed my arm. His high-coloured face and increasing confidence were so terrifying they got the better of me. I could hardly get the words out loud enough when I tried to shout, 'Let me go!'

Any worry about a scandal left my mind. All I wanted was to be out of Cyrille's grasp and back at Lucile's apartment, warm and safe in my bed. I didn't care if I never went to another ball again.

The smell of alcohol on Cyrille as he pressed himself against me brought me back to my senses. I struggled against him with all my strength. We knocked into the walls, then got caught up in the flowing drapes, before crashing into the desk and sending the fine stationery scattering over the floor. To my horror, Cyrille landed his slobbery mouth on my lips.

At that moment, the door flung open. A woman screamed. I turned to see three figures in the threshold: Edith Fouquet, Marthe and Lucile.

'*Mon Dieu!*' Madame Fouquet cried.

Marthe smiled and then burst into fake sobs.

But it was the look on Lucile's face that was worst of all. She had gone deathly pale. Her eyes rolled back as she brought her hand to her head. Then her knees buckled and she fainted.

CHAPTER THIRTEEN

KRISTINA

Paris, November 1928

Kristina was putting on her earrings when she heard Max's and Serge's voices rise from the nursery.

'I'm sure that's not how you fold it, Max,' Serge said.

'It is. Kristina showed me. You can't fold it too big because she's only a few months old.'

'Well, tuck it under her leg then,' suggested Serge, 'otherwise I can only see it leaking and the poor thing will be left lying in a wet bed.'

Kristina smiled. They sounded like two grandmothers bickering. But baby Nadia could not have had a more devoted father and godfather in Max and Serge. Their willingness to share the responsibility for Nadia had given her time to paint. Magnificently too. She had three small oils and one large one on show tonight. Maybe at last she would make a significant sale.

'I'm ready,' she said, coming out of the bedroom and smoothing her embroidered Georgette dress.

Their young maid, Colette, came up the stairs holding a pile of freshly washed nappies.

'Now, you are sure you'll be all right looking after Nadia tonight?' Kristina asked her. 'We are just around the corner if you need us.'

Colette's grin brought out all her dimples. 'I'll be fine. I've got ten younger brothers and sisters. I've done all this before.'

Kristina smiled then called out for Max and Serge. 'We'd better get going!'

The door to the nursery opened and Max and Serge backed out, both waving at Nadia before finally shutting the door.

'You look beautiful,' Max told Kristina, taking her arm.

They moved towards the stairs. Serge followed after them, but suddenly stopped and felt around his pockets before pulling out a silver rattle.

'Her favourite toy,' he said, heading back towards the nursery. 'She can't be without it.'

Kristina and Max looked at each other and chuckled.

Their five-year-old marriage was a happy one. Max and Serge were now well known in the art world as discoverers of exceptional talent, and they all had enough money to live well. Even with an economic depression looming over the world, Bergeret & Lavertu still managed to find collectors whose fortunes were so large their lifestyles were impervious to the ups and downs of the markets. Now the dream of owning a beautiful gallery on Rue la Boétie did not seem so far-fetched. The icing on the cake of Kristina and Max's blissful union had been the birth of their beautiful daughter, Nadia.

'Serge would have made a wonderful father,' Kristina whispered to Max.

Max nodded. 'I know.'

Since Madeleine had left, there had been no word from her or any news about the child. Every year, on the estimated date of the child's birthday, Kristina would light a candle and say a prayer for it. She didn't need to wonder if Serge still thought about it. Whenever they were together and they saw a young child about the same age as his would have been, a look of intense pain would come to his eyes and he would go quiet.

'Why doesn't he marry?' Kristina asked Max. 'He's handsome, good at business and kind. We know so many women who would be pleased to have him as a husband.'

Max shook his head. 'Kristina, don't. Please. It's Serge's life. I think he prefers to be alone.'

Kristina conceded that seemed to be the truth. Besides, he was so helpful with Nadia, she wasn't sure what she would do without him.

*

The exhibition hall was already crowded when Kristina, Max and Serge arrived. The guests sparkled like stars in their evening clothes and the chatter was enthusiastic. Lucien Pluet, one of the furniture dealers who was collaborating with the exhibition, made his way through the throng to them.

'It's wonderful, isn't it?' he said, grasping each of their hands in turn. 'What a brilliant initiative of Bergeret and Lavertu!'

'I hope they will be able to see the furniture,' said Serge, trying to look over the heads of the people. 'I didn't quite expect so many to attend. There must be at least seven hundred.'

A reporter from *Le Figaro* approached Max, notebook and pen in hand. 'What made you decide to put antique furniture and modern paintings together in the one exhibition?'

'We want people to stop viewing paintings as merely interior decoration,' Max told him. 'Or think that modern art doesn't belong with Louis XVI furniture. We want to show how beautifully they can work together. Modern art is a celebration of life and ideas.'

'And you, Madame Bergeret,' the reporter asked Kristina, 'what do you have to say about the exhibition? Do you like to see your paintings displayed this way?'

'Why yes, I do,' she answered. 'In fact, I adore it. Bergeret and Lavertu are known for their taste, their first-rate eye, their commercial astuteness. Anybody who wants to start a modern collection is in safe hands with them.'

Serge winked at her, and she knew she had done well in representing them.

Other reporters wanted to speak with Max and Serge, so she moved away from them and joined the bustling spectators. She was pleased to see the art critics from *L'Illustration* and *Paris-soir* looking at her works with what seemed to be favourable eyes. A cluster of people were gathered around her major piece in the exhibition: a large oil painting depicting women dancing together in a forest and titled *The Joy of Life*.

'It's magnificent!' she heard a woman say. 'Oh, it's just wonderful. I must have it!'

She turned to see a well-dressed couple admiring her painting. They were exactly the sort of people she needed to buy one of her works and display it in a prominent place in their home.

The man made his way to the painting to take a closer look. He squinted at the signature – *K. Belova* – before running his eye over every inch of it. After studying it this way for some time, the man called Serge over. 'My wife and I would like to buy it. Tell me about the artist.'

Kristina's heart skipped a beat. Serge's face lit up with delight. He and Max loved the painting. 'An extraordinary talent,' Serge said. 'She—'

'She!' the man exclaimed, like someone spitting out something rotten. 'A woman?' He shook his head. 'I don't want a painting by a woman. It's a bad investment. I'd be the laughing-stock of everyone who visits my drawing room.'

Kristina's spirits sank. She felt like a hamster on a wheel. No matter how hard she worked, she never went anywhere.

'Now that I look at it, I see it is quite amateurish,' the man continued, 'and naïve.'

Serge's face turned red right to the roots of his glossy hair. 'Amateurish? Oh no, quite the contrary. This is the work of a great painter.'

The man let out a hearty laugh. 'Now you are playing with me,' he said to Serge. 'Everyone knows there are no great women painters. Their brains aren't built for genius. That's not to say they don't do flowers or small children justice. But this is a large painting, an ambitious work. The kind that dominates a room. Only a man should dominate a room.'

Kristina fixed her gaze away from the scene and over the heads of the other attendees as if she was a bird preparing to take flight. She wanted to cry but refused to let herself break. This is what had plagued her ever since she went to art school. Her paintings were considered 'great' until someone found out her sex. It pained her to have to sign her works for the exhibition 'K. Belova' instead of her full name. She was Kristina. She *was* a woman. The change of the signature showed that the only difference to a painting's worth was perception. 'There are no great women painters,' the man had said. But there were, and even more so for having so many things thrown against them − not being admitted to art schools, or being pawed at by male tutors and derided by male students when they finally were; being considered too delicate to paint nudes and having to take life-drawing classes with a cow as a model instead. Or not being able to paint outside their homes without the risk of being molested or considered immoral. And there was no hope for their talent at all if they were saddled with domestic duties. All this, and yet there were still Suzanne Valadons, Sonia Delaunays, Marie Laurencins and ... Kristina Belovas. For she did feel the greatness in her, and it needed not only to be expressed but recognised.

★

'Kristina,' Max whispered in her ear the following morning as the grey November light crept through the gap in the curtains.

'Yes?'

'I have to see a collector this morning about the paintings he purchased from the exhibition.'

Kristina squeezed her eyes shut again, knowing that they weren't hers. All those months of work and the only painting of hers that had sold was a small oil of a woman clutching a bouquet of flowers. 'It's so pretty,' the buyer had said. 'I'll give it to my daughter to hang above her dressing table.'

'Serge is going to the Hôtel Drouot. There is a Manet up for auction and he wants to buy it. But we have a tight budget until we receive the payments for the paintings from the exhibition. Can you please go with him and make sure that he doesn't mortgage everything we've got to obtain it?'

Kristina smiled and turned over to face him. 'Isn't that what you did to buy my paintings when we first met?'

Max chuckled and tucked his arm around her. 'Yes, I did. But what a priceless treasure we got in return. Seriously though, when he really wants something, he can ... *change*. And things are different now. There is Nadia to consider. We can't be out

205

on the street eating beans while waiting for our cashflow to become steady again.'

'Yet you're letting him go to London next month after the last time when he temporarily sent us broke?'

Max kissed her on the forehead. 'He's going to London with a strict budget and can't sign off on anything without my approval.'

'All right,' she told him. 'I'll go.'

★

Serge seemed excited by the idea of Kristina accompanying him to the auction. As they rode in the taxi together to the ninth arrondissement, he told her:

'The Hôtel Drouot is nothing like the hallowed institutions of Christie's or Sotheby's. You'll see. There is always something fascinating to look at.'

Indeed, when Kristina and Serge walked through the main pavilion of the auction house, she thought it resembled a flea market. The only difference was that the price tags were considerably higher. Fine art, furniture, marble busts and heirloom jewellery filled every room. But after becoming used to the tasteful way that Bergeret & Lavertu exhibited their artworks, Kristina was slightly disturbed to see that priceless paintings were often stacked against each other, that jewellery was jumbled together on trays and some of the display cases were dusty.

'It's like a bazaar or a souk,' she said to Serge as they made their way through the crowd, which was a mix of dealers, curiosity seekers and tourists.

'Yes,' he said. 'That's why I make sure I only ever come with one object in mind. It's easy to get carried away. I often have to rein Max in, you know.'

206

'He says the same thing about you!'

Serge laughed. 'The truth is, we are as bad as each other. Out of the three of us, you are the most level-headed, Kristina.'

They took their seats in the auction room and Serge looked about him. 'There are three other dealers,' he whispered to her. 'This is going to be tough.'

'What is so special about this painting?' Kristina asked him. 'Apart from the fact it's a Manet?'

'While Manet is famous for his controversial *Olympia*, art connoisseurs love his flowers for the fact that they draw on the old masters for structure, but Manet also gives them a modern cast.'

The bell rang and the auctioneer began to describe the items in the lot, including a Venetian armorial cartouche and a pair of Roman granite columns. When the Manet was brought to the block and the auctioneer described it as being in excellent condition and one of the finest examples of Manet's work, Kristina noticed a distinct charge in the atmosphere. But most of all she saw that beads of sweat had broken out on Serge's forehead although the room was chilly. Before the bidding started, he took out a handkerchief and dabbed at his face and neck. His hands were trembling.

'Are you all right?' Kristina asked him.

He barely nodded and seemed to be in a trance-like state.

As the bids for the Manet began to rise higher and higher, Serge's trembling increased. His legs jiggled up and down and his pupils enlarged so that his eyes seemed to have turned black.

It's like watching a drug addict, thought Kristina. Was this what Max had been worried about? At what point would she need to stop him? Max hadn't said.

She was thankful when Serge made the highest bid and the auctioneer dropped the hammer and the ordeal was over. Serge slumped back in his chair, almost catatonic. When the auction was done, he sat up again, his eyes back to normal and his voice even.

'Well, we have it,' he said cheerfully. 'The Manet is ours! And under what I'd expected we'd have to pay for it.'

Serge sounded like himself again, but Kristina remained unsettled. The auction had shown her a different side to him. It was exactly as Max had said – when Serge really wanted a piece of art, something in him changed.

CHAPTER FOURTEEN

EVE

Paris, June 1946

The morning after the Fouquets' ball, I sat in front of Marthe de Villiers, Madame Fouquet and Lucile like a doomed aristocrat before the Revolutionary Tribunal. And like those hapless victims of the past, I too knew that it was a mere formality and that my fate was already sealed, no matter the evidence presented or the pleas made.

'What a scandal!' said Madame Fouquet with a shiver full of repugnance. 'And in my home! The one I welcomed this young woman into as a complete stranger in a spirit of generosity. Why, I heard that young Hubert Thirard was so taken with her that he asked his mother for permission to court her. It's one thing for her to have led a doddery old man astray … but to have almost destroyed that young man's future is unforgivable.'

Marthe stopped weeping her false tears for a moment and frowned. 'My husband is *a hero of Verdun*, Edith,' she said. 'It's taken me years to nurse him back to a state of equilibrium since he received that terrible injury in the service of France. Then this woman destroys all my efforts for her own personal gain.'

Although they had formed an alliance, it was obvious that Marthe and Madame Fouquet were not friends. They were united in their ambition to keep certain people out of their circle of society. I was sure that if Lucile's friends had known about Cyrille's previous pursuits of young women, then Madame Fouquet would certainly have known too. It was not my having been caught in a compromising position with Cyrille that irked her, but that her ball had been infiltrated by someone who was of an 'inferior' class.

The only one who could save me was Lucile. If she would address the difficulty with a firm hand, the other two women would have to back down. But when I tried to catch her attention, she stared at her coffee cup, which Madame Fouquet promptly filled. Without my guidance, she seemed to have turned into a lump of dough, entirely unable to direct her own thoughts and therefore was easily led by Marthe and Madame Fouquet.

'It's a terrible shock, my dear,' Madame Fouquet said to Lucile, 'to be treated so terribly by someone you were only trying to help. But young women like that never change. You should never let *servants* get the upper hand.'

The word 'servant' hit a nerve. They might have been richer and more powerful, but I wasn't going anywhere quietly.

'Lucile,' I said, 'you must know that I would never have anything to do with Cyrille de Villiers. The man is completely odious. *He* launched himself at *me*. Marthe set us up.'

'Oh, the cheek!' said Marthe. 'Not only a tart but a liar! She was after his money.' Then weeping into her handkerchief again, she added, 'What have I done to deserve this? I've been a loyal and loving wife.'

'I can't bear to hear any more of this,' said Madame Fouquet. 'I have a hairdresser's appointment at eleven o'clock and a luncheon at twelve. Action must be taken now. Lucile, get your maid to pack some things for Mademoiselle Archer and give her money for a fare back to Australia, where she belongs.'

'Lucile,' I said, trying to keep my nerves steady, 'remember what you told me at the Ritz on my birthday.'

But trying to appeal to any sense of loyalty in Lucile seemed to have the opposite effect. She clenched her fists and said in a low voice, 'I'll tell Odette to pack a small suitcase for you and give you your allowance for the month. Then you must never contact me again, or I'll call the police.'

Her coldness shocked me. 'Lucile!'

'"Madame Damour" to you, young lady,' said Madame Fouquet, rising from her chair. 'Now off you go without a fuss.'

I stared at Lucile, unable to believe she was doing this to me. But then she raised her eyes and said with perfect clarity, 'One more thing, Eve. Please leave the ring I gave you with Odette before you go.'

★

I sat in the grimy café on Rue Gabrielle feeling defeated. The coffee I was drinking was gritty and burned like mustard in my throat. The waiter was surly and unkempt, but it was better to sit there than in the dingy room I had rented above it that smelled like a wet dog.

I sensed someone approaching and looked up to see Georges. He was dapper as usual and out of place in a café with a floor covered in pigeon droppings.

'What a lovely venue you've chosen,' he said. 'I hope it doesn't reflect a permanent mood.'

'Is it possible to think about someone and have them appear?' I asked.

'Were you thinking about me, Eve?' he asked with amusement. 'I hope those thoughts were good ones and that you don't feel about me the way you must feel about my aunt. I'm appalled at her ungrateful behaviour, after all you've done for her.'

'Thank you for coming. I didn't want to disappear without saying goodbye to you.'

He took out his handkerchief and wiped the chair opposite me before sitting down and signalling to the waiter.

'I wouldn't order here if I were you,' I told him. 'They're still using acorns.'

Despite my warning, Georges ordered a coffee and a baguette. Then he turned to me. 'To live a satisfying life, one should taste bad coffee now and then. It sharpens one's appreciation of a good brew. Just like every exceptional person should have their share of failure. It makes them hungrier for success. By the way, you have failed spectacularly, Eve. I must congratulate you.'

I clenched my jaw. Nobody could hate the word 'failure' more than me. 'It wasn't my doing.'

'I didn't mean anything against you,' he replied as the waiter placed his coffee and limp-looking baguette before him. 'I was referring to your valiant attempt to turn my aunt into a sensible woman.' His eyes roved over my dress and he gave a delighted laugh. 'You spent a lot of money on that, didn't you? Let me guess – my aunt gave you enough money for a week's rent and you've spent half of it already on a dress.'

'Two weeks' rent, and I've spent nearly all of it.'

Georges nodded as if he thoroughly approved of my reckless behaviour.

'I'm glad you find my situation amusing,' I said. 'But I can't think straight unless I'm well dressed.'

'That's very French of you, Eve. If I appear at all amused by your predicament, it's only because I know it's temporary, and I look forward to seeing how you will get yourself out of it. Anyway, I'm glad you sent me a note and didn't just vanish into thin air.'

'I'm sorry I can't come with you to the Anglo-French Legal Conference dinner now. It might have been fun.'

'Why on earth not?' he asked.

His remark confused me. 'Well, apart from the fact I don't have anything to wear, I am something of a pariah.'

Georges leaned forward and tapped my arm. 'The fact that you have caused a scandal only makes you a far more fascinating companion. Besides that, I can help you with the dress. Choose any gown you like and have the bill sent to me. And while you are at it, find yourself a decent place to stay at my expense.'

I pressed my lips together. It was a kind offer, but it was different to have a man pay for me than for Lucile to provide for me. I didn't want to be indebted to Georges that way. When we battled our wits against each other, it made us equals. His financial assistance would change that.

He must have sensed my discomfort because he quickly added, 'You know it's not charity I'm offering you. It's a straightforward transaction. Otherwise, I would instead be wasting money lying on the couch of an expensive psychiatrist desperately trying to overcome my shame at having such a silly aunt.'

Despite my dour predicament, I couldn't help but laugh. 'I wouldn't like to see that, Georges, as you are the sanest person I know. But I can't accept your offer. I need to get out of this mess myself.'

'And I have no doubt that you will. But you can't stay in this dump. It's not safe. So in the meantime ...' He reached inside his jacket for his wallet, but I put my hand on his arm to stop him.

'It's a lot like where I grew up,' I said. 'I know how to survive.'

Georges met my gaze and took in the firmness of my words. The truth was, that moment when Lucile told me to give back the ring she'd gifted me for my birthday had strengthened my belief that I could only rely on myself. For it seemed clear now that relationships between human beings were purely 'transactional' and only worked harmoniously when there was a mutual advantage to be gained. I had decided that I would never reveal to Serge that he was my father. He hadn't wanted to take responsibility for me as a child, so why would he wish to do so now? Why would I make myself so vulnerable only to be abandoned again? Even Georges thought people didn't do things out of pure motives. All the promises Anthony had made me – and that I had believed – were nothing but a necklace of pearls of bitterness for me to wear now. I didn't need to add any more strings to it. If I wanted loyalty, I'd more likely get it from a dog or cat or a chicken than a human being.

Georges took a sip of his coffee without wincing. 'Then let me try another way. It seems that you have a very good sense of art and have formed an alliance with a dealer who has some legal issues to overcome. Why don't I offer my services to him pro bono on the condition that he take you on as an apprentice? It seems you would have a much better chance at creating the independent life you desire, and one surrounded by the beauty you crave, in his employment than in that of my aunt.'

A spark lit in my heart. I did love art and I did have a natural flair for knowing what was good and beautiful. If I were to be Serge's apprentice, then I could be near him without ever having to reveal I was his daughter. And Georges was probably right, I would be much happier surrounded by art than a bunch of socialite vipers.

'I can see you are warming to the idea,' said Georges, taking a bite of his baguette which did not emit the delightful crunching sound usually associated with French bread. He chewed until he managed to make himself swallow it. Then he fixed a mischievous grin on me. 'You see, there isn't any problem in the world that can't be solved over a good cup of coffee and a fresh baguette. Let's go see Serge Lavertu now, shall we?'

I felt a surge of gratitude well in my chest. 'Thank you, Georges. I appreciate it.'

'Don't thank me, Eve—'

'I know,' I said, resisting the temptation to wipe away a crumb that had attached itself to his chin, 'it bores you.'

CHAPTER FIFTEEN

KRISTINA

Paris, May 1939

'Not there. Up to the next floor please,' Kristina said, directing two red-faced furniture removalists carrying a heavy walnut bookcase up the staircase. It was probably not their favourite job to furnish a six-storey house, and they would face worse troubles when the piano arrived, but they were being paid well for their efforts.

'Kristina, come look!' Max called from the street.

She wiped her hands on her apron and descended the stairs again. Outside the building at the gallery level, Max was watching a workman screw into place the bronze plaque for 'Bergeret & Lavertu'. It was a proud moment and had been years in the making.

Max put his arm around her shoulders and kissed her on the cheek. 'Rue la Boétie,' he said proudly. 'Remember this is where you came to look for me after I took all your paintings? You thought Serge and I were important art dealers then. Well, now we are.'

The street was elegant and calm, with the kind of spotlessness that wouldn't be found in Montparnasse. The windows were cleaned daily, and the name plaques and doorknobs polished to a high shine each morning. Dirty puddles and horse manure had no place on the street and all the pedestrians who graced it wore clean tailored clothes that fitted exquisitely.

Kristina rolled her shoulders as if to shake off a slight tension. She could feel that all eyes were on them, the newcomers to the neighbourhood. Some of the galleries had been handed down from father to son for years in that fine tradition of succession that the French valued so much. The top art dealers of Paris were a tight-knit group but not a welcoming one. Bergeret & Lavertu still had a lot to prove. Max and Serge would have to watch their backs.

Nadia came out holding Ginette's hand. They were sisters but looked completely different. Nadia was dark like Max, and Ginette was fair like Kristina, with a head full of fluffy curls that made her resemble a dandelion.

'Look, Mama and Papa, I painted Tulipe,' Ginette said, holding up a piece of paper.

Tulipe was the family's pet rabbit, the successor to Leo who had lived to the ripe old age of eleven. Ginette's art was as delightful as her personality. She'd painted Tulipe's body with remarkable accuracy for a six-year-old, but the rabbit's teeth looked like a human's and Tulipe was grinning in a way that reminded Kristina of Max. She had to bite her lip to stop herself from laughing.

'We should frame it for her, Papa,' Nadia said. 'Can we?'

Nadia was quieter and more serious than Ginette. She looked after her younger sister with all the care of someone who had been left in charge of a rare and precious diamond.

'Of course we can,' said Max, taking the painting from Ginette and kissing both girls on the top of their heads. 'We shall hang it next to the Kandinsky that Uncle Serge spent a fortune on.' Then with a wink at Kristina he added, 'You can hardly tell the difference.'

'Where *is* Serge?' she asked. 'I don't know where he wants his furniture placed and he's so particular about things.'

'At the Hôtel Drouot,' replied Max. 'There are two Matisses up for auction.'

'He'll be gone for hours,' she said. 'And the movers won't be that patient. I'll tell them where I think his furniture should go, and no doubt he'll change his mind as soon as he sees it.'

★

Later, when Kristina was in the kitchen of the apartment above the gallery helping Colette unpack cutlery, Sonia arrived looking fashionable in a Hungarian-style silk blouse and slim black skirt. She had an assortment of fabrics over one arm and a bottle of Dom Pérignon in her free hand.

'Today I paid your husbands the last of the loan they gave me. So we are going to celebrate.'

'*Husband*,' Kristina corrected her, although she knew Sonia had used the plural deliberately. Max and Serge had lent Sonia money to open her own atelier, which was now a thriving interior-design company. 'How was Barcelona?' she asked, taking the champagne bottle from her friend and handing it to Colette.

Sonia dropped the fabric samples on top of a box and moved a stack of cookbooks so she could sit down. 'Full of brilliant surrealists doing incredible things. The Barcelonians are refreshingly innovative and daring. The avant-garde designs have already been a hit with my customers.' She stopped a moment to admire the Art Deco bracelet she was wearing. 'And how did your exhibition go? I was sorry to have missed it.'

Colette popped the cork of the champagne and handed Kristina and Sonia a glass each.

'It was a resounding success,' Kristina said, taking a sip of her drink. 'Nearly three thousand people came to look at my paintings and the art critics finally proclaimed me a "genius".'

'And ...?'

Kristina put down her champagne glass. 'And as with my previous exhibitions, I didn't sell anything significant. In fact this time, I didn't sell anything.'

Sonia arched one of her perfectly groomed eyebrows at her. 'Not even one painting?'

Kristina shook her head. She had been blessed with many good things in life – wonderful parents, good health, a happy marriage and children – but what she dearly wanted seemed to elude her. She had painted nearly every day since the time she could hold a paintbrush, and just when it seemed she was about to go somewhere with her art, she found herself back where she had started: nowhere.

'Well, it's not a lack of talent,' said Sonia matter-of-factly. 'The best of France's art connoisseurs have bought your works – Édouard and Beatrice Fould, Count Étienne Beaumont, the Rothschilds.'

'Those who love art love my work,' she agreed. 'But I can't make a name for myself selling one painting a year. It doesn't matter if the critics say I'm brilliant, art buyers still don't see a female painter as a good investment.'

Sonia smoothed her skirt thoughtfully, then a mischievous glint came to her eye. 'Why don't you concentrate on flowers – or children? Something more romantic and domestic like the ones you painted when you were at art school to make some money on the side. That's what people expect of a "lady painter". They don't want brilliant and daring art created by a woman.'

Kristina's spine prickled. 'Seriously? Is that what *you* would advise me? The champion of the cubists, expressionists and futurists?'

Sonia shook her head. 'I would advise you to do what Serge is always telling you to do – to keep going. The success you want will come eventually.'

'I'm surprised Serge hasn't given up on me. I'm the only painter he represents who never makes him any money.'

Sonia shrugged and looked around the room. 'So, you are seriously all going to live here together in this house? That will get the gossips talking. They already see you as a threesome.'

'Nobody thinks like that but you, Sonia,' Kristina said, irritated that she had brought up the subject again. 'Serge is like the brother I never had. Nadia and Ginette think of him as their uncle. And he has his own apartment on the third floor, below ours. We're hardly living together.'

Even as she said it, Kristina knew it was not as straightforward as that. The best times were always when it was the three of them together. After dinner, they would sit and talk for hours about everything from music to books to politics. As much as she and Max loved each other, husbands and wives could rarely keep their conversations so stimulating after years of marriage. What Kristina felt for Serge was something more than she would have felt for a brother. She had learned it was possible to love a man without being his lover.

'Don't you wonder why Serge has never married?' Sonia asked.

'Serge's passion is for his art,' Kristina replied, picking up her glass of champagne again and taking a sip. 'Not everyone is suited to matrimony, something you're always saying yourself, Sonia. Sometimes I think there was more between him and

Madeleine than he ever told us, and that perhaps she broke his heart in a way that can't be fixed.'

Sonia studied Kristina. She seemed on the verge of saying something but then thought better of it. She reached for her fabric samples and placed them on the table, holding up textured crepes, velvet and silk. 'Come on, let's choose the materials for your curtains and upholsteries. They aren't going to make themselves.'

★

The following week, Kristina was playing hide and seek with Ginette and had just managed to pull her by her squirming legs from under the sofa, when the new secretary Serge had hired came upstairs to see her. Inès Bonne was well presented, with never a hair out of place. Everything about her was tidy and precise, from her tailor-made suits to her white lace blouses to her neat handwriting.

'Madame Bergeret,' she said, 'there is a visitor downstairs. Monsieur Martin La Farge. I told him that Messieurs Bergeret and Lavertu are away on business for the day, but he says he came to meet you.'

Her gaze dropped to the dust and rabbit fur stuck to the front of Kristina's blouse. Kristina brushed it off. She would have to remind Colette that she needed to clean *under* the furniture as well as around it.

'Monsieur La Farge wants to meet me?'

Martin La Farge's gallery was diagonally across the street from Bergeret & Lavertu. One couldn't fail to notice the Fragonards and Bouchers he had displayed in the windows. He had been born into an old established family, and it was those families who made up his lucrative clientele.

'He says he has already met Messieurs Bergeret and Lavertu and it is you he wants to welcome to the neighbourhood.'

'He probably wants to get a look at our inventory,' Kristina said with a rueful laugh. 'And thinks that I will be more gullible than my husband or Serge.'

A mischievous smile danced on Inès's perfectly made-up lips. 'You are probably correct, Madame Bergeret, so perhaps we shouldn't leave him alone downstairs too long on his own.'

Kristina realised Inès was not as uptight as her impeccable appearance suggested.

'Very well,' she said. 'I'll meet him. Let's go.'

Inès nodded and reached up to take something from Kristina's hair. 'Permit me,' she said, pulling out a dust ball. 'That's better.'

Martin La Farge was holding a bouquet of white calla lilies. He was as handsome as Michelangelo's *David*. It was impossible not to notice. He was tall and blond with the glowing skin of someone who spends a great deal of time at health spas. But there was something slightly obscene about his good looks. His only physical defect was a slight bend to his nose which suggested it had once been broken.

'Madame Bergeret,' he said, holding out the lilies. Then suddenly looking contrite, he added, 'Or do you prefer to go by your artist's surname, Belova?'

'Bergeret is quite all right. I only use Belova to sign my paintings.'

'I must congratulate you on the success of your exhibition. Such wonderful reviews.'

'Thank you,' she replied, irked by the flattery in his tone.

Martin La Farge would have known that she hadn't sold a thing, but she wasn't going to let him make her cower. She passed the flowers to Inès who went in search of a vase.

'Your husband and his partner have done very well,' Martin said, looking at one of Léger's early still-life paintings hanging on the wall. 'Dealers rarely prosper from modern art and not everyone has the patience to nurture an artist through their early years, giving them stipends and a shoulder to cry on.'

Martin La Farge's voice was so even and so cultivated it was almost impossible to take offence at the note of condescension in it. Perhaps he hoped that Max and Serge wouldn't last long on Rue la Boétie. But Kristina knew they would prove him wrong.

'The dealers on Rue la Boétie always help each other out,' he continued. 'Sometimes we will have a special client who will want to add a particular artist to their collection. If we have nothing available, we might do a swap with another gallery. The Wildensteins and I have always worked together this way. I hope that your husband and Serge Lavertu will work with me in the same spirit of cooperation.'

Kristina didn't want to answer for Max and Serge, but she sensed Martin La Farge was a man who would always do what was necessary to accomplish his ends.

He glanced towards the staircase as if he hoped she might invite him to inspect the old masters exhibited on the next floor. But when she extended no such offer he continued to stalk around the lower gallery, his eager eyes travelling between the paintings and sculptures. Then he stopped and furrowed his eyebrows at her painting of Madeleine hanging above the cashier's desk. It was the one she had painted just before Madeleine left, depicting her as Eve fleeing the Garden of Eden. Even if someone had offered her a million francs for it, Kristina would not have sold it. The first night she slept in the new apartment, Madeleine had come to her in a dream and Kristina was sure that her long-lost friend had died and had come to say goodbye. The painting reminded Kristina of Madeleine's promise to be her guardian angel.

'Who is the model?' he asked.

'A friend,' she answered.

Martin La Farge's brow furrowed. 'When did you paint it?'

'Years ago,' she said, reminding herself that she didn't have to tell him anything, regardless of his commanding tone. He came across as a man who expected women to do his bidding, so no doubt the depiction of a powerful Eve irked him.

Little footsteps sounded on the stairs and Ginette appeared in the doorway, cradling Tulipe securely in her arms. She must have become bored waiting for Kristina to return. At the sight of her, Martin's eyes glazed over and he seemed to have trouble breathing.

'Well, I mustn't keep you any longer. I wish you all the best in the neighbourhood. Tell your husband and Monsieur Lavertu that they can call on me anytime.'

Inès returned with the lilies in a vase in time to see Martin hurry out the door. Kristina smoothed down Ginette's hair and patted Tulipe.

'He's an odd man,' Kristina said to Inès. 'He had the strangest reaction to Ginette. He acted as if he were allergic to her.'

'They're all a bit eccentric on this street, Madame Bergeret,' Inès said drolly. 'It comes from a life of bubble baths and eating caviar for breakfast.'

Kristina laughed at Inès's comment. But her mirth was cut short when the telegram boy arrived from the post office. Kristina opened the message, and her hand flew to her mouth when she read the words:

Come home. Papa dead.

★

The sunset sparkled on the water with such beauty it was almost painful. Summer was fading. Kristina felt it in the softening sunlight and the tinge of coolness in the evening breeze. She stood on the terrace of the Villa des Cygnes watching Nadia and Ginette playing in the garden with Tulipe, a scene that normally would have filled her with joy, but that evening her heart was laden with melancholy. It was as if she knew that their happy carefree days were coming to an end. Her father had been barely sixty-five when he died in his sleep from a heart attack.

'Kristina,' her mother called from inside the house. 'I found something your father would have liked you to have.'

She turned to see Yelena holding out a blue presentation box. Kristina took it from her and opened the lid. Inside was a gold brooch set with a large ruby and a cluster of pearls. She recognised it as having once belonged to her paternal grandmother. Since her father's death, her mother had been giving things away and it unsettled Kristina. It was as if Yelena was intending to follow him to an early grave and was divesting herself of her worldly goods. Kristina couldn't bear to think of losing her too and reached out and grasped her mother's hand.

'Why don't you come and live with us in Paris? I don't like the idea of you being here alone.'

Yelena shook her head as if the idea was impossible.

'We have plenty of room, and you would be near the children,' Kristina insisted. 'You could come back here in winter when it turns cold in Paris.'

'No,' Yelena said, gently releasing her hand. 'I feel him here. He loved this place so much.'

Kristina didn't push the matter. Her mother would have her reasons and Kristina would have to respect them. Yelena had become a stranger to her in some ways. Their relationship felt lopsided since Mikhail had died, as if Kristina was having to get to know her mother again and figure out who she was without her father. She took the brooch and pinned it to her blouse, although it was too heavy and ornate for the light fabric. It was as though the weight of her father's death was tugging on her heart.

'Thank you,' she said.

Yelena smiled and looked away.

It wasn't simply that Yelena was living alone with the aid of only Lorenzo and Suzanne that was worrying her. It was also what was happening in the world. Hitler's army had invaded Czechoslovakia, and Poland would certainly be next. France was very likely going to be sucked up into another war with Germany.

Nobody had any idea what to do – to carry on normally and risk being taken by surprise? Or to prepare for the worst and somehow invite bad luck? Movie stars were gathering in Cannes for the film festival while extra trains had been put on to take worried tourists away from the coast. The casinos and hotels were being commandeered for use as hospitals and refugee centres, while rich American heiresses were still dancing at the nightclubs in Antibes. Max had just sold a Modigliani to a friend of the Duke and Duchess of Windsor who couldn't see what 'all the fuss' was about.

'They built the Maginot Line for a reason,' the collector had told Max. 'It's France's insurance policy against invasion by the Krauts.'

He was referring to the concrete battlements, obstacles and weapons installations that France had constructed along the border with Germany. It was considered the most advanced fortification ever built in the history of the world.

Kristina had read in the newspaper that Louvre officials were moving precious artworks out of Paris, including the *Mona Lisa*, and the stained-glass windows from Notre-Dame, and people were being advised to keep their children in summer camps for fear Paris would be a target for bombs and gas attacks. Max tried to ring Serge to find out what was happening in the city, but long-distance calls couldn't be placed and there was no reply to the telegram he sent.

'I'll go back to Paris for a few days and see what is happening with the gallery,' Max told Kristina. 'I'll collect the children's winter clothes and return as soon as I can.'

'I'm coming with you,' she said. 'The girls will be safe with my mother.'

Although she hated the idea of being separated from her daughters, at that moment it seemed even more unbearable to be without Max.

On the train back to Paris, everyone in the carriage wore an expression of utter shock.

'How can this be happening? It's madness,' said one woman. 'It's been a beautiful summer. Why on earth go to war?'

After that came a long period of silence as the others disappeared into their own thoughts, until a ruddy-cheeked man looked over the top of his newspaper and said hopefully, 'According to the astrologer in *Le Journal*, there won't be a war because Hitler's and Mussolini's horoscopes show no sign of it.'

Kristina and Max arrived in Paris in the evening to find that the city of lights was shrouded in darkness. Sandbags had been stacked around statues and important buildings. At the station entrance they were handed brochures on what to do in case of gas or bomb attacks. There were no taxis to be found and they had to walk the long distance back to the apartment.

They found Serge sitting in the kitchen eating soup by candlelight.

He was relieved and apologetic when he saw them. 'It's been impossible to make private telephone calls out of Paris and it's forbidden to use phones in cafés or hotels,' he explained. 'The postal service has gone to pieces. Nobody's saying it, but you can see the city officials are expecting Paris will be attacked. Colette and Inès have gone to check on their families. I've put most of our inventory in storage at Wacker-Bondy's but have kept a few paintings in the gallery so we can still run the business until we're sure things are as dire as everyone believes.'

Max and Serge spent the rest of the evening looking at the paintings on the walls of the gallery by torchlight, discussing which they should take down and pack away and which ones might be safe to leave until the last moment. They spoke in whispers as if the Germans had their ears to the walls and were listening.

Kristina felt as if she was having a bad dream. All of this was too familiar to her. Surely she wouldn't be forced to leave her home again like she had during the Russian Revolution?

The following day was balmy and the sky a translucent blue. It seemed impossible that such a perfect day could bring with it death and destruction. Kristina kept her mind from morbid thoughts by packing up the silverware and other valuables into suitcases that they could take in Serge's car if they had to flee the city. Then she went to the stores and lined up with hundreds of other women for sugar, flour, rice and matches.

'I'm taking the family photograph albums only,' said the woman next to her in line. 'It's those you love who matter most in the end.'

The woman's manner was cheerful. Kristina tried to match her optimism with a brave smile of her own, but she felt as if she'd swallowed a small rock and now it was stuck in the pit of her stomach.

She had only just arrived back at the gallery when Serge returned from delivering a Matisse to a customer at the Hotel Ritz. He held up a copy of the afternoon newspaper.

'They've done it,' he said. 'Hitler has invaded Poland. France and Britain are at war with Germany.'

For the rest of the afternoon, Kristina, Max and Serge stayed glued to the radio. The announcer sounded exhausted, and Kristina imagined his hands trembling as the broadcasts were handed to him. Then what they had been dreading came: a general call-up of men aged twenty to forty-five years of age would commence at midnight.

'Our country is in grave danger,' the announcer said. 'We must all do our duty with pride and dignity.'

She turned to Max and Serge. Serge was forty-six years of age and would not be required for active service, but Max was only forty-one. But out of the two men, it was Serge who looked the most distressed.

That evening, Kristina prepared supper while Max took a bath. She had a sharp ache in her temple that wouldn't budge no matter how much she massaged the spot. It was as if she had to concentrate very hard to stop herself from shattering.

Serge continued the job of packing away the silver and other valuables in crates. He looked at her and stood up then took her hands.

She let out a sharp sob. 'I couldn't bear it if—'

'Don't think of that,' he said, squeezing her fingers. 'We must be brave for him, Kristina. We must *both* be brave for him. We cannot think of him in any other way than coming back safely to us.'

Her fear suddenly turned to outrage. 'What are the Germans thinking! They should know what war means, the pointlessness of it all. Are the wives and mothers of the country so willing to be widows? And to see their children killed and maimed?'

Serge pulled her to his chest and held her tightly. 'It may come to nothing,' he said, although he didn't seem so certain himself. 'Surely even Hitler is not such a fool.'

In the early hours of the morning they went in the car to the Gare de l'Est, guided only by moonlight. The shop shutters were closed, and the streets were quiet and eerie. The lampposts had been fitted with padded sleeves to prevent fatalities should anyone crash into them during a blackout.

When they arrived at the station it was packed with people. Some men were already in uniform while most of the others, like Max, were still wearing their civilian clothes. Next to them were women with stricken faces. Everyone was trying to look brave, but the strain was showing in their trembling lips and the anxious twisting of hands.

Suddenly one woman let out a wail that seemed to speak for everyone gathered. 'My husband fought in the Great War, wasn't that enough? Now you want to take him when he has children to feed!'

Max pulled Kristina into his arms as if to shield her from the horror. 'Keep painting,' he whispered in her ear. 'You must never stop painting.'

He turned to Serge. 'Look after Kristina and the children.'

'As if they are my own,' Serge replied, fighting back tears.

The enlisted men were called to board the train just as sunrise began to shine through the glass ceiling of the station. The red glow made it seem as if everyone had suddenly caught on fire. Max embraced Kristina and Serge. For a moment it was as if the three of them were safe in a cocoon, shut off from the world outside. But then he released them and turned to go.

For Kristina, it was terrible to watch him moving further and further away from them, knowing they might never see him again.

CHAPTER SIXTEEN

EVE

Paris, June 1946

As Georges and I made our way to Saint-Germain-des-Prés, we laughed at the terrible coffee and bread we'd shared together.

'Well, I hope that is the last time you are going to cause me indigestion, Eve.'

'I warned you not to order anything.'

But our mirth was cut short when we reached Serge's gallery. The closed sign hung on the door and when we peered inside, we saw that all the paintings were gone. For one wildly optimistic moment, I thought perhaps Serge had sold them all to an enthusiastic buyer. But the scraps of packing paper scattered across the floor and the upturned drawers of his desk told a more foreboding story.

'Mademoiselle Archer!'

We turned to see Madame Bonne hurrying towards us. Her face was drawn.

'What's happened?' I asked her.

Her lips pursed and she looked away, hesitant to tell me.

'Is Serge all right?'

She looked back to me, her eyes glistening with tears. 'He has been arrested.'

'Arrested?'

Madame Bonne trembled as if something terrible inside of her was bursting to get out. 'Yes, but on charges that couldn't possibly be true. Charges *I know* can't possibly be true. *National disgrace.*'

I knew 'national disgrace' was a crime that had been specially legislated for those who collaborated with the Germans.

'What exactly is he accused of?' Georges asked Madame Bonne.

'Selling an important artwork to the Nazis.'

Georges grimaced. 'Well, that's a fine of one million francs and being banned from running a business for ten years.'

'It will break Serge if that happens!' I cried.

'Now don't panic, Eve,' Georges said. 'Nearly all the dealers in France had their fingers in the Nazi pie during the war and I'm not aware of any of them losing their business or spending time in jail. I'll see if I can sort the matter out this afternoon.'

Madame Bonne's face contorted into a grim expression. There was something she wasn't saying.

'What is it?' I asked. 'Is it worse than collaboration?'

She drew a breath. 'It wasn't just any Nazi that he is accused of selling the painting to. It was Hitler.'

★

The sight of Fresnes prison gave me the chills. Its dark walls and narrow barred windows were Dickensian. Although the day was sunny, the buildings that comprised the complex seemed to be encased in a halo of mist, as if they were emitting the misery of the souls trapped inside. In a twist of fate, the prison that had been used to incarcerate members of the Resistance during the war was now the place for detaining collaborators.

Georges was waiting for me at the entrance. After Madame Bonne had given us the terrible news, he'd asked me to meet him there at two o'clock. In the meantime, he would make some telephone calls to investigate the matter. I had never seen him look so grim. If it wasn't for his height and perfectly tailored suit, I may not have recognised him at all.

'The charges are far graver than I thought,' he said.

I felt myself pale. 'So Serge will lose all his property and be banned from practising his profession?'

'He will be executed as a war criminal if found guilty.'

His words hit me like a shockwave. 'War criminal? Surely that is an overstated charge. He didn't kill anybody.'

'That's precisely it. He *has* been charged with murder.'

This time the ground really did roll under my feet. I'd barely come to terms with Serge being arrested and now Georges was speaking of murder!

'Of who?' I asked.

'Édouard and Beatrice Fould. The original owners of the painting.'

'He couldn't have,' I said, a tremble in my voice. 'I don't believe it.'

'Don't or won't, Eve?' asked Georges. 'They are not the same thing. How well do you know Serge Lavertu? You've been in France less than a year.'

I bowed my head. It was true that I hardly knew him. 'He doesn't seem the type to commit such a heinous crime.'

'Good god, Eve, that is the case with half the criminals that are sent here,' said Georges, his mouth narrowing to a thin line.

'People can always surprise you when money is involved. We are talking about a painting worth a fortune.'

'Not Serge,' I said with conviction. 'Oh god, this is terrible. We must help him.'

'All right,' said Georges, looking towards the entrance. 'I'll go inside. You wait for me here. Fresnes is no place for you.'

While going into a prison was the last thing I wanted to do, I willed myself to be strong.

'I'm coming with you. I have food, soap and fresh clothes.' I held up the package Madame Bonne had given me. I didn't add that I *needed* to see Serge for myself. I couldn't help my mother now, but I could help my father.

'The place is infested with fleas and rats. You may see things you'd rather forget.'

'I'm coming with you,' I insisted.

Georges shrugged and indicated towards the direction of the gate. 'Then I will make no other attempt to dissuade you.'

He produced a document from his jacket pocket and showed it to the guard, who then opened the gate and ushered us to proceed. We were met by another guard who took us to an anteroom and opened the parcel Madame Bonne had given me. He took out the shaving mirror and razor, before handing it back. Then he directed us to follow him through an iron gate that creaked when he opened it and onwards through a narrow corridor, at the end of which was a room with nothing in it but a table and four chairs that were all chained to the floor. My eye followed a cockroach as it made its way across the peeling paint on the walls.

The guard left and we remained for what seemed like an interminable time before he returned with a dishevelled and demoralised-looking Serge. His suit was crumpled, and a grey two-day growth had sprouted on his normally clean-shaven face. But it was the chains around his ankles and wrists that caused me to gasp.

'Eve!' he cried out, looking both relieved and confused.

Relieved, no doubt, that he had not been deserted but confused as to why I should show up to see him.

'Hello, Serge,' I said. 'This is a friend of mine, Georges Camadeau. He's a lawyer. We're here to help you.'

A look of recognition and a slight smile came to Serge's face. 'I remember you, Monsieur Camadeau. I was a witness at the inquiry into that butchered Degas.'

'Indeed. I'm sorry that we meet again in these circumstances.' Georges turned to the guard and indicated the chairs. 'May we?'

The guard gave a nod and allowed Serge to take a chair while Georges and I sat down on the other side of the table.

'Let's start with the details, Monsieur Lavertu,' said Georges, taking a notebook and pen from his pocket. 'You are aware of the charges against you?'

'A distressing claim that I murdered Édouard and Beatrice Fould,' replied Serge, 'but no details beyond that.'

Georges read from his notes: 'According to the Foulds' gardener, François Gattolin, on the tenth of September 1943, you and a Madame Kristina Bergeret arrived at the Fould residence in Nice around midday and, along with Monsieur Gattolin and two maids, commenced packing away the Foulds' art collection with the expectation of the couple leaving Nice that night to avoid deportation by the Germans. Sometime in the afternoon, Madame Bergeret left by bicycle to attend to domestic matters at her home, but you remained behind. Monsieur Gattolin says he spent several hours with you building a false wall to hide the most important artworks behind. When you finished, you suggested that Monsieur

Gattolin and the maids go to their respective quarters and sleep for the next few hours as a storm was brewing and Monsieur Gattolin would need his wits about him to drive the couple along the back roads to Saint-Martin. But when Monsieur Gattolin re-entered the house at three o'clock in the morning, he found the maids fast asleep and the Foulds gone. He concluded you must have decided to drive the couple yourself.'

Serge paused before responding. 'I left Édouard and Beatrice about one o'clock in the morning and returned to the villa where I was staying as a guest of Kristina ... Madame Bergeret. The plan we had decided upon was for the gardener to drive them to Saint-Martin from where they would make their way to Italy, and I assumed that was what had happened.'

'Did you make any attempt to find them after the war?' asked Georges, writing down what Serge was telling him.

'Yes, through the Red Cross. But they had disappeared without a trace. I thought perhaps they had been caught and deported, but there were no records of them in the camps. In the end, I could only assume they met some bad end on their way out of France.'

'And their artwork?' Georges asked. 'What happened to the art you hid?'

'I reported it to the Artistic Recovery Commission soon after the liberation. But it had been stolen, as was the art at Madame Bergeret's villa. Both houses were occupied by the Germans towards the end of the war and were looted. Madame Bergeret was sent to a camp and I joined the Maquis.'

Georges leaned back in his chair and regarded Serge carefully. 'The Foulds never left their villa. Their decomposed bodies were found two days ago in a disused well on their estate.'

The room seemed suddenly airless. A palpable sense of foreboding came over me and I thought I might pass out.

Serge's face was a study in anguish and it took him a few moments to compose himself enough to speak. 'Someone must have informed the Germans that the Foulds were leaving.'

'The Germans wouldn't have killed them and hidden their bodies in a well,' said Georges. 'They would have deported them along with all the other Jews they were sending east.' Georges glanced at me before turning back to Serge. 'You may not like what I'm about to say, but I have to inform you that if you are guilty, Monsieur Lavertu, this is going to be a lot easier if you admit it.'

It wrung my heart to hear Serge's innocence questioned but he remained steadfast.

'Édouard and Beatrice were my friends,' he said, lifting his chin. 'I never betrayed them and I certainly did not kill them.'

Georges softened his manner. 'It's not a matter of whether I believe you. I'm asking questions that the examining judge will want answered. There is also the painting from the Foulds' collection that was sold to Hitler's art dealer – Hedy von Rittberg. A rare Botticelli that Monsieur Gattolin said Édouard Fould was so attached to, it was the one artwork he intended to take with him as he fled for his life.'

Serge was quiet as if he were remembering the events of the night. Then he sighed deeply. 'In the end he saw the wisdom in entrusting it to me. It would have been stolen or damaged if he tried to take it over the rugged mountains on foot.'

'And yet you sold it to Hedy von Rittberg?'

'Not quite. I never sold the original. That was stolen. I sold von Rittberg a copy of the painting.'

'A fake?' I asked. 'You sold Hitler's art dealer a forgery?'

Serge nodded.

'Well then,' said Georges, putting aside his pen and leaning back in his chair. 'You'd better start by explaining how you ended up selling a forgery of a rare and beautiful masterpiece to Hitler's dealer – and how on earth she fell for it.'

PART II

CHAPTER SEVENTEEN

KRISTINA

Nice, June 1940

Initially it was all good news. *Vive la France! We are winning! France triumphed before, and she will triumph again!* The French people were assured the country's tanks were superior and that the German army was retreating in the face of the French army's might.

But the refugees pouring into Nice told another story. They were coming from everywhere. At first from Belgium and the Netherlands, and then the north of France and from the towns that bordered Italy. Tired, weary, carrying what was left of their possessions in wheelbarrows and prams. Those with money may have found a hotel room, while others were left to sleep under the palm trees in the parks. Kristina saw them whenever she went to run errands in town – women staggering under the responsibility of finding food and shelter for their young children, elderly parents and bickering in-laws. Their homes were gone, and their husbands and older sons were at the front. They waited in line for hours outside the hospital or the Town Hall for food packages. Sometimes all they could get were two boiled eggs to share between a family of six. Kristina was haunted by their dazed, hopeless expressions.

'I can't bear it,' said Yelena at breakfast one morning. 'It reminds me of fleeing Russia.'

Kristina's mother found the suffering of others so unbearable, she volunteered at a soup kitchen run by a Catholic priest to help the refugees. And it was from them that she would convey the horror stories to Kristina and Serge.

'The German pilots targeted innocent civilians,' she told them one evening when she returned home looking wan and exhausted. 'Women, old people, children – they gunned them down indiscriminately on the roads. And now refugees are starting to pour in from Paris. I'm sending Lorenzo back to his family in Italy. If Mussolini joins the war, who knows what will happen? We'll have to manage ourselves with just Suzanne to help for a while.'

Kristina was glad that Nadia and Ginette had eaten early and were already in bed. She had tried to shield them as much as possible from the calamity that was unfolding, but she wasn't sure how much longer she would be able to do so. She turned to Serge who looked as shocked as she felt. The war was truly here now. For the past year, they'd held the belief that it might be averted, that the Germans might come to their senses or that Hitler might be assassinated. After the initial flurry of preparations – air-raid drills, blacking out windows and buying gas masks – autumn, winter and most of spring had passed by uneventfully. In Max's letters from the Maginot Line, he'd written about soldiers dying from boredom not bullets.

Now she hadn't heard from him since his last leave over a month ago. 'Keep painting,' Max had reminded her when he'd left. But how could she paint when the future she had imagined for herself and her family was now only a great, uncertain hole?

After Yelena retired for the evening, Kristina sat up with Serge in the drawing room, discussing the latest events. He paced the floor, stopping every so often to peer through the blackout curtains at the sea.

'Perhaps we should leave?' she suggested. 'Take Mama and the children and go to Portugal.'

But Serge continued to pace and didn't answer her. His expression was stern and a bit sad. She knew he was thinking about his beloved paintings. What came to be known as the 'Phoney War' had gone on so long, he had been forced to return to Paris to do business so they would have some money. He'd held exhibitions and sold some paintings, and for a while it seemed things might even return to normal. But when the Germans came through the Ardennes in a blitzkrieg, he'd had to flee with only a couple of canvases rolled up in his suitcase. The car had been requisitioned and he'd come on a crowded train where the only room available for him was in a toilet cubicle. The rest of his paintings, apart from the ones in storage at Wacker-Bondy's, were on the walls of the gallery. They were like his children. He felt as frantic about their welfare as Kristina did about Nadia and Ginette.

'You can't go back to Paris,' Kristina said. 'Please tell me that's not what you're thinking.'

Serge stopped his pacing and turned to her with a pained expression on his face. Then the tension seemed to go from his body and his eyes filled with tenderness.

'I promised Max I would look after you and the children,' he said. 'And I will. I'll look after you until the very end.'

Kristina's heart swelled. She sensed a deepening of the profound connection they shared, the intense desire they both felt to protect each other. Serge had chosen them over his beloved paintings, and that meant everything to her.

★

In the middle of June, the radio that Kristina, Serge and Yelena gathered around each day brought them the worst news: Italy had declared war on France. The Germans had marched into Paris and Marshal Pétain, who had replaced Paul Reynaud as prime minister the day before, was seeking an armistice. All fighting was to cease.

They stared at the radio and then looked at each other in disbelief, their faces pale and their lips clenched. Nobody moved or spoke. Kristina could hear her daughters playing outside. Ginette was skipping rope and chanting: *Chocolate cake, when you bake, how many minutes will you take? One, two, three, four …* They had no idea that their sweet childhoods had just been taken from them.

'It's over?' Yelena asked, finally breaking the silence in the room. 'It's over already?'

'It must be a lie,' said Serge, his voice hoarse. 'France was not losing the war. Why the sudden capitulation?'

Kristina's mind turned to Max. At least if an armistice was called, he would come home. Unless he was dead. She squeezed her eyes shut. She couldn't allow herself to even think that.

★

'Have you heard any news?' a pregnant woman asked the group of housewives waiting outside the bakery. Kristina was there, not because she needed bread, but because she was getting more accurate news from the women of Nice than from any other source. Since the armistice, the country was divided, with the Germans occupying two-thirds of the north and the new French Vichy government occupying the south. News from the north was slow in coming and letters were censored. Some soldiers were gradually returning after demobilisation, but they only brought with them tales of slaughter and a sense of demoralisation.

'The Maginot Line!' spat a grey-haired woman with bitterness in her eyes. 'The Germans not only bypassed it, they wheeled around and took the soldiers guarding it from the rear. The rumours are that nearly two million French soldiers are now prisoners of war. What was it all for?'

Kristina's legs felt leaden as she climbed the hill back to the villa. The physical absence of Max had been hard enough to bear. She missed having him to talk to and his tenderness and caresses. But now this? Was he still alive and a prisoner? Injured and suffering? Or—? She stopped herself from following that last, terrifying thought. It was the not knowing, and the inability to find out, that was almost driving her crazy. She stopped. On the pavement ahead of her someone had painted a large 'V' in red. She didn't know what it stood for. Perhaps the new Vichy government? But then she saw one on a building and another on a tree. The letters seemed to be leading down a laneway. Against her better judgement, Kristina followed them. Then she saw painted on the side of a building:

Vive de Gaulle! Vive l'Angleterre! De Gaulle, c'est la liberté!

Who was de Gaulle and why did he represent freedom? The message was also in support of France's former ally, Britain. It was a dangerous act of subversion, as the French were now supposed to be cooperating with the Germans. Kristina quickly returned to the main street. Somehow, despite all her troubles, the message had lifted her spirits.

She had no sooner walked in the door than Suzanne asked if she could speak with her. Kristina ushered her into the drawing room.

'My brother Jerome is in a camp near Paris,' Suzanne said, holding out a card with the Red Cross emblem at the top. Beneath it was a short message: *I am a prisoner and I am in good health.*

It was such a brief message — all Suzanne's brother had been permitted — and yet it was everything. Kristina could see the relief and hope on the maid's face. She took her hand and squeezed it.

'I'm very happy for you and your family,' she told her.

Then more sadly, Suzanne said, 'I must go back to my home in Saint-Agnès. With my father and brothers away, my mother is managing the grocery store by herself.'

'Of course,' Kristina told her. 'I wish you well.'

Suzanne nodded and turned to leave. Then she looked back to Kristina. 'I wish you well too. I hope Monsieur Bergeret returns home soon.'

Kristina waited for Suzanne to close the door behind her then went to the window. The Mediterranean was still so peaceful, so blue. It was difficult to believe that they were all living in hell.

★

One evening, when Yelena was serving the soup for dinner, her hands began to tremble as she lifted the ladle.

'Here, let me do that,' said Kristina, taking the ladle from her and urging her to sit down.

Since the war had started, Kristina had noticed her mother growing frailer at an alarming rate. Her skin was like parchment, dark veins visible beneath the surface. They had all lost weight from the food restrictions, but Yelena's thinness was palpable. It filled Kristina with sadness. How would she hold up if she no longer had her mother? Could she stand on her own? She realised she would have to, otherwise who would look after everybody if she broke down?

She noticed Nadia studying her. She was twelve years old and slowly blossoming into a young woman. The war was taking away from her the years that should have been full of joy and discovery. Kristina didn't want her to be burdened with any more hardship than she was already experiencing. So she plastered a smile on her face.

'Will we leave some for Papa?' asked Ginette, when Kristina placed the soup in front of her. 'He will be home soon.'

Max had been in the army for nearly a year, and at eight years of age, Ginette had seemed mature enough to accept that he was away fighting to keep them all safe. But her sudden request had a note of desperation in it. Kristina glanced at Serge, tears filling her eyes.

Although there was barely enough food for them all as it was, he stood and held out his bowl for Kristina to fill. Then he placed it on the stove to keep warm.

'Yes, sweet Ginette,' he said. 'We must remember your father tonight and every night. For while we may not know exactly when he will come back, we must be ready for when he does.'

★

The following morning, Kristina and Serge went to see Édouard Fould. He had contacts in the government and they hoped he might be able to help them find out more information about Max.

'If your husband is a prisoner of war, Kristina,' he said with a voice full of regret, 'it will be a long wait. I've read the terms of the armistice. The return of French prisoners of war depends on a peace treaty, and in my opinion the British will fight to the bitter end. If the Americans join the conflict and add their resources, which I believe they will, this war could go on for years. The Germans will use the French POWs to mitigate their labour shortages from having so many of their own men mobilised.'

'France will collapse,' said Serge, horrified. 'We don't have enough farm and factory workers. And we are paying the Germans millions of francs a day to occupy us.'

Édouard nodded. 'Exactly. France will collapse.'

'We should have kept fighting, like Britain,' Kristina said.

Édouard turned to her. 'Not every Frenchman has given up. There is de Gaulle in London.'

There was that name again. 'Who is he?'

'A dedicated soldier and an intelligent man,' Édouard explained. 'He was promoted to general only a short while before the defeat. He escaped to London and has called all those who wish to keep fighting for a free France to meet him there.'

'Well,' she said, remembering how the 'V' signs had uplifted her, 'if not all French people have given up, then neither should we.'

★

A few weeks later, Kristina and Yelena were in the garden pruning the roses. She had an urge to apologise to the plants for her inexpert hands, but she didn't want to lose this precious inheritance because they had been her father's pride and joy.

'*Bonjour*! Madame Bergeret!'

She looked up to see a young woman waving from the gate. She was smartly dressed in a nipped-waisted suit. Kristina wondered how she knew her name.

'*Bonjour*, mademoiselle,' she said, putting down her secateurs and approaching the gate. 'How may I help you?'

'I am Renée Masset, Inès Bonne's niece.'

'Yes!' Kristina said, opening the gate. 'How is she? I hope she's all right managing the gallery on her own?'

'My aunt is quite all right, although Paris is different,' Renée said with a slight shiver. 'It was right of Monsieur Lavertu to be wary about travelling there. It's almost impossible to come to the free zone. I only received special dispensation because I'm a dermatologist, deemed to be an essential service.' She reached into her purse and gave Kristina a letter. 'This is from my aunt to Monsieur Lavertu. I must return to Paris in three days' time. I'll come by here before I go and collect your reply.'

Kristina thanked Renée, and after she left, ran inside to show Serge the letter.

'From Inès?' he asked, putting down the screwdriver he'd been using to fix the frame of a painting.

'Come, let's sit in the library,' she told him.

They sat down in Mikhail's favourite overstuffed armchairs. Kristina folded her hands in her lap with nervous expectation. Serge's own hands trembled as he slipped the letter out of the envelope. Then he exhaled and read Inès's message.

Dear Monsieur Lavertu,
I hope that you and Madame Bergeret are in good health. Has there been any news of Monsieur Bergeret?

Here in Paris, the German soldiers are behaving with restraint. So far there hasn't been any trouble. They stand for the elderly on buses, step aside for women on the pavements, and address shopkeepers in polite – and often perfect – French. There are many here who are happy for their businesses. Signs reading 'German spoken here' are appearing everywhere. But

*the exchange rate between the franc and the Reichsmark means
everything the Germans buy is a bargain. Carloads of loud crass
Berliners arrive in Paris on the weekends to snap up everything
they can set their eyes upon. Several have knocked at the gallery
door, so I have put up a sign that we are closed for stocktake.
But I won't be able to keep that up for long before I am arrested
for being uncooperative with our occupiers.*

*Then yesterday, I had a visit from Monsieur La Farge.
He told me that all businesses owned by Jews will soon be
'Aryanised' as they were in Germany, and he made an offer to
buy everything in the gallery including the building. The gall of
the man! His offer was perhaps just over a third of the worth of
it. I reminded him that half the business is owned by Monsieur
Bergeret and that if he so wishes, Monsieur Lavertu could sell
his share of the business to his partner. Although he appeared to
concede to this, I was left with a lingering feeling that it is not
the last I will hear of the man.*

*Please advise me what you would like me to do. I can pack
up the rest of the paintings and put them in storage, or send them
to you in Nice — although I think there is a good chance they
would be stolen en route. For while the other galleries on Rue la
Boétie are doing a roaring trade with our occupiers, I cannot but
feel a bad storm is coming. The swastika hangs from every public
building, and each day we are subjected to the sight of German
soldiers parading in goosestep along the Champs-Élysées …*

Serge looked up at Kristina, a deep frown on his face. They
had already discussed the trouble that was brewing. Pétain had
only been in power for a month when the Vichy government
had begun imitating the draconian Nazi laws against Jews.
Those who had been naturalised recently were stripped of
their citizenship, while French-born Jews were ousted from

the army, civil service and universities. Ordinary people were losing their livelihoods and being plunged into poverty. Martin La Farge's warning that the gallery was under threat of being Aryanised soon was most likely true.

Kristina shared the sense of foreboding Inès had described. Serge's heritage hadn't been an issue before. He was a Frenchman just like any other Frenchman. Thinking about the German refugees who had poured into Paris after Hitler rose to power, she realised many of them had been just like Serge: non-religious people who had been considered normal citizens for decades. But that didn't stop the terror that had been unleashed on them.

'As long as Max remains a missing soldier or a prisoner of war, his business interests are in my hands,' she told Serge. 'But as I'm not French, I'm not sure how much longer that will be the case.'

Serge came and knelt before her. The pain in his eyes was heartbreaking. 'I'm losing everything,' he said. 'Max, and now the gallery.'

She held him to her. 'You haven't lost me or the girls, Serge. We'll get through this somehow. Max will come back, and de Gaulle will defeat the Nazis. Then life will be beautiful again, just as it was before.'

★

'Mama,' Nadia called, pulling her head back in from the upstairs window. 'Mademoiselle Masset has returned.'

Kristina had been busy letting down the hem on Nadia's best dress. She was growing so tall, like an ostrich. Kristina went to the window to see Renée at the gate. It was almost four months since she had taken their letter back to Paris, instructing

Inès to put everything in storage, and they had not heard from her in that time.

'Come in,' Kristina said, opening the front door for her. 'Would you like tea? We don't have real tea unfortunately, but we do have some dried linden leaves.'

'I can't stay,' Renée said. 'I'm meant to be in Menton by tomorrow. But my aunt said this letter is extremely important.'

'Thank you.'

Renée left and Kristina went searching through the house to find Serge. But he wasn't in the library or study.

'Serge!' she called, but when he didn't answer she couldn't restrain herself. She opened the letter. The first line made her heart sink.

The Gestapo came and took it all. Everything, not just the paintings, but all your furniture and that belonging to Monsieur and Madame Bergeret …

'It's bad news, isn't it?' asked Serge, appearing in the doorway. 'I can tell by your face.'

She read the rest of the letter out to him.

They said that as you are a Jew and have not been heard of for some time, they had a right to requisition everything as 'abandoned property'. I wanted to protest that you were in Nice, but then thought better of revealing your whereabouts. Instead, I made the argument that the Bergeret family were not Jewish and therefore they had no right to take their things. The man who was heading the requisition approached me menacingly and then struck me across the face. In all my life, I have never been hit by any man and the shock was as bad as the pain. After that I remained silent, because I knew that I had two things over them – I had already checked on the paintings at Wacker-Bondy's and added your favourite Monet and Signac to the collection, and, with no clients, I'd had the time to photograph and record your inventory. That catalogue is now safe inside your violin, which is hidden at the back of my mother's linen closet.

I am sorry I could not save your gallery and home. I believe that evil eventually burns itself out and one day France will be restored. I hope the catalogue will allow you legal claim on all that has been so wrongly taken from you. Until we meet again in happier times, please think of me always as a true and loyal friend.

Affectionately,

Inès Bonne

'Good, dear Inès,' said Serge. 'If ever I find that Nazi who struck her, I'll kill him with my bare hands.' He looked at Kristina. 'I'm sorry, because of me they have taken everything of yours and Max's too.'

'Because of you? No!' Kristina said. 'Because of the Nazis. They try to make everything look legal, but they are common thieves. What they have done to you they will do to the Wildenstein, Seligmann and Bernheim-Jeune galleries too. Only the Aryans like Martin La Farge will remain.'

★

It was a sorry little tart that Kristina and Yelena made for Ginette's birthday, but they did the best they could with the ever-decreasing rations. They had saved up the flour allocations to make a rather dry pastry – butter and vegetable oils being in short supply – which they hoped the jam created from the last of the apricots from the garden would improve.

Ginette, who loved to be the centre of attention, seemed content enough to have her family around her, but Kristina wondered what her young mind made of this strange new world where there was always fear in the atmosphere, and small pleasures like walking along the seaside were no longer possible. She could only hope whatever deprivations her children lived with, it would not be a lack of love and affection.

Since Max had been mobilised, Kristina had been given a small military allowance. Now they no longer had the gallery, she was trying to make it stretch to keep everyone fed. She had so many worries that concentrating on painting was near impossible. She spent most of her day lining up for food or ration cards. But even if she had been able to paint, modern art was considered degenerate by the Nazis and she couldn't hold an exhibition.

When her allowance didn't arrive one week, she assumed it was an administrative delay. She went to her father's library and stared at the Ilya Repin painting of Tolstoy he'd brought with him from Russia. Mikhail had treasured it, not only because the artwork was so finely rendered, but because both men had been his friends. 'Did you know it took Ilya ten years to paint that?' he would always say. The galleries and second-hand shops of Nice were full of beautiful paintings and objets d'art that the refugees had been forced to sell at bargain prices. It had been the same for the White Russians after the revolution.

'You're not going to sell your father's paintings,' Serge said firmly when she put the idea to him. 'If we run out of money, I'll sell the Matisse I've hidden away in the cellar first. It will fetch a good price.'

'I thought the Germans weren't buying degenerate art?'

'They aren't, but the French who can afford it are buying it by the truckload. Nobody trusts the currency anymore, so they're buying art as an investment. The French art market is raking in millions.'

Kristina considered the paintings that had been stolen from their gallery. Then she thought of Martin La Farge, who was flourishing while Serge was struggling. It was hard to believe there were people becoming millionaires by buying and selling art, while so many other French people were starving.

'You can't sell the Matisse either,' she said. 'You like it too much. That's why you have hung on to it for so long.'

Serge smiled whimsically. 'I'm an art dealer, Kristina. The paintings I like best are the ones I can sell.'

★

When her next payment did not arrive the following week either, Kristina went to the military office in town. There was a long queue, and she took a ticket and waited for an hour between a matronly woman and a young woman with a child. A clerk called her number, and she showed him her identity card and papers. Then she had to return to her seat. A moment later, the young woman was called up. She spoke to the clerk and then emitted a terrible shriek and crumpled to the ground. Two other women rushed to help her up.

'A death notice,' said the matronly woman, leaning closer to Kristina. 'They have been so slow to issue them. It's been torture. I don't know where my son is.'

Kristina murmured her sympathy, but when the matronly woman was called up, there was no news for her and she left. Kristina sat on the hard bench for another five hours. Her head began to throb and her mouth was so dry, her tongue felt like sandpaper. The other women came and went around her but she didn't dare leave.

As the crowd began to thin, an elegantly dressed woman sized her up from across the room and then stood and approached her. 'The allowance they pay is pathetic. How are we supposed to live? I've heard Paris is full of prostitutes now – respectable women trying to feed their families.'

Kristina didn't want to hear any more of what the woman had to say and was relieved when the clerk called her back to the counter. His face was harsh as he shoved her allowance notice back to her. Stamped across it in red was one word: Cancelled.

'What does it mean?' she asked, thinking of the woman who had received the death notice.

But the clerk dismissed her abruptly and waved to the next person to come to the counter. Dazed, she sat back down on the bench, her eyes searching the papers that had been handed back, but they gave no clues.

'If they suddenly cut off your allowance it means your husband has escaped from a German camp,' the elegantly dressed woman whispered to her.

'From a prisoner-of-war camp?' Kristina asked. 'But isn't it the duty of a soldier to try to escape if held captive?'

The woman nodded. 'Yes, in a normal war. But France is in bed with the Germans now. Your husband's escape would be seen as an act of treachery. The Germans want his labour.'

The woman's number was called and she stood up. 'Well, goodbye, madame,' she said. 'I wish you well.'

*

It was early morning and the air was still. Kristina and Serge left the house with the painting by Modigliani that Serge had brought from Paris, rolled and hidden in a suitcase. They were on their way to see a collector who had agreed to buy it at a good price. The bus arrived and they climbed on board, alighting a few stops from the Promenade des Anglais just as the sky was lightening to a magnificent silvery blue.

'Take my arm,' Kristina said to Serge.

She hadn't asked him for the comfort of his touch – they often walked arm in arm outside the house. Jews were forever being stopped and having their papers checked. Serge was not as well known in Nice as he was in Paris and had never practised any religion except the appreciation of art. He'd also been savvy enough not to register himself as of Jewish heritage with the Town Hall. But lately, the police had been dragging men off the street and forcing them to pull their trousers down. If they were circumcised, they were beaten and arrested. Because Kristina was so blonde and tall, she hoped that they'd be left alone if they were perceived as a couple.

'Where are you going so early?'

The policeman appeared out of nowhere. Kristina pressed herself closer to Serge.

'To the train station to visit my parents in Cagnes-sur-Mer,' she said.

'I wouldn't go anywhere today if I were you,' he said. 'Stay off the streets until after four o'clock and stay away from hotels.'

'Why, what's happening?' Serge asked, realising, as Kristina did, that the policeman was trying to warn them away for their own good rather than arrest them.

The sound of trucks rumbling along the Promenade broke the stillness of the air.

'Go!' he said.

They didn't wait a moment longer. They turned back in the direction of the bus stop as three open trucks, the type used to transport soldiers, roared by them and came to a stop outside a small narrow hotel. The door to the café opposite opened and a grey-haired woman beckoned to them.

'Get off the street!'

They bundled inside and she locked the door behind them, wiping her hands on her broad hips.

'It's a raid,' the woman said.

Peering from behind the lace curtains, the three of them watched as policemen in blue Vichy uniforms jumped out of the trucks. One of them, red-faced and thick-necked, pounded on the hotel's front door.

'Open up! Police!'

A strained minute passed before it was opened by a terrified-looking concierge hurriedly pulling her shawl around her shoulders.

'Monsieur, it is early ...'

But the woman had no chance to finish her sentence before the policeman roughly pushed her out of the way and stormed into the hotel. The others followed behind. The next moment there were shouts and the sounds of wood splintering and glass breaking.

Kristina's eyes travelled to the top floor. A young woman in a nightdress was climbing out a window. She placed one foot on the ledge and grabbed the sill to lift herself. At first, Kristina thought she intended to hide herself from the police on the narrow balcony. Although her attempt would have been futile, Kristina mentally urged her on, wondering how secure the drainpipe was and if the woman was strong enough to inch her way down it. But it seemed she had another intention. The woman closed her eyes tightly then opened them again. After a moment's hesitation she launched herself from the balcony. Her scream as she plummeted to the pavement below sent waves of horror through Kristina. She stared at the spot where the woman now lay, her eyes staring at the sky. Perhaps she was still alive and needed help? Kristina grabbed for the door, but Serge and the café owner pulled her back.

'There is nothing you can do for her now,' said the woman. Her tone was harsh, but her voice caught as she spoke. Her distress showed in her eyes.

The inhabitants of the hotel filed out, guarded on all sides by the police. The men had their hands on their heads and the women were clutching children. They were forced to clamber onto the backs of the trucks. An old man saw the body of the woman on the pavement and held his hands to his face before crying out. 'Monsters! You are monsters!'

If Serge and the café owner hadn't kept their hold of Kristina, she might have run out on the street and screamed curses at the police too. The misery on the faces of the captives reminded her of sheep she had seen on the back of farmers' trucks on the way to the slaughterhouse. They sensed they were doomed but they were powerless to do anything about it. The policemen took out a blanket and rolled the dead woman up in it, her bloodied hair protruding from the end. They threw her body on the last truck, under the feet of the people on it. Their action was so callous it left Kristina trembling. It was only after the trucks rumbled away that she realised she'd clenched Serge's arm so hard, he was bleeding through his shirt.

'I tried to warn them,' the café owner said, her voice low and despairing. 'Some of them listened and left yesterday. But the others ... they simply couldn't bring themselves to believe their own countrymen would do this to them.'

Kristina was still too shocked to react but Serge was instantly curious. 'How did you know there would be a raid?' he asked.

The woman fumbled in her sleeve for a handkerchief and dabbed her eyes. 'I heard it on the radio.'

'The BBC?' Serge asked.

The woman seemed to regret her unguarded confession. She looked from Serge to Kristina uncertainly. It was illegal to listen to the BBC and she could have been thrown in prison if they decided to report her. But Serge was quick to reassure her.

'You were brave to try to help the Jews,' he said with an earnestness that was disarming.

The woman shrugged off the praise. 'We must resist the Germans and we must resist the Vichy government.'

With the police and the trucks gone, the woman unlocked the door for them. But Kristina sensed her reluctance to let them leave. After witnessing such a distressing event together, a bond had formed between them.

'I won't open the café today,' the woman said. 'I only have chicory coffee to offer you, but I have some pastries that will go to waste if we don't eat them.'

Kristina and Serge followed her through a curtain and into a small kitchen. The walls were covered in travel posters and a rack was laden with well-worn copper pots and ladles, but the cabinets and shelves were almost empty, a testament that all foodstuffs were in short supply.

'What's in there?' she asked Serge, pointing to his suitcase.

'A canvas,' he said matter-of-factly. 'I sell paintings.'

'By who?'

Serge smiled kindly. 'Modigliani.'

The woman's eyebrows shot up. 'Modigliani! Why, he came here often when he was in Nice!' The ice broken, she nudged Serge with her elbow. 'I can tell you some stories. My name is Moira, by the way.'

Kristina and Serge introduced themselves and over the chicory coffee that Moira managed to make taste pleasantly nutty, and butter-less croissants, they listened to their hostess's lively stories.

'Modigliani wanted to paint me,' Moira said. 'But I always refused. He was talented but cruel to his models.'

Serge, usually reluctant to gossip, agreed with her. 'I'll never forgive his treatment of Jeanne Hébuterne,' he said, his brow furrowed. 'She was a loyal and kind woman. I have … I had one of her paintings in my possession. She was a very talented expressionist.'

As Kristina listened to Moira and Serge speak, her mind calmed, although the sadness from what she had witnessed remained. She rested her head on Serge's shoulder and shut her eyes, hoping when she opened them again it would be in a different world where young women didn't leap to their deaths to save themselves from worse horrors.

When it was time to leave, Moira went into the pantry and returned with a handful of pamphlets with the words 'Help the Jews' printed on them.

'Put them in your suitcase,' she told Serge. 'Leave them on bus seats and put them in letterboxes.'

Kristina wasn't quite sure if she was ready to be part of the Resistance. She had her mother and daughters to think about. But Serge accepted the pamphlets and put them in his suitcase.

'Come back soon,' Moira said as she waved them goodbye. 'The more of us who resist, the sooner the Germans will go.'

It was a sad and sombre town they walked through after wishing Moira goodbye. The streets were empty except for a few people scurrying in and out of doorways like nervous mice. The patrons of a restaurant they passed looked dazed. There was no friendly chatter between diners or clinking of glasses. The atmosphere was foreboding and Kristina and Serge spoke in muted tones.

'We'll leave the collector for another day,' he said. 'I don't think we should get the bus back either. It could be commandeered by the police.'

The journey on foot back to Mont Boron seemed to take longer than usual. Kristina's throat was parched, and her heels were raw from her shoes rubbing against them. Serge took her arm to help her up the hill. When they finally reached the villa, Yelena was standing at the gate, biting her thumbnail and looking on the verge of tears.

'I was beginning to think something had happened to you,' she said, her voice brittle with nerves. 'Come inside, quickly.'

'I'm sorry we're late. There was a raid in the town,' Kristina told her.

'I know,' she said. 'That's why I was so worried.'

But Kristina sensed her mother's distress was caused by more than their late return. If she hadn't heard Nadia and Ginette playing in the garden together, she would have panicked that something had happened to them.

'Mama, what is it?' she asked. 'You seem in a state.'

'The police raided the soup kitchen,' she said. 'It was terrible.' She lowered her eyes and her nostrils quivered slightly.

'Oh,' Kristina said, taking her hand and squeezing it. She'd forgotten it was Yelena's day at the kitchen.

'Come upstairs, there is something I need to show the both of you,' she said.

Yelena led them up the stairs to Mikhail's observatory. With so much on their hands with no servants, Kristina couldn't remember the last time any of them had gone there.

Yelena took a key from her pocket. Since when did she lock the room? She pushed open the door, and in the fading daylight, Kristina saw a dozen faces staring back at them. There were three women and one old man, but the rest were small children – the youngest, a girl, looked to be no more than two years old. They were so pale and bedraggled that for an odd moment, she thought she was staring at ghosts.

'One of the policemen turned a blind eye when I got these people out the back door,' Yelena said.

The group wore the same beaten expressions as the people Kristina had seen taken away on the trucks. Their humanity had been stripped from them. Yelena ushered Kristina and Serge into the room and picked up the little girl. She buried her face into Yelena's neck, terrified.

'Her mother thrust her into my arms and begged me to take care of her,' Yelena said. 'How could I refuse?' She nodded towards the people in the room. 'We must help them.'

Kristina balled her hands in her pockets and thought of Ginette and Nadia downstairs, barely able to conceive the strength – and desperation – of the woman who had entrusted her child to a stranger.

'It would be inhumane not to help these people,' agreed Serge, a note of determination in his voice. 'We have to help.'

Kristina's attention settled on a young woman who resembled her long-lost friend, Madeleine. She sat with her hands between her knees, prayer-like, and rocked back and forth. The bushy-eyebrowed old man next to her looked the same age as Kristina's father would have been if he was still alive. The others stared at her with pleading expressions, as if one word from her could save or condemn them.

She thought of the pamphlets Moira had thrust on them earlier, and her reluctance to take them. The horror was impossible to ignore any longer, no matter how frightened she felt. The stinging truth of it was etched on the faces of the people in front of her and it was not going to go away without action.

She looked at Serge then her mother, and nodded. They were part of the Resistance now. There would be no turning back.

CHAPTER EIGHTEEN

KRISTINA

Nice, June 1946

There were times since being liberated from the camp when Kristina left her body, and this was one of them. Only a moment before she had been sitting in a chair in what had been her father's observatory, while Eve Archer had paced the floor relating everything Serge Lavertu had told her about what had happened during the war.

'The Resistance?' Kristina had asked incredulously. 'We were in the Resistance?'

Everything that she knew about herself before her memory stopped in 1923 – and even more so of her mother – seemed to indicate that the courage required to stand up against the Germans during the war would have been beyond either of them. In the hospital in Switzerland where she had been sent to recuperate, she'd heard story after story of the most abject brutality. She'd only had to look at the scar on her head and her own skeletal body to believe them.

'Yes,' Eve said, looking out the windows towards the sea. 'That's why you were sent to the camp. Someone betrayed you.'

Kristina knew she lived in the body of a woman who had been a mother. She could feel her daughters, but she couldn't remember their faces or voices. Lorenzo had told her things about Nadia and Ginette, but with great reluctance for fear of distressing her. But the love was strangely still there, the deepest love of a mother who cannot lose the connection to her children.

A terrible thought occurred to her.

'Is that why the Nazis—'

Then *whoosh!* Kristina was out of her body and across the other side of the room, observing her physical self still sitting in the chair. It was a terrifying sensation, as if time was all happening at once and the world was spinning. Although each experience frightened her, Docteur Gabriel had assured her it wasn't an entirely unusual phenomena. 'Especially in those who have sustained head injuries or suffered great traumas. It sometimes occurs right before they remember something too devastating to recall. The American writer Ernest Hemingway wrote about his own experiences of this after suffering mental distress from shellfire in the Great War.'

'Possibly,' Eve was saying, still with her back towards the physical Kristina who was staring blank-eyed in front of her. 'Serge didn't say anything about it.'

As Eve continued to speak, the disembodied Kristina remembered the time when she had thought there was no point to living anymore. She had lost everything and was only a burden to Lorenzo, who should have been living his twilight years in peace. One evening at sunset, she'd gone to the rooftop terrace and stood at the corner where it overlooked the side of a sheer cliff. All she had to do was step out and all her troubles would cease. But something – or someone – had pulled her back. She'd heard a female voice whisper, 'No, it's not your time, Kristina. You still have things to do.'

After that experience, she'd wondered if it had been an angel that had spoken to her. At the time she thought perhaps the angel had meant that she still had a masterpiece to paint and that her life's work was not yet finished. But now as she watched the distressed Eve pacing, she believed that perhaps the sole purpose left to her was to save Serge Lavertu. Maybe it was possible that in this disembodied state, rather than in her physical body with its damaged brain, she could find the past again.

But then Eve turned around and saw that Kristina wasn't moving and let out a cry.

'Madame Bergeret!' she screamed and shook Kristina's shoulder desperately.

Kristina heard Lorenzo's footsteps lumbering up the stairs.

I must go back now, she thought. *I'm scaring her.*

Then *whoosh!* Kristina was back in her body staring out at the concerned faces of Eve and Lorenzo. She was panting and weeping. She felt nauseous and the pain in her head felt like she was being suffocated.

'It happens sometimes,' Lorenzo told Eve. 'Docteur Gabriel says that when she has one of these seizures, she must have nothing but bed rest for at least a day.'

After bringing her water and letting her catch her breath, and seeing she was too weak to move, Lorenzo and Eve brought up a mattress for her. Then they carted up another mattress, and Kristina understood that Eve intended to watch over her.

The young woman placed a cool compress on Kristina's forehead. 'I'm sorry,' she said. 'I didn't mean to cause you harm. I didn't know you had seizures.'

The past is somewhere, Kristina tried to say, but she couldn't get the words out. Her tongue felt thick. She must have bitten it.

Her whole body felt heavy and she was starting to drift into sleep. As her eyelids fluttered, it was no longer Eve watching her. It was Max. But he wasn't the fresh-faced Max she remembered. He was older. Harder.

'What happened?' she asked him. 'What happened to you and our daughters?'

CHAPTER NINETEEN

KRISTINA

Nice, November 1942

'It's like a dream,' whispered Gretel, one of the refugees Kristina was sheltering at the villa. They were carrying their baskets of black-market potatoes and leeks from the Gambetta district.

Kristina understood what she meant. The Promenade des Anglais had been renamed the 'Avenue de la Victoire' by the occupying Italians, but exactly whose 'victory' was being referred to wasn't quite certain. They passed people who only a few months ago had been forced to wear a yellow star, but were now lounging in deckchairs and enjoying the view of the Mediterranean. The cafés too were full of Jewish refugees. Children in Judaic school uniforms walked freely in the street and a new cultural centre had been opened. The Jewish community in Nice was flourishing again, while in every other part of France it was being annihilated.

'Yesterday, I went to the synagogue with Ruth,' Gretel continued. 'And there were Carabinieri outside of it. I froze, thinking we were about to be arrested, but they were there to make sure nobody harassed *us*.'

'Well, we have *something* to thank Mussolini for,' Kristina said. 'If we're going to be occupied by one of the Axis countries, then let it be the Italians.'

They turned a corner and nearly ran into a bridal party on their way to a wedding.

'*Mazel Tov*,' Gretel said, wishing the bride good luck. Then she turned to Kristina. 'The Italians are even marrying Jewish girls. Hitler must be fuming.'

A loud wolf-whistle sounded in Kristina's direction. She turned to see a group of Italian soldiers eyeballing her. '*Sei bellissima!*' one of them shouted. 'Are you free tonight?'

She turned away and she and Gretel walked on. 'They are like undisciplined schoolboys,' Kristina said. 'With those smooth olive complexions and big dark eyes, they should be at home with their mamas, not fighting a war. When I need to bribe one of them to look the other way, I only have to offer him a bottle of perfume. They must bathe themselves in the stuff. The whole city smells of Pour Un Homme de Caron.'

'Perhaps Ruth and I should stay,' Gretel said. 'We have already fled one country. Why should we flee another?'

Kristina stopped and looked at Gretel firmly. 'Hitler let Mussolini have Nice on the condition he enforce anti-Jewish laws, which the Italians have not done. Now the success of the Allies changes everything. Mussolini will side with whoever he thinks is going to win, and if Italy changes sides, the Germans will swarm in with a vengeance. This situation is unstable and we need to get you both to Switzerland as soon as we can.'

Gretel's face pinched at the harshness of her tone, but Kristina couldn't allow her to be lulled into a false sense of security. She didn't tell her that the Italians were no angels — there was a dark side to their occupation too. The OVRA was as brutal as the German Gestapo. She'd heard through her contacts at the mayor's office that the British and de Gaulle had been sending in agents to train the French Maquis in sabotage. The railway lines and stations on the Côte d'Azur were constantly being blown up by the Resistance. The Italians hunted the agents down and tortured them. Outside their interrogation centre hung a sign with an ominous quote from Dante's *Inferno*: *Abandon all hope ye who enter.*

They reached Moira's café and took their baskets to the kitchen. Moira eagerly turned them upside down to divide the produce between the three safe houses she was helping.

'Is this all you could get?' she asked, disappointed. 'Those bottom-pinching *macaronis* might be helping us smuggle people out but they aren't doing anything to prevent us from starving. They stole my tomatoes, those *bastardi*! I went out to the vegetable garden this morning and the vines have been stripped bare!'

'I'm going to the countryside tomorrow to try and get some olives and beans,' Kristina told her.

Gretel sighed. 'After this war is over, I'm never going to eat another turnip.'

Kristina sat down in a chair feeling like a withered flower. She spent so much of her life looking for food, she even dreamed about it. It was true they had a powerful man in Nice helping with their operation – a dynamic Italian Jewish businessman named Angelo Donati. But while he could help with bribes, transport and forged papers, he couldn't produce food where there was none to be had.

'The night we heard on the BBC that the Allies had taken North Africa, I thought, at last there will be food!' said Moira. 'I didn't realise it meant we would be cut off from wheat and vegetable oil and just about everything else.'

'The quality of French bread has plummeted to the point where if I wasn't starving, I wouldn't touch it,' Gretel said. 'It is being filled out with who-knows-what and smells like a swamp. If you buy it in the morning it's putrid by the afternoon.'

'I miss Russian Borodinsky bread,' Kristina sighed, remembering the malty rye dough sweet with molasses and coriander. 'If we had a loaf of that we could survive for a week on it.'

Moira looked her up and down. 'Kristina, you are *too* thin. Are you not eating at all? How is your mother?'

Kristina's heart pinched. Yelena was dying. Her doctor had warned her to prepare herself.

'She fades a little more every day, but helping the Jewish people gives her an interest in life. Every so often she perks up and seems like her old self again. Sometimes I find her at the stove trying to create something edible out of the few ingredients we have, or reading to the Jewish orphans we're sheltering.' Kristina's voice caught in her throat. 'In those moments I can almost convince myself that my mother is going to live forever.'

Gretel rubbed Kristina's arm. She had been a nurse in the Great War and helped Kristina bathe her mother when Yelena didn't have the strength to do it for herself.

'It's life, my dear,' said Moira, patting Kristina's hand. 'You still have your daughters.'

Kristina blinked away her tears. 'At least the "sweet little mouse" still comes to visit,' she said. 'This time she left malt syrup on my doorstep.'

For the past few months, weekly packages of vitamin supplements and cans of food – impossible to get in France – had been placed on the doorstep of the villa.

'I wonder who it is,' said Moira. 'A friend of your mother's?'

Kristina shook her head. 'If it was a friend, why not simply give it to me? The maple syrup was from England and a brand you can't get in France. Besides, whoever it is, they are scaling the gate to put it on the doorstep.'

'It must be someone who knows all that you are doing to help people and that your mother is dying,' said Gretel. 'A member of the British Resistance perhaps?'

She thought about that sign outside the OVRA interrogation centre. *Abandon all hope ye who enter.*

'I hope not,' she said. 'That would put us all in grave danger.'

★

Gretel stayed to help Moira, and Kristina returned to the villa. She was surprised to find a black car parked out the front with a chauffeur leaning against it. Who had a car, let alone a chauffeur these days? Although the Italian occupation reduced the chances of Vichy raids, they still weren't unheard of. Kristina raced into the house and was relieved to find it calm and quiet. That meant all their 'guests' had gone into hiding. She walked into the drawing room, and to her surprise saw Serge sitting there with a woman dressed in an elegant silk suit.

Serge rose from his chair when he saw her. 'Kristina, look who's here.'

The woman stood, and Kristina blinked. It was Sonia. Her skin was luminous with none of the pallor of someone suffering wartime deprivations. She was more beautiful than she had ever been.

'Sonia!'

They embraced. Sonia smelled like a bouquet of iris. On the table was a tray of tea that emitted such a delectable aroma that Kristina assumed Sonia must have brought it with her.

'Look at you,' Kristina said as they sat down on the sofa together. 'You look marvellous!'

Sonia smiled and reached into a bag beside her, producing a presentation set of Chanel perfumes for Kristina. 'And I brought these for Ginette and Nadia,' she said, opening up some packages wrapped in tissue paper and holding them out. They were undervests made of such fine wool they felt like silk to touch.

'These are beautiful. Thank you,' Kristina said, before the realisation came to her. Sonia must have kept her Paris store open – that meant she was trading with the Germans. Her stomach tied itself in knots. Of course, that explained how well she looked and her beautiful clothes. Kristina quickly put down the gifts on the table in front of her.

Sonia noticed but didn't remark on it. 'I saw that the gallery has been sold and I had to come and see you. I didn't expect to find Serge here as well. He tells me that you haven't heard anything from Max.'

Sonia's voice conveyed genuine concern, but Kristina couldn't meet her eyes. They used to be such good companions when they were younger, in those days when every evening started with drinks at La Rotonde. But something in the pit of Kristina's stomach told her she could not trust her friend now.

Sonia was watching her carefully. 'Nothing at all?'

'Why didn't you expect to see Serge?' Kristina asked.

'Because she thought I'd be in New York to avoid … all the *trouble*,' Serge said lightly. 'But I told Sonia that I promised to look after you and the girls and that's why I'm here.'

Kristina realised that he sensed something was wrong too, but he was playing the game better than her.

'How are Édouard and Beatrice Fould?' Sonia asked her.

'Like everyone else. Under strain,' Kristina replied.

'They'll have to sell their art collection, of course.'

Kristina knew that Sonia had never liked the Foulds. Was she gloating – or was there something else behind her question? 'You mean before it's stolen by the Germans?' she said, irritably. 'Like the paintings in our gallery were?'

Serge sent Kristina a warning look. But she was tired and hungry, and worried about her family. She had no patience for whatever game Sonia was playing.

Sonia's mouth pinched. 'You are judging me, aren't you, Kristina? You think less of me because I'm still doing business in Paris. You forget that I employ fifty women in my company who might otherwise be left destitute if I closed. Do you think I should toss them out to earn money as prostitutes? I have my own mother to take care of, and quite frankly I refuse to throw away everything I've worked for simply because the French government opened the doors for the Germans to occupy the country.'

'I don't judge you,' Kristina lied. 'I think we're all doing the best we can.'

'Kristina's tired,' said Serge. 'Yelena hasn't been well, and the strain of not knowing where Max is has taken its toll on her. Of course, there is no harm in selling furniture and home decorations to the Germans. For goodness sake, you're not peddling weapons or *spying* for the occupiers.'

He laughed warmly and, after a moment's hesitation, Sonia did too.

'Well, I'd better get going,' she said. 'I've borrowed the chauffeur and car from a client who wants me to do up her holiday house. But I wanted to take the opportunity to see you first.'

'We are glad you came,' said Serge.

Sonia turned to Kristina and her voice had a slight edge to it. 'I haven't forgotten that your father was generous to my mother and me for many years,' she said. 'You can always come to me for help if you need it.'

Kristina needed help. But not from Sonia.

Seeing that Kristina was on the verge of saying something that would inflame the situation, Serge took Sonia by the arm. 'It's been wonderful to see you again,' he said.

After Sonia drove away, Kristina turned to Serge. 'You think she was spying on us with those questions about Max?'

'Yes.'

'Why?'

'I don't know, but I think on this occasion it might have been just as well that we don't have a clue where he is.'

★

'Mama!'

Kristina blinked open her eyes. Nadia was standing next to her bed, the winter morning light giving her skin a silvery glow. The burgundy silk-velvet opera coat she was wearing accentuated her willowy elegance. For a fleeting moment, Kristina thought she was *Snegurka*, the snow-maiden of the fairy tales her mother used to read to her when she was a child.

'What is it, darling?' she asked, struggling to raise herself.

Without enough fuel for heating, the villa was icy cold. The unusually bitter winter was taking everyone who did not have the strength to resist it. The funeral parlours in Nice were churning out coffins in all sizes. The smallest ones were displayed in the windows as if they were gift boxes. The refugees staying at the villa went about in cushion covers, tablecloths, even Afghan blankets that had formerly been wall hangings. When everyone wandered down to the dining room for meals, they resembled a bizarre fantasy play where the household furnishings had come to life.

Kristina peered more closely at Nadia through the gloom. Her trembling lips and wide eyes could mean only one thing.

'Grandmama?' she asked, her voice catching.

Nadia nodded, and the panic that ran through Kristina gave her the strength to free herself from the igloo of cushions she used to insulate herself. 'Is she still breathing?' she asked, standing up.

'Just.'

Serge and Nadia had taken turns with Kristina in watching over Yelena during the night for the past few weeks, ever since she had lost the use of her legs and become bedridden. They had been warned another stroke could be imminent. For weeks, Kristina had known this moment was coming. Gretel had explained the death process to her before she'd left for Switzerland. Kristina thought she was prepared. She was sure that God would give her the strength to face it. But now her legs were like jelly as she followed Nadia down the hallway to her mother's room.

Lying in her bed, Yelena was swaddled like an Egyptian mummy. Despite her illness her face was regal and beautiful. Kristina sat down next to the bed and tenderly touched her mother's forehead. Nadia was right, her breathing was faint, and for a moment Kristina thought she'd already expired.

'Mama?'

Yelena's eyes fluttered open and she turned to her. Kristina knew it was selfish, but she needed to be alone with her mother. She touched the hot water bottle by Yelena's feet.

'Could you boil some more hot water for Grandmama, darling?' she asked Nadia.

When Nadia went to complete the task, Kristina took her mother's bony hand from under the coverings and gently caressed it.

'My beautiful daughter,' Yelena whispered, her voice full of infinite love. 'There is something I want to tell you.'

'Yes, Mama?'

'Max might not come back, and he would understand if you and Serge were to be married. He'd make a good husband and a good father. Life is too hard to bear it all alone.'

Kristina lowered her eyes. Why was her mother saying this now? It seemed everyone had assumed there was more between her and Serge than friendship, even her own mother.

'Mama …' she started to say, but Yelena took a sudden deep breath. A flash of anguish crossed her face and a rattling sound rose in her throat. Kristina squeezed her hand tightly. There had been many times when she had wished her mother's suffering might be shortened, but now the moment of farewell was imminent, she had an urge to beg her not to go. The sound stopped and Yelena's chest collapsed as the air – and her life – rushed out of her. She sank into utter stillness, her eyes half-closed as if she were dreaming.

'I love you, Mama,' Kristina said, closing her mother's eyes gently. She stared at her mother's peaceful face, feeling too bereft and exhausted to even cry.

*

They buried Yelena next to Mikhail in the Russian Orthodox cemetery on the hill of Caucade. Kristina clung to her shawl as it flapped about her in the strong sea breeze, sounding like a sail in her ears. Ginette looked up at her. Her daughter's baby face was gone; her expression was fixed and serious. Kristina glanced at Nadia and recalled her beautiful voice when she had sung at the service. It was angelic, like the heavens had opened. When had Nadia learned to sing so exquisitely? Kristina had been so busy finding food for everyone, obtaining papers and caring for her ailing mother, that she had failed to notice her own daughters were changing. Yelena had been there for them the past year far more often than she had. Now Yelena was gone, Kristina knew she would have to be a better mother, but had no idea where she would find the strength.

As the priest sang prayers and waved his incense burner over the grave, her eyes travelled to the view of the Mediterranean and the city below, so quiet from this height. From a few metres away, she saw something move out of the corner of her eye. She squinted. A man in a dark suit stood half-hidden behind an olive tree. *It couldn't be!*

'Max!' she gasped.

Serge glanced at her, as if he thought she had uttered her husband's name out of grief. He wrapped his arm around hers to give her comfort.

'It's Max, over there, can't you see?' she whispered.

She broke away from him and went running in the direction of the olive tree, but Max disappeared like a mirage. She surveyed the cemetery, peering at the crumbling headstones with their Orthodox crosses and statues of angels. There were so many places to disappear into the shadows behind the mausoleums and orange tree groves.

'Max!' she called.

For a moment she thought she was hallucinating. Then she heard footsteps on gravel.

'Max! Why are you hiding from me?'

She spun around but there were no more sounds, only the wail of the wind and Serge's footsteps as he caught up to her.

'Kristina,' he said, his voice full of concern.

'It was Max. I'm telling you,' she said. 'He was here, watching us.'

★

At the wake, people handed Kristina cups of mint tea and whispered among themselves about the strain she had been under. But she knew her own husband when she saw him.

'Maybe it *was* Max ... or his spirit at least,' suggested Moira when the mourners were gone and she and Kristina were alone cleaning the dishes in the kitchen together. 'Sometimes the dead visit when they sense we need them. I felt my husband get into bed and curl up beside me for many years after he died.'

Max wasn't dead, Kristina was certain of that now. She wondered how long he had been watching them. He'd come to the funeral to pay his respects. She was also sure now that it had been Max leaving the parcels on the doorstep when Yelena was ill. She also believed she knew the reason the French government had stopped paying her army wives' allowance. Max had escaped the prisoner-of-war camp and gone to London to join de Gaulle with the other Frenchmen who had refused to accept the armistice. But he was back in France now at the same time as the Allies were stepping up their sabotage activities, and the Italians were cracking down mercilessly on them.

Oh god, Max please be careful, she thought.

★

After that day at the cemetery, Kristina looked for Max everywhere. There were times when she thought she'd spotted him slipping out the back door of a café just as she arrived, or vanishing into a crowd a few metres in front of her. Once she thought he'd brushed past her when she was waiting in line for ration stamps. *Max!* She'd lost the place she'd been holding for two hours to run after him. She turned the corner where he had gone only to discover an empty laneway. She dreamed of him too. She'd see him up ahead of her on the Promenade and would run up to him and touch his shoulder. He'd turn and smile when he recognised her, reaching for her and telling her that he loved her and that they'd be together – a proper family again – as soon as the wretched war was over. When she woke up after those dreams, she was filled with two contradictory feelings – peace and uneasiness.

She left a letter for him on the doorstep each night in the same place where the packages for Yelena had appeared. She'd rush downstairs at the break of light to see if it had been collected, and her heart would shatter all over again when she saw that it was still there.

'I believe you, Kristina, when you say you saw Max,' Serge told her one morning when he found her holding her letter in the garden and crying. 'But you must stop waiting for him. He has important work to do and so do you. If he hasn't revealed himself to us, then there is a reason for it.'

She took Serge's hand, and they sat together on the garden bench.

'I feel a terrible dread in my stomach,' she told him. 'Bastille Day was such a show of strength by the Niçoise. But things with the Italians have turned grim.'

On Bastille Day a crowd of people, including young children, had marched to Place Masséna, singing 'La Marseillaise' and waving tricoloured flags. It was a carnival-like atmosphere not seen since before the war. People fearlessly shouted 'Vive de Gaulle' and 'Down with Vichy and Hitler'. The Italian soldiers were armed but did little to restore public order. Kristina had felt that the war was petering out then and she had allowed herself to feel hopeful again.

'What's happened?' Serge asked. 'What have you heard?'

She winced as she told him. 'Moira sent word that the mayor has been forced to stand down and hundreds of resisters have been rounded up.'

Serge's face fell. 'It's a disaster. We must be very careful then,' he said.

'There is more,' she told him. 'According to the underground, four men acting as spies for de Gaulle and the British have been arrested by OVRA. What if Max is one of them?' she asked, squeezing his hand tighter. 'I can't bear to think what he might be suffering.'

★

With the raids and arrests, it would have been wiser to have stayed at home. Kristina didn't dare ring Moira in case the telephone had been tapped. But she couldn't settle her racing mind. Finally, she took an old bicycle from the garage and rode towards town. She was taking her life into her hands riding the rusty contraption downhill. The tyres had been repaired so many times, they had more puncture patches on them than rubber. But before she could reach the outskirts of the city, she was stopped by an Italian soldier.

'Papers please, signora.'

She hardly ever got asked for her papers, but she promptly produced them. While the soldier perused them, she looked past him to see that the streets had been barricaded. A transport of long-range guns was moving through and there were soldiers unrolling barbed wire on the beach. She knew better than to show too much curiosity about what was happening.

But after the soldier gave her papers back and waved her towards a detour, a woman bumped into her shoulder. '*Pardon*,' she said, and then whispered, 'The Resistance blew up the railway depot. The Germans can't move their troops.'

The war, which had been kept away from Nice for almost a year, was coming close again. With the tension in the air, Kristina decided it wasn't worth taking the risk of drawing attention to Moira. She went to the Russian Orthodox church instead. It was a little piece of Russia on French soil, with its six gilded domes and coloured ceramics. Her parents had helped fund its construction. Inside the carved wooden interior, with its icons and flower frescoes, she felt serene, which was unexpected because she'd been feeling so fraught only a few moments earlier. She lit a candle for Max and then prayed with all her heart.

Please bring my husband, and my children's father, safely home to me.

*

Moira warned Kristina not to become attached to the people who she sheltered at the villa, but that was impossible for her, especially the children. One evening the following summer as she and the others sat together in the dining room, the doors and windows shut despite the stifling heat, she found herself looking at the refugee children with a deep sense of love. There was Hermine and Joséphine, the ten-year-old twins whose mother had never come home from work; Herschel, who had been smuggled by an escape line to Nice after his German-Jewish parents had been rounded up in Paris; and the youngest, six-year-old Aline from Belgium, who often asked Kristina when her mother was coming to collect her. They were all brave children but if one of them started crying from homesickness, then it brought a waterfall of tears from the others, which Serge, Nadia and Kristina would do their best to comfort.

But sometimes, after they had settled the children down, they themselves would have to retreat to various corners of the villa to weep. How could humans be capable of inflicting such horror on each other? Kristina wanted to wrap each of the children in her arms and keep them safe forever, but she knew the day would come when she would have to entrust them to others further along the escape line so they would have some chance at survival. Just as with the others who had stayed at the villa, they would have to leave, and she wouldn't hear any more news of them. Then more children – and perhaps some adults – would be sent and Kristina would become attached to those new ones as well, and the cycle of worry and loss would begin again.

They had just finished their dessert – an unusual treat of cream of wheat with raisins – when a massive boom sounded in the sky followed by a series of crackles.

'What was that?' asked Nadia, her eyes wide with fear.

Serge ran to peer out the blackout curtain, while everyone else looked to Kristina for the command. She had been drilling the children for weeks. 'Police!' meant they were to scatter and disappear behind the secret walls Serge had installed. 'Air raid!' meant everybody had to run to the cellar where the walls had been reinforced with sandbags. But the sound coming from outside was neither the police nor an air raid. It sounded like firecrackers and flares.

'The Italians!' said Serge. 'They are celebrating.'

Kristina's mind raced, wondering what they were celebrating. An Italian holiday? The end of the war? What?

'Go to the observatory,' she said to the children, including Ginette, whose eyes were bright with excitement at the idea of fireworks. 'You can watch from the windows. But you must do everything Nadia tells you to.'

Kristina and Serge ran to the garage. At an exorbitant price, they'd managed to buy an old Peugeot with a charcoal gasifier fixed to it now gasoline was impossible to obtain. It was slow but when they had to move people about, it was faster than going on foot. As they drove into the city, they could see the bars and cafés were full of Italian soldiers. A group of them crossed their path, dancing the tarantella, while another stood on the side of the road singing 'O Sole Mio'.

Kristina wound down the window and called to him. 'What's happened?'

'*Mussolini è finito!* Mussolini has been voted out by the Grand Council.'

'What does that mean?' she asked him. 'Are the Italians going to continue fighting with a different leader?'

But the soldier only shrugged his shoulders. Serge parked the car and they got out and hurried towards the Promenade, stopping soldiers along the way to ask them whether they were staying or leaving. One of the soldiers grabbed Kristina's waist and twirled her in a dance. 'It means I'm going home to my wife and children! I'm going back to my village!'

Kristina looked to Serge. If they didn't have the Germans on their doorstep, it would have been good news for everybody.

'We'd better get back to the house,' he said, 'and start making plans to get the children out of Nice immediately.'

CHAPTER TWENTY

EVE

Paris, June 1946

Georges slipped the guard a few notes to give us extra time to
speak with Serge. Then he came back and sat next to me.

'So, Monsieur Lavertu, you say that you were part of the
Resistance? Unfortunately, all of France claims that they were in
the Resistance, even the worst of collaborators. Who is there to
vouch for you? We have limited time to put together our case and
it seems those you helped came and went under false names and
who knows where they are now – or if they are still alive? What's
most useful for our case is your claim that the painting you sold
was a forgery, and you knew it to be such when you offered it
to Hitler's art dealer. While that doesn't automatically negate the
murder charge, it does cast some doubt on the prosecutor's case.
Most likely the police had an art expert examine the painting
first before a judge approved the warrant for your arrest.'

'Was that expert's name Martin La Farge, by any chance?'
asked Serge. 'The man who stole our gallery and won't give it
back?'

'Are you saying you have enemies who might wish to frame
you?' asked Georges.

Serge sighed. 'The art world is vicious. I am the only dealer who fought with the Maquis, I had my art stolen by other dealers, including Martin La Farge, and can prove it, and I am a Jew.'

'Very well,' said Georges. 'I'll see if I can persuade the judge to give us more time. I need you to tell me everything you remember about the circumstances of the forgery. I'll ask Eve to write your testimony down. Let's start with who painted the fake Botticelli.'

'Kristina Bergeret did,' said Serge. 'But she had artistic qualms about copying another artist's work. So she included in it, and other paintings she forged, what she called a "time bomb" – a clue that only she would be able to reveal after the war to prove the paintings were fakes.'

'Well, then she will be able to vouch for you!' I said, feeling suddenly more hopeful. 'And she will be able to support your claim of having been involved in the Resistance.' I turned to Georges. 'We think Kristina is in Nice. I'll send a telegram to her today and if she responds, I can go there straightaway.'

He nodded. 'Yes, I think that is wise.' Then he scribbled in his notebook before passing it to me. He had written:

Listen to this story very carefully. When you see Madame Bergeret, her version of events must match Serge Lavertu's. If she has a very different recollection of events we can't use her as a witness.

289

CHAPTER TWENTY-ONE

KRISTINA

Nice, August 1943

Kristina answered the telephone to find Moira on the line. 'Come straightaway. A new supply of coffee is here,' she said, sounding unusually breathless. 'I don't know how long it will last.'

'Coffee' was their codename for Angelo Donati's Resistance contact from the Town Hall. They never used real names over the telephone line, well aware that operators were in the employ of the enemy to listen in on calls.

'I'll be right there,' Kristina told her. 'I don't want you to run out.'

Vittorio Melato was a kind-looking man who before the war had been a popular city official. But from the haggardness of his face, it was clear that this was not a meeting for pleasure.

'I don't need to tell you, Madame Bergeret, that the situation in Nice is now grave,' he said, when Kristina entered Moira's kitchen. 'The Gestapo are already here, preparing the way for the Germans to occupy us, and when they do there will be round-ups. With the Germans losing the war, the raids have grown even more vicious. We have heard stories of them bashing babies to death in front of their mothers.'

'Will they never give up?' Kristina exclaimed, anger burning in her blood. 'They have no chance of winning the war now. Why not surrender and spare millions of lives, including their own?'

'Hitler is insane and will not surrender,' said Vittorio. 'He will fight to the very last German. But I do have some good news. Signor Donati has pulled off an incredible feat. The Italians have agreed to allow Jews safe passage through Italy and then on to Africa. We have secured four transport ships. The British and Americans have promised naval and aerial protection. Instead of saving handfuls of people at a time, the escape line will now be able to undertake a mass evacuation.'

'That is a miracle!' Kristina cried. 'Signor Donati should be made a living saint.'

Vittorio laughed. 'He has been a light for us all. He is in Rome now, making the final arrangements. Until then we must get everyone ready. We have five thousand passports printed so far and the mayor's office is burning the Jewish registration papers the Vichy government forced people to submit at the start of the war.'

'I know you have your hands full, Kristina,' Moira said, 'but can you squeeze in some more people at the villa? We are bringing in refugees from the countryside to have them ready to leave from Nice.'

'How many?'

'Five adults.'

Kristina's resources were stretched to the limit, and each extra person added to the risk of discovery for everybody. But how could she refuse at such a crucial time?

'Yes, I can manage that for a short time,' she said.

Vittorio sighed. 'And I must burden your generosity with another request too, Madame Bergeret, this one from French intelligence in London. The Maquis has picked up two of de Gaulle's agents. One has been sent back to Britain but the other is too badly injured to be moved. He was shot escaping from Italian custody. A Resistance doctor performed surgery on his wounds, but he can't be left at the hospital where the Gestapo would be sure to find him. He needs somewhere to convalesce.'

A tiny glimmer of hope flared in Kristina's heart. 'One of de Gaulle's agents, did you say? What is his name?'

'Philippe Delphy.'

So not Max then. She turned away to hide her disappointment. 'Of course we will help. You've done so much to help us.'

★

At one o'clock in the morning a car arrived with its headlights off. Two men in dark suits got out. Kristina and Serge watched, hidden in the garden, as the men helped a third man out of the back seat. He couldn't stand on his own and they had to hold him upright. They got him only as far as the gate before he collapsed in a faint. Kristina stood up, intending to go and help. Serge pulled her down again.

'Wait,' he whispered. 'The pass phrase.'

He was right. The men could be from the Gestapo and this could be a trap. They couldn't trust anybody.

Serge approached the men and Kristina heard the pass phrase: 'We've taken a wrong turn. Can we stay here for the night?' When the men lifted the agent, he gave out a muffled cry of pain. One of the men went back to the car and got a blanket. They lay the injured man on it and they all carried him into the house. When Kristina went inside, they were lifting him upstairs to the bedroom she'd prepared – the room she had once shared with Max but couldn't bear to be alone in now. The journey was difficult and slow. When the men turned the corner of the first landing, the injured man gave another stifled cry. Kristina began to wonder whether she was up to taking care of someone so badly injured. Dealing with her mother's last few weeks had been difficult. But what choice was there? This man had sacrificed so much, they had to help him.

Upstairs, the men laid the agent on the bed. He murmured something incomprehensible.

'Do you have something for his pain?' Kristina asked.

One of the men reached into his pocket and took out a handful of vials, which he pressed into her palm. 'He's had surgery, but only give him the morphine if the pain is unbearable,' he said. 'The other medicine is penicillin. It's as hard to come by as hen's teeth but infection is a greater danger to him than pain. If anything goes wrong, call this number. You need to memorise it. We don't write anything down.'

As she committed the number to memory, the seriousness of the situation weighed on her. To be caught hiding one of de Gaulle's agents would most certainly result in torture and a gruesome death.

'*Bonne chance*,' the men said to their colleague, and then without another word they left. Serge went to see them out.

The injured agent groaned again. Examining him in the dim lamplight, Kristina could see he'd been beaten badly. His eyes were no more than slits in his black and blue face. She thought of Max and prayed that if someone discovered him in a similar condition, that they, too, would risk everything to help him.

'We won't let anything bad happen to you,' Kristina whispered. 'We are here to help.'

He reached out a trembling hand and squeezed her fingers. '*Merci*,' he said, in a faint, almost imperceptible, voice.

Kristina dipped a cloth into the water bowl beside his bed and squeezed some drops into his mouth. Her eyelids started to droop from exhaustion.

Serge returned. 'We can't do anything more right now for him than let him rest,' he said. 'You'd best go to bed, Kristina, and we will see how things are in the morning.'

★

When Kristina opened her eyes at dawn, her first thoughts were about the injured agent. She hadn't been able to see the true extent of the man's injuries by lamplight. She had an ominous feeling that he may have perished overnight and she would find him stiff and cold in the bed. She went to the room where the agent was and gingerly pushed open the door. To her surprise, the man was sitting up and looking around the room.

'What miracle is this?' he was mumbling to himself. 'I'm home.'

Kristina's pulse quickened. She flushed hot then cold.

'Max?'

He turned to look at her. Although his bruised face was still unrecognisable, even in daylight, his smile was unmistakable. 'Last night I thought I was dreaming,' he said. 'But it's true. I'm home.'

Her heart exploded with a joy that had no words. She knelt down beside him and took his hand, staring at him in wonder. It was as if she had been sitting in the dark and someone had flicked on the light and startled her. When her voice returned, she managed to stutter, 'But they told me your name was Philippe Delphy.'

'That's my codename.'

Yes, of course, she should have known that. She was so overcome by the miraculous way he had been restored to her, she could only say, 'I knew you would come back. I always knew it.'

She looked down and saw what had been done to him. The skin of his hand was covered in burn scars: purple craters that curled inwards at the edges. The nails of his index and middle fingers were missing. But she didn't want to ask him about the injuries just yet, sure that her rage at the answer would spoil the moment. Instead, she let her heart swell with how much she loved him and gratitude for whatever divine grace had brought him back.

Serge walked into the room with a towel and a bowl of water. He stopped when he saw Kristina kneeling next to Max. 'Is everything all right?'

'It's Max. He is back.'

A frown rippled Serge's forehead, as if he was wondering if Kristina had gone mad, driven too far by her fantasies about Max returning.

'Serge?' Max said. 'Is that you?'

Serge froze to the spot, his eyes filling with tears. At that moment the sun rose above the sea and filled the room with light. It reminded Kristina of the day at the station four years earlier, when they had said goodbye to Max, and the sun had come up as he was getting on the train. It had made everyone look as though they had caught fire. But now Max was back, that very same sun seemed to shine more brilliantly for Kristina than it ever had before.

★

It was painful to watch Max eat. His jaw had been broken and reset and he'd had stomach surgery because of the bullet wounds. Adding to his poor condition was the fact that he'd been starved for several weeks. He could only take tiny teaspoons of gruel, and he winced with each mouthful. Kristina had to keep reminding herself to simply be grateful he was alive, and that he was doing his best to recover.

Serge looked on, offering a serviette when Max dribbled food down his chin. 'It seems you are a master at escaping, my friend,' he said. 'First from a German prisoner-of-war camp and then from the Italians. Five shots are a lot of bullets to take and to keep running.'

'I had you both to come back to,' he said. 'And Nadia and Ginette.'

'The girls prayed for you every day,' Kristina said. 'I'll call them in after you've finished eating.'

'No!' said Max. Then realising he may have spoken too harshly, added, 'When I'm better. I don't want them to see me this way.'

'They won't care, Max,' she assured him. 'We have been a safe house for Jews on their way out of France for some time now. They have seen a lot, and aren't babies anymore.'

Kristina was proud of her daughters' maturity, but it saddened her too. The war had made them grow up too quickly.

Max nodded. 'I've missed a lot.' Then he turned to Serge. 'Thank you. I asked you to look after my wife and children and you did.'

★

Although Kristina didn't say it to Max, she was concerned about how Ginette might react when she saw her father.

296

Nadia, she knew, would be brave. But when the girls came into the room, Ginette sat next to Max and looked at him with nothing but adoration. She produced a painting she had made of Tulipe, who was now a geriatric rabbit who stayed in an enclosure in Ginette's room for fear that somebody would try to eat her.

'This is a beautiful piece of art,' Max told her. 'You have your mother's talent. When you grow up, you will no doubt become a famous artist.'

Ginette beamed brightly at the compliment.

Kristina noticed Serge slip from the room. She found him, sitting in the garden and staring out at the sea. She sat quietly beside him.

'I should have married Madeleine,' he said. 'I should have tried to have a normal life and a family.'

Kristina put her hand on his shoulder. 'You were prepared to do all that. Madeleine was the one who ran away.'

'I often wonder what happened to the child. Did Madeleine keep her, or did she give her away?'

She wasn't sure what to say to Serge. They'd had this conversation many years before but now it seemed to have a particular urgency for him again. She put it down to the high emotions of Max's return, and the fact they were both out of their minds with exhaustion and hunger. For while she believed that Madeleine was a good person in her heart, she was too troubled to be able to take care of a child. It was most likely the child had been given up to an institution long ago. And as for Madeleine, if she had wanted to be found, she would have written to them.

'You'll always be part of our family, Serge,' Kristina said. 'Even with Max back, nothing changes between you and me. You've been my protector and support.'

He looked into her eyes, and she hoped he understood. Their love for each other may not have been romantic or sanctified by marriage but it was very real.

*

Moira was all smiles when Kristina told her the news about Max.

'It's incredible! I have never heard of such a thing!'

Kristina remembered the candle she'd lit in the Russian Orthodox church and the peace she had felt afterwards. 'It was divine intervention.'

A mischievous smile came to Moira's face. 'Well, let's drink to the divine,' she said. 'I have a bottle of Italian grappa I was saving for after the war, but why not celebrate now?'

As the two women drank the 'firewater', it felt to Kristina like a breath between sprints – a moment of light-heartedness in a life of terror. Of course it didn't last. No sooner had they put down their glasses than Vittorio from the Town Hall arrived, dishevelled and feverish.

'It's off,' he said. 'The evacuation is off. The Italians have signed an armistice with the Allies.'

For Kristina, the news was a terrible blow to their already precarious existence.

'Signor Donati has had to go into hiding,' Vittorio continued. 'The Germans tried to assassinate him.'

'But many of the Italian soldiers are still here,' Kristina said. 'Won't they fight for the Allies now?'

Vittorio shook his head. 'They outnumber the Germans, but they are surrendering in droves. They want to go home.'

'Surely there is time to get the people we're hiding out?' said Moira. 'We have everything prepared. We can put them on trains and get them out to Italy tonight. The Allies can work out what to do with them from there.'

Vittorio was on the verge of tears. 'The Germans have taken over the railways already.'

All Kristina could think about were the children and adults hiding at the villa. They had been living in uncomfortable, cramped conditions, bearing it all because they believed ships were coming soon to take them somewhere safe. There was no choice now, Kristina realised, but to hunker down and hope that the storm would pass over them.

★

'Where are Édouard and Beatrice?' Max asked Kristina, when she told him about the armistice.

'They are still in their home here in Nice.'

Max shifted himself to sit upright, a move that caused him to wince in pain. 'Please tell me that's not true. Why didn't they leave months ago?'

'When the Italians came, life went back to normal for Jewish people. They believed Donati would protect them.'

Max shook his head. 'They have to get out *now*. They are a target.'

'All Jews are targets,' said Serge, bringing in a clean pair of pyjamas for Max.

'They are on a list,' Max said. 'French intelligence in London have known for some time that the Nazis have been sending trainloads of art to Germany. They already have their hands on the Rothschild and Schloss collections. They will certainly be after the Foulds' art. Hitler has plans for a Führermuseum, a super art museum in Linz. They know about Botticelli's *Flora* and it's on Hitler's prize list – if Göring doesn't get his greedy hands on it first.'

Kristina and Serge listened with shock as Max described the extent of the art that was being looted from German occupied territories, from museums and art galleries but particularly from Jews. In Paris, the stolen artworks were assessed by a team of Nazi art historians before being sent on to Germany.

'We've lost everything we stored at Wacker-Bondy's,' he told Serge. 'Martin La Farge led the Gestapo straight to it for a generous ten per cent commission of artworks that he wanted.'

Serge looked beaten, as if he had just been told that his best friend had died.

'He got our art gallery as well,' he said.

Kristina didn't want to ask Max how he knew about the extent of the looting. It was clear he was privy to de Gaulle's intelligence, and she sensed it was better to know as little about Max's mission as possible.

★

The Foulds' mansion was not shut up like other mansions along the Côte d'Azur. The shutters were wide open revealing sparkling windows. A gardener was on his knees weeding a flowerbed while two maids were beating a mattress as if they were expecting overnight guests. One of them stopped when she saw Kristina and Serge approaching and showed them inside, where they found Édouard smoking a cigarette and reading a newspaper in the drawing room. Beatrice was beside him, working on a tapestry of the Notre-Dame cathedral. Kristina and Serge stood speechless when they saw what was hanging on the walls. Some of the most priceless artworks from the Foulds' collection, ones that they had helped pack away so carefully the year before, were on display again in the room. A portrait by Cranach – a favourite artist of Hitler's – hung above a bureau. It was as if it had been placed there as a taunt.

'It was lonely without them,' said Édouard, indicating the paintings. 'We like to have them around like old friends. Speaking of which, we haven't seen you two for a while. Let's have some champagne, shall we? The cellar is full of the stuff, and we may as well enjoy it before the Krauts get here.'

Kristina glanced at Beatrice, who shuddered. She looked pale and worn, a woman defeated.

'You're both in grave danger,' said Serge. 'We can't tell you exactly our source, but it comes from someone in contact with French intelligence in London. You are on a list for deportation.'

'Words, rumours, talk,' said Édouard, signalling to one of the maids. 'I've probably been on that list a long time.' The maid approached and Édouard told her to bring two bottles of Veuve Clicquot.

Beatrice looked on the verge of tears. The image came to Kristina of those women who decided to go down with their husbands on the *Titanic* when they could have got in a lifeboat. Maybe they did it for love, or fear they couldn't survive without their husbands, but it would have been a terrifying choice just the same.

'They want your art,' Serge told Édouard. 'It doesn't matter about all your international connections. They won't protect you here. They've already plundered the other Jewish collections and arrested two of the Schloss family in Nice. They will be coming for you too soon, no doubt.'

Édouard sat back and grinned. 'For all his vitriol against us, it seems that Hitler thinks the Jews have excellent taste.'

Was his obstinacy the result of a distressed mind? Kristina wondered. But it wasn't just his life that was on the line, but his wife's too.

'You and Beatrice still have a life ahead of you,' said Serge. 'I don't think your son would have wanted you to just sit here and wait to be murdered.'

Beatrice let out a muffled sob. Kristina sidled up to her and whispered, 'Go and pack two bags. Just clothes, food and whatever money you have to hand.'

After Beatrice left to carry out her task, Kristina sat down next to Édouard and placed her hand on his back. 'Everything has been very hard. We have all suffered constant shocks. But you must pull yourself together. You won't get a second chance. You must leave now.'

Kristina inwardly lamented that the Foulds had not left the previous August when they had the chance. They could have gone through Italy and crossed into Switzerland by car. Now the only way to get them out was with a *passeur*, a guide, who would pick them up at Saint-Martin and take them across the high peaks of the Mercantour alps and into Italy, where hopefully the Red Cross would be able to help them get out of Europe. The trip would be arduous, and she wasn't entirely sure the Foulds were up for it. But they had no choice now. To stay was far more dangerous.

Édouard looked around him. 'What would they do with all this beauty? Those Nazis and their black hearts.'

He let out a heart-rending sob and leaned on Kristina in a way that broke her heart. But she was relieved he was giving voice to his pain. Once it was expelled, she hoped he'd find the strength to leave.

Serge took a breath, as if determined to keep his mind on practicalities. 'Your maids and your gardener can help me crate your artworks. We can hide them in various places around the property. I can take some back to the Villa des Cygnes. I may even be able to build a false wall for you here as I've got rather good at constructing them. But give Botticelli's *Flora* to me now. That's the painting Hitler and Göring are competing over and will stop at nothing to get.'

Kristina was surprised. Taking the Botticelli was not something she and Serge had discussed beforehand.

Édouard straightened. '*Flora* must come with me. It's the only thing I have left of my son.'

'The guide who will be taking you through the mountains is paid, not a member of the Resistance, so he won't want any trouble,' Serge told him. 'You'll have to travel through the alps on narrow trails. The lighter you pack the better.'

Édouard covered his face with his hands and said nothing.

Then to Kristina's surprise, Serge changed his stance. 'All right,' he said. 'Take it.'

Everyone helped with carting crates from the garage into the house. But after a couple of hours, it was clear the Foulds, along with their maids and gardener as well as Kristina and Serge, were not enough hands for the job. They ended up performing a triage on the artworks, sorting them by their value and counting as losses what they would have to leave to be taken by the Germans.

Serge regarded two run-of-the-mill pastoral scenes. 'They might distract the Nazi looters from the real treasures,' he said hopefully.

Édouard took *Flora* down himself, rolled it and embraced the painting like a child before putting it in a cylindrical case. Serge pulled Kristina aside. 'That priceless Botticelli is going to end up at the bottom of a ravine when the guide gets sick of Édouard struggling to keep up. Or worse, some mountain bandit will assume it's an expensive artwork and slit Édouard's and Beatrice's throats for it.'

'I'd leave the subject alone, Serge,' she said. 'We've tried already. If you push it, he might refuse to go again. And right now, people are more important than paintings.'

★

It was getting late and Kristina had to get back to the villa to prepare food for Max and the others.

'Take Beatrice's bicycle,' Serge told her. 'I'll come later and bring what artworks I can in the car and hide them at the villa.'

When Kristina embraced Beatrice before leaving, she thought it was like holding a frail, frightened bird.

'We'll meet again in better times,' Kristina told her.

She sincerely hoped they would, but her stomach was in knots as she climbed on the bicycle and sped away from the villa.

★

It rarely rained in Nice but the downpour that evening was torrential. The wind rattled the windows and the house seemed to shudder with each blast. Serge hadn't returned for dinner. Kristina hoped it was only because he'd decided to continue hiding the Foulds' artworks until the morning. She rolled over several times, finding herself annoyed with Édouard for putting everyone in danger, even though part of her sympathised. Why should he and Beatrice flee their home and live in fear when the Germans were losing the war anyway? She heard a car approach and peered out the window to see Serge pulling into the driveway. She was surprised he'd driven through the blinding rain like that, but perhaps it had been safer to do so rather than when the Germans were out on patrol. She went downstairs and waited for him to come into the house. He was carrying something under his arm when he stepped through the door. It was the cylinder in which Édouard had packed the Botticelli.

'I didn't expect you to be awake,' he said, his shoes squishing on the tiles before he took them off.

'The painting?' Kristina queried. 'You brought it?'

He nodded. 'In the end, Beatrice convinced Édouard it was foolish to take it. I built a false wall, but it was a rush job and, although we moved cupboards in front of it, I'm not convinced it will fool the Germans enough to save the artworks behind it. So, he finally agreed to let me bring *Flora* and some other works here and gave me a letter as proof that he entrusted part of his collection to me.'

'Come to the kitchen,' Kristina said. 'You must be freezing.'

She took a towel from the cupboard and put it over his shoulders. 'Édouard was so adamant that he was going to take the painting, I can't quite believe even Beatrice managed to change his mind.'

He shot her a look. 'Well, she did. So let's drop the subject. I'm exhausted. Édouard was so slow, moving about the house and forgetting things. It was as if he was getting ready to go on summer holidays rather than fleeing for his life.'

'The war has done something to his mind,' Kristina said, putting the kettle on the stove to make tea. 'He wasn't himself when I saw him today. None of us are.' A fierce gust of wind blew against the house, making the walls shudder and the windows vibrate. 'I hope the Foulds will make it,' she said. 'I don't know if this is a good night or a bad one to set out.'

Serge looked away. 'We can't think about that now. We did our best.'

★

'Fear and hunger. Fear and hunger, that's all the Germans have brought us,' said Moira as Kristina worked beside her in her kitchen, slicing the tops off the withered carrots they had managed to buy on the black market and cutting up a cabbage that had long lost its crispness.

The garden at the Villa des Cygnes was full of planted carrot tops that would eventually sprout leaves from which seeds could be harvested to grow more carrots. It was a process that Kristina's father might have enjoyed in peace time, but it was painfully slow when everyone was hungry.

'The Swedish Red Cross brought preserves and gingerbread into Nice yesterday,' Kristina said, 'but the only one who qualifies for food packages is Ginette.'

There were fourteen of them at the villa now, all trying to survive on the barely adequate ration cards of four. If it wasn't for what Kristina could scrounge on the black market, they would all have perished from starvation long ago.

'I have to tell the children to stay away from the windows and to play quietly, lest someone come unnoticed to the house,' Kristina said. 'And yet, I find myself feeling sorry for the German soldiers who have been sent to Nice. Some of them are almost children themselves. They look bewildered and lost. Like naïve farm boys.'

'They are boys who do what they are told,' Moira said, with a note of warning in her voice in case the youthfulness of the soldiers caused Kristina to drop her guard. 'That makes them especially dangerous. You wouldn't feel sorry for them if they were about to shoot you.'

Moira put the vegetables in the boiling water and shook her head. 'My mother would turn in her grave if she saw me putting cabbage in a pot-au-feu, but desperate times mean we can't be fussy now.'

'It looks more appetising than the potato peel soup and stale bread we ate yesterday.'

Moira took a cloth and wiped down the table. 'Hunger can turn us into monsters. The Germans are offering people extra ration tickets for denouncing Jews and their helpers.'

Although Kristina was sad that Tulipe had died from old age the previous week, she was relieved too. She had been turning a blind eye to Ginette taking a precious carrot or turnip to feed her pet. One of the refugees, thankfully moved further down the escape line before the last intake, had discovered Tulipe one day and made everyone take a vote on whether they should kill the poor old bony rabbit to make a stew. Luckily, no one supported her.

Kristina looked out the window and her mind wandered to that morning when Ginette had found Tulipe stiff and cold. To comfort Ginette, Kristina had suggested they have a funeral to remember the sweet and affectionate rabbit. Afterwards, she and Serge had moved a large square of cement over the burial site and placed an urn on top, not so much as a memorial but because they feared someone would dig up the rabbit's corpse and eat it.

★

Kristina drove home with a portion of the stew Moira had made hidden under a blanket on the front passenger seat. She'd had to take a long detour because the Germans weren't only starving the population of Nice, they were turning the beautiful natural coastline into a defence line. They had blown up lighthouses to stop them being used as reference points for enemy aircraft, and had cut down ancient trees to make way for blockhouses, trenches and tunnels. Ugly concrete walls curved around the coast. Even the beach was mined. Max believed they were seeding the explosives at a hundred devices per acre. Rumour had it that the Germans had plans to blow up the whole city when they retreated from it.

Out of nowhere, a black Citroën closed in behind Kristina. The driver beeped the horn aggressively. She glanced in the rear-view mirror to see the surly faces of men who could only have been Gestapo agents. She had no choice but to pull over. Her thoughts scattered and it was difficult for her to think clearly. They would take the stew, no doubt. But it was a loss she could bear. It was the discovery of the false papers stashed under her seat that was terrifying. She prepared herself for the worst, but the Gestapo didn't stop. The Citroën roared onwards. She drew a breath to calm herself and whispered a quick prayer of gratitude. But then the sound of vehicles approaching made her look up again. Three army trucks driven by German soldiers and crowded with people of all ages – dejected, frightened, battered – passed by. They were Jews from a round-up. After they passed, Kristina beat her fists against the dashboard.

'*You are monsters!*' she shouted after the Germans. '*Monsters!*'

★

When Kristina pulled up at the villa, she gave the stew to Nadia to take to the kitchen and went straight upstairs where she found Max struggling to get out of bed.

'Darling, don't do that,' she told him. 'One of us will bring you something if you want it.'

'What I want is to help you, Kristina. You are practically skin and bones.'

'You'll help me by getting better. Now lie down.'

She took off her shoes and curled up on the bed next to him. His swelling was finally starting to come down and he was yellow instead of purple. But it was still painful for him to be touched. She lay close enough to feel the warmth of his skin but not to make contact. They looked into each other's faces, and Kristina was moved to see that even though they had been separated for over four years, he still looked at her with love in his eyes.

'Max,' she said softly, as if saying his name would keep him with her forever.

He lifted his hand and stroked her cheek with his finger. 'At least tell me what your worries are, Kristina. Don't carry your burdens all by yourself.'

She waved the question away. She didn't want to say that her main worry was him. She had drilled everyone to vanish to their hiding places should the Gestapo appear at the gate. But what would they do with Max? He could barely move. Moira was trying to get false papers to say that he had been in an accident at a factory. But they were taking forever to get done.

'It's money,' she said, naming her second greatest worry. 'When there is some food it's exorbitantly expensive. I could sell the piano, but it would probably only buy me a bunch of grapes. Besides, the second-hand stores are full of Steinways and playing it is one of the few pleasures Nadia has left. Then there are the *passeurs*. The people on the safe-house chain do everything they can out of their sense of compassion, but the *passeurs* smell our desperation and take everything we've got. And they won't take children. Our escape line doesn't have the money, so we hide Jews and try to keep everyone fed. Every day I wake up thinking I can't do it anymore. Only God gives me the strength.'

Max stretched his arm out slowly so that it circled her head. 'I've been looking at that painting of Serge you have hanging over the dresser.'

At first Kristina was hurt. Why was he talking about a painting when she had just poured out her heart to him. But her eyes followed his gaze to the painting Serge had finally agreed to sit for, only with Tulipe instead of Leo. They did it not long after Max went missing and Kristina was distraught. Serge had suggested it as a distraction. Together they had absorbed themselves in studying everything they could about Leonardo da Vinci's technique so that Kristina could use it perfectly to imitate the master himself.

'It's not your usual style,' Max said.

'I painted it in homage to da Vinci's *Lady with an Ermine*. It was a little joke I was making with Serge.'

'Tell me how you did it?'

'I wrote to a friend from the Louvre to see if they could tell me what size the original was and I learned it had been painted on a walnut wood panel. Serge helped me with the chemical composition of the paints. I spent hours studying the peculiarities of da Vinci's style and learning about the techniques of the period. After much practice imitating da Vinci's brushstrokes, I was confident enough to attempt the painting.'

'Despite the fact it's Serge with Tulipe, it *could* be a da Vinci,' said Max. Then struggling to push himself up higher on the cushions, he said, 'Go get Serge. I know a way that we can make money. *A lot of money.*'

★

Serge rubbed his chin and leaned back against the windowsill. 'It's one hell of a risk to take, Max. It would be dangerous enough to draw attention to ourselves by selling the originals.'

'The way things are going, we have nothing to lose,' Max replied. 'And if any artist can pull it off, it's Kristina. She studied the masters as a student and she's a perfectionist.'

'You can't be serious!' Kristina said.

'I am serious,' said Max. 'Why should we be starving here while other dealers are making millions of dollars in Paris?'

'They are making it from stolen art, Max,' she reminded him.

A sly grin came to his face. He looked more like himself again than ever. 'But we will make it from *forgeries* – it's not the same thing. We will be the Robin Hood, Little John and Maid Marian of the French art world. We will be cheating the Nazis to save the very people they are persecuting.'

Kristina could see Max's point. They had already broken so many rules, they would be executed if they were discovered. What difference would it make if it were for hiding Jews or forging art? The punishment would be the same. But Serge would have to agree to the scheme.

'What do you think?' she asked him.

A smile crept across his face. 'What do I think?' he asked. 'I think, my dear friends, that it will not only bring us an income but it will be a delicious form of revenge.'

CHAPTER TWENTY-TWO

EVE

Nice, June 1946

I had to let Georges know about Kristina's amnesia as soon as possible. When she looked better the morning after her seizure, I told Lorenzo I needed to telephone Paris.

'I am sorry, Mademoiselle Archer,' he said. 'There is no telephone. All the lines were cut when the Germans retreated and they haven't been fixed yet.'

'I'll have to call from the post office then. When is the next bus into town?'

'This afternoon.'

'But I must telephone Serge's lawyer this morning.'

It looked like my only option was to walk. But the idea of it was unappealing as I wasn't wearing practical shoes and the warm morning was foreshadowing an even hotter day ahead.

Lorenzo coughed into his fist. 'There is a bicycle. You can use it to get into town then catch the bus back here,' he offered.

'Would you mind getting it for me while I fetch my handbag?'

When I returned to the front of the house, Lorenzo presented me with a contraption that looked more like an eggbeater than a bicycle. It didn't have any rubber on the wheels.

'The Germans took Madame Bergeret's bicycle during the war and left this one,' explained Lorenzo. 'It has steel tyres because rubber was in short supply.'

It was no surprise to me that the Germans would have got rid of it. With no rubber on the tyres the suspension would be terrible. The fixed gears meant it would be impossible to ride up a hill. But it was a long walk to the centre of town, and time was of the essence.

I rode the bicycle around the courtyard a few times to get my balance before leaving down the villa's private road. As I reached the intersection to the main road, a woman driving a black Renault turned towards the villa. Our eyes met and the way she stared at me gave me the chills. But I didn't have time to think too much about who the visitor might be, I was more concerned about surviving the trip down the steep winding road on a bicycle with bald tyres that squeaked like rusty bedsprings.

When I approached the Promenade des Anglais, the grinding of the bicycle's tyres was so loud a group of glamorous suntanned people lying on the beach turned around to look at me.

'*Mon Dieu!*' one of them said. 'I thought we were rid of the Nazis.'

It was a relief to finally reach the post office, but as I stood in line I felt as if my thighs were on fire. I would have to find a pharmacy to buy talcum powder to stop them rubbing otherwise I would be walking like a cowboy for days.

'What have you managed to find out?' Georges asked, when the operator put my call through.

'Kristina has lost her memory,' I said. 'She doesn't remember what happened during the war. She knows about Serge but can't recall anything about him. She can't even remember her own children. It's some sort of amnesia.'

Georges paused before asking: 'Amnesia? Doesn't that go away?'

'According to her butler, Lorenzo, she has shown some signs of improvement since she returned to Nice. But they have been slight.' I took a breath and forced myself to say the words that terrified me. 'Her brain may take months to heal … or it may never heal at all, and those memories might be lost forever.'

Georges's silence made my own fears roar louder in my ears.

'She's our main witness,' he said in a tone so serious, and so unlike his usual sanguine self, it filled me with dread. 'We go to court in three weeks.'

'Three weeks! I thought we had months, and that meanwhile Serge would be released on bail.'

'The French judicial system is different from the Australian one,' Georges quickly explained. 'It functions under the Napoleonic code. The examining judge is already processing evidence to report to the judge who will preside over the case in court.'

'Three weeks is unreasonable! Regardless of the court system, shouldn't there be a fair trial?'

Georges's hesitation to answer worried me.

'What is it?' I asked him. 'What are you not telling me?'

'We are being rushed and the examining judge is being rushed too. It smacks of political expediency.'

'You mean they are going to use Serge as an example? That this is going to be some sort of show trial?'

'What I'm saying is that we are going to need the strongest case possible if we are to have any chance of winning this.'

My legs trembled and I thought I was going to be sick. The seizure Kristina had suffered the previous day looked so dangerous it could have been almost fatal. But it seemed to me the only hope we had was if I could persuade her to go with me to Paris and see Serge. Perhaps then she would remember more about what happened during the war.

After I rang off from Georges, I turned towards the pharmacy with the intent of buying the much needed talcum powder. A woman crossed my path and stood in front of me. I recognised her as the dark-haired woman I'd seen turning into the villa's private road. Had she followed me?

'Excuse me, mademoiselle,' she said, with the faintest inflection of a Russian accent. 'Who are you and why are you visiting Kristina?'

Her arrogant manner was off-putting and I was inclined to walk past her, but she put her manicured hand on my arm. Despite the heat of the day, her touch was ice-cold.

'Who are *you*?' I asked.

'Sonia Vertinskaya. Kristina's told you terrible things about me, hasn't she? But I understand she has some sort of damage to her brain and that she can't remember things? She doesn't remember that we were friends and that I helped her during the war?'

My ears pricked up at her last statement. 'You helped her? Do you mean by rescuing Jewish people?'

Sonia nodded. 'Yes, that's right. I help her still. Lorenzo gave me a self-portrait she painted and I had it auctioned for her anonymously at the Hôtel Drouot in Paris. Otherwise, she and that poor old man would have had nothing to live on. I'd help her more if she'd let me. I happen to know of a very good specialist in London who can restore people's memories. I would be willing to travel there with her and pay for anything she might need. Lorenzo is open to my help, but Kristina keeps pushing me away.'

I wavered. The fact that the woman knew about Kristina's Resistance work was a godsend. But something about her approach made me wary.

'And you haven't said your name yet, mademoiselle?' she added.

'I'm Eve Archer,' I ventured cautiously. 'Why did you say Kristina was saying awful things about you?'

'Because with those sorts of injuries, the person always turns on the person closest to them.' She smiled, treating me to a flash of gold dental work. 'I have a suite at the Hôtel Negresco. Why don't you come and have a drink with me? I'll tell you all about it.'

If I wasn't so desperate for any information that might help Serge, I probably would have declined. Instead, I nodded.

Sonia's suite was lavishly decorated with items that did not belong to the hotel – antique Chinese screens, Syrian embroidered fabrics, and a large leopard-print rug.

'What does the doctor think is wrong with Kristina? Is her memory loss permanent?' Sonia asked, pouring a glass of chilled rosé, which the bellboy had brought to the room.

'No one knows.'

She offered me a seat. 'Are you here because of Serge Lavertu?'

I hesitated a moment before answering. 'Yes.'

'He's as guilty as hell, you know,' she said, stretching her arm over the back of the sofa. 'Everyone in the art world knows it. He'd kill his own mother to get his hands on a painting he wanted. Nobody would dare cross him at an auction. If he was after a painting, it was safer to let him have it.'

I flinched and Sonia noticed.

'Oh, I'm sorry,' she said. 'Are you a friend of his?'

'Yes.'

She eyed me carefully. 'Well, you can't have been friends long otherwise what I said wouldn't have shocked you.'

I'd walked straight into a trap, and I knew it. I wasn't going to say anything more until I discovered exactly what Sonia Vertinskaya was after. Then the answer hit me.

'Are you testifying *against* Serge Lavertu at the trial?' I asked. 'If you are, I don't think I should be here.' I stood up to leave.

Sonia stood up with me. 'He is going to frame Kristina,' she said. 'That's why I'm concerned. If she can't remember anything, she's an easy target.'

'He didn't know that she'd lost her memory. No one knew until I came here.'

'Didn't he?' replied Sonia, racing to the door ahead of me. 'Serge Lavertu says a lot of things and I'd be wary if I were you. He knew perfectly well Kristina has amnesia. It was what he was counting on when he sent you here.'

I rushed into the corridor and hurried to the elevator. As I pushed the buttons, Sonia leaned against the doorway of her room. 'It was a pleasure to meet you, Eve Archer. You are rather famous in Paris, you know. That little thing with Cyrille de Villiers. Are you going to be a character witness in the Serge Lavertu trial? Are *you* going to say how reliable and trustworthy he is?'

The elevator arrived and I jumped inside. When the doors closed, I could smell Sonia's musky perfume clinging to me. I had never wanted to have a bath so much in my life. It was a relief to get back out on the street. But as I walked the bicycle to the bus stop, I realised I had been the winner in that exchange with Sonia Vertinskaya. I hadn't told her anything she didn't already know, but she had told me something important. She had something to hide, and she had wanted to make sure Kristina didn't remember it.

★

I took my seat on the shady side of the bus back to the villa, and even there the leather scorched my back and legs. I kept my eyes peeled to the view outside. Palm trees lined the wide boulevard, and then as the bus wound its way uphill and around bends, lemon and orange groves came into view. I was struck by all the things I'd been too wrought-up to notice the first time I travelled up the hill, including the brightly coloured stucco mansions and the large gardens, full of pine and fig trees. Nice had once been a sleepy fishing village before it was discovered by the English and the Russian aristocracy and the opulence of their homes remained. We passed a woman on a bicycle, and I was taken by her flowing floral dress and the wide-brimmed hat that bounced on her head as she pedalled. How I would have enjoyed coming to Nice for any other reason than the one I was here for. It might have been an exciting adventure. Instead I was in one of the prettiest parts of France, feeling the weight of the world bearing down on me.

But the war had come to Nice as well and there were signs of that too. Some mansions had been reduced to rubble, and on some properties, barbed wire and other barricades remained.

As we progressed up the hill, the passengers got off at various stops and soon I was the only one remaining. Finally, the bus driver pulled over and turned to me.

'This is the last stop before I turn around, mademoiselle. The Villa des Cygnes is up that private road. I'll help these passengers with their bags and then I'll get your bicycle down for you.'

318

I looked out the window to see Kristina and Lorenzo standing under a palm tree with two suitcases next to them. I recognised one of the suitcases as mine. Kristina was holding Flora in a wicker carrier.

'I've decided to come with you to Paris,' Kristina said, as I stepped out of the bus. 'Perhaps it will help me remember.'

She still looked wan from her seizure the previous day.

'Are you sure?' I asked.

'Yes,' she said, as the driver took the suitcases and put them in the undercarriage before taking the bicycle off the rack and leaning it against the tree.

'You'll take good care of her, won't you?' said Lorenzo, with the voice of a man who was entrusting his most precious possession to a stranger.

'I will. I promise,' I told him.

Kristina and I took our seats on the bus with Flora's carrier perched on the seat in front of us. As the bus turned around we waved farewell to Lorenzo who looked bereft. I only hoped everything would somehow turn out right, and Kristina would be returning to him soon.

I took her hand. 'Thank you,' I said.

'You are welcome,' she replied, squeezing my hand back. 'I have to try to help. From the way you've described it, me remembering something is the only chance Serge has got.'

CHAPTER TWENTY-THREE

KRISTINA

Nice, August 1943

If Kristina needed more motivation to go along with Max's plan, it came the following week when she was heading towards Moira's café to deliver a bag of walnuts. They had been given to her by a farmer and were worth their weight in gold. But before she reached the café, a man stepped from a doorway and grabbed her affectionately by the shoulders.

'Good morning, Lydia,' he said, kissing her on both cheeks. 'I was beginning to worry you had already come and I'd missed you.'

She had never seen the man in her life. She wondered if he was drunk when he linked his arm with hers and escorted her to the opposite side of the street. 'I'm afraid that café is closed at the moment,' he said, 'but there is another one further on. The coffee is roasted acorn, but you wouldn't know it from the careful way they brew it.'

Then she caught on to what was happening when he nodded towards Moira's café. The windows were broken. There was a black Citroën waiting outside with two men in it, no doubt watching the café to see who would arrive. When Kristina and the stranger reached the other café, he chose a table right in the middle of Nice's best-known collaborators, as if seating themselves in the midst of their enemy was the safest place to be.

'It's a good idea that you have your relatives stay with you,' he said, signalling the waitress and continuing to speak in code. 'It's times like this that families need to stick together. Nobody would want to be travelling under the present circumstances.'

The people at the table closest to them got up and left, and he was able to speak more freely. 'The biggest Nazi monster, Alois Brunner, is here,' he said, while pointing to items on the menu. 'He's set up his headquarters at the Hôtel Excelsior. It's become a processing office for Jews who have been discovered. Already twenty-seven train cars have left for the camps. They are killing children with injections of strychnine, then sterilising their mothers and sending them to brothels in the east.'

'What happened to our friend?' she asked, referring to Moira.

The man shook his head and Kristina's heart sank. She understood Moira had been arrested and the fate that awaited her was grim. A German soldier sat down next to them and she had to rapidly blink away her tears. Moira's laughter and the conversations they'd had in her kitchen were some of the few comforts she had known in recent times. She was a good woman and a brave soul.

When Kristina and the stranger parted, she took a different route home to avoid walking past the café again. She was in too much shock to express her grief over Moira, but one thing she knew was that she was not going to let her daughters grow up in this kind of world. In honour of Moira she would fight the Nazis tooth and nail. Or in her case, with a paintbrush.

★

At first Kristina thought she wouldn't be able to do it. She stared at one of the Foulds' Rembrandts on the easel in front of her and her hand trembled. It was a different style of art from her own, so dark and gloomy. Yet the more she studied Rembrandt's work, the more she came to appreciate it. He lived in a world without streetlights and electricity. Rooms were illuminated by candles and firelight. His clients were sombre Dutch protestants. Hence the browns and blacks he used. As she slowly imitated his brushstrokes, she began to appreciate his attention to detail and the emotional intensity captured in his portraits. As she painted on, she imagined her work hanging in the homes of Nazis – or even better, their museums! The thought of making fools out of them while stealing their money filled her with a sense of pride.

'For Moira,' she said, as she laboured over her work.

'That's good!' Serge said when she showed him the finished portrait. He studied it from every angle. 'So good it would get past half the dealers in Paris.'

'Only half?' asked Kristina.

'There are minor flaws in the face. But so minor I am sure they will disappear with practice. Let's see if you can copy the portrait Rembrandt did of his wife, Saskia.'

'But where will we get smalt?' she asked, naming the grittier blue Rembrandt used and which turned brown and translucent over time.

'Let Max and I worry about the paint compositions,' said Serge. 'It's how we first cut our teeth in the art world. You focus on the technique.'

The idea of selling forgeries of old masters to the Nazis seemed to energise Max too. Despite the severely rationed food, he was making a speedy recovery. After a week he was able to walk slowly down the stairs to the cellar, where he and Serge were experimenting like a couple of mad scientists to produce paints that matched or substituted those used by Rembrandt. Kristina and Nadia were sent out to search the markets and junk shops for old paintings whose canvases and stretchers could pass off as authentic for the forgeries. Then using soap, pumice stones and coarse brushes, Serge and Max removed the layers of paint except for the priming layer. It was painstaking work, especially as the canvases were already fragile with age, but Kristina often caught them grinning at each other like two mischievous schoolboys.

'Why do you do that?' Nadia asked them one day. 'Why not just paint over them?'

'Because of the possibility that someone will insist on getting the painting X-rayed before they buy it.'

'I feel sorry for the artist whose work you are destroying,' she said.

Serge put down the pumice stone and wiped the dust off his fingers. 'Well, it's a lesson to not produce second-rate paintings.'

Kristina cringed. Picasso was still painting masterpieces in his Paris studio despite the war, while she – in between forging great artworks – was producing ubiquitous flower paintings to sell to the mistresses of German soldiers in an attempt to keep food on the table.

Max sensed her dismay and guessed the cause of it. 'After the war, you will be painting again,' he told her. 'And your work will be greater than ever because you will have so much to convey.'

★

'What is that smell!' Kristina asked, coming down the stairs to investigate the unpleasant chemical odour. 'I can't concentrate with it wafting up the stairs.'

She had been aware of banging and hammering sounds emanating from the cellar, where there was an old-fashioned Russian stove that hadn't been used for many years. The door to the cellar opened and Max and Serge burst out, coughing and laughing at the same time. She warned them that the noxious smells probably travelled all the way to their neighbours' houses, but they were too excited to consider it.

'We've done it!' Max cried. 'We have perfected the hardening process!'

He plunged himself into the smoky dungeon again and returned with the first Rembrandt portrait Kristina had painted. Oil paint took three days to become touch-dry, but decades to truly harden. That meant that recent forgeries could be detected with a simple alcohol test that would lift the unsettled paint. Max and Serge had been experimenting with ways to dry the paint faster, but so far the results had been disastrous – singed canvases, blistered paint and blanched colours. But the Rembrandt had lost none of its intensity.

Max and Serge slapped each other on the back with pride. But Kristina's stomach turned, as the reality of what would come next bore down on her. She would be the one taking the paintings to dealers and negotiating the prices. She wasn't a natural saleswoman and found it difficult enough to hawk her flower paintings at the markets. Now she would be in direct contact with Nazis, and if something went wrong, what then?

'You must worry less, Kristina,' Max told her with a twinkle in his eyes. 'If we had any doubt about these paintings passing as authentic works, we would not be sending you out into the world with them.'

Serge also did his best to reassure her. 'The best museums around the world, including the Louvre, are full of forgeries,' he said. 'Museum directors and specialists make errors of judgement all the time. And if a painting that has had pride of place in a gallery proves later to be a forgery, what museum director is going to destroy his reputation to admit it?'

Max nodded his agreement. 'Your painting is the very best of forgeries, but *you* must believe in it for this to work.'

Kristina saw his point but she had other qualms too. 'I don't mind cheating Nazis,' she said. 'But what does it say about me as an artist to copy others?'

'Kristina!' Serge said. 'You are following in the path of all the great men of art! Michelangelo used to forge old masters when he was young, and age them with smoke and dirt to pass them off as original.'

'Then you must have bought forgeries too at some stage,' said Nadia, coming down the stairs.

Kristina smiled at her daughter's astuteness, then looked back to Max and Serge. 'Have you?'

'Of course not,' said Serge.

Max shook his head. 'Serge and I worked our way up to our position. We know all the tricks and deflections. We've always bought paintings for their beauty and uniqueness. We wouldn't have bought an artwork we didn't like, regardless of the artist. Dealers like Martin La Farge see the artist's signature first and that makes him more liable to be taken advantage of.'

★

When Kristina returned to her studio, she sat for a long time looking at the Rembrandt before her. He had been a brilliant painter but had also suffered as a human being. He was plagued by mental illness all his life, his moods swinging from exuberance to periods of dark depression. She wanted to pay homage to him rather than simply copy his work. While she accepted she needed to 'borrow' his style to save lives, she didn't want her work to hang in place of his own. Great works were sold and resold so many times it was impossible to tell where her forgeries might end up after the war. What if they went to Allied countries like Britain, America or Australia, that had sacrificed men and women to save France?

It was then that she decided she would give each forgery a 'time bomb'. She would make a tiny mark – a personal signature of her own – on all the forgeries so they could be identified as fake after the war. The idea pleased her, and she went to the open window to breathe in some fresh air, turning over in her mind what that mark would be. Then a smile broke out on her face. She knew exactly what she would create and marvelled at her own brilliance.

CHAPTER TWENTY-FOUR

EVE

Paris, June 1946

It unnerved me that when Kristina looked out of the taxi on our way to Inès Bonne's apartment, she wore the expression of someone who was seeing Paris for the first time. She didn't look at it as someone who was returning to a place where she'd spent most of her adult life and brought two children into the world. Her gaze flickered over the red-brick buildings and Baroque church of the Marais district with the curiosity of a tourist. When we arrived outside Inès's apartment, I didn't ask Kristina if she remembered it. I didn't want to prompt her to have memories that weren't her own, as that could prove disastrous under the pressure of being in court. Paris was a different city to the one she had known when she was young and in love.

The taxi driver put down our suitcases and I took Flora's carrier from him. The rabbit looked around with curiosity while Kristina had an expression of deep concentration etched on her face.

'Who is Inès Bonne again?' she asked.

I was careful not to use the word 'friend' as it seemed to inflict pain on Kristina when she couldn't remember someone who had been close to her. 'She was the secretary at the gallery on Rue la Boétie.'

I had called Inès from the station in Nice to warn her of Kristina's memory problems and to caution her not to overwhelm her. But as soon as Inès opened the door, the normally restrained secretary threw her arms around Kristina in a warm embrace.

'You have returned!' she said, tears pouring down her cheeks.

Kristina froze, not showing even a glimmer of recognition. It wasn't how I'd hoped things would proceed. 'Perhaps we should go inside,' I said.

Inès's apartment was a reflection of her personality – an environment of perfect housekeeping with polished floors and gleaming windows. A plate of freshly baked shortbread sat on the dining table. The place was immaculate, and I wondered how she would cope with Kristina's rabbit, but she seemed genuinely delighted by the animal.

'Who is this?' she asked, looking in the carrier. 'Hello, you sweet thing. What's your name?'

'Her name is Flora,' Kristina answered with a nervous smile.

The significance of the name wasn't lost on Inès, who flashed me a quick glance before taking the carrier and setting it on the floor. She opened the door and Flora stepped gingerly out.

'We'll let her explore the apartment at her own pace, shall we?' suggested Inès. 'I have a sandbox in the kitchen and some straw.'

I grimaced as I looked at her freshly swept carpets. Flora was a rabbit, not a house-trained cat. But then seeing my consternation, Inès said, 'Kristina has always had such clever and well-trained rabbits. Far better behaved and mannered than most children. Except for Nadia and—'

Inès stopped herself and blushed from the collar of her dress to the top of her head. 'Oh, I'm sorry,' she said, looking mortified.

'Of course you knew them,' said Kristina, regarding Inès with renewed interest. 'Do you have a photograph of them?'

Inès looked uncertainly at me. I nodded. There was no cure for Kristina's sort of heartache, and it didn't seem to do her any good to try and shelter her from it.

'Yes,' she told Kristina. 'I have an album.'

'I'd like to see it, if that's all right?' Kristina replied.

'Of course it is. Please sit and make yourselves comfortable. I'll put the kettle on and then go get the album.'

After the women sat down at the table and the tea was poured, Kristina stared at the cover of the album as if she were perched on top of a diving board, about to take the plunge.

'I want to hear about my daughters, Madame Bonne. Please tell me about them.'

The older woman placed her hand on Kristina's arm. 'Call me Inès,' she said, 'and your two girls were the most beautiful children I have ever known.'

Kristina opened the album and the three of us looked at the portrait-sized photograph of a small blonde girl holding a rabbit while sitting in the lap of a pretty dark-haired girl a few years older. Kristina studied the picture with the utmost diligence while Inès desperately tried to hold back her own tears.

'When was this taken?' Kristina asked.

'A short while after you all moved into your home on Rue la Boétie,' Inès told her.

'They look happy, don't they?' Kristina said.

'They were very happy children. Clever and good-natured.'

Kristina squeezed her eyes shut for a moment. The deep sorrow on her face made me realise, perhaps for the first time, the extent of what she had lost – the most precious part of her existence. It made me want to fix every moment – good or bad – of my own life in my memory, for the loss of so much a part of oneself must be as devastating as to lose all one's limbs.

When Kristina opened her eyes again, she turned the page to look at the next photograph. It was of Max and Serge standing in front of the gallery.

'That's Max!' she said, her face brightening. Her finger hovered over the photograph for a moment, as if she would like to run it down her husband's handsome face. Then pointing at Serge, she asked, 'And who is he?'

Her question drove the air out of me.

'That's Serge Lavertu,' said Inès.

Kristina turned to me but I couldn't hold her gaze. It didn't bode well that she hadn't recognised the man she'd come to Paris to save.

★

I had wanted to go see Georges, but Inès suggested that we take a walk with Kristina to Serge's gallery in Saint-Germain-des-Prés and then to Rue la Boétie to see if anything stirred her memory. However, the walk produced no recollections for Kristina and we returned to the apartment where Inès made us *la soupe au pistou* and we drank a bottle of pinot gris. The wine, along with the weariness of travel and the summer heat, caused us all to doze. Inès put us up in her guest room, and Kristina and I lay down on the narrow single beds with a table and lamp between us.

As I drifted in and out of slumber, I heard Kristina talking in her sleep. She was mumbling names: 'Max' and 'Nadia and Ginette', and then after a long pause, 'Serge'. I sat up, watching her fluttering eyelids. It seemed to me that if Kristina could dream about them, then they must still be in her memory somewhere and we only had to find a way for her to access them.

I listened for a while longer, hoping to hear more names, but Kristina appeared to have drifted into a deeper phase of sleep. I lay back down, eventually feeling the slow tide of drowsiness wash over me. But before I lost consciousness, Kristina began to toss and turn. Suddenly she said out loud, 'We must find Monsieur Lapin!'

I turned over and looked at her. 'Who is Monsieur Lapin?' I asked.

But Kristina neither answered nor stirred. 'Lapin' was the French word for rabbit. Was she talking about a former pet rabbit? I didn't know. But the way Kristina had emphasised the name made it seem very important.

I settled back down into the bed. But sleep was impossible now.

Who on earth is Monsieur Lapin? I wondered. *And how will we find him?*

CHAPTER TWENTY-FIVE

KRISTINA

Paris, November 1943

Paris that November was not the city Kristina had known and loved. All its happiness and gaiety had been destroyed – at least it appeared to have been from the careworn look of the people on the streets. They moved about slowly, without the vivacity she had always associated with the City of Lights. The beautiful parks were now vegetable gardens, and rose vines no longer twisted themselves through balcony railings. In their place were scraggly tomato vines. Paris's cats, that had always delighted Kristina when she would spot one sunning itself on a windowsill or doorstep, had disappeared. They had gone into cooking pots along with the thousands of pigeons that used to grace the pavements. When she reached 21 Rue la Boétie, she clutched her precious package of the forged portrait of Rembrandt's wife and almost cried. Gone was the plaque Max had so proudly screwed next to the door announcing the arrival of 'Bergeret & Lavertu'. Instead it was 'The La Farge Gallery'. It was a testament to the dissolution of a life she had loved. But Serge and Max had been adamant that Martin La Farge would be their first victim, and not only for reasons of revenge.

'How pleased he will be to see you, Kristina,' Serge had said, 'and offer his assistance to a woman who possibly has a few valuable paintings stored away in Nice. He has no idea what I brought south. And he can only guess that with your husband missing, you are desperate.'

'*It would be unchivalrous not to come to your aid, Madame Bergeret,*' said Max, imitating Martin's affected manner of speech.

'I suppose he would think it will make him look better after the war when we claim our gallery back,' Kristina agreed.

'Precisely,' said Max.

The corners of Serge's lips turned down as if he had caught a bad smell. 'He'll probably tell you that he can discern a painting as an original *by the prickle of recognition that runs up my spine, as if I am recognising an old friend on the street.* He's bought plenty of fakes in the past.'

'Excellent ones, mind you,' added Max. 'The man doesn't refuse easy money. If he can pass something off as genuine, he will.'

Now as she stood before their old gallery, she remembered what Nadia had asked her before she left. *If a forgery is so good that it can pass the most expert examination, doesn't that mean it's also a work of genius?*

'*Bonjour*, Madame Bergeret,' Inès said with a wink as she opened the door for her. She had ingratiated herself with Martin to continue to work as the gallery's secretary, with the aim of keeping track of all the stolen art he sold. It was Inès who had arranged the appointment for Kristina.

'Ah *bonjour*, Madame Bergeret,' said Martin, as he came down the stairs. For a fleeting moment, Kristina nearly lost all sense of calm, and wanted to attack him for taking away not only her husband's business, but her family's home. By force of will she managed a sober nod.

'A Rembrandt?' he said, guiding her towards his office. 'Is it from your husband's collection?'

'My father's,' she said. 'He was a great lover of art.'

The statement was her own idea and temporarily threw Martin. If the painting belonged to Serge or Max, she figured he might try to have it declared an 'abandoned good' and claim that the Nazis already owned it. But if it was an inheritance from her father, he couldn't do anything but buy it lawfully.

'Your father was a collector?' he asked, pulling out a chair and offering it to her.

'Yes, of a small but very valuable collection,' she replied, keeping the facts deliberately vague. 'He was very particular about what he acquired.'

Martin watched her closely, lapping up what she was saying.

The Rembrandt was packaged in layers of brown paper. Kristina placed it on the table before Martin and watched as he untied the string and unwrapped it. Everything was so quiet in the gallery compared to the agitation she felt inside.

Martin grew up in a family with wealth, she heard Max's voice say in her head. *But he proved incompetent to run family affairs, so they bought him a prestigious gallery to run instead.*

Would he be incompetent enough to fail to recognise a forgery? she wondered. What about her 'time bomb'? Max and Serge had not been able to find it and she had refused to divulge where it was hidden. 'It's like a magic trick,' she had told them. 'If I reveal the sleight of hand, you'll see it every time.'

She had to remind herself to keep breathing, although her pulse was throbbing in her ears.

He placed the painting on an easel and turned his desk lamp towards it for better lighting. Then he put on his glasses and stared at the painting for a good few minutes before speaking.

'There is a touch of overpaint, some sort of restoration around the face, but that's not uncommon, especially in a painting of this age,' he said.

Despite her nerves, Kristina almost laughed. The 'touch of overpaint' had been Serge's suggestion. It would have been unlikely for a real Rembrandt to have passed between different owners in perfect condition.

He looked over the painting again before returning to his desk and thinking about something. Kristina wondered if he was feeling 'the prickle up his spine' that Serge had mentioned. But he gave nothing away on his poker face. Then he took out a notepad, wrote down a number and passed it to her. He had offered 400,000 francs, far less than the painting was worth on the heated Paris market. Serge had warned her that Martin would try something like that.

'It's lower than I anticipated,' she said.

'The Paris market is flooded with paintings. It's the best I can do.'

'Flooded with Rembrandts?' she asked with an innocent air.

The fact that Martin wanted the painting and was blatantly lying to her gave her more confidence to call his bluff. She wrote down one million francs and passed it to him. Max had told her to believe in her forgery, and she did. Asking less for it than that would scream it was a fake.

He looked at her figure and crossed it out. Replacing it with 800,000 francs. She had to decide whether to accept the price or insist on a higher one. Not accepting it meant she might have to approach another dealer and go through the whole ordeal again. She decided to keep up the bluff.

'It's as high as I am prepared to go,' he said, sensing her hesitation.

'I understand,' she said in a tone of infinite regret. 'I do have an appointment with Monsieur Gleize tomorrow afternoon. Perhaps he will be able to offer the price I am asking.'

Monsieur Gleize was a notoriously crooked art dealer with links to the German ambassador. She had no intention of going to see him, but Martin didn't know that.

'All right then,' he said. 'I agree to your asking price.'

Max had coached her about how to react if such a scenario unfolded. *Don't look surprised or relieved – that would be suspicious. Simply seem pleased and maintain an air of decorum.* In their normal lives, Max and Serge had never made that much of a profit on a painting. If they sold a work for an artist, they received a commission. If they bought something at auction, they had to take the risk that they would be able to resell it at a higher price to recoup their initial outlay. That Kristina had made a million francs in less than half an hour for something she had painted herself was staggering, but she couldn't show it.

While Inès typed up the paperwork, Martin guided Kristina around the gallery. The tour brought back painful memories, but she held her chin up and looked at each painting carefully. No doubt much of the art had been stolen from Jewish collections and she felt that having sold Martin a fake was in some small part a way to avenge them. She had made one million francs to help the escape lines save the very people Martin and his ilk were exploiting.

After the paperwork was completed, Martin gave her a cheque. She bid him goodbye and walked hurriedly down the street, her legs trembling. She wanted nothing more than to get back to Inès's apartment and curl up under the bedcovers. Then she became conscious of a car following her. The Gestapo? Had they been on her trail all the way from Nice?

For a split second she experienced panic at the idea of being caught and tortured, but then a familiar woman's voice called out to her. She turned around and saw Sonia waving from the window of a chauffeur-driven black Renault. The driver left the car idling and stepped out and opened the door for her.

'Hop inside!' said Sonia. 'It's cold today but lovely in here.'

Kristina wanted to refuse and to tell Sonia that they were no longer friends, but the nervous tension of the morning and her empty stomach left her unable to think fast enough. As if she was watching herself from afar, and having no power over her actions, she slid into the seat next to Sonia.

'Where are you going, Kristina?'

'Marais.'

'Have you eaten? Why don't we have lunch together?' Then without waiting for an answer, Sonia leaned towards the driver. 'The Ritz,' she said. Turning back to Kristina, she smiled. 'We haven't seen each other for a long time. We should celebrate our reunion.'

★

In the midst of starving Paris, the Ritz was as it had always been. Under the towering blue ceiling, the gilded mirrors of the dining room glimmered with a celestial glamour. White-gloved waiters delivered warmed plates of *filet de sole* in white wine to the city's most acclaimed writers, fashion designers, film stars and industrialists. The air was tinged with the scent of Turkish tobacco, not the linden-leaf cigarettes that were smoked by the people on the streets. Everywhere she looked, Kristina saw high-ranking Nazis. But when she recognised Hermann Göring sitting only a few tables away, she thought she might be sick. Despite his flaccid face and obese figure, he was the second most powerful man in Germany after Hitler and the worst art thief. Max had told her that Göring's personal art dealer would show up during raids on Jewish collectors to pick out the best artworks for his master while families were beaten and thrown out of their homes. The thin, effeminate mouth that he was now stuffing with foie gras must have also barked diabolical orders. Kristina had to use all her willpower to stop herself from letting her disgust show on her face.

A waiter came and set down a plate of asparagus in Hollandaise sauce on the table. She thought of the hundreds of pointed stakes that had been cut from Nice's trees and implanted at angles along the beach. The Niçoise called them 'Rommel's Asparagus', but Kristina judged it unwise to mention that joke in the current environment.

'You are in Paris selling some paintings?' asked Sonia.

There were no fresh lines on her olive skin and her dark hair was luxurious. Sonia did not bear the marks of a woman living with wartime deprivations.

'I have to keep things going,' Kristina said. 'I have two daughters to support. The cost of heating the villa is enough to break me.'

'I might be able to help you,' Sonia said. 'I have a client from Munich who buys for an important man. It's been mainly fabrics and porcelain, but Frau von Rittberg does deal in artwork. She will be down in the southern zone soon. I can set up a meeting for you, but she'll want something spectacular — something nobody else has. Do you have any works to offer that will satisfy that requirement?'

Kristina found it strange that she used to consider Sonia a friend, but she couldn't allow her to think that she didn't trust her. She took a sip of her champagne cocktail to give herself a moment to think. Serge had brought a Manet to

the villa during the Phoney War, and the Fould collection
he had personally salvaged included a Fragonard, an artist
favoured by the German market. She had come to Paris to
pass off a forged Rembrandt to Martin La Farge and been
paid a princely sum for it. She hadn't intended to make a
business of forgeries. But she tried to think like Serge and
Max. They would see that selling a forgery to Sonia's friend
would be a marvellous opportunity to exploit the enemy.
Kristina had never heard of an art dealer named von Rittberg,
but the Paris art market was so hot that dealers were turning
up everywhere all the time.

'Frau von Rittberg's client can afford the very best,' Sonia
said, pushing her case a little harder. 'Money is not a problem if
the painting is extraordinary.'

For a moment, Kristina felt like a collaborator in the midst
of other collaborators, and an opportunist driven by greed. Her
pride almost pushed her to refuse, but then she realised how
much it would help the Jewish refugees.

'All right then,' she said. 'Please arrange the meeting.'

'Good,' said Sonia as the waiter placed a braised duck in
front of her and ratatouille in front of Kristina. After living on
a starvation diet, Kristina should have found the taste of sautéed
eggplant, zucchini and bell peppers satisfying. But listening to
Sonia's tales about the wives of German officials who now made
up her clientele left her feeling queasy. Sonia didn't seem to see
any problem with helping the women decorate apartments that
had been stolen from Jewish families. The more she went on,
the harder Kristina had to press into her seat to stop herself
from standing up and slapping her.

★

'Do you think it might be a trap?' Serge asked, looking from Kristina to Max. 'I'm sure Sonia is collaborating with the Germans as a spy.'

Max thought about Serge's question. 'I think it's far less dangerous than what Kristina has been doing in hiding Jewish refugees. She would only be offering an artwork, and she did well in Paris with Martin La Farge. It sounds like whoever this von Rittberg is a dealer for has an enormous amount of cash behind him that could save a lot of people, as well as buy food for the Maquis and their families. I would not put Kristina in such a position if I thought it could go wrong.'

Max was a natural adventurer and self-confident in a way Kristina had never been. She couldn't tell if the knot in her stomach was from her intuition warning her of danger, or whether it was her natural timidity.

'I can go with you, Kristina,' Max said tenderly. 'And you can say no if you don't want to do it.'

'Are you mad?' Serge exclaimed. 'Look at you! You've got cuts all over your face and you walk with a limp. Everything about you screams "escaped agent". I'll go with her.'

'You call me mad,' said Max. 'If some German makes you pull down your pants, we'll all be lost.'

'Stop it, please!' Kristina said to them. 'I can go by myself. While I don't trust Sonia either, I don't think it's a trap. My impression was more that Sonia wants to get this woman in her good books, and I guess she could sense how desperate I am.'

'Well, we are only going to sell forged paintings to the enemy, we agreed on that,' said Serge. 'But we want something we can make significant money with and then be done. Because the more we put ourselves out there, the greater the risk something will go wrong.'

'*Flora*,' said Max, after a moment's consideration. 'We should do *Flora*.'

'You want me to forge such a masterpiece?' Kristina asked.

Max's eyes were alight with mischief. 'It's the perfect choice. Very few people have seen it. The painting has not been photographed for a catalogue, it's only described in the Foulds' inventory. If the dealer should – by some miracle – identify our version as a fake, the blame can be put on David Fould and the officials who viewed it at the Louvre, not you.'

'No,' Kristina said, looking away and shaking her head.

The Rembrandt had been nerve-racking, not only for its intricate detail but the chemical composition of the paint. But Botticelli? His style was supernaturally unique. There was an atmosphere to his work that she couldn't reproduce. No other mortal could.

It was Serge's turn to bolster her confidence now. 'You can do it, Kristina. I agree with Max that *Flora* would be the perfect painting to forge, but there is something else to consider too. This war is almost over. When the Nazi monsters are out of here, I plan to contact the press and let them view the paintings you forged and see if they can tell which one is the fake and which is the original. It's a chance to make you famous. The fact that you have planted a "time bomb" that will go off only when you reveal it, will make it all the more exciting!'

Max clapped his hands and paced the room. 'Brilliant!' he said.

'I want to be famous for my art not my infamy,' Kristina protested. 'And the fact that the Germans are losing the war has made them even more brutal. They'll only leave when the Allies force them to retreat, and we've been waiting for the Allied landing for months now.'

Max and Serge said nothing. They were leaving the choice to her. Kristina thought back to the defining moments of her life: her family fleeing Russia; going to art school; meeting Max and Serge; joining the Resistance. They were moments that if she had not taken certain turns, her life would have been completely different. She sensed that she was facing one of those defining moments now. When Donati had organised the ships to get the Jewish people out of Nice, she'd felt elated, as though good things could actually happen. Then fate turned against him. But what about her? If she sold a Botticelli to the Germans for its current market value, she may not change the course of the war, but she would change the course of hundreds of people's lives. Her heart pounded and blood surged through her veins as she thought about Moira and the Jewish woman who had jumped from the hotel window during the raid. She felt keenly every bit of rage and sorrow that she had endured through the last three years of Nazi terror.

She turned back to Max and Serge, not timid, but full of fire. 'I'll do it,' she said.

*

Although Kristina had made her decision and stuck by it, it didn't stop her from sometimes being paralysed by fear that she would fail everybody. Her courage and cowardice ran alongside each other, like two ponies pulling a cart. But the more she stared at Botticelli's *Flora*, the more she came to believe that his painting had a life of its own. It filled her with beauty and light and a sense of spring coming. The colours were vivid and the lines ravishingly sensual. The whole work glimmered. It took some practice to bring Flora's slightly flattened figure to life, to outline her and then paint her in the perfect pastel colours that were Botticelli's signature. But after several nervous attempts, her own masterful technique began to flow and she found herself believing in her talent again. Despite the high stakes, Botticelli's playfulness was contagious, and Kristina painted in her 'time bomb' with a cheeky confidence and a conviction that Botticelli would have approved of the practical joke.

When she was finished, Max and Serge went over the painting with a fine-tooth comb.

'It's perfect,' said Max, hugging Kristina to him and kissing her cheek. 'And neither Serge nor I can find the clue you have planted.' Then with a broad grin, he added: 'Serge has come up with a forgery of his own.'

'I'm coming with you to see von Rittberg,' said Serge, looking mildly embarrassed. 'Should any Nazi make me pull down my pants, I have a letter from a Resistance doctor to say I was recently circumcised due to venereal disease.'

*

Kristina and Serge stood before the doors of the hotel room in Cannes where Frau von Rittberg had agreed to meet them. They gave each other one final reassuring glance before Serge knocked on the door. Kristina quickly crossed herself and silently prayed for all to go well.

A moment later the door was opened by a maid. 'Madame von Rittberg is expecting you,' she said. 'Please come inside.'

She ushered them into a salon where a woman of about sixty was waiting. She had immaculately dyed black hair and not a skerrick of make-up except for a slash of lipstick.

'Please, have a seat,' she said, indicating a sofa.

Kristina and Serge settled themselves among the cushions while Frau von Rittberg took an armchair upholstered in blood-red velvet.

'Cigarette?' she asked, holding out a gold shell filled with Swiss cigarettes.

They declined, and Frau von Rittberg took one for herself and lit it. 'A rare Botticelli,' she said. 'I'm trembling with excitement.'

Kristina's fingers were numb although the room was adequately heated. Her throat felt scratchy, and her mouth was dry. It was lucky it was Serge who would do the talking, for she was sure she would have stuttered if she had tried.

'You won't be disappointed,' Serge said. 'It's on par with the *Birth of Venus* and *Primavera*.'

The telephone rang but Frau von Rittberg chose to ignore it. 'May I ask how you acquired it?'

'From someone who needed to leave the country, *in a hurry*. I have the bill of sale here as well as the painting's provenance.'

For a brief moment, Kristina drew strength from the thought of Édouard and Beatrice safe somewhere out of France. One day they would all meet again and wonder at how their Botticelli painting had saved so many lives. That is, provided all went well now.

Serge reached into his jacket pocket and took out the fake bill of sale as well as a cooked-up history of ownership. They had been printed by the same forger who made the false papers for the Jewish refugees. Frau von Rittberg perused it briefly, clearly not too concerned if it had been stolen or if the seller had been given a fair price.

'And how much are you asking for it?'

'Three million francs,' said Serge, with remarkable composure.

344

Kristina couldn't have swallowed if she had tried but Frau von Rittberg didn't even flinch. 'Then show it to me,' she said.

Carefully and with great reverence, Kristina and Serge undid the wrapping and lifted the painting from it, placing it on the stand Frau von Rittberg indicated.

Her eyes widened then softened again, like the flame of a fire. She stood up and looked over the painting.

'Every element is beautiful, don't you agree?' asked Serge. 'From Flora's lovely face to the exquisite detail of the flowers and plants.'

'Bring it closer to the light, please,' she said, pointing to a window.

Serge obliged by moving the stand and painting to the place Frau von Rittberg suggested.

She took a magnifying glass from her pocket and examined the painting, square by square. She was more thorough than Martin La Farge had been, which made Kristina think she was no run-of-the-mill interior designer. Her observation was confirmed when she noticed the pink marble Venus on the mantelpiece and the Indian Buddha holding a lotus leaf next to it. Everywhere she looked there was some sort of marvel – an Egyptian mask, enamel boxes, Lipchitz fire dogs. Frau von Rittberg was an experienced collector.

'The gentleman you are buying for,' Serge asked, 'is he an art connoisseur?'

A mysterious smile came to her lips. 'He trusts my judgement entirely. I am a good friend of his fiancée. We are almost family. Now explain to me again how this painting came from Italy to France.'

As Serge began a fictional tale about a grand tour, Frau von Rittberg went to a desk and took from the drawer a small bottle of alcohol and a cloth. 'May I?' she asked looking at Kristina.

Max and Serge had assured her that the ageing process they had perfected meant the paint would pass the alcohol test, but they had never demonstrated it for her. She knew everything depended on what would take place in the next few minutes and how well she played her part.

'Of course,' she said.

Frau von Rittberg poured some alcohol onto the cloth and dabbed at a corner of the painting. The cloth came away clean. Whatever that foul-smelling process Max and Serge had come up with was, it had worked. Then she stood back and regarded the painting for a long time.

'This is not the work of a student or a follower of Botticelli,' she said with both awe and conviction. 'This has a presence that only Botticelli could convey. Looking at it is like being seduced by the artist. I feel that he is taking my clothes off, slowly, one item at a time.'

Kristina bit down on her lip and didn't dare look at Serge.

Frau von Rittberg turned and smiled at them. 'And you haven't offered it to anyone else?'

Serge shook his head. 'We don't work that way. We speak to only one client at a time.'

She regarded him for a moment before saying, 'Then I will honour you by not trying to negotiate a lower price.'

It was the only moment in the whole procedure that made Kristina doubt Frau von Rittberg's competence. A dealer who doesn't try to negotiate a lower price is not a dealer.

Frau von Rittberg picked up the telephone and spoke to someone in German, a language neither Kristina nor Serge understood, except Kristina picked up one word: *dringend*. It meant 'a matter of urgency'. She'd heard it uttered in German bulletins on the radio before the French translation was given. Kristina pushed back a wave of fear. Frau von Rittberg put down the receiver and turned to them, but then the telephone rang again. This time she spoke at length in an excited voice. Kristina did her best not to think about what would happen if things went wrong. But when Frau von Rittberg put down the telephone receiver the second time, she looked pleased.

'I think it is time for champagne,' she said. 'The money will be transferred to you no later than tomorrow but on the condition that I take possession of the painting now. You'll be given all the paperwork and a deposit today of course.'

'Those terms are acceptable to us. I am very pleased for your client,' said Serge.

Kristina murmured her agreement. Art dealers normally didn't pass on priceless paintings until the full payment was received, but in that moment she'd have agreed to anything just to get out of there. She wondered if Serge had felt the same way. Whoever the buyer was, he obviously had blind trust in Frau von Rittberg to part with that much money without viewing the painting himself.

Frau von Rittberg opened the champagne bottle and poured them each a glass. 'I'm glad we settled things quickly,' she said. 'I want to take the painting with me to Berlin as soon as possible. The Führer is impatient to see it.'

Kristina didn't believe her ears at first. But Serge's sudden pallor confirmed that she had heard correctly.

'The Führer has a lot on his mind at the moment,' Frau von Rittberg continued. 'But the search for great works for the Führermuseum must continue.'

Kristina took a gulp of champagne. She tried to take in the reality of what had just happened. But even after repeating it to herself a dozen times in her head, she still couldn't believe it. Surely she'd wake up and see it all as some strange hallucination.

'Indeed,' said Serge, his face frozen. 'I've heard that the museum will be quite something.'

It was then that the identity of the buyer cemented itself as a picture in Kristina's mind: the pale, penetrating stare; the hair combed to one side; the toothbrush moustache. But most of all the hate and evil that emanated from the man. The acceptance of the fact of what had occurred was so shocking, Kristina felt dizzy with it.

They had just sold her forgery of Botticelli's *Flora* to Hitler.

CHAPTER TWENTY-SIX

EVE

Paris, June 1946

'Eve! I'm delighted you are back!' Georges said, ushering me into his study. 'I've got some good news. I managed to persuade the examining judge to give Kristina Belova a chance to study the two paintings Serge claims she forged — the Rembrandt that Martin La Farge purchased and sold to a collector, and the Botticelli that Serge and Kristina sold to Hedy von Rittberg. Perhaps Kristina will remember the clue she planted in them if she sees them.'

I sat down in the chair he offered me. 'That's wonderful.' But my enthusiasm hit a false note. Kristina hadn't recognised her own daughters or Serge in the photographs Inès had shown her. Paris wasn't familiar to her, and when I had asked her on the train from Nice about the 'time bomb' in the forged paintings, she had no recollection of what I was talking about. So Georges's 'good news' really didn't mean anything. It was all starting to seem hopeless.

Georges leaned against his desk and scrutinised me. 'Eve, what's wrong? You look like you are about to cry.'

'No, I'm not,' I lied, choking up even as I said it. 'I haven't slept very much, that's all. Hasn't anybody who Serge and Kristina rescued been found?'

'No, and I don't think we can count on it in the short amount of time we have. People had false papers, and records were destroyed at the time to keep them safe. Many of them have gone to live in the United States and even China and the Middle East.'

'What can we count on then, if Kristina can't remember anything?'

Georges grimaced. 'A miracle – and I don't like our chances of that.'

It felt as if all the wind had been knocked out of me. 'If Serge is condemned as a murderer then I won't be able to believe in justice anymore – or miracles.'

'Eve ...' Georges hesitated. 'You *are* in love with Serge Lavertu, aren't you? Now don't deny it – I saw the way you looked at him when we went to Fresnes prison.'

'The way I looked at him?'

Georges waved his hand. 'With longing in your eyes, as if he were the only man in the room. I don't blame you. He is sophisticated and charming, but under the circumstances I should counsel you against your infatuation, if it is at all possible to counsel people to be sensible when they have fallen in love.'

'He's my father, Georges.'

For a moment Georges looked exactly like the French saying: *Un berger qui a perdu ses chèvres.* A shepherd who has lost his goats. In Georges's case, he had to coax his herd from hilltops, valleys and meadows before he was able to speak again.

'Your father!' he cried. 'Gracious! But neither of you said anything about it.'

I fiddled with my sleeve. 'He doesn't know. My mother left France when she was pregnant, and I came to Paris to find him. Then I saw how he was struggling, and I didn't want to burden him until I could make something of myself.'

'You were doing that for him?'

'Yes, and of course for myself too. I thought if we could both go up in the world then we could live happily as father and daughter.'

Georges drummed his fingers on his desk. 'Where is your mother now? Still in Australia?'

'She ... killed herself. I haven't told him that either.'

Georges digested what I'd said and then looked at me with sympathy. 'I'm sorry, Eve. I wish I had known.'

It occurred to me that I often told Georges things I wouldn't say to anyone else. 'You understand I can't tell him any of this now, not when he has so much else on his mind.'

Georges gave a sad shake of his head. 'Of course not, and it's not my story to tell anyway.' He bit his lip. 'It's a brutal world. France is a country that knows that well. But I will promise you one thing, Eve,' he said, looking into my eyes, 'I will do everything in my power to save your father.'

I was touched by the kindness in his words. 'I know you will, Georges.'

CHAPTER TWENTY-SEVEN

KRISTINA

Paris, June 1946

'Take your time, Madame Bergeret,' Georges told Kristina as they stood in the anteroom in the Palais de Justice looking at two masterpieces claimed to be by two of the world's greatest artists - Botticelli's beautiful *Flora* and Rembrandt's moving portrait of his wife, Saskia — but which Serge Lavertu was adamant had been painted by her.

Eve was with them. While the young woman wasn't exactly wringing her hands, her desperation was palpable. But Kristina was not so much trying to remember painting the works, as to actually make herself *believe* such a thing was possible. Because even if she had copied each of Botticelli's and Rembrandt's brushstrokes to perfection, the paintings before her had none of the flatness of imitation. And they were vastly different from one another: Botticelli painted for the flamboyant Medicis and the Catholic church with its pomp and colour. Rembrandt's patrons were sombre protestants and his dark colours reflected that. Yet the paintings shimmered with life, as if they had each been animated by the soul of their creator.

More than a year had passed since Kristina had been rescued from the concentration camp. Docteur Gabriel had told her that most improvements in amnesia were seen in the first months after the incident that caused them. 'After that,' he explained, 'further recovery is unlikely.' She squeezed her eyes shut, as if she might be able to force herself to have a seizure. Perhaps an out-of-body experience would allow her to travel back to the past. But she couldn't conjure up such a condition; they happened spontaneously and she wasn't a magician.

She studied the paintings again – this time with an art critic's eye. She remembered that Botticelli sometimes placed himself in a work, as he did in *Adoration of the Magi*. But Flora was not her, nor were any of the nymphs. Rembrandt's Saskia was most certainly his wife. The paintings were both rich with blooms and she looked for an image of herself hidden among the petals, but found none.

The awful burden of having a man's life dependent on her memory weighed on her again and she could feel herself begin to panic. But before the terror reached a crescendo, another sensation took over. She was somewhere else, no longer in the anteroom and no longer with Georges and Eve.

She was standing at the bottom of the staircase at the Villa des Cygnes, and the pretty dark-haired girl she knew from Inès Bonne's album to be Nadia was talking to her. *If a forgery is so good that it can pass the most expert examination, doesn't that mean it's also a work of genius?*

Kristina could hear Nadia's voice clearly. She sensed her own feet on the tiled floor and the fabric of the clothes she was wearing against her skin. But more importantly, she could feel the bond between her and her daughter. It was an invisible thread that could not be broken.

What is this? she wondered. A hallucination? No, it was too real and vivid for that. It was a memory. The first one to appear out of the mist of everything that had happened between 1923 and 1945. It was only a flash – just seconds – yet she experienced it like a triumph and was hungry for more.

She turned to Georges and Eve. 'Can I see Monsieur Lavertu … Serge, I mean?'

Eve and Georges exchanged a glance between them. They looked uneasy. It wasn't until they went to Fresnes prison together that she understood why.

★

Kristina looked up from the enclosed courtyard to the three levels of cells on either side. *All those doors!* she thought. Behind each one she sensed a soul. Someone with a story. Someone who was suffering. She felt their misery as acutely as if it was her own – the loss of freedom, the monotony, the starvation … the fear. Then she knew why it felt so familiar.

'I was held here, wasn't I?' she asked the guard who was escorting them up to the second level. The air was so fusty she could hardly breathe. The place smelled like a sewer and they were all sweating. Then she recalled someone telling her that the prison was built over a swamp. But who was that? When was that?

The guard nodded grimly. 'If you were a resister and you were sent to a concentration camp, it is possible you passed through here first to be interrogated. But there won't be any record of it. The Germans burned the evidence of their atrocities before they left.'

He took them to an empty cell that was used as a conference room. It contained only a wooden table and chairs. Another memory sparked in Kristina's brain. Uniforms. Germans. Flashes of light in her eyes. Docteur Gabriel had said that the loss of her memory might have been induced by trauma – a shutting out of something that was too horrific to remember. She realised that if she eventually remembered Serge and recalled the 'time bomb' she planted in the forged paintings, other nightmares might resurface. Would she be able to bear them?

'Are you all right?' Eve asked, squeezing her arm.

There was a jug of water on the table and Kristina was desperately thirsty. But no one drank from it. None of them could afford to get dysentery with the trial less than three weeks away.

Then a tall man was brought in by the guards. There were chains around his wrists and ankles. His clothes hung loosely, but he maintained an air of dignity about him despite his condition. He looked at Kristina with such feeling her heart nearly broke.

'Kristina,' he said tenderly.

He had the same expectation in his eyes that Inès Bonne did – waiting for her to do or say something – but what? She was not the Kristina he knew. She was a woman who went to sleep one night in 1923 and woke up in the future with no recollection of what happened in between.

'Do you know who I am?' the man asked.

'Serge Lavertu.'

Her declaration cut the tension in the room, but she only knew it was Serge because of the photograph Inès had showed her. He sensed this and she saw it shocked him. Eve said she had warned him of her condition, but Kristina understood that it must be very difficult to comprehend. Yet he recovered himself and seemed intent on comforting her.

'The self-portrait I bought at Hôtel Drouot was very beautiful. I'm glad you are painting again.'

Somehow the idea that *he* bought her painting made her happy. 'I'm sorry that I don't remember you,' she said.

'I know,' he replied.

Their eyes met and she understood. This man loved her. She wanted to be free from her mental prison as surely as he wished to be released from his physical one, but neither of them had the key. Tears welled in her eyes.

'It's all right, Kristina,' he said. 'I'm happy knowing that you're safely home and that you are painting again. Better than ever.'

He tried to lift his hand to touch hers, but he couldn't because of the chains. So she reached out to touch him. As she felt the warmth of him under her fingertips, a name suddenly came out of the mist of her mind. 'Monsieur Lapin,' she said.

His face instantly lit up and despite the dire circumstances, he laughed.

Eve piped up then. 'Who is Monsieur Lapin? Kristina mumbled his name in her sleep the other night.'

Serge turned to her. 'It was the nickname of a portrait she painted of me holding her pet rabbit. She did it during the war in the style of Leonardo da Vinci's *Lady with an Ermine*. The official title was *Frenchman with a Rabbit*, but we called it "Monsieur Lapin" for short. It was a joke between us, but she went to enormous lengths to pay tribute to da Vinci's work. She even painted it with monocular perspective.'

'Where is the painting now?' Georges asked, suddenly animated. 'We could use it to show that Madame Bergeret is capable of reproducing works from the Renaissance.'

'It was probably stolen, like almost everything else in the villa,' Kristina said. 'My butler reported the theft to the Artistic

Recovery Commission but only a few of my paintings have been returned and nothing like the one you are describing.'

Georges turned to Eve. 'We must find that painting.'

The guard indicated that their time was up. As Serge was led away, a deep feeling welled in Kristina's heart. She may not remember a thing about him, but she knew that she loved him as much as he loved her. She would not abandon him, no matter how difficult the trial got. She would go through any ordeal for him, as she believed he would for her.

CHAPTER TWENTY-EIGHT

EVE

Paris, July 1946

The trial was scheduled to start at two o'clock in the afternoon. Lunch at Inès's apartment was a horrid, nervous affair of stilted conversation. I forced myself to eat some potato and leek soup, which then sat uneasily in my stomach. It was decided that Georges would meet Serge as he arrived from the prison, while Kristina, Inès and I would go to the Palais de Justice by the Métro. We were surprised to find the carriages congested at that time of the afternoon. I sat squashed between a businessman in a suit and a chef in a white uniform, who left a trail of white flour on my black skirt where his leg pressed against mine. Then to our even greater surprise, everyone poured out of the train at the same stop: Cité.

'*Mon Dieu*,' Inès whispered to me. 'They are *all* going to the trial.'

As we approached the monumental Palais de Justice with its fluted columns and statues of imperial eagles, we saw that a large crowd had already gathered in the courtyard in front. Georges had warned us that the trial would attract the public. The Foulds were greatly admired for their philanthropy and

358

the French had not completely tired of letting the blood of collaborators. But I had not imagined anything like the spectacle before me. Because the Foulds had been murdered in Nice, the trial would normally have taken place there. But the Ministry of Justice had deemed the trial to be in 'the public interest', so it was taking place in Paris instead. Terrible pictures rose in my mind of the French Revolution and mobs cheering as aristocrats were led to the guillotine.

Kristina stopped in her tracks, afraid to go on. She had brought a large tapestry bag with her and was clinging on to it as if she was protecting a child. I took her arm, and we pushed our way through the crowd towards the massive iron gates along the Boulevard du Palais. Inside the building there were so many people waiting to get into the courtroom that there would be only standing room left. It was as if all of Paris society had turned up for the opera – the women magnificently turned out in silks and brocades, feathers and pearls. I spotted Marthe de Villiers and Madame Fouquet among them. It struck me how those women who had orchestrated my downfall were back again to see someone else condemned. Did it make them feel superior to stand in judgement of others? I was sickened that only a short time ago I had wanted to be accepted by them. I didn't care about any of that now.

Georges appeared from the courtroom wearing a long black cloak with a white jabot. With his towering height he was impressive in appearance, and I hoped the jury would be swayed by him.

'Come inside,' he said, ushering us in front of him. 'They have one woman on the jury, a nurse. The rest of them are men – bakers, factory workers, mechanics.'

I understood the significance of what Georges was telling me. The woman was one of the first to be selected for a jury under the new rights granted to women after the war. Something they had been denied for many years for many reasons, one of them being that it was argued women would be too soft on criminals. The nurse might feel she had something to prove. The men would have had to have been directly involved in the Resistance to serve on the jury, but would any of them believe Serge had been a genuine member of the cause too?

I followed Georges to the desk where he and I would be sitting for the defence. Kristina and Inès took their places at the front of the spectator seats. The press corps was already in place, eager to grab the starring by-lines of the day. One heavyset reporter elbowed his colleague.

'Look, Camadeau has a pretty young woman with him. Do you know who she is?'

'Mademoiselle,' his companion called out to me. 'What is your name and are you free for dinner tonight?'

Georges answered for me. 'This is Mademoiselle Archer, my associate. And no, she is not free for dinner tonight or any night, thank you.'

Suddenly the doors opened and the public rushed into the room, pushing each other to get the seats that offered the best view. The prosecutor arrived in his red robe, and although he nodded courteously to Georges and me, I couldn't forget that this was the man who was going to do everything in his power to have Serge condemned. A bell rang and two gendarmes led Serge into the accused box behind us. He was wearing a freshly pressed navy suit and silver tie that Inès had selected. Although he had been unjustly imprisoned, he had no air of bitterness about him. I admired him for his brave face, and I decided I would never show him the weight and worry I carried in me.

'*Bon courage*,' Georges said to him.

Serge's appearance had stirred chatter among the spectators but he paid them no heed. Instead, he looked up at the ceiling. My eyes followed to where he was looking. It was a fresco depicting King Louis XIII, known as 'The Just', taking his vows.

'It was commissioned during the occupation. The paint still isn't quite dry,' Serge whispered, as calmly as if he were taking in a painting at a museum. 'And now I will be judged by the very men who served under the Germans.'

The presiding judge, named Clouzot, and the magistrates and jurists entered the room and everyone rose to their feet. Then the trial began.

Judge Clouzot turned to Serge and spoke gravely. 'Your name is Serge Lavertu, you were born on the second of September 1893 in Barbizon. You are an art dealer, and you reside in Paris.'

Serge confirmed the details, and then it was the court secretary's turn to read out the charges. I cringed as I heard the words 'collaboration', 'theft' and 'murder'.

From there the trial proceeded like a macabre opera with its own overture, recitative, aria, chorus and ballet. Judge Clouzot questioned Serge at length, using the report the examining judge had prepared. In the Australian court system, only one judge presided over a trial to even-handedly orchestrate the proceedings. But in the French system, not only would the prosecutor question the accused, the judge would as well, and even individual members of the jury.

Nonetheless, Judge Clouzot's questioning should have been impartial, with the aim of creating an atmosphere of 'discovery', but clearly it was not. He hinted that Serge was not a man who revered art and beauty, but a man who worshipped money enough to kill his friends.

'Those who saw you at auctions at the Hôtel Drouot describe you as a dealer who "salivated over a painting that he knew he could sell at three times the price for which he acquired it". Other dealers were frightened to bid for a painting if they knew they were up against you.'

Serge showed no animosity in his answer. 'No, the money was never the main thing,' he said. 'Although no dealer who wants to stay in business buys a painting without some consideration of a profit. If faced with two clients who desired the same painting, I usually erred to the side of the one who would appreciate the work more over the one who offered the highest price for it.'

The only time Serge became ruffled was when the prosecutor directly accused him of killing Édouard and Beatrice Fould. 'Never!' he replied, raising his voice. 'Why kill a man and his wife who entrusted me, their friend, with not only their artworks, but their lives!'

'You have no proof of any of this,' the prosecutor reminded him. 'Judge Regis in his report wrote that you claim there was a letter from Édouard Fould entrusting you with the collection, including the Botticelli, but that has mysteriously disappeared.'

'The Germans looted everything at the Villa des Cygnes,' Serge replied. 'Including important documents.'

When Georges stood up it was like the opera shifted again. 'Ladies and gentlemen of the court, if Serge Lavertu murdered the Foulds and stole their artwork, where are all the paintings? Where is the money? It's not enough to say, "Oh, he has them stashed away in banks in Switzerland," when there is no proof. On the question of how he acquired a pistol, the prosecution claims that it could have been easily obtained from the Italians who discarded weapons as they left France. But such a claim is true of *all* the citizens of Nice! I object to how these proceedings are being run. The evidence is purely circumstantial. Serge Lavertu himself was robbed blind by both the Vichy government and the Nazis. He lost his gallery. His own inventory was looted by the Germans. Surely someone who has been an exemplary businessman, a good citizen and a member of the Resistance can hold his head up wherever he goes and not have to be burdened with such outrageous accusations ...'

After a short intermission it was time for the witnesses. There was Sonia, who painted a picture of Serge as a money-grubbing dealer. 'Serge Lavertu never liked me because I looked out for Kristina's interests. I could see that he intended to exploit her. She was terribly naïve. I warned her several times that he was trying to come between her and her husband. Do I believe that Kristina could have been persuaded to paint forgeries? Never!'

The testimonies of the Foulds' two maids, who had apparently heard nothing the night of the storm, had clearly been written for them by the prosecution to collaborate with the theory that Serge had an opportunity and a motive to kill the Foulds. I had to force myself to think of something else when the police detective described the gruesome discovery of the Foulds' bodies.

But the most damning evidence came from the Foulds' gardener, who no doubt had been spurred on by the prosecution to put the most sinister spin on all Serge's actions that fateful day. 'He seemed keen for Madame Bergeret to return to her home as if he wanted to have her out of the way' and 'No, if anyone else had come to the villa that night I would have heard them arrive as my cottage is next to the gate.'

Georges had warned me the gardener and maids might give biased testimonies. 'Honest people making statements in perfectly good faith constitute the worst danger. They may have good intentions, but they only saw part of what took place. While they seem to be reporting the facts truthfully, their recollections have been tainted by the prosecution, and by their own desire to see justice done.'

Then, with a renewed sense of drama, the paintings were brought into the court by attendants and set on easels – not only the Botticelli and the Rembrandt, but Kristina's portrait of Max and her self-portrait in front of a dressing-table mirror that had been returned to Serge by the Artistic Recovery Commission.

When everything was in place, the prosecutor announced, 'I now call on Monsieur Martin La Farge.'

Like a knight charging into battle, Martin swept into the courtroom. Whispers of delight were exchanged among the female spectators, forcing Judge Clouzot to call for order. Martin reached the stand and looked around the audience, giving nods and waves to his admirers.

'Monsieur La Farge,' said the prosecutor, 'you are considered one of the foremost art dealers in Paris. You have been in the art business for how long?'

'Thirty years.'

'Thirty years!' repeated the prosecutor. 'So you are certainly no novice. In November 1943, you bought the painting on the right, *Portrait of the Artist's Wife*, from Madame Bergeret, which you believed came from her father's collection. The defendant claims it is a forgery painted by Madame Bergeret. Do you agree that it is a forgery?'

'Absolutely not,' said Martin, jutting out his chin. 'If I had, I should not have paid the sum of money I did.'

'And how much did you pay for it?'

'One million francs.'

Gasps sounded around the room at the mention of such a substantial amount. I glanced at the jury. One of the men, grey-haired with long sideburns, folded his arms and frowned. Another looked with disdain from Martin to Serge. In the minds of men who would never earn that amount of money in their lifetimes, and in a country where people were still dying from malnutrition, one million francs was an obscene amount of money to pay for a painting.

I took a piece of paper and wrote down: *The jury is becoming alienated by the sum of money involved. Martin La Farge is a rich man. Make sure they know Serge has nothing. He sacrificed it all for the Resistance. He is a Jew who had everything taken away from him – by Martin La Farge who presently lives like a king!*

I passed it to Georges, who nodded. He probably didn't need legal coaching from me, but I was beginning to feel powerless in the face of the calamity that was unfolding before my eyes and had to do something.

'Indeed, I very much doubt anyone would pay that amount of money if he thought he was purchasing a fake,' said the prosecutor, looking around the room for effect. 'But could you explain to the jury why you are so certain?'

Martin smirked in a way that riled me. 'Look at it,' he said, pointing to the portrait. 'Rembrandt is the most renowned painter of the past four hundred years. A master. See the detail in the bouquet the subject is holding, the way her gaze is not direct but looking at someone just to the right. It's intimate and moving.'

'And you don't believe Madame Bergeret could have made an excellent copy of the painting?' asked the prosecutor.

Martin turned to Judge Clouzot. 'May I?'

'Proceed,' said the judge.

Martin approached Kristina's paintings and gave a faint sigh. 'And here we have the work of Madame Bergeret painting as Kristina Belova. Not a master by any means, not even close.

She's a good enough modern painter, but she doesn't have the technical skill to reproduce a Rembrandt. At least one that would get past me.'

Laughter arose from the audience. For the first time since the ordeal began, Serge looked angry. I understood why. Martin was going further than proving his point. He was trying to destroy Kristina's revived career by publicly dismissing her talent.

'Objection!' said Georges, standing. 'Those portraits were painted at the very beginning of Madame Bergeret's career, when she had only just started her studies in Paris. Why not look at her later works, like *The Joy of Life* ...'

'Or *The Flight of Eve*,' I said under my breath.

'Objection overruled,' said Judge Clouzot. 'Please proceed, Monsieur Prosecutor.'

'The defendant also claims that Madame Bergeret added a certain element to each painting so they could be detected as forgeries. And yet you have not found any such element on examining these paintings, have you, Monsieur La Farge?' He then indicated Kristina. 'And Madame Bergeret has no memory of it.'

'Objection!' called Georges. 'Madame Bergeret has no memory of it because, as confirmed by the doctor's examination in Judge Regis's report, she is suffering amnesia.'

'Convenient for Lavertu!' muttered one of the press reporters.

'Order!' said Judge Clouzot. 'I am warning you, Monsieur Camadeau, if you persist with these unnecessary interruptions I will have you removed from the court.'

Judge Clouzot's clear bias inspired Martin to even greater arrogance. He took out a magnifying glass from his pocket and waved it for effect. 'Neither I nor the two other experts from the Louvre could find any such element as a supposed "time bomb" in either painting. We have gone over the works several times, inch by inch, and found nothing. It's a ridiculous notion.'

'Thank you, Monsieur La Farge,' said the prosecutor. 'That is all.'

It was Georges's turn to question Martin. 'Monsieur Lavertu claims that he used certain processes to make sure the canvases passed through the standard alcohol and X-ray tests to detect a forgery. He also says it was impossible during the war to obtain the exact paint pigments that Rembrandt or Botticelli would have used, and that the paintings can be proved to be forgeries if they are submitted to a proper chemical test. Yet both you and the Louvre have refused such tests.'

'We are not going to scrape paint from valuable masterpieces in order to substantiate what we already know,' replied Martin irritably. 'All the other evidence combined is enough to say that both the Botticelli and the Rembrandt are authentic.'

'You are not prepared to risk minute damage to a painting, but you are prepared to have a man condemned to death by denying him the evidence that may save him?'

Out of the corner of my eye I noticed Kristina staring at the paintings, willing herself to remember something. The tapestry bag on her lap moved. At first I thought it was a hallucination brought on by the strain I was under, but then two long ears appeared, followed by a furry caramel head and a pink twitching nose. Kristina must have brought Flora to the court with her for comfort. Unnoticed by Kristina, the rabbit wriggled out of the bag and onto her lap. From there it leaped to the centre of the court.

People whispered and tittered when they spotted Flora. 'Look, somebody brought their dinner,' said one of the reporters, eliciting laughter from the room.

I stood up to retrieve Flora but before I could grab her, she hopped straight towards Martin. A look of horror came to his face and his whole body jerked. A cry that sounded like something between a yell and a sneeze came out of his throat. It was then I remembered he suffered from leporiphobia, an irrational fear of rabbits. He tried to run away but tripped in his effort to flee and knocked over the Rembrandt.

'Get it away from me,' he screamed.

One of the gendarmes made a grab for Flora but she slipped from his hands. Luckily, Inès caught her and managed to carry her back to Kristina, who pressed Flora to her chest.

'It's a rabbit!' Kristina cried out.

Her claim brought jeers and laughter from the spectators, while an attendant hurriedly righted the Rembrandt portrait and helped Martin to his feet.

'Order!' demanded Judge Clouzot. 'It's quite obvious it's a rabbit, Madame Bergeret. Now please remove it from this courtroom immediately.'

But the look on Kristina's face told me there was something else she wanted to say. 'Monsieur President, I meant that the clue in the painting is a rabbit. I can prove it to you.'

Judge Clouzot looked outraged, but with all eyes on him it was impossible for him to refuse. Kristina handed Flora to Inès and picked up the magnifying glass Martin had dropped.

The entire courtroom held its breath while she examined the Rembrandt.

'There in the bouquet!' she said triumphantly. 'A rabbit's face and ears painted in white with a single line.' She moved to the Botticelli painting. But as much as she scanned the magnifying glass over the painting, she couldn't seem to find the same clue in it. The courtroom was silent, their attention riveted on Kristina. But the pressure flustered her and I could see she was beginning to panic.

'Well, get on with it,' said Judge Clouzot.

Kristina's face suddenly lit up. 'And there!' she said at last. 'In the fold of Flora's drapery. Exactly the same rabbit.'

The prosecutor took the magnifying glass from Kristina and looked to where she pointed. The astonished expression on his face confirmed her claim. The magnifying glass was then passed to Judge Clouzot and each member of the jury as they filed past the painting to look at the new discovery.

'Once you see it, you can't not see it,' said the female jurist.

The press corps went wild. Camera bulbs flashed like lightning strikes.

Kristina looked at Serge and smiled. Both of them were trembling with excitement.

Judge Clouzot returned to the platform and banged his gavel. 'Order! Order in the court!' He glared at Georges and then the prosecutor. 'In my chambers at once!'

★

While the rest of us waited in the courtroom, I listened to the two journalists debate about what was most likely to happen next.

'The fact that Lavertu insisted from the beginning that the paintings were forgeries, and that the experts were wrong, strengthens the case that he's telling the truth.'

'Not necessarily,' replied his colleague. 'It could be argued that he kept the originals to sell later while taking advantage by selling forgeries of them. It simply means the charge of national disgrace will be dropped, but the charge of murder will proceed.'

'But that would be all circumstantial, with no evidence to support it at all. If they follow that line, it would be obvious that Judge Clouzot and the prosecutor are building a dubious case against Lavertu and they have already decided the outcome of this trial.'

I waited in tense anticipation for what seemed like an eternity. Then the door to the courtroom opened and Judge Clouzot, the prosecutor and Georges returned. Georges would not meet my eye when I looked at him.

'The trial for the charge of murder will proceed,' announced Judge Clouzot. 'Prosecutor, please give your closing statement.'

Shocked and surprised murmurs sounded through the courtroom.

Georges stood up. 'Monsieur President, I object. The enormity of the charges against the defendant should guarantee the strictest and most impartial of trials. Why in France, of all countries, would we pervert the process of justice that has defined our soul for decades!'

'Objection overruled,' said Judge Clouzot. 'Monsieur Prosecutor, proceed with your closing argument.'

The prosecutor, who had seemed so confident at the beginning of the trial, now looked unsettled. He stuttered as he repeated the same arguments he'd used in his opening statement. It was as if he had lost the conviction that Serge was guilty or that justice was being done.

Now everything rested on Georges's closing argument. 'How is it possible that a respectable and honest man may find himself accountable before the court?' he asked the jury. 'It would take some wretched stroke of fate that he should find himself mistaken for a dubious character, let alone a murderer. Yet, ladies and gentlemen of the court, I can assure you that such unthinkable incidences do occur and there is a name for them – miscarriage of justice!'

I was proud of Georges, so eloquent despite the dire turn of events. The eyes of the reporters and the spectators were glued to him.

'France will bear the scars for many years of the *épuration sauvage*, when a desire for revenge got the better of our ideals of truth, equality and justice. All that was required to see an innocent person wrongfully convicted was a vengeful crowd. But there can be no miscarriage of justice today, since the guilt of the defendant, far from being confirmed, remains seriously in question. There is no evidence other than circumstantial, no witness to the actual crime, nothing in the defendants' longstanding relationship with Édouard Fould and his wife to suggest such a heinous crime would be committed. There are no money trails to Swiss bank accounts, or even a lavish lifestyle, that might indicate that Serge Lavertu profited from the crime he is accused of. Rather, before you stands a hero of the Resistance. A man who sold a fake painting to Hitler to gain funds for an escape line to help his fellow citizens. He deserves the *Légion d'honneur* not the farce that has been this trial.'

I knew Georges had given his argument everything. It was out of his hands now. He sat down next to me and we watched Judge Clouzot, the magistrates and jurists file out of the room. Serge was escorted out by the gendarmes and Georges indicated for me to follow them. Inès stayed with Kristina, who looked bewildered, as if wondering why the very thing she had come to Paris to do hadn't seemed to have made any difference.

'What happens now?' I asked Georges as the guards closed the doors behind us.

'The magistrates and the jury will go to Judge Clouzot's chambers, where he will explain the implications of an innocent or guilty verdict.'

'Will he be fair?' I asked.

Georges acknowledged my doubts with a grim nod of his head. 'We must remain steadfast in hope, Eve,' he said, indicating the room where Serge was being held. 'For his sake. Now let's go see him.'

But no sooner had we stood up than the bell sounded calling us back to court. Was it possible that a verdict had been reached so quickly? I knew that in France the jury's decision did not have to be unanimous and there was no such thing as a 'hung' jury, but even so, I would have expected a much longer deliberation.

We took our places in the courtroom and Serge was brought back in.

Silence fell over the assembly. The pens of the journalists were poised above their notepads. The court secretary's fingers stayed suspended over the keyboard of his stenograph machine. The jurists stared blankly in front of them. The spectators leaned forward in anticipation while Kristina and Inès clung to each other. I stopped breathing. The courtroom had turned into a painting – an impression of a moment in time.

Judge Clouzot turned in Serge's direction. 'Will the defendant please rise.'

Serge stood as he was directed. Judge Clouzot cleared his throat. 'The court has given its declaration by a majority that you, Serge Lavertu, have rendered yourself guilty of murder ...'

I felt myself blanch. My mind went blank. I saw the judge's mouth moving but I didn't hear another word of what he said. The court broke out in pandemonium. Some cheered when Judge Clouzot pronounced a sentence of death, while others swayed on their feet as if they couldn't believe what they were hearing.

When Judge Clouzot asked Serge if he had anything to say, Serge only looked him in the eye and said, 'You have misjudged me.'

The two gendarmes took him by the arms and led him from the courtroom.

Georges turned to me, his face ashen. Then standing head and shoulders above everyone, he said in a booming voice, 'This is a travesty of justice! We have forty-eight hours to appeal. And appeal we will!'

He turned to me. I knew that no matter what we did to save Serge, we were fighting something beyond the course of justice. Something corrupt and tainted. The trial should not have happened in the first place. Serge had been set up. But was forty-eight hours enough time to find new evidence that would change anything?

'I must see him. I must tell him that he's my father,' I said.

Georges nodded. 'I will arrange it.'

I turned to Kristina who was weeping in Inès's embrace.

Kristina, I inwardly prayed. *Please, please remember something else of significance. Something that can exonerate Serge completely.*

CHAPTER TWENTY-NINE

EVE

Paris, July 1946

When I went to see Serge at Fresnes he was brought in wearing rough prison garb. The chains around his feet made him shuffle in tiny steps. He had a diary tucked under his arm. When he reached his chair, he handed it to me.

'Ever since I saw Kristina, I have been writing in this diary for her,' he said. 'I've shared everything I remember about her life with Max and her children. I've written about her parents and an account of what she did in the war – the people she helped, and our friends Moira, and Édouard and Beatrice Fould. But most of all, I wrote about *how much she was loved.*'

The diary was weighty, thick with words. Serge had poured all his love into it. Here he was, in chains and condemned to death, and yet thinking of Kristina.

'You are loved too, Serge,' I said.

He shook his head sadly. 'Anybody who loved me is dead ... or can't remember me. I won't be missed, and strangely, that is a comfort somehow.'

'I love you.'

'Eve,' he said, his voice full of compassion, 'you did everything you could. I haven't even had a chance to thank you.'

I shook my head and breathed deeply before plunging forward. 'I should have spoken sooner,' I said, a tremble in my voice. 'I'm Madeleine's daughter. *Your daughter.*'

Serge went still, like an image frozen in time.

'After she left France, my mother went to Australia with Efron Archer, where I was born,' I continued. 'I was given his name but I wasn't Efron Archer's child, although for the first seven years of my life I believed I was. I was yours.'

Serge stared at his hands as if trying to take in what I had told him. 'Madeleine had a girl,' he said, shaking his head. 'I always thought the child would be a girl. That's how I imagined her.' Then he looked up at me and his eyes filled with tears. 'How I imagined *you*, I should say. You have no idea how often I've thought of you, but I believed you were lost to me forever. And yet, here you are ... like an angel.' He paused, thinking. 'It's a miracle. I've been praying for one, only God has answered a different prayer to the one I was sending.' He smiled gently. 'This is a far, far better miracle. But how did you find me?'

'My mother ... Madeleine, told me all about you. She told me how wonderful and talented you were.'

'She did? But I thought she hated me.'

'Why?' I took from my purse the letter my mother had written before her death and passed it to him. 'She asks you to forgive *her.*'

Serge read the letter, his face clouding over when he reached the end. 'Did she ...?'

'Yes, she took her own life.'

He shook his head. 'She was beautiful, and funny, and clever. We all loved her.' His eyes took on a faraway look. 'She sang like a nightingale.'

'She sang?' It was news to me. My mother had hated any sort of singing. I wasn't even able to hum nursery rhymes without eliciting her irritation. 'My mother wasn't a well person. She drank.'

Serge looked at me sadly. 'I think things happened to her that would make anyone lose their sanity. Her family was ... well, they were abusive. She was afraid of them. I believe that's why she ran away. She was afraid they would harm you.'

'Do you know who they were?'

Serge shook his head. 'She would never say. After she left, we found a picture in her room of an old woman with a baby we assumed to be Madeleine. They were standing in front of a grand house with a mansard roof and a bronze equestrian statue of Marcus Aurelius near the door. Kristina told me that Madeleine had known love only from her grandmother, and that her father and brother were brutes.'

We both sat quietly for a moment, absorbing what we had revealed to each other. My mother had said that she had come from a rich family so the grand house had probably been her family home. But she would never tell me her family name, so I didn't see any way I would ever find out who they were. But there was another more pressing question to ask.

'Did you love her?'

He nodded. 'Yes, very much. But not in the way she needed. I believe I hurt her deeply.'

'How? What happened?'

Serge shifted as if he had borne the weight of his guilt for a long time. 'One night when we were both sad, we tried to find comfort in each other's arms. And for one passionate moment in time, we did, and it was beautiful. It was the night you were conceived. But in the morning, I realised I'd made a terrible mistake. I could not give her as much of myself as she wanted, and she took it as a rejection.'

I nodded towards the letter. 'Whatever happened between you, she forgave you. And she wanted me to come to you.'

Serge looked into my eyes. 'I wanted to be your father more than I have ever wanted any painting,' he said. 'But now they'll take everything from me, I can't even give you an inheritance.'

'It doesn't matter. I never wanted anything from you other than to hear what you've just told me – that you thought of me and wanted to be my father.'

Serge nodded towards the diary. 'I'm even more glad I wrote it all down now. I've written a lot about Madeleine. Kristina loved her too – and you. She used to light a candle for you every year on what she thought would be your birthday.'

His face crumpled into tears, and I wept too. We cried until we were both spent, and afterwards, even in the dirty and sordid atmosphere of Fresnes prison, the air felt as fresh as spring. I realised that all the pain of the past had been washed away and everything was anew. Whatever happened, for however brief it might be, Serge and I finally had each other.

CHAPTER THIRTY

KRISTINA

Paris, July 1946

Kristina was lying in her bed in Inès's guest room, half-dozing, when Eve came in looking unusually dishevelled. Strands of hair had fallen from her chignon and her lipstick had faded. She seemed very young and vulnerable, and it stirred something maternal in Kristina. She raised herself into a sitting position and patted the space on the bed next to her. 'Come sit with me,' she said. 'It's been a distressing day.'

Eve took something from her purse, a diary, then handed it to her before sitting beside her. 'Serge wrote down all the things he wants you to know about your life.'

'When did he do it?' Kristina asked, looking at the diary in wonder.

'He said he's written in it every day since you first visited him.'

Kristina turned to the first page.

Let me start by telling you things about yourself, Kristina. You liked to paint in the morning. You were often the first to rise and you would go to your studio and work until you produced something you considered worthwhile. Nature was a wonder to you, and you could spend an hour studying a rose or a leaf. If a bird appeared, you would watch it with fascination, whether it was a rare European roller or a common street pigeon. You brightened everyone's lives with your inner beauty and kindness. The sound of your voice would bring a smile to everyone's faces — Max, your daughters, and even your pet rabbits adored you. Whatever and whoever you enfolded in your heart, blossomed in the joy of its existence ...

Kristina brushed her fingers down her throat. 'It's beautiful,' she said. 'He's written beautiful things about me.'

'I think he's written the truth about you, Kristina. You are beautiful.' Eve bit her lip, thinking a moment, then added, 'Before you read more, I want you to know that Serge is my father. Madeleine was my mother. He said he's written about her in the diary, but I haven't read any of it yet.'

Kristina studied Eve, taking in this new information. 'You and Serge look very much alike. I am surprised I didn't make the connection sooner.'

'We have things in common too, you and I,' Eve told her, almost shyly. 'You see, there's so much I don't know about my mother's life before she came to Australia, so much that's a mystery to me. Sometimes I think I know how you feel when you say you're missing parts of yourself.'

Kristina handed the diary to her and leaned back on the pillows. 'We will discover the past together then.'

Time stood still as Serge's words brought the past to life. Sometimes Eve read to Kristina and then Kristina would take over. They laughed at the story of Serge arriving home from a trip to find Max had hocked his furniture so he could buy all

Kristina's paintings, and about Kristina and Serge's rescue of Leo the rabbit from his would-be butcher.

'So that's where my love of rabbits started,' said Kristina.

She and Eve smiled at the stories of Nadia and Ginette, whose personalities Serge so vividly described that they burst like sunshine from the pages. Then they read with heavy hearts the grim days of the war. The diary was a testament to love.

Although you cannot remember any of these things for now, you carry your loved ones in your heart, as I carry you in mine. I will now face the darkest night with courage because of you. I will wait for you in that land where we can never be separated or lose each other again.

'It is a glorious gift he has given me,' said Kristina, her voice trembling with emotion. 'He has given me back my life.' Then looking at Eve with glistening eyes, she said, 'He means this as a parting gift, but neither of us can lose him, not now.'

'No, not now. Not ever,' agreed Eve.

Kristina felt so drawn and tired. Eve saw it and helped her under the sheets. But before she drifted off to sleep, she took Eve's hand.

'Serge wrote so many wonderful stories. Some of them happy and others sad. But he didn't write about what happened to Max and my daughters. Why is that? It's something I have to know.'

CHAPTER THIRTY-ONE

EVE

Paris, July 1946

I was too overwrought to sleep. I walked to Georges's apartment and saw that the light was still on in his study.

'Come in, Eve,' he said. His face was pale with fatigue. He looked as exhausted as I felt.

'You're still up?'

'Sleep and I are not seeing eye to eye,' he answered, ushering me into his study. His desk was piled with teetering stacks of paper. 'I have written to the president,' he said. 'I have interviews with *Le Monde* and *L'Aurore* tomorrow.'

That Georges was not giving up touched me. 'I don't know what I'd do without you, Georges. No other man would have worked this hard to save him.'

He frowned. 'Eve! You've gone as white as a sheet. Sit down.' He led me to a sofa by the fireplace. 'I think a drop of brandy is the thing,' he said.

He went to his drinks cabinet and poured two glasses, setting one on the table in front of me. I took a sip, but to my mortification, tears started to fall down my cheeks and I was unable to make them stop. The last thing I wanted to do was blubber like a child in front of Georges.

'I'm about to lose the only family I have,' I said. 'I'm all alone in the world.'

Georges sat down next to me and nursed his drink in his hands. 'You're not alone, Eve. You have me.'

Our eyes met. He put down his drink and tilted his head close to mine. Then on some impulse, which had no logical explanation, our lips met and we kissed. With hesitation at first, but when neither of us put up any resistance, our embrace grew more ardent. We pulled tightly against one another. I could feel the warmth of him through his shirt, his heart beating fast against my chest. Georges's kisses moved down my neck and the sensation of his warm lips on my skin was heavenly. Then the realisation hit me. I was doing the same thing my mother had done with Serge. She had destroyed her friendship with him by trying to lose her wretchedness in lovemaking. I could not make that mistake with Georges.

'No,' I said, pushing him back.

He immediately broke away and almost leaped to the other side of the room.

'Good god, I'm sorry,' he said, running his hand through his hair. 'I don't know what came over me.'

My heart was pounding. But it would not be fair to let him take all the blame. 'It wasn't only you. It was me too. But I don't want to lose the most loyal friend I have because of some foolish romantic impulse.'

Georges, normally so urbane and unshakeable, looked dumbstruck. 'Your most loyal friend?' He paced the room. 'How very well I understand you,' he said. 'You're my most loyal friend too. I am quite sure that even if I lived to the end of time, I'd never find another Eve Archer.'

'And I would never find another Georges Camadeau,' I told him.

A smile tickled his face. 'A lovely young woman like you could have any man at her beck and call if she wanted.'

I shook my head. 'That's not true. I was very much in love once. But he didn't want to marry me. Not a nobody without a family name.'

Georges sat down in the armchair opposite me. 'You know, Eve, we do have an awful lot in common. Why do you think I had to leave South America in such a hurry? I fell in love with a beauty who kept begging me to rescue her from her "brute of a husband". I nearly got shot by the man when it turned out he wasn't really a brute at all, and she had no intention of leaving him for me. He was far too rich. We both know the hurt of being used.'

'That woman was an imbecile, Georges,' I said. 'She might have been beautiful, but she had no sense if she didn't run away with you.'

Georges laughed before turning serious again. 'And in your case, Eve, whoever the man was, he was a stupid fool. He didn't know what a treasure he had.'

Our eyes met, and I was sure we were in danger of losing our heads again when there was a loud knock at the door.

'Who could that be at this hour?' he exclaimed, looking irritated. 'I'd better answer it. My maid has already gone to bed.'

Georges went out into the hall and opened the door. To my surprise I heard the voice of Odette, Lucile's maid. 'You must come as a matter of urgency, Monsieur Camadeau. I have a taxi waiting downstairs.'

'Why? What's happened?' he asked.

'Your aunt tried to kill herself.'

I went into the hall. Odette gave a start when she saw me, but her attention was on Georges whose face had crumpled with distress.

'Was she serious?' I asked Odette, not able to believe Lucile had any reason to take her own life. It seemed out of character for the woman I knew.

'Yes,' she replied. 'The doctor said it was a lethal dose of Veronal and that if I hadn't found her in time, she would most certainly be dead.'

★

We arrived at the apartment to find Lucile's physician, Docteur Vadim, and a nurse in attendance.

'We pumped Madame Damour's stomach,' Docteur Vadim told us. 'It wasn't pleasant, but she will survive.'

'Why did she do it?' asked Georges.

Docteur Vadim shook his head. 'She wouldn't say. She is in good health and is a woman of means. Perhaps it was the result of a personal crisis. I believe she had a significant birthday this year.'

I was only half-listening to the conversation. I was too occupied looking at the apartment's décor. Simulated leopard fur carpeted the floor, and the walls were papered in blue foil. My gaze travelled from the furniture, which had been upholstered in red velvet, to the alarming sight of a stuffed Australian emu by the fireplace.

'It's hideous,' I said out loud.

Georges nodded, grim-faced, thinking I was talking about the situation with Lucile when in fact I was wondering how she'd managed to turn the beautiful apartment I had created into a showy bordello in such a short space of time. Then I noticed the art. It was everywhere. Some of it good and some of it terrible. But it was the sheer amount of it that was shocking. There had to be over five million francs worth of artwork hanging on the walls, busily arranged like a jigsaw puzzle so that it was impossible to take in the details of one painting at a time.

'Odette,' I said under my breath, 'what happened here? Has Lucile gone mad?'

'It's terrible—'

But before she could continue, the nurse came out of Lucile's bedroom. 'You may see her now,' she said.

Docteur Vadim urged Georges and me to go into the room. 'I'll be waiting out here if you need me.'

The first thing I noticed about Lucile's room was that all the walls were mirrored. It made it seem that the profusion of objets d'art had multiplied themselves. Everywhere I looked there were Venetian masks, crystal sconces and giant seashells. In the middle of this hell, raised on a bed on a pyre-like platform and covered in scarlet chintz, lay Lucile.

'Oh!' said Georges, finally noticing the change in interior design for himself. He warily picked up an African chief chair and placed it next to the bed. 'Aunt Lucile?' he said, taking her hand. 'You've given us a terrible scare.'

'We had no idea you were so unhappy,' I added.

Lucile didn't seem surprised to see me. If anything, she looked relieved.

'I've been foolish,' she said. 'I thought he loved me.'

Georges and I exchanged a glance. Lucile had a lover?

'Who is this cad?' asked Georges. 'What is his name?'

'I can answer that,' I thought, sure it was the insipid Cyrille de Villiers who had seduced Lucile. No doubt Marthe had tried the same trick on her that she used on me to destroy my ambitions in society.

Lucile squeezed her eyes shut and opened them again. She looked so vulnerable that, despite the fact she had mercilessly thrown me out on the streets, I felt pity for her.

'Martin La Farge,' she said so quietly it was almost a whisper.

'Martin La Farge!' I repeated, flabbergasted. If Lucile had said she'd had a tryst with His Highness the Aga Khan, I would have been no less surprised.

Tears came to her eyes. 'He made me feel beautiful. Loved.'

At least I understood that sentiment, but still, I wouldn't have touched Martin La Farge with a barge pole for all the love in the world.

'Aunt Lucile,' Georges asked, becoming less emotional and more like a lawyer, 'did you give him money?'

She nodded sheepishly. 'I bought all these paintings from him. He promised me he would make me the "Queen of Paris Salons". Then he brought his friend Sonia Vertinskaya to decorate the apartment.'

'With every piece of junk she couldn't sell from her warehouse,' I said.

Georges sent me a reproachful look and I decided I would bite my tongue.

'Then,' said Lucile, her voice trembling, 'I went to surprise him one afternoon with a gift of a Mauboussin tie-pin he had admired. I found him ... well, I found him with Madame Vertinskaya.'

'We will go to the police,' said Georges. 'This matter can be handled discreetly.'

Lucile suddenly looked alarmed. 'No, you don't understand,' she said. 'He's dangerous.'

'What do you mean?' asked Georges.

'He tried to blackmail me,' I said. 'I don't blame Lucile for feeling frightened.'

'Is that what happened to you, Aunt Lucile? Did La Farge blackmail you over something?'

Lucile grimaced. 'Last week, before everything unfolded, I went to a dinner at his home in Neuilly. Madame Vertinskaya was there, along with Marthe and Cyrille, the Fouquets, Judge Clouzot—'

'The presiding judge of Serge's court case?' I asked.

Lucile nodded and then continued, 'There were two Germans there as well. Martin referred to them as Herr Roth and Herr Schwarz, but I sensed those weren't their real names. They were heavily bandaged, and Marthe explained they'd just had plastic surgery. Then at the end of the evening Martin proposed a toast to "the Führer and the Fourth Reich".'

'A Fourth Reich! They were fascists?' asked Georges, frowning.

Lucile bit her lip. 'I didn't quite understand until afterwards that they were using my money to get high-profile Nazis out of Europe and to South America.'

'Did they threaten you?' Georges asked.

'Only after I caught Martin and Madame Vertinskaya together. I burst into a tirade of jealous anger, and Martin grabbed me by the throat and said if I told anyone about what I'd seen at the house, he would have me killed and fed to the crocodiles at the zoo.'

My mind was working overtime, and I could see Georges's was too. There was some connection between this fascist group, and Serge being framed for stealing the Foulds' art collection and for their murder.

'Aunt Lucile, I will organise police protection,' said Georges. 'But you must tell me everything.'

Lucile burst into sobs. 'No! I'm so ashamed.'

'Tell me,' he urged.

'All right,' said Lucile, kneading the bed clothes with her fingers. 'One night, when Martin thought I was asleep after we ... well, he took a phone call downstairs. It was Sonia Vertinskaya he was speaking to, and I heard him boast to her that he made a fortune during the war informing Hermann Göring where to find hidden Jewish art collections. Göring would pay him by letting him choose any modern art in the collections he wanted. But then, when Göring started to fall out of favour with Hitler,' Lucile looked from me to Georges, 'he decided to go it alone one time. To take an entire collection for himself.'

Lucile reached to her bedside table and passed Georges the copy of *Le Monde* that was lying there. On the cover was a story about the court case and a picture of Édouard Fould, standing in his private gallery next to a work by Manet, *A Portrait of a Woman Reading*.

'What are you trying to say, Aunt Lucile?' asked Georges.

With a grim expression on her face, Lucile pointed to something across the room. We turned to see the same portrait hanging on the wall opposite her bed. All the pieces of the puzzle were coming together. Martin La Farge was responsible for the death of Édouard and Beatrice Fould and the theft of their collection.

'I paid nine hundred thousand francs for it. I sold my house in Chantilly to buy it,' Lucile said.

Georges stood up. 'I'll need you to make a statement to the police first thing in the morning.'

Lucile's eyes flew open with alarm. 'I can't,' she said tearfully. 'I couldn't bear the scandal.'

Georges's face turned stern. 'You will have to, I'm afraid,' he said. 'A man's life is at stake.'

★

'What do you want at this time of the morning?' asked Judge Regis when he walked into his drawing room. 'It's just past sunrise. Couldn't it wait?'

'My apologies, Monsieur Judge, but I'm afraid it couldn't,' said Georges. 'The matter has become more than an innocent man wrongly found guilty. It is a matter of French security.'

Judge Regis invited us to sit down. I watched his round face go from interested to perturbed to shocked at what Georges explained to him.

'And Madame Damour is willing to give testimony to these claims?'

'She is,' said Georges.

Judge Regis sat back and drummed his fingers on his knee as he considered the matter. 'I've always harboured doubts about Judge Clouzot but I never had proof. But this is corruption at the highest level. If you want a warrant to have La Farge's house searched for other paintings from the Fould collection, which he may not even be hiding at his residence, the only one who can grant it is the president. As you say, this matter now involves French intelligence. It's beyond the powers of the Ministry of Justice.'

'How soon do you think you can speak to the president?' Georges asked. 'We only have forty-eight hours to appeal. And as there has been little respect for the due processes of the law so far, I am concerned that Serge Lavertu's life is in imminent danger if he is held captive in Fresnes.'

'Indeed, he appears to have been this organisation's scapegoat,' agreed Judge Regis. 'But the president is currently in Spain and will not return until tomorrow. Meanwhile, we need to gather as much additional evidence as we can. La Farge may try to argue that the Manet painting came to him through another dealer.' He turned to me. 'It would certainly help if that letter Édouard Fould wrote entrusting his collection to Monsieur Lavertu could be found. Does Madame Bergeret still not know what happened to it?'

'It seems it disappeared when the Germans occupied her villa,' I told him.

'Well, let's do what we can without it for now,' said Judge Regis, 'and pray that God helps us.'

★

Georges and I went straight from Judge Regis's home to Inès's apartment. To our surprise, it was Kristina who opened the door and invited us inside.

We explained to her what we had found out from Lucile and that we'd taken her statement to the examining judge in Serge's trial.

'It's going all the way to the top,' I told her. 'To the president.'

She looked from me to Georges. 'I woke up early this morning and couldn't sleep. You see, I think *Frenchman with a Rabbit* is still at the villa. I dreamed of Max, and he told me I must go back there to get it, that the painting will save Serge. But I don't know how.'

'But didn't you say you and Lorenzo searched the villa everywhere?' I asked.

'Everywhere except the cellar, which the sappers told us was probably mined. They said it would be a complex job to clear it and that they would come back to do it. But they never did.'

We had very little time, and I didn't think Kristina's dream of some mystical message was going to be a strong enough reason for Georges agreeing we should go to Nice and possibly waste our efforts on a futile mission. But as the saying goes, desperate times call for desperate measures.

He looked at his watch. 'There is a train leaving for the south in an hour,' he said. 'We can't afford to leave any stone unturned.'

★

The cellar of the Villa des Cygnes was dim and neither Georges nor I dared touch the light switch. The only source of illumination was a narrow, frosted-glass window. But as our eyes adjusted to the gloom, certain objects stood out – overturned wine racks and old armchairs covered in layers of dust. Cobwebs dangled from the ceiling, and I wondered what creepy-crawlies were hiding under the rubble. As if to answer my question, a rat appeared from a crevice and scurried up a plank before disappearing through a broken pane in the window. Georges directed his torch towards the far end of the room where a large cupboard stood. I could see why the Germans had left it. It was too big to move and too ugly to covet. Kristina, who was at the front gate waiting for the Nice police lieutenant to arrive, had told us it had been used to store empty wine bottles.

'What time is it?' I asked Georges.

He glanced at his watch. 'Just after four o'clock.'

'The police lieutenant was supposed to be here two hours ago. We'll miss the train back to Paris if he doesn't come soon.'

The lieutenant in question had been a sapper with the French army during the war and was supposed to be an expert in defusing booby traps left by the Germans. The British sappers who'd hurriedly cleared the villa after the war, had only said it was a possibility that the cellar was booby-trapped as well. But even the slightest chance of being blown to smithereens should have been enough to deter us. Still, my mind travelled to Serge sitting in Fresnes, waiting for his execution for all he knew. We were dealing with far darker forces than we had imagined, including a corrupt judge, and time was of the essence.

An anxious thought jabbed at the edge of my mind. What if those fascists got wind of what we were up to and hastened Serge's execution? A dismal picture of Serge being led towards the guillotine filled my mind with such revulsion that my fear of being blown to pieces all but vanished.

'I'm going to open the cupboard myself,' I said, climbing down the steps.

Georges tugged me back. 'Don't be a fool, Eve.'

'But we don't even know if the cellar is booby-trapped,' I protested. 'We might be scaring ourselves over nothing. Serge's life is at stake.'

I tried to move forward again but Georges held me even tighter. 'I'll go,' he said. 'You go outside and wait with Kristina.'

'I'm not leaving you. I'll shine my torch to help you find your way.'

Georges sucked in his lips as if to steady himself and began picking his way gingerly through the toppled racks. His foot struck a box of bottles that rattled on impact. The loud noise made both of us start.

'Be careful,' I said.

Georges continued with caution and after a few tense minutes, reached the cupboard. He shone his torch around the doors and hinges as well as behind and on top of it.

'I can't see any wires,' he reported. He put his hand on the knob. I sucked in a breath, wondering if this might be our last earthly moment together. I was overcome by a sudden urge to set things right with him.

'Georges?'

He glanced back over his shoulder. 'Yes?'

'About last night. When we kissed, it was ... nice.'

'Yes, I agree it was rather pleasant, Eve. But perhaps we can talk about it another time?'

Given the circumstances, I saw the wisdom in his suggestion. 'Ah yes, all right.'

Georges prised the doors open ever so slightly and peered into the cupboard. 'So far so good.'

As Kristina had said, the cupboard was filled with crates of empty wine bottles. From the thick coat of dust that covered them, I held out hope that the Germans had never touched them. Georges took the crates out cautiously, placing them on the floor next to him before shining his torch into the cavernous interior. He tapped his knuckles against the back of the wardrobe.

'There is something there!' he said, reaching into his pocket and taking out a screwdriver.

'I'm coming to help,' I said, clambering over the rubbish in the cellar with a foolhardy eagerness.

Georges undid the screws that held the back of the cupboard in place, and together we lifted it out to reveal a large square object wrapped in burlap and tied with string.

'Ah-hah!' he said.

It was most certainly a painting. Georges took it out and carried it above his head as he made his way back towards the steps. 'Follow my path exactly,' he advised. 'Don't let your caution drop.'

But I was no longer watching him. I was looking at another object that had been placed at the back of the wardrobe. At first I thought it was a beach umbrella, but when I shone my torch over it, I saw it was something cylindrical wrapped in brown paper. I lifted it out and followed Georges.

In the dining room, Kristina and Georges carefully unwrapped the large painting. We all gasped when we found ourselves looking at the portrait of Serge with Tulipe. Despite having been hidden in less than ideal circumstances, the painting was undamaged. Kristina studied it as if she could almost see herself painting it.

'Well, it's a nice painting,' said Georges, grimacing. 'But I don't see how it helps now. You've already convinced everyone of the fact you forged the paintings used in the trial.'

'Let's undo the frame,' she said.

We left it to Kristina's expertise to loosen the frame. In between the stretcher and canvas, she pulled out a folded piece of paper and handed it to Georges. He frowned at first and then his eyes opened wide.

'"I, Edouard Fould, entrust my entire collection of artwork along with my wife's collection to our good friend, Serge Lavertu …"' he read.

He handed it to me. Age had turned the paper yellow but the writing was clear. '"If we should fail to return, we request that our collections, including Botticelli's *Flora*, should be donated to the Louvre,"' I read out.

I looked at Georges and Kristina. 'If the Louvre believes it's going to inherit the entire collection, they'll start doing everything to track it down.'

Georges nodded. 'It's a good thing.'

Kristina's eyes drifted to the other package I'd brought up from the cellar. A strange tingling feeling came over me. Georges reached for it and cut the string, while Kristina slowly unravelled it, revealing a goddess in a diaphanous gown. The three of us stared at it, bedazzled. It was the original painting, *Flora*.

'Max must have put it there,' said Kristina. 'I never knew.' She smiled. 'That's why I saw him in my dream.'

★

Although we caught the train on time, my heart was racing. My eyes constantly drifted to the luggage compartment, terrified someone would snatch away the two paintings. Serge had called Judge Regis from the station to tell him what we had found and that we were on our way back to Paris. Yet, as long as Serge remained in Fresnes, a sense of foreboding hung over me. Mentally I urged the train on, and each stop was torture.

Kristina stared out the window, looking upset and confused.

'Are you all right?' I asked her.

She turned to me, tears welling in her eyes. 'I remember,' she said. 'I remember what happened. I always knew the paintings were in that cupboard. I helped put them there.'

CHAPTER THIRTY-TWO

KRISTINA

Nice, October 1943

Three days after Kristina and Serge had sold *Flora* to Frau von Rittberg, the remaining payment still hadn't arrived. They had received a deposit of three hundred thousand francs in cash, and nearly died from nerves when it was delivered to Frau von Rittberg's room by an SS officer who had taken his time counting the money out. The delay could simply be a banking hold-up due to the war. But a niggling doubt bothered Kristina: What if Hitler had other art dealers in Berlin examine the painting and they declared it a forgery? Or if they looked closely at the faked provenance and told Hitler that *Flora* was the Botticelli from the Foulds' collection that he and Göring had been in competition to find. Serge showed his usual calm when she voiced her worries to him and Max one afternoon while they were playing cards in the drawing room.

'There is another possibility you haven't considered,' Serge said, sending a smirk to Max. 'The Germans think they have cheated us and have no intention to pay. They'll assume we have no redress and we won't be able to pursue the matter in court. But who's going to have the last laugh in the end?'

'Three hundred thousand francs for the escape line is a lot of false papers and bribery money,' Max said. 'Besides Martin La Farge's cheque has cleared. I don't know which is funnier, Hitler "stealing" a forged painting or La Farge paying full price for one.'

He and Serge laughed like mischievous school boys.

'I'm glad you two find it funny, while I'm losing sleep,' Kristina said. But she smiled too, there was something special in those moments when Max and Serge were together. Their warm regard for each other, as well as the way they could be arguing passionately one moment and then enthusiastically discussing a painting the next, spoke of a bond that was deep and lasting. To her it was priceless.

★

The following day, Max called to Kristina from the cellar. He was standing over the oven that he and Serge had used to dry the forged paintings.

'Do you feel like painting some more fakes?' he asked her.

'Not really.'

He smiled. 'I've hidden all the valuable paintings behind false walls. But I thought it would be good to have some decoy paintings hung around the house. They don't have to be perfect copies, but good enough that any looters might make off with them and not look too carefully for hiding places.'

'Are we expecting looters?' she asked.

'The Germans are taking over houses even outside of Nice now. This one, with its perfect view of the bay, will most certainly be on their list. When our "guests" leave, you and the girls must leave too, along with Serge. It's no longer safe for you to stay here. The Germans are getting more desperate. If they

397

uncover the identity of an agent, they will arrest his family and torture them for information – or worse. And Serge is Jewish. Someone will denounce him sooner or later.'

Kristina felt a tinge of apprehension. 'Max, you're not leaving?'

'I must now that I'm well enough,' he said, barely able to meet her eyes. 'I have to join de Gaulle in London.'

All Kristina could think of was the dull and aching void of the days during the war when she did not know where Max was. Although they were in danger, it was easier to bear it when they were all together. But she could see that he had made up his mind.

He opened the old cupboard against the back wall of the cellar. 'I've hidden the letter from Édouard Fould entrusting his collection to Serge between the frame and stretcher of *Frenchman with a Rabbit*. I'll make a false back to the cupboard and hide the painting behind it.'

'Why did you hide the letter in my painting?'

'Because we can't lose that letter and it's not safe to take it with us or even deposit it in a bank. The Germans will empty every drawer and rip up every loose floorboard in the search for hidden valuables. This is the best hiding spot I can come up with. Should they open the back of the cupboard, they will simply see—'

'A painting not worth looting.'

'That's not what I meant,' said Max.

'But you're right. A Kristina Belova painting doesn't face the danger of being sold far and wide like a Vermeer or even a degenerate Picasso. They might palm it off to a second-rate dealer in Nice who won't be able to sell it – or they will simply leave it.'

Max put his hand on her shoulder. 'Stop it, Kristina. This is painful enough as it is. I'm hoping they won't discover the painting in the first place, that's why I'm making such an effort to hide it. But if they do, yes they are more likely to leave it or sell it locally than they would a Vermeer or a Picasso. Not because it's a lesser painting, but only because you aren't a well-known artist *yet*.'

Kristina turned away and squeezed her eyes shut so he wouldn't see her bitter tears. He wrapped his arms around her and kissed her tenderly on the forehead.

'You have given yourself selflessly to save others these past three years. After the war is over, you will paint again,' he told her. 'I will see to it that you have no distractions. Together, Serge and I will make you the best-known painter in France: A place you deserve far above any other artist I can think of.'

*

The entire household ate dinner together that night, the adults trying to effect calm for the sake of the children. Despite all the difficulties, it had become comfortable hiding away from reality in their little oasis. Now they were about to venture out into the world and go their separate ways. Kristina sensed the danger, but also a profound feeling of loss. She perhaps would have preferred it if they could all have stayed in their little cocoon forever. But as Max had pointed out, the house was a target and there was no choice now but to go.

Their lovemaking that night was sweet, gentle and sad. Kristina and Max lay awake afterwards, bathed in the moonlight, and Kristina thought how the moon softened the edges of things. She drifted off and woke sometime later. But when she reached out for Max he was gone, and she immediately sat up. She knew the planes came from London when the moon was bright, and wondered if he'd thought it was easier to leave her without saying goodbye. But then she heard Max and Serge talking quietly in the garden. She pulled her robe around her and went downstairs to find them.

The French doors were open, and Max and Serge were standing together, their heads close and their voices soft. Kristina leaned against the wall and watched them from a distance. This parting was painful for them too. They were like two trees whose roots had grown together. They supported each other in sunshine and held together in storms. Kristina was about to go back to bed, to leave them the moment for themselves, when they moved closer together and kissed. Not a kiss of friendship, but a passionate kiss. One that was lit by a fire within.

Her eyes opened wide, unable to comprehend what she had just seen. Her thoughts rolled out in so many directions, she couldn't keep track of any of them. She stifled a scream as she felt her entire life splinter into pieces. Everything she believed collapsed around her. She was not losing Max to the war, she had been losing him every moment of her life, and to the person she had trusted most.

'Kristina?' said Max, peering into the darkness of the house.

His voice sounded far away, muted by the blood rushing in her ears and the ache in her chest. She thought that the three of them had understood each other, but it seemed they were all living parallel lives. Maybe Max and Serge had never felt the same way she had about them. Perhaps they had pitied her or worse — perhaps she had been something of a joke. Poor, innocent, naïve Kristina. She wanted to hide and pretend she never saw anything so that life could go on as before. But her anger at their betrayal got the better of her. She strode out into the garden, not knowing what she would say or do.

They turned to her, and their faces fell.

Max stepped towards her. 'Kristina!'

'I saw!' she gasped. 'I saw!'

She was so shaken with rage and hurt, it was all she could say. She had loved them both and had never questioned the integrity of their foundation.

'Kristina, I'm sorry,' Serge said, tears in his voice. 'This is my fault. Not Max's. I took him by surprise. He has never ...'

'I trusted the both of you,' she said through gritted teeth. Then directing her full fury at Serge, she said, 'You'd better leave.'

His face dropped. Those simple, cold words with their tone of dismissal cut him deeper than if she had plunged a knife into him, and she knew it. They signified a change, a death of love and companionship. He glanced at Max then turned to leave. Even in her own hurt, she felt torn apart. She wanted to call after him, *Don't walk away. I can never stop loving you.* But she was too confused and couldn't get the words out.

Then she heard the car motor start up and the sound of tyres on gravel. Serge was gone.

Her tears were falling freely now and she turned to Max. 'Our children. I thought we would be growing old together. Was it all a lie?'

His expression was tortured. 'No, Kristina. It was never a lie. You haven't lost anything. Not me or Serge.'

'He's gone.'

'He'll come back.'

'You were kissing him.'

Max came near and she lifted her hurt gaze to his eyes.

'Kristina, you are loved,' Max pleaded with her. 'You have two men in your life who love you more than anything else in the world. Neither of us would ever want to hurt you.'

His voice was muffled by the cacophony of thoughts in her head. She caught only snatches of what he was saying, but it was clear he was reassuring her that the bond between the three of them was irrefutable and that nothing could break it.

It was a single gunshot that made them both jump. Then the sound of someone pounding on the front door. They ran to the side of the house and crouched down behind a bush. Then they saw that all they had been dreading for over a year had taken shape in the form of an SS officer in a grey-green uniform standing on the doorstep. He was tall and intimidating, and from the light of the torch he held, Kristina saw that he wore a pair of frameless glasses that gave him an air of cruelty. Behind him were four German soldiers holding machine guns. She realised the sound of the gunshot she'd heard was one of them shooting the lock on the gate.

The lights went on and to Kristina's horror, one of the Jewish refugees, Sarah, opened the door. Why, after all the drilling, would she have done such a thing? Kristina couldn't fathom it.

The officer held up a piece of paper to Sarah's face and yelled, 'All occupants are to come into the courtyard now!'

Sarah, clearly panicked and not thinking straight, called out Kristina's name. For a terrible moment she worried that Sarah would call out the names of the other refugees as well, but thankfully she didn't. Then, because Kristina hadn't responded, she called out for Max.

'Monsieur Bergeret?' the officer asked her. 'We weren't aware there was a Monsieur Bergeret residing here.'

Sarah instantly realised her mistake, but she couldn't think fast enough on her feet to come up with a lie. *Delay. Say something*, Kristina prayed. Sarah needed to stall so as to give the others time to make their beds and go to their hiding places. It had to appear that it was only Kristina and her daughters living here. Sarah could try to pass herself off as their maid, but she faltered under the SS officer's gaze.

Kristina moved forward. She would have to delay the Germans herself. But Max pulled her back.

'No, an agent is a much more important catch,' he said.

Their eyes met and she understood he intended to sacrifice himself, and that she would not lose him because of Serge. She would lose him because of the Germans.

'I love you, Kristina. I've always loved you,' he said.

A chill ran down her spine when she sensed someone behind them.

'Get up!'

She hadn't noticed the fifth soldier. The one who had been searching the garden and had found them. She and Max only had seconds to reach for each other's fingers and squeeze them before the soldier pushed them out into the open.

The SS officer was surprised to see them. He looked over his shoulder and gave a command to one of the soldiers: '*Geheime Staatspolizei.*' The Gestapo.

Kristina anticipated that they would take both of them, but the soldier grabbed only Max. With the help of another, they forced him into the car. He turned and looked at Kristina for one brief moment. It was a parting look that spoke of an end of a journey together and the pleasure that they'd shared for a time. It said, *I'm sorry I hurt you. Forgive me. I love you*, and answered, *I know. I love you too.*

The car drove away, and Kristina knew then that they would never see each other again.

'On your knees!' the SS officer screamed, grabbing her by the hair and pushing her to the ground. Two trucks arrived, and she assumed someone had denounced them and they had come for the Jewish refugees. But instead, a familiar figure jumped out of the cabin of the first truck. He was so blond he practically glowed in the dark. Martin La Farge. The SS officer went to meet him.

'So you believe this is where the Fould collection is being hidden?' he asked Martin.

Suddenly Kristina understood. The Germans had not come for the Jews, they had come for the art. The soldiers shoved Sarah out of the way and stormed into the house. Kristina could hear them emptying cupboards, breaking and pushing over furniture. Nadia and Ginette were brought out, dazed and confused. They were forced to kneel either side of Kristina. Nadia was brave, her face expressionless, but Ginette was weeping. Kristina longed to hold her, to comfort her. To whisper to her to be calm and not allow herself to be noticed or to show fear.

Then there was a sudden silence. All noises coming from the house had stopped.

'*Obersturmführer!*' one of the soldiers shouted. The next moment, the other Jewish adults staying with them were marched out. They looked straight ahead, not at Kristina, and she understood. They had surrendered themselves to try to save the children who must still be hiding somewhere. Kristina prayed with all her heart that angels would protect Hermine and Joséphine, Herschel and Aline.

While the soldiers continued their raid, Martin La Farge stood by the truck smoking a cigarette. He must have seen Kristina and the girls. He must have known this was her house. Had he realised she'd sold him a fake painting and this was his revenge? But then the SS officer had mentioned the Fould collection. However, Serge had only brought a small part of it back to the villa – the rest was still hidden at the Foulds' home. A thought began to turn in her mind, but before she had a chance to make sense of it, the SS officer yanked her up by the arm and forced her into the house.

'You've been hiding Jews!' he screamed in her ear.

Then he dragged her into the library and she saw that they had smashed through the false wall behind one of the bookcases. In the space were the children, huddled together like frightened rabbits in a burrow. She knew then that all hope was lost.

The children were dragged out, so frightened they were silent, even little Aline did not cry. Kristina was watching everything she had worked and hoped so hard for disintegrating before her eyes. They would find the art now, but what did art matter? It was those helpless children, and her own, that were important. The SS officer dragged her back to the courtyard.

'Jewish-loving whore,' he hissed in her ear.

She heard Ginette cry out, 'Mama!'

Two shots rang out in the dark.

Then all went black.

CHAPTER THIRTY-THREE

EVE

Paris, July 1946

Georges, Kristina and I arrived in Paris in a sombre mood the following evening. Remembering what had happened the night she and Max were arrested had left Kristina almost comatose, and delays due to repairs on the train tracks meant the trip between Nice and Paris had taken longer than expected.

'We had better get her straight to Madame Bonne's apartment,' said Georges quietly. 'And ask her to call a doctor.'

'Kristina's banishment of Serge saved his life. He wasn't there when the Germans came,' I whispered back. 'But he must carry the guilt of it. At least now Kristina can tell him that she and Max were reconciled before he was arrested.'

What Kristina had revealed about Serge did not change my love for him. I finally appreciated what my mother had come to see about their relationship: *I understand the reasons why you couldn't love me the way I loved you, and I forgive you for them.*

After settling Kristina with Inès, Georges and I headed to Judge Regis's house. There were two burly men wearing trench coats waiting in the garden and another two policemen standing by the door.

'French intelligence,' whispered Georges, indicating the two men in the garden.

'Is it a good sign?' I asked.

'I would hope so.'

The butler led us to the drawing room where Judge Regis was waiting for us. 'I have news for you,' he said. 'French intelligence observations of Martin La Farge's house in Neuilly-sur-Seine have revealed an interesting coming and going of high-profile visitors, including Judge Clouzot. We have also received word that Martin La Farge and his lover, Sonia Vertinskaya, intend to leave tonight for Switzerland.' He nodded towards the door. 'We should go with the officers outside for the arrest. The president demands that I be present as the examining judge of the case. Clearly, he thinks I'm the only incorruptible member of the Ministry of Justice.'

★

Judge Regis sat in the front passenger seat of Georges's car while I took the back. We followed behind the police and intelligence agents.

'Martin La Farge is going to try to move the collection to Switzerland tonight,' Judge Regis told us. 'We were tipped off by the furniture removalist company – the same company that helped him loot Jewish homes during the war. The owner offered information in exchange for clemency. We are hoping to catch La Farge red-handed.'

'Did the removalists witness the murder of Édouard and Beatrice Fould?' asked Georges.

Judge Regis shook his head. 'They were there to do the looting and were called in after the fact.'

'What about the gardener and the two maids? Wouldn't they have heard trucks arriving?' I asked.

'Not necessarily,' said Judge Regis, 'if the storm that night was loud enough.'

'So surely all of that, combined with the fact that Martin La Farge had a reason to cast suspicion on Serge because he wanted to keep the gallery he'd gained during the war, turns the tide of assumed guilt to him?' I asked, finding it frustrating that it had been so easy to convict Serge, but the evidence for placing the guilt on Martin seemed to require watertight evidence.

'That's not all,' said Judge Regis. 'He hated Serge Lavertu for another reason. His sister, Madeleine La Farge. He apparently blames Lavertu, along with the Bergerets, for corrupting Madeleine and seducing her into their bohemian way of life.'

My reality shifted. 'His sister?' I echoed faintly.

Georges glanced at me in the rear-view mirror, puzzled by my reaction.

All three cars pulled up behind a grove of trees. One of the agents walked over to the car and signalled for Georges to wind down the window. 'We'll walk the rest of the way. There are ten policemen already stationed around the property to assist. We'll lead and you follow behind in case of gunfire.'

Up ahead of us, I saw a house with a mansard roof and an equestrian statue of Marcus Aurelius near the front door. I buckled at the knees as the awful truth loomed over me. This was my mother's childhood home exactly as Serge had described it.

'Are you all right?' Georges asked. 'Who is Madeleine La Farge, by the way? Has Serge ever mentioned her?'

I shook my head. 'We'll talk about it later.'

Georges turned his attention back to Judge Regis. 'You didn't tell us about Sonia Vertinskaya. What's the story there?'

'She worked as an informer for the Gestapo, afraid that they would close her business and arrest her mother if she didn't.'

'Do you think she's aware that Martin La Farge might have had something to do with the murder of the Foulds?' Georges asked.

Judge Regis shrugged. 'Even if she didn't know beforehand, I'm quite sure she has learned the truth by now.'

The gates had been left open by the removalists. Martin was standing by the truck supervising the loading of the crates of what was almost certainly the Foulds' art collection. I cringed now that I saw the family resemblance. He shared my mother's perfect features and her Nordic blondness. It was his broken nose that had thrown me. No wonder my mother had run away from her family with a brother like that.

Sonia came out of the house carrying a Louis Vuitton cosmetic case. The intelligence agents turned around to us and nodded.

Then, like a storm of swarming wasps, they and the police converged towards Martin La Farge. Sonia saw them coming and went running back into the house. One of the policemen ran after her, but Martin was surrounded.

'Martin La Farge,' announced the police sergeant. 'You are under arrest for the murder of Édouard and Beatrice Fould.'

Martin said nothing at first, only put his hands in the air. His face hardened, and I thought he was going to start resisting. But then Sonia was brought out of the house by the policeman. She was wrestling with him and shouting expletives. A slow smile came to Martin's face.

'The game is over, my dear,' he said. 'They know all about what you've done. I can't cover for you anymore, I'm afraid.'

Sonia stopped resisting and looked at him. '*Connard!*' she cursed. 'You poor excuse for a man!'

And I had to agree. Martin La Farge was not only a murderer and a thief, but he had no honour. Not even to his lover. I felt tainted knowing that I was related to him.

Not able to bear seeing anything else, I turned and walked back towards the car. Georges ran after me. 'Eve, don't you want to see the art? They're opening the crates now.'

I turned and looked at him.

'What is it?' he asked.

What would he think of me when I told him the truth? It was one thing to be born poor, quite another to be related to a monster — a man who had betrayed his country, committed cold-blooded murder, been responsible for the deaths of innocent children, and who knew what other dark deeds? But Georges deserved to know the truth before he developed any further feelings for me.

I nodded back towards the house. 'The man they just arrested … *is my uncle.*'

CHAPTER THIRTY-FOUR

KRISTINA

Paris, July 1946

Kristina opened the door and Serge stood before her, holding a bouquet of Sterling Silver roses. Although his suit drooped from his thin shoulders, he looked debonair with his clean-shaven face and a gardenia in the buttonhole of his jacket. She invited him inside then put the flowers in a vase and set it on the table.

'Is Inès here?' he asked, looking around.

'No. She thought we might like to be alone and went to stay with her mother. But not before cooking a quiche and baking an almond cake. She thinks you need fattening up.'

Kristina poured them a glass of wine each and they sat down on the sofa. Their meeting alone wasn't as awkward as she feared it might be. It felt very much that they had been on intimate terms for years. Perhaps everything she needed to know was imprinted on her soul, and it didn't matter if her mind could produce the exact pictures or not.

'Thank you for the diary,' she said. 'It was a beautiful gift.'

'I can't imagine what it would be like to not remember your life,' he replied, his eyes looking deeply into hers. 'Sometimes I think I remember too much, too vividly.'

'It's like the destruction of a library of rare books, ones that can never be replaced,' she told him.

She realised she had never articulated what it felt like so well, not even to herself, to have lost so much that was precious. But she looked at Serge and saw that at least one of those precious books had returned to her.

He put his hand on her arm. 'But some memories have started to come back to you, haven't they? Eve tells me you remembered why I wasn't at the villa when you were all arrested.'

'Yes, I remember.'

His eyes filled with tears. 'I am so sorry, Kristina. So sorry that I lost control. It was not Max's fault. It was mine.' Then he fixed his mesmerising green eyes on her. 'But I loved you too, Kristina. Very much. Perhaps even more than Max.'

They sat together in the quiet of the apartment, among Inès's polished and perfectly dusted furniture. Then Flora appeared from the bedroom. She scampered across the carpet and began circling Serge's feet.

'That means she likes you,' Kristina told him.

'Your rabbit caused quite a stir in the courtroom.'

'Her timing was impeccable.'

They smiled and fell into another comfortable silence. Kristina knew she must ask him the saddest question of all. But if she was to start a new life, she must let go of the old one.

'Serge, where are Nadia and Ginette buried? And what happened to Max after he was arrested? Please tell me.'

Serge closed his eyes for a moment. The memory that was lost to her caused him suffering. 'I returned to the villa the following morning to try to make amends with you. I found Nadia in a terrible state ... and Ginette.'

Kristina clenched her fists but nodded to urge him to continue. She was afraid of what she would hear but she didn't want him to stop.

'Nadia passed away soon after and I buried the girls in the garden. In the same place where you and I buried Tulipe. I thought they would have liked that.'

'So, they were so close by, and I never knew,' Kristina said thoughtfully. 'You buried them in the garden of the home where they had been loved. Thank you. And Max?'

Serge shook his head. 'There is no record of him. Hitler had a policy of *Nacht und Nebel* for Allied agents. Making them disappear in a way that nobody, especially their families, would ever know what happened to them.'

'He was the Devil incarnate. He knew destroying the memory of someone was the ultimate cruelty.'

Serge took her hands and held them. She suddenly felt very tired.

'May I lay my head on your shoulder?' she asked.

He nodded and lifted his arm so he could encircle her in his embrace. 'Kristina, I want to take care of you. Keep the villa by all means, but come live with me in Paris. Lorenzo can come too. Judge Regis says I will have the gallery back by next week. You can paint again. I promised Max I would look after you, and I will.'

'Will you be my art dealer?' she asked. 'Max promised me that after the war you two would finally make me famous.'

He shook his head. 'I'm too old. Paris is destroyed. New York is the art capital of the world now and I don't have the energy to sail back and forth across the ocean. But Eve does. She will represent you. You must have noticed that when she gets behind something, she stops at nothing until she succeeds.'

Kristina laughed. 'I have noticed.'

'I want to share my home and my daughter with you, as you and Max always shared everything with me,' Serge said. 'Please say yes.'

'Yes,' she said, burying her face deeper into his shoulder.

He gently stroked her hair. 'Ours is an unconventional harmony. People won't know what to make of it.'

Kristina looked up at him. 'After how I have seen people behave, I don't care what anybody else thinks is "normal". I'd rather have our unconventional bond than their hatred and murderous ways any day. Love is love, Serge, whatever form it takes.'

'Yes, love is love,' he said.

She closed her eyes and drank in the peace of being with him. Even when she'd had no memory of him, she had longed for Serge. And now she had found him again.

CHAPTER THIRTY-FIVE

EVE

Paris, July 1946

After forty-eight hours of plunging into melancholic depths and soaring to dizzy heights again, Georges and I decided the best thing we could do was to have a quiet dinner at La Tour d'Argent.

'Do you mind if we see Aunt Lucile first?' he asked, opening the car door for me.

'Of course,' I told him.

We were both pleased to find that Lucile was up and sitting in the drawing room sorting through her button collection.

'Ah, Aunt Lucile, you are looking much better than when we saw you last!' said Georges, kissing her on both cheeks.

Lucile asked Odette to bring us a bottle of champagne. 'I want to celebrate a second chance at life,' she said, 'with two people who are dear to me.'

She looked meaningfully in my direction. 'I have something for you, Eve,' she said. She went to the bureau and brought back the ring she had given me for my birthday.

'Please take it as an apology for how badly I treated you.'

'You have nothing to apologise for,' I told her firmly. 'You did me a favour. You made me stand on my own feet.'

'Do you think you might come back?' she asked hopefully. 'I miss you.'

I put the ring on my finger and showed it to her. 'I'll come back to visit, as a friend. A *true* friend.' I looked around at the hideous furniture Sonia had palmed off onto her. 'And I'll help you sell these things and return your apartment back to how you liked it – the way it was before the war.'

'But you thought it was so old-fashioned,' said Lucile.

'It doesn't matter what I think. It's your home. I'd like to see you happy here.'

Georges watched our exchange with a smile on his face. 'I hope we shall come to visit you often, Aunt Lucile.' Then pointing to a box of sterling silver buttons with a lady's cameo portrait on them he said: 'Now explain to us what all these buttons are and where they came from. I don't believe I've ever seen these ones before.'

There was a knock at the door and Odette came into the room. 'I'm sorry to disturb you,' she said. 'Monsieur Camadeau, your maid is on the telephone.'

'My maid?' replied Georges. 'What on earth has happened now?'

He went out into the hall and I heard him say, 'Oh, I completely forgot about it. Thank you for reminding me. Yes, do lay out my suit. I shall be there shortly.'

Georges had overlooked some engagement, that much was clear. I was disappointed, because after all we'd been through, I was hoping to spend some time with him alone. I was still reeling from the shock that Martin La Farge was my uncle.

'Eve, tonight is the Anglo-French Legal Conference dinner,' said Georges, coming back into the room. 'Are you still up to coming with me as my companion?'

'I don't have anything to wear.'

'Yes, you do,' said Lucile. 'I didn't give away any of your clothes. They are in your wardrobe, as well as your shoes.'

'Good,' said Georges to me. 'Why don't you get ready here? I'll come back and pick you up in an hour.'

I had serious doubts about going to the dinner, but I didn't want to disappoint him. I bathed and put on the silver and white lamé evening dress I had worn for Lucile's fiftieth birthday party.

But when Georges picked me up in his car, nervous butterflies filled my stomach.

'I don't think I should go with you tonight,' I told him. 'They'll celebrate you as the lawyer who saved the life of a Resistance hero. But me? They will still see me as the woman who created a scandal at the Fouquets' ball.'

Georges glanced at me. 'I think the Fouquets are the ones who should be embarrassed. They were funding a network to help high-profile Nazis escape from Europe. And, I should remind you, that it was you with your dogged determination that saved Serge.'

'To be Serge Lavertu's daughter is something to be proud of,' I said, 'but I'm plagued by shame at being Martin La Farge's niece. I went to the library yesterday and looked up Marcus Aurelius. I wanted to know why his statue was outside my ancestral home. I never found that out, but I did discover a quote by him that I wrote down: "The best revenge is to not be like your enemy." I think that's what I have to do. To make sure I in no way resemble the other members of the La Farge family.'

'Eve, we have been over this a dozen times,' Georges said, reaching across and squeezing my arm briefly before taking the wheel again. 'What La Farge has done has nothing to do with you.' Then after a moment's reflection and with a smirk, he added, 'On the plus side, you are also related to Marthe and Cyrille de Villiers. Just think of that!'

'I'd rather not!' I cried.

'Well, please stop obsessing that you are some sort of liability to my reputation. I shall be very proud to introduce the associate who worked with me on the most intriguing legal case of the year. Besides, you look very beautiful, and it would be a terrible waste for you to sit at home in that dress.'

I looked out at the view of Paris and the Jardin des Tuileries as we passed by. My life and my beliefs about it had been challenged in the last couple of months. I wasn't the same cynical young woman I had been when I first came to Paris. A brief picture of Anthony flashed up in my mind, but I pushed it away. 'That sounded almost sentimental, Georges,' I said. 'I thought you were against sentimental attachments?'

He laughed. 'Did I say such a thing, Eve? What a fool I am. Besides, I should remind you, it was you who resisted me.'

'I didn't want to make the same mistake with you that my mother did with Serge, and destroy a friendship that means more to me than gold.'

Georges turned the corner and the grand Hôtel du Louvre appeared before us, its second Empire façade shimmering in the fading evening light. He stopped the car and gave his keys to the valet before opening the door for me.

'Life isn't as straightforward as we would like it to be,' he said, guiding me up the red carpet to the entrance. 'The results of any endeavour can be quite unpredictable. Often we don't know how things will turn out until we try.'

Spectacular was the word to describe the glittering ballroom we were ushered into by the hotel attendant. My eyes took in the elegant marble columns and gold chandeliers. Tables covered in heavenly white cloths circled a dance floor, and a band was playing Cole Porter songs. The guests were exquisitely turned out in satin and silk. Paris was ready to be glamorous again.

But as Georges and I made our way to our table across the other side of the room, the stares began. There were subdued gasps of surprise and whispers. People moved back at our approach. A sense of humiliation crept across my skin. It was exactly the derision I had feared. They meant to cut me.

Then the room fell completely silent. I stopped in my tracks, mortified. I was a tarred woman, and nothing could save my reputation, not even the company of a celebrated lawyer. I wanted to turn and run away, like Cinderella fleeing the ball. The fairy-tale heroine had been sensible enough to know she was out of her depth.

'Please, let's go,' I begged Georges.

Suddenly, from the silence, came the sound of someone clapping. They were joined by another and then another as people turned around or rose to their feet. Soon the entire room had burst into applause. It was so loud it sounded as if it was bouncing off the walls. Georges and I had no other choice but to acknowledge the veneration with slight bows. I felt both elated and humbled.

'And there we have it,' said Georges, turning to me. 'What I have been trying to explain to you all along. Despite all protestations to the contrary, there is nothing Parisian society appreciates more than a truly memorable scandal.'

The band began to play 'Let's Do It (Let's Fall in Love)'. Couples made their way to the dance floor.

Georges offered his hand. 'I think they are playing our song,' he said. 'Shall we dance, Mademoiselle Archer?'

I took his hand and let him lead me out onto the dance floor. He was right, of course. The results of any endeavour can be quite unpredictable. Often we don't know how things will turn out until we try.

'Yes, Monsieur Camadeau,' I said, leaning into his embrace as we moved to the music. 'I think we should.'

BOOK CLUB QUESTIONS

1. How much did you know about life in France during the Second World War before reading *The Masterpiece*? Did you learn anything new that surprised you?

2. Is *The Masterpiece* a love story? Why or why not?

3. There are several twists in the novel. Which one surprised you the most?

4. Do you think striving to be part of Paris high society was a worthy goal for both Eve and Lucile? Were they always destined to fail?

5. Kristina's genius as an artist is dismissed by many collectors because she is a woman. Do you think perception is more influential than talent in one artist becoming more successful than another?

6. Mirrors and rabbits are recurring motifs in the story. What do you think they represent?

7. Do you agree with Kristina's statement that 'the past is a mirror we look into to make sense of who we are today'? Docteur Gabriel thinks it's a blessing that Kristina doesn't remember her trauma. Kristina believes it's a curse not to remember it, because whether something is good or bad, it is still part of her life and experience. Who do you agree with more?

9. In France there were those who actively resisted the occupation and tried to help Jewish people, those who collaborated with the Germans, and those who tried to keep their heads down and get through the ordeal. Giving consideration to the terrible fate of resisters who got caught, and the significant money that could be made by collaborating, which group do you think you would have belonged to? What do you think of the choices made by Kristina, Max, Serge and Sonia?

AUTHOR'S NOTE

I am often asked about what inspires me to write a certain book. In the case of *The Masterpiece*, it was two intriguing men from history.

The first was Paul Rosenberg, one of the most important French art dealers of the twentieth century. He had an elegant art gallery at 21 Rue la Boétie and represented artists such as Pablo Picasso, Henri Matisse and Marie Laurencin. While Serge Lavertu is a fictional character and not a thinly disguised Paul Rosenberg, I did have Serge voice some of Rosenberg's philosophies, including the notion that no artist is ahead of their time — it is the public that must catch up — and that antique furniture and modern art complement each other perfectly. Rosenberg fled to New York before the German occupation of France, but his gallery in Paris was Aryanised and his artworks stolen from the bank vault where he had stored them. While he was never part of the French Resistance, his son, Alexandre, was a lieutenant in the Free French Forces. As part of the D–Day invasion of France, Alexandre stopped a train that was heading for Germany with looted goods on board. When the train's box cars were opened, Alexandre was surprised to see some artworks that he knew were part of his father's collection. Rosenberg spent many years after the war trying to recover paintings from his collection that had been scattered over Europe.

The second inspiration for the story was a Dutch artist (or con–artist) named Han van Meegeren, arguably one of the most brilliant art forgers of modern times. A 'failed' artist, van Meegeren took his revenge on the art world by forging paintings by the greatest artists of the Dutch Golden Age and passing them off as 'previously undiscovered works' to collectors and museums. Van Meegeren made a fortune, but things came undone for him during the Second World War when the Nazi art plunderer Hermann Göring purchased van Meegeren's forgery of Vermeer's *Christ and the Adulteress*. After the war, van Meegeren was arrested for treason for selling cultural property to the Nazis and faced the death penalty. He had to then convince the authorities that he had painted the work himself. I found the dilemma a delicious inspiration for my own story of Resistance heroes forging art for more altruistic reasons.

The artist Kristina Belova is a composite of female modern artists including Natalia Goncharova, Zinaida Serebryakova, Amrita Sher-Gil and Suzanne Valadon, who achieved some recognition in their day but never became household names in the way their male equivalents did.

Writing about historical events such as the Second World War and the Holocaust can be heavy-going at times, so I like to balance my stories with snippets of humour, satire and whimsy. But those notions are often inspired by facts. Leporiphobia is a real affliction, for instance, and art dealers have been known to sometimes add their own touches to a painting if they think a collector will prefer the 'improved' work. Readers who may be wondering if a shot-putting concert pianist is even a possibility will be interested to know that the inspiration for Fanny Toussaint was Micheline Ostermeyer, a great niece of French writer Victor Hugo. She did indeed win the Premier Prix at the Conservatoire de Paris in 1946 and then went on to win gold medals at the 1948 Summer Olympics in shot put and discus throw, and the bronze medal for high jump.

I often tell the stories behind my stories in my Substack newsletter, 'Glamour comes from the word Grammar', so be sure to subscribe to it for more:

belindaalexandra.substack.com

ACKNOWLEDGEMENTS

I am very grateful to all the wonderful people who helped bring *The Masterpiece* to fruition, particularly my long-time publisher, Anna Valdinger, and ever-supportive literary agent, Catherine Drayton. I am very fortunate to have such enthusiastic champions of my writing. I'd also like to thank the supportive team at HarperCollins Publishers Australia, including senior editor Madeleine James, marketing manager Kate Butler, and publicity manager Hannah Lynch.

Thank you to Dianne Blacklock for her expert structural and copy editing of the manuscript. She is the next best thing to a literary fairy godmother. Special thanks also goes to my first reader, Roslyn McGechan, who despite two cataract operations read through the manuscript with me not once but twice. Thank you also to proofreader Pam Dunne for her attention to detail.

I'd also like to express my gratitude to those who helped me with my research for the book, including Carmen Maravillas, Lilli Testa, Kay and Michael Donovan, and Professor Rita Shackel of the University of Sydney Law School who, despite a heavy workload, gave me excellent feedback on my legal scenes. I'd also like to thank the staff at Ku-ring-gai Library for their wholehearted help in finding even the most obscure of historical material.

Last but not least, I'd like to thank my gorgeous family and friends for their love and support. They make all the hard work worthwhile.

With love and thanks,
Belinda XX

Discover the world of Belinda Alexandra ...

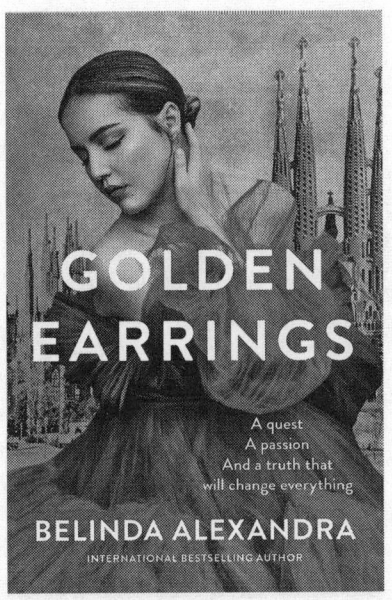

Discover the world of Belinda Alexandra ...

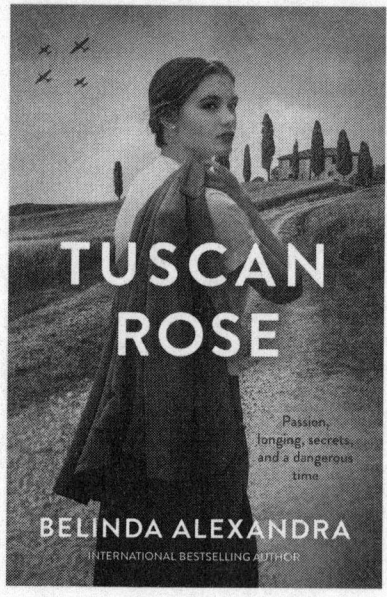

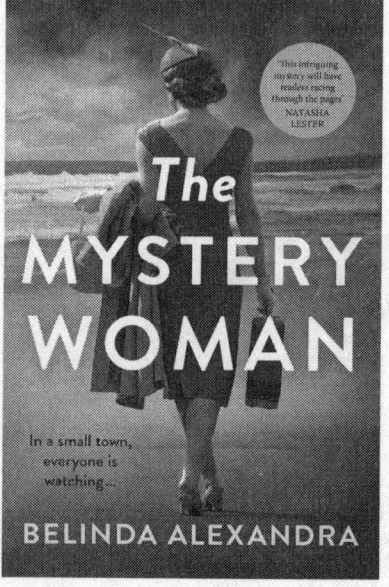